Earth and Mind

Book Two of The Quinate's Faithful

Brendan Corbett

Illustration © Tom Edwards

TomEdwardsDesign.com

Editor: Celestian Rince

celestianrince.com

Blood and Flame / Brendan Corbett

ISBN: 979-8-9901899-9-7

CONTENTS

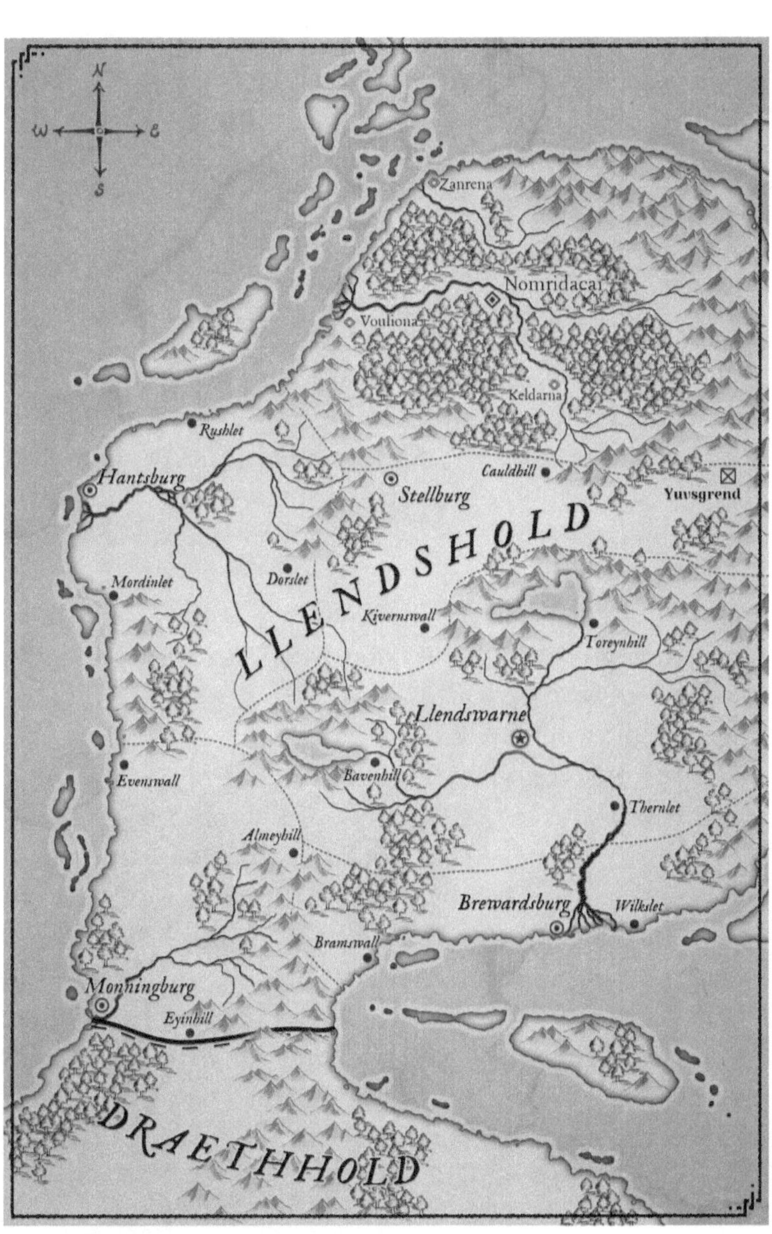

N
W
E
S
Zanrena
Nomridacai
Vouliona
Keldarna
Rushlet
Cauldhill
Yuvsgrend
Hantsburg
Stellburg
LLENDSHOLD
Mordinlet
Dorslet
Kivernswall
Toreynhill
Llendswarne
Evenswall
Bavenhill
Thernlet
Almeyhill
Brewardsburg
Wilkslet
Bramswall
Monningburg
Eyinhill
DRAETHHOLD

CHAPTER 1

"Grandfather, where are they going?"

The old Fae sat by a knee-height table between a packed dirt path and the front of his home. He ran a hand through his wispy hair as he watched the village Elder lead a procession of two Mages with gourds at their hips, a deer, and half a dozen children—about twelve years old, of a similar age to Ami—through the streets of Keldarna.

"Matters of those born above us," he said, tugging at an earring dangling from his earlobe, which stretched from this ear down to the base of his neck. "It's nothing for you to worry about, Aminantskeilara."

Ami set a basket of feathers on the table beside a stack of arrow shafts. Her grandfather mindfully rolled the wooden rods over the table one at a time, inspecting for warps.

"What do you mean, it's nothing for me to worry about? The Elder is leading a group of kids my age with Mages, and I heard nothing about what they're up to."

"You are young, but you will learn in time—we need not know everything of the world around us. We can find happiness in our days as they come and go by doing the things we are able to do, changing the things we are able to change, being with the people we love to be with."

Ami frowned, though a smile swiftly replaced her bitter expression when her grandfather affectionately pinched her chin. "Did I bring enough feathers? If that's all you need, I'd like to go for a walk."

Her grandfather's hand fell away as he inspected her face. A tangle of short black hair sat atop her head. Earrings, made by Ami herself, ran from the top of her ears all along the lobes. Her slender nose and low cheeks framed broad eyes. He knew at a glance that Ami's head was full of schemes, yet he knew better than trying to stop her from whatever she had set her mind to.

"You brought plenty, and of the most excellent quality! Stretch your legs as young people need to do, but I beg of you, please stay out of trouble, my little feather."

"It's trouble that always seems to find me, not that I go looking for it," Ami said with a smirk and wink.

She gave her grandfather a hug, then scurried off into the village of Keldarna.

Ami slipped around wooden buildings with domed roofs painted in green. While the walls bore little in the way of decoration, doors came in a myriad of colors. Residents carved and painted to their satisfaction, bringing a vibrance to the village. Shops, in the form of tables with simple cloth canopies, were erected outside homes and offered food and wares of every kind. Ami waved and bowed and smiled as she passed familiar faces. Weaving through the streets, she meandered as if to enjoy a lazy, sunny day, but her outward appearance masked a focused determination.

At the edge of a crowded avenue, Ami ducked into an alley. She hastened her steps, hurrying down the path between the backs of buildings, until she reached the edge of the village. After mindfully checking to see if she had been followed, she scurried away.

Ami crossed the fields of berries and grain which covered the few hundred yards between the outskirts of Keldarna and the edge of the Nomridian Forest. She skipped past the gatherers, who were far too busy to pay her any notice. Inside the forest, she used thin leather ties to pull in her poncho and billowy pants.

Ami took a moment to appreciate her surroundings. She had spent countless hours roaming among the vines and ferns and lichens which hung from the forest of dead trees. Every nook, every cranny, every hollow of a tree was a tiny world she could lose herself in; over the years, she had become as familiar with the forest as she was with the village of Keldarna. Soft moss coated decaying trunks and the ground. On quiet days, Ami would take off her boots to enjoy the embrace of the plush tufts of green. Today, however, Ami dashed into the woods.

Following a trail of footsteps and snapped branches, it took her a matter of minutes to find the procession as they plodded along. Hiding in the shadows of trees, Ami glared at their ponchos with envy. The silken fabrics in bright colors sported intricate patterns and decorative trim. She looked down at her own simple, green poncho, with its worn and tattered hem.

"All of short names," Ami muttered under her breath. "What is going on? Why bring only those born into privilege? Where are the rest, those like me?"

Ami stalked the group, grateful for the singing birds, bounding deer, and buzzing insects that covered the sounds of her every move. Nearly half an hour later, the Elder came to a halt. The Mages stood by his side, facing the six children. Ami scaled a nearby tree then deftly climbed across branches and vines until she was nearly on top of the group.

The Elder stood at the heart of a small clearing; moss-covered stones paved the ground. Behind him, a cairn of oval stones rose to shoulder-height. The sight perturbed Ami. She wondered how it was possible she had never seen the peculiar clearing, despite this part of the forest being all but a second home.

"Welcome, my young friends. We have brought you to this most sacred of secrets, a place hidden, protected, warded from the gaze of unwelcome eyes." The Elder, his thick brow furrowed, motioned to the cairn. "You stand before a former mana source. In ages past, mana once flowed from within these stones. Though it is now dry, we revere its memory, a sign of the gift given to us all by the Five."

Ami suppressed a snort, indignant that the Elder would call it a gift for all when the cairn was hidden, and only a few stood before it now.

"You six stand here because you have been deemed worthy to taste mana, to determine if you are attuned to the gift of the Five. Those who are so blessed will become Mages. You all were born into families of quality, yet as a Mage you will be elevated further. Though we must not get ahead of ourselves; Hawel and Yorin are here to assist with the ceremony."

Deemed worthy? Ami's nostrils flared as she silently fumed over the Elder's words. What had they done to be considered worthy? All she saw were children from wealthy families. Was that all it took to be seen as worthy? To have the fortune of a high birth?

"We will offer a sacrifice in the place where mana once flowed endlessly," said Hawel, pulling errant strands of long, sleek brown hair behind his ears. He watched as his counterpart brought the deer before the altar. "In doing so, we thank the Five for providing us with mana through the creatures of the forest, even if the source no longer flows."

Yorin knelt and pet the deer's head.

"We raise these delicate creatures with care and make their every moment pleasing. We do this to honor their sacrifice and to ensure they are a sufficient offering to our dearest God of the Five, Mizaina. It is from her that we draw our ability to do magic."

Hawel drank mana from one gourd, then grasped a second at his hip tightly. He raised a bloodstained hand and held it over the deer, speaking as he gently waved his hand back and forth.

"Mizaina, grant your peace to this creature of your woods."

The deer sighed and closed its eyes as Yorin drew a curved dagger with a gem-encrusted handle. She slit the animal's throat and lowered it onto the cairn in a single motion. Blood trickled over stone as the deer's legs twitched and quivered. Hawel raised a bulbous empty gourd with an open top and whispered too softly for Ami to discern his words.

A cloud appeared above the lifeless deer. Blood flew upwards from the carcass as if it rained into the cloud, which swirled and churned. A thin stream of shimmering liquid flowed into the empty gourd. The mana shed wisps of ash as it flowed through the air, dusting the ground in powdery grey. A few minutes later, the cloud dissipated.

Hawel filled a shallow, palm-sized silver bowl with mana from the gourd, then corked the vessel. Meanwhile, Yorin returned to the deer and pressed a wooden cup against the slit in its neck, gathering a few drops of blood.

The Elder paced in front of the nervous youth. "You have witnessed the formation of mana, the coalescing of the Five's greatest gift. We must never forget that it comes at the price of a life. It is now time for you to drink. All who are attuned will be trained as Mages, the most venerated members of our society.

"And yet, the Gods act in ways we do not fully understand. Not all will respond to mana. There is no shame should this be the case; it means only that the Gods have another purpose for you. We will grace you with a softened memory, and you will return to the path you were on before this day."

Hawel presented the bowl to the first of the young Fae. "Gwin, drink, and let us examine your connection to the gods."

Ami's face twisted with glee when the boy trembled. Gwin had often gone out of his way to stop by Ami's home to make fun of her, or worse, her grandfather. He would confidently boast of the certainty of his future all while speaking ill of Ami's life sure to be spent fletching. She wished she could see his face flushed with fear, though the youth stood with their backs to Ami.

"Worry not, my young friend," Hawel said reassuringly. "Attunement, or lack of it, is no condemnation of your character, and no harm can come from drinking mana. You have nothing to fear."

Encouraged, Gwin reached out and cradled the silver bowl in his hands. He breathed in deeply, then exhaled slowly from his mouth. Hawel nodded, and the boy drained the bowl.

Ami leaned forward on the branch until she risked falling, staring intently at Gwin. Hawel took the bowl back as the boy hunched over, staring at his hands. He jumped to his feet, laughing uncontrollably.

"Praise be to Mizaina!" declared the Elder. "Praise be to the Five! A soon-to-be Mage joins our fold this day."

Yorin stepped forward and dipped her thumb into the pot of blood. Ami fought back a giggle when the Mage wiped the blood on Gwin's face, knowing his distaste for touching anything he considered dirty, whether that be mud, blood, or those of a low birth like Ami. Still, the boy stood proudly while the Elder and Mages proceeded down the line.

The taste of mana filled three more of the youth with joy, though two smiled hesitantly after taking a drink.

Yorin took the two unattuned to the edge of the clearing, nearly beneath Ami. The Mage knelt and placed a hand on a shoulder of each.

"I see the sadness in your faces. Remember, you are to be looked upon no differently than before. You have shown courage in joining us and drinking mana. You exposed yourselves before the Five in the most raw and vulnerable of ways, and in doing so, have proven the quality of your hearts. Feel no shame. Feel no sadness. Feel only joy that you took steps that few ever will."

Ami scowled at the coddling. She had been made to feel lesser nearly every day, and yet these two would return to lives of comfort. Ami wanted to scream when Yorin muttered a spell to rejuvenate the sad youth, easing their heartbreak and embarrassment. The Mage patted their heads then led them into the forest, back to Keldarna.

Once Yorin was out of sight, the Elder spoke.

"You four have taken your first steps on the path to becoming Mages. Your future is boundless! As you train and grow in skill, we will observe and study you to understand where your strengths lie. Some Mages serve as leaders among our scouts, others serve as healers, some stand proud as the strongest of our guards. Others—as Hawel, here—will find themselves training to become an Elder.

"You will enjoy an elevated status, commensurate with the greatness that is this gift from the Gods. And yet, you will be duty-bound to our people. Never forget that you serve the Five through your service to the Fae, and that service begins today. Now, let us return. Training begins tomorrow. Tonight, celebrate with your families. Revel in the glorious gift which the Five have bestowed upon you!"

The four youth happily skipped and laughed and cheered as they headed back towards Keldarna with the Elder.

Hawel tarried with the silver bowl still in his hands. He set the dish upon the top of the cairn. Taking hold of his mana-filled gourd, he poured until the iridescent liquid dribbled over the edge and dampened the cold carcass of the deer.

"Mizaina, blessed of the Fae, our closest and dearest of the Five, we leave this offering for you and the forest. Thank you and all the Five for the gift of mana. Thank you for blessing us with these new Mages. May we always serve our people in your name, and bring joy to you in all we do."

Ami rolled her eyes as she lay on her back, cradled by the branches of the tree. The sun descended as she struggled to digest what she had witnessed.

Though she had seen Mages before, the secret of their selection was ever a mystery. Ami had been struck by the occasional, passing hope that she might one day become a Mage, yet the lack of status of her birth prevented her from ever truly considering it a possibility. Now, seeing the simplicity, the inequity of the process sent her mind reeling.

The late afternoon sun filled the forest with a vermillion glow. The hoots of early-waking owls replaced the chirping of birds, and the squeaks of darting mice faded. Ami watched as a lizard scurried across a vine, then leapt between branches, snagging a beetle on its way. A cool evening breeze rustled vines in the forest, reminding Ami of the lateness of the hour.

Rolling off the branch, Ami landed deftly on her feet. She surveyed the clearing from behind a ruffly fern. She had neither heard nor seen a Fae since Hawel left; still, she mindfully searched for any sign of a disturbance.

Ami bounded out from behind the fern and strode into the clearing. She halted halfway to the cairn, all but expecting an unseen Fae to appear and condemn her presence.

"Hello?" she ventured.

The hooting of owls and rustling of vines in the early evening breeze were the only reply.

Ami marched over to the cairn. She peered inside the bowl; despite being in the shade and going untouched for hours, the mana shone like mother-of-pearl and swirled lazily. Then Ami noticed the smell. It was sweet and vibrant, like the scent of freshly opened flowers carried on a warm spring breeze. She stared at the bowl. In that moment, a tangle of conflicting thoughts and rage filled her mind. Unable to resist any further, Ami snatched the bowl and drank the entirety of its contents.

Ami set the bowl back atop the cairn.

"Thanks for the offering, Hawel," she said with a chuckle. "Gift of the Gods indeed, I wonder-"

A sudden warmth in Ami's gut sent her doubling over. She felt a surge of energy run through her veins and spread across her entire body, as though she were made of dry grass and a fire had been lit in her belly. The joyous brightness sent her laughing and dancing around the clearing.

Ami's excitement tapered when her eyes landed on the deer. She stared into its cloudy, open eyes.

"Sorry, friend. I can't help but think it wasn't a worthwhile trade for you to give your life for *them.*"

Ami gently closed the deer's eyelids, then brushed its cheek with her still-tingling hand.

A pair of chipmunks scampered by, snapping branches and rustling shrubs on their way. Brought back from her daze, Ami looked up to the darkening sky. Knowing her grandfather would be worried if she was gone much longer, she hurried back to Keldarna.

Ami strolled up to the village when two guards marched out. They wore earthy brown ponchos over chain mail shirts, with plates protecting their elbows and knees. Steel helms with tall crests wobbled above their heads. Broad round shields hung from their backs and black scabbards shrouded swords with sweeping, curved tips.

Uncomfortable in their presence, Ami moved to skirt around the guards when they blocked her way.

"Hello?" she asked, brow furrowed indignantly. "In case you've forgotten, I live here. Why are you stopping me?"

"Stay there."

Ami scoffed and moved to pass by when a guard lowered his spear, holding the point inches from her chest. Ami's head pounded and her heart raced as she froze in place with hands clasped over her stomach.

The second guard took hold of a hollowed gourd attached to a string. He spun the gourd rapidly, releasing a shrill whistle, before returning it to his belt.

The three stood in silence for a few minutes until the Elder and Hawel marched out from Keldarna.

"What's the meaning of this? Why demand my attention? Why are you holding a child at spearpoint?" the Elder demanded. He looked closer when a guard nodded at Ami; the Elder's body tensed. "Aminantskeilara, is it? You there, go find her grandfather. You know of him; he's the old fletcher."

Ami chewed at her lips. Her mind was a blur, wondering why the guards had stopped her, if they somehow knew what had happened in the forest. She suppressed the overwhelming urge to vomit as a guard marched into the village.

"What's going on? Why are you sending a guard to get my grandfather? I was on my way to him anyhow."

"Do not speak until you are spoken to," Hawel cut.

The last rays of evening sun brightened pillowy clouds in the sky when Ami's grandfather appeared with the guard. On seeing Ami, his shoulders slouched and his face drooped.

"Grandfather!" Ami shouted. "What's going on?"

She took a step forward when the guard raised his spear to block her way.

Her grandfather sighed deeply. "You already know. We can see it in your eyes."

"What do you mean?" Ami said, casting her gaze down to a pebble on the road.

"There is no point in deception, no point in lying, little feather. We must all live with the consequences of our actions, no matter our intention. Elder, what is to become of Ami?"

"I have more than half a mind to order her execution, and my remaining thoughts are near equally unpleasant," the Elder growled.

Ami thought it perhaps a poor joke, but her grandfather's lips quivered and tears rolled down his cheeks. She hardly remembered the last time he cried. The sight sent her heart racing, more so even than the Elder's harsh words.

"What have I done to deserve death?"

"You stole!" shouted the Elder. "And it was not a simple theft, Aminantskeilara. You, in all your unworthiness, stole the most sacred of all things. You stole mana, and worse still, you stole mana left as an offering to Mizaina, while trespassing in a sacred place. Banishment is the least severe punishment I am considering. You had best pray to the ones you stole from that mercy finds its way into my heart."

"Banishment to Human lands?" Ami's grandfather stammered. "Elder, please... I know your judgement to be true, that she must live with the punishment you decide, but banishing her there... she is a foolish child. To send her to Llendshold is to send her to death."

"You say this, as one with a reputation for being a Human-lover?" questioned the Elder.

"I believe our peoples are stronger when we see each other as equals, yes. But to send a child to live among Humans, without protection?"

The Elder crossed his arms. "No one said you have to stay. Since you like the Humans so much, you are welcome to join her."

"Elder, if I may," Hawel said, stepping forth. "True as it is that she drank mana and desecrated the source, and though she is lowborn, we cannot deny the glow in her eyes. I would contend that her birth does not absolve her of the necessity of repenting for her foul acts. Death or banishment would not serve as repayment for what she has done."

"What then do you propose, Hawel?" asked the Elder.

Hawel stared at Ami. "Aminantskeilara, tell us of what you felt when you drank mana."

"It was like... like my whole body was alive, in a way I never felt before. I felt so warm, I still feel warm, like there's something inside me ready to break free. I'm sorry, if I knew, I never would have-"

"Silence." Hawel rubbed his neck while glaring at Ami. "We should train her."

"What?" the Elder spewed.

"Through her training, she will learn to serve. And through her service, there will be penance in droves. Never as the highest of the Mages, but as a servant, to the Elder."

Ami's chin quivered as her anger boiled over. "Why was my drinking of mana a desecration? Why were there only highborn with you? Why would you not have invited others like me? What makes me unworthy of receiving a gift from the Five!?"

"That you have to ask is all the answer you deserve," the Elder said coolly. "You have lived among the Fae your entire life, and still choose to ignore our ways. A pathetic specimen. Hawel, I see the value in your determination. If trained, she will be your responsibility. Her failings will be your failings."

Hawel bowed his head. "This is no act of charity, Elder. I will extract all that is owed due to her transgressions, and I aim to see her debt repaid tenfold."

The Elder leaned by Ami until his mouth was an inch from her ear, his breath tickling her skin. "You will train among your betters, Aminantskeilara. You will never stop being a lowborn. You do not deserve this; you stole it, and you will never deserve it. Never forget that."

Ami's grandfather's face twisted and shifted, bounding between joy and fear, relief and worry. "Does this mean..."

"Yes," Hawel replied. "Training begins at first light."

Back home, Ami's grandfather spoke only when he absolutely had to, though he cooked one of her favorite meals: crisped sausages atop a bed of foraged berries, roast tubers, and sauteed greens. The food made Ami feel only more guilty, and she slept hardly a wink that night.

Her grandfather's wistful look in the morning had done little to encourage Ami as she left their home. Now, she stood by a pond, far from the other four youth who huddled together, whispering as they stared and pointed at Ami. She clasped her arms tightly together as discordant emotions tore at her heart. Rage at the Elder, excitement at the prospect of becoming a Mage, and sadness at her grandfather's quiet formed a cloud over her head.

Hawel strode into the field. He set down a hulking pack and motioned for the youth to gather near him. Ami hurriedly complied.

"I prefer to not waste time mincing words you are unlikely to remember or care for. I will provide you with books to study on your own. Time with me is expressly for practicing magic. We begin with a simple spell: summoning fog. The presence of water will, of course, make such spells easier. As you are novices, I expect no more than a patch a few feet across. I will demonstrate, and you are to replicate. With magic, you must properly complete the hand motions and the words in concert. Observe and remember, that you don't waste mana."

Hawel's fastidious, militant gestures wasted not a second of time nor an inch of motion. He uncorked a gourd then drank a sip of mana. As he returned the gourd to his belt with his right hand, his left clasped a gourd with a spike at the end. He squeezed, then raised his bloodstained palm.

"Mizaina, may your waters rise, and hold steady."

Hawel waved in a broad circle as he spoke, then closed his fist. He abruptly swept his hand in an arc, and a fog surrounded the perimeter of the field.

"Take a gourd of mana and a spiked gourd, then practice. I will walk among you. The opening gesture determines the shape, while the closing gesture determines the scope of the fog. Do not waste mana. Conclude your spell with a small circle in front of yourselves."

Ami made for the pile of gourds inside the pack, but the other students cut her off, snickering as they turned their backs to her. Ami tapped her foot while waiting, then finally took up the last of the gourds. She happily hooked them to her belt, though the cold metal spike gave her pause; the star came to a sharp point about a quarter of an inch from the gourd. She questioned the necessity of piercing her own skin, but figured the ability to control magic would be well worth the pain.

Ami eagerly downed a sip of mana, licking her lips as the power embraced her. She raised the gourd and pored over the spike. Was it better that it was so sharp as to pierce skin easily, or would it be better if blunted as to not plunge too deeply, she wondered?

Exhaling slowly, Ami threw her hand onto the spike.

Tears filled her eyes as she gasped and pulled her hand to her chest. Blood dribbled out from between her fingers.

"Too deep," Hawel said loudly. "You are to make blood flow, not gut yourself. Inelegant, as I expected from you."

Ami's face burned as the others laughed. "You never told me-"

"I will not trouble myself with the troubles of a lowborn. These others have learned these basic principles over the years. You ask why you don't deserve this? Prepare to see at every turn, Ami. You took what is undeserved, and as such, you will learn in this way. Now, let us see your attempt at the spell."

Hawel stood with his arms crossed while the rest of the students gathered around. Ami raised her quivering hand, still dripping blood.

Ami mimicked the spell as best she was able, nearly jumping with glee when a thin haze of mist appeared. It lingered for a breath until a breeze carried it away. She grinned and looked at Hawel, expecting praise.

"Meager. I asked for fog, and you created no more than a bluster of spit in the wind."

"That was my first time," Ami protested.

"Do not waste mana, Aminantskeilara," Hawel said, speaking over Ami. "You already stole mana. Be mindful, and try harder, lest you be branded a waste as well as a thief. You four, carry on. I'll watch over you, as I'm sure we will see better results."

Ami watched as Hawel knelt by the other youth, encouraging them and guiding them with gentle touches, despite their pitiful, unsuccessful attempts. Fueled by hatred, Ami took a drink of mana. She roared the spell, pulling forth a more complete cloud. For hours she repeated the spell, ignoring the sounds of the forest, ignoring the words of the others practicing their spells, ignoring the searing pain in her hand.

Taking the last sip from her gourd, Ami allowed the mana to swirl around her tongue before swallowing and closing her eyes. She exhaled slowly through her nose until her chest and throat burned, then breathed in rapidly.

"Mizaina, may your waters rise, and hold steady!"

Ami opened her eyes to see a dense cloud of grey, swirling like a miniature hurricane. She stared into the eye, entranced, as if she could see her future inside; a future where she was a person of import, of status; a person who took what she had deserved; a person recognized for what she was capable of instead of condemned for the status into which she was born.

In the distance, Hawel offered not the slightest reaction to Ami's success. He motioned for her to take a fresh gourd of mana.

At the end of the day, Hawel invited the students to join him by the pack of now-empty gourds.

"Stand in a line. Well done. You are now Apprentice Mages, and may keep your spiked gourds. In time, you will carry mana with you every day, but it will be some time before you earn that right. Hold your hands out, palms up."

The students swiftly complied; dried blood covered Ami's palm and the star-shaped puncture ached. Hawel took the wooden lid off a stone cup and scooped out a glob of ointment with a flat spoon. He walked down the line, shaking a drop onto the outstretched hands. When he reached Ami, he positioned the loaded spoon over her hand. Ami's hand twitched, aching for relief, when Hawel abruptly wiped the ointment back inside the cup then sealed the vessel.

"Why? Why don't I get any of the ointment?" Ami pleaded.

Hawel sneered. "You are a thief. This ointment is a reward. A thief should be rewarded for their ill-gotten gains no more than a murderer should be given a knife and their freedom as punishment. Should you receive ointment because your hand hurts? I think not. Your hand will be allowed to scar, a permanent reminder of your transgressions. And a painful one, as you must be ready to break the skin again tomorrow."

That evening, Ami sat on the hearth close by the fire, her gaze lost in glowing embers. Her grandfather adjusted a hunk of roasting meat; bread already waited alongside berries and greens.

"So that's how your day was."

Ami sighed and wiped away a tear that ran down her cheek.

"Yesterday you gained both a blessing and a curse, and both will be with you forever, little feather. Come, let me see your hand."

Ami winced as she uncurled her fingers.

"It will scar," said her grandfather, "and I'm sure it will ache mightily as you train these coming years, but perhaps I can ease the pain a little."

Ami's grandfather bustled about, gathering up strange leaves from jars and soaking them in oil. He layered a few of the leaves over her palm, then wrapped them snug with a bit of cloth. Though the wound smarted, the leaves cooled and numbed her hand.

"Ah, a moment."

The old man rifled through a drawer of fletching supplies. He returned and tucked a round, carved wooden owl charm into Ami's pocket, then took her hands in his. Ami instantly relaxed; his hands, though aged and rough, were as gentle as a spring breeze.

"I am old, Ami. Know that I will always be with you; if not in person, then in your heart and in your mind. But if there are days where it feels like I'm far away, that little friend will keep you company."

The sun hung low on the horizon. Ami knelt atop a hill, with her hands in her lap. Her eyes were fixed on the owl charm, worn smooth from the decade of carrying it. She rolled the wooden token around. The owl slid about as if it were dancing around the scar on her palm. She wished for nothing more than to feel her grandfather's touch one last time.

Clenching her fist, Ami looked ahead. Below her vantage point was an enormous fortress. Sheer stone walls rose three stories high above a deep ditch, covered with low roofs. A prominent turret jutted out at each corner. More than one hundred Paladins were reportedly stationed inside. Many of their number patrolled the walls and peered out from the turrets, though Ami hardly thought such a prominent guard was necessary. The mountains were too steep and rocky to approach from the north or east, a wide open field stood between a forest and the walls to the south, while the path west wove through farmland on its way to the coastal village of Mordinlet.

"Caudro, you big, stupid, occasionally handsome hunk of a man, what have you gotten yourself into? What have you gotten *me* into?" Ami muttered. "I'm sure Hawel will love this, me thieving yet again. I hope Imreia's informants were right, otherwise I will have taken the most inconvenient of trips, all for naught. It was Dara and Wynne who committed to finding you, and Imreia who funded this little jaunt; but Aminantskeilara, did you really have to volunteer for this? I'm to break in to a Paladin fortress and steal a Paladin. I sailed on the Andaira, Caudro, with Catarin! All to save you. Of all the sour parts of the Quinarium, what misfortune could possibly have led you to joining the Paladins?"

Chapter 2

"Pick up your feet!"

Caudro stumbled, unable to find his footing as two Paladins dragged him by the shoulders. They surged down the cold stone halls until they reached a room filled with prison cells. The Paladins yanked open a door of iron bars, then threw Caudro inside.

His face smacked the cold stone floor. An overwhelming white blinded Caudro. Ringing filled his ears as the world spun around him. His mind roamed as he faded in and out of consciousness. Caudro pushed off the floor, attempting to stand, but his arms gave out. He struck the ground once more, and the world went black.

The sun blazed above as Caudro's cheek bounced off the hot stone path. Touching his cheek, he felt warm blood smearing the dirt and grit on his face.

"Get back here, boy!" the shopkeeper shouted. "I'm not half done with beating you! Not going to let your thieving little hands get away this time! Come here!"

On hearing the voice, Caudro recognized the all-too-familiar memory. His childhood self scrambled away, not caring as the coarse stones scraped his hands and knees. He looked over his shoulder to see a shopkeeper, whose tunic was hemmed halfway down his thighs; the portly man was red in the face. Caudro resented the sight of someone clearly well fed taking offense at him stealing to stave off hunger.

"No use running, boy!" The shopkeeper reached out, his grubby hands nearly grabbing hold of Caudro when the man abruptly stood tall. "Oh, the Quinate bless me this day! Good sir, excuse me! Good sir! Oh, thank the Five. I found this thief, and am presently in need of the Quinarium's righteous judgement. Worthless guards haven't done a thing to thwart the thieving which has plagued me so!"

Caudro brushed his wild, unkempt hair from his face. He scanned the street until he spied a nearby Paladin. Caudro held his breath; though he had seen the warriors of the Quinarium from afar, he had never been so close to one.

The Paladin's breastplate shone beneath the sun, the steel nearly as bright as the white symbol of the Quinarium painted across the front. Overlapping metal scales adorned his tunic, which covered his upper arms and thighs. The Paladin's domed helmet was tucked beneath one arm, and a shield was pulled tight against his back. A short spear was slung over his shoulder, held in place by a rope. A sword hung from a belt, with a dagger on the Paladin's opposite hip.

The Paladin's plated greaves clinked with each step as he approached. He raised a hand when the shopkeeper began to speak.

"Boy, do you deny the theft?"

The middle-aged man, with a grizzled face bearing scars from battle and short hair, should have instilled fear. Instead, Caudro felt oddly comforted by the Paladin's voice and a gentleness in his eyes.

"No."

The Paladin knelt on the street beside Caudro. "Tell me, why did you steal?"

"I'm hungry."

"It is the Confessor's duty to ensure all are provided for, as the Quinate intend. Have you sought refuge at the Sanctuary?"

The Paladin looked over his shoulder at the imposing stone building, which stood taller than the walls surrounding the village. Columns lined the exterior, which was absent decoration. Caudro glared at the Sanctuary; home to the Confessor, who preached endlessly inside of the grace and generosity of the Quinarium.

Caudro's eyes drifted back to the Paladin. He caught sight of a wooden charm hanging from a braided cord around the man's neck. He couldn't tell if it was meant to be a dog or a cat, but he found it curious that an Agent of the Quinarium would wear such jewelry.

"I stay in the Sanctuary, yes, but they rarely have enough food. The Confessor says we are to be grateful for what we get."

The Paladin rose and faced the shopkeeper. "These are difficult times for many. And it is in difficult times that we must all look to the wellbeing of those around us. Shopkeeper, do you attend Sanctuary, that you might listen to the words of your Confessor, and heed his messages?"

The man's chin rose and fell like a bird pecking at dirt for worms. "I... ahem. Well... of course I attend. When I can."

The Paladin's face was as still as stone. "You call upon the Quinate, ask for righteous judgement to be delivered, yet you do not regularly attend service in the Sanctuary?"

"As you said, times are difficult for many," the shopkeeper said indignantly. "I can't leave my shop for hours at a time. Thieves like this miscreant will empty my shelves and leave me with nothing!"

"Do not blame your lack of piety on a child. The boy looks to be no more than ten years of age."

"Ten is plenty old to know right from wrong. And lack of piety!? Five above, I have never been so slandered, and by a Paladin. Who do you report to, that I might express my dissatisfaction?"

The Paladin blinked slowly; his face was otherwise blank and emotionless. "If you dare to call upon the Five again in the name of your self-serving arrogance, I will be sure there is nothing left of your shop to steal from. You, boy. What is your name?"

"Caudro... sir."

"You may call me Jarain." The Paladin knelt again and his expression softened. "Caudro, as you have stolen, I must, unfortunately, offer you a choice of penance. The normal punishment, as meted out by the village guards, would be for a finger of your choosing to be taken. However, it is your good fortune that I am present, as I can offer an alternative: you may instead pledge to become a Paladin. I will take you to the fortress at Mordinlet, with all your fingers intact.

"There, as a Paladin Trainee, you will see the true grace of the Quinarium. You will never go hungry. You will never be without a bed to sleep in. Your life will be filled with purpose as you serve the highest order, the Quinarium, in reverence to the Quinate."

"But what about him trying to steal from me? What about the things he undoubtedly stole in days past?" the shopkeeper grumbled.

Jarain raised his hand again. "Speak with the Confessor if you are so wronged as to need restitution. As for this choice, it is Caudro's, not yours."

As he looked into the Paladin's eyes, a confusing, foreign sensation overtook Caudro. For the first time, he felt the pull of hope, and he smiled.

Caudro closed his eyes, then opened them to find himself sitting at a long wood table. Some twenty young boys and girls of a similar age flanked him on either side. In the dining hall, with its vaulted ceiling and surrounded by Paladins, they felt absolutely miniscule. Caudro looked down at a bowl of gruel. Though the food was humble, the portion was generous and he eagerly dove in. While the children ate, a Paladin marched before the table. She tilted her head back and spoke to the ceiling, her voice husky and bold.

"I am Scireth, and it is my duty and pleasure to serve as head of this fortress. Welcome. Welcome and rejoice! It is by the light of the Quinate that you find yourself here in their house, among their Faithful. Listen as you fill your bellies, for your training begins now."

The Paladin paused, prompting the eating children to freeze. She grinned and resumed her march.

"Above all, three tenets rule a Paladin's life. The first of the tenets is to *adhere to the Paladin's oath*, which in turn has three parts: abandon your past, serve in the present, and forgo the future.

"To abandon your past, any attachments you have to the way you lived, the person you thought yourself to be, will reshape you into an empty vessel. To serve in the present, to dedicate yourself to the Quinarium, will fill the empty vessel with the righteous purity of the Quinate. To forgo your future is to acknowledge that you exist to serve the Quinarium. Letting go of hopes and dreams—aside from becoming a Paladin—will focus your purpose, your resolve, and enable you to pour out the contents of the vessel you have become, enriching all of Llendshold. You will become an unrivaled agent of the Gods!"

Scireth paced for a minute to the scraping of spoons in bowls.

"The second tenet is *fealty to the Five*. We Paladins are servants of the Quinarium, and through it, the Quinate. Through our service to them, through total dedication, a never ending celebration of their grandeur, our lives gain meaning without equal! The Five are all and without them, we are nothing. It is through their infinite, boundless grace that we rise. If you dedicate yourself in totality as you study in these halls, you will even be able to hear their words."

Hands clasped together, Scireth halted her march and surveyed the children. She smiled reassuringly.

"Third and final of the tenets is *strength eternal*. A Paladin is the hardened armor, the protector of the Quinate's fold across all of Llendshold. A Paladin is the sharpened spear, ready to be thrust into the hearts of those who stand in defiance of the divinity of the Quinate. You will become fearsome warriors, the hands which carry out the will of the Five through the orders of the Quinarium.

"Eat well, my young Trainees. Your true lives begin tomorrow. As They speak!"

"So we listen!"

The Paladin turned to leave. She took a few steps, but halted when a bit of gruel splattered across the floor. A boy wheezed as he fought to stifle his laughter, his spoon still in hand.

Without a word, Scireth strolled around the table until she stood beside the boy. In a flash, she grabbed hold of the boy's hair and slammed his forehead onto the table. The Trainees all flinched. Tears erupted from the boy's eyes as he clutched his head. Caudro rubbed his own forehead as fear gripped his heart.

"You all have been given an immeasurably valuable gift," Scireth said, her voice calm and even. "Should any of you make light of this again, I will personally see to your punishment."

The footsteps of the Paladin marching out echoed as Caudro's mind drifted. A year of servitude passed in a flash. From sunrise to sundown, he scrubbed halls, washed dishes, fed animals, hauled supplies, polished armor, and sharpened weapons.

The blur of memories slowed and cleared, and Caudro found himself standing beside Jarain outside the gates of the fortress.

"Your combat training begins tomorrow," the Paladin said.

Uncertain how to respond, Caudro nodded.

"Ever quiet, my young friend. Speak honestly. What are you feeling?"

Caudro shrugged. His head tilted down until he stared at the tips of his boots. "I'm... scared."

"Appropriate," Jarain said with a chuckle. "You are to take your first real step towards becoming a Paladin. If you are to serve as a protector of those needing protection, you must become skilled at combat. Only the Blood Mages at the Academy of Ramaia train more than Paladins. And yet, this moment is daunting for you, as it should be. Not all will pass the training, as you know."

"What becomes of the ones who fail?" Caudro asked.

"The Quinarium provides," the Paladin whispered.

Jarain looked out over the rolling fields which gently sloped down to the village of Mordinlet and the coast beyond. White-capped ocean waves rolled endlessly to the horizon.

"Allow me to offer you a bit of advice: right now, in this moment, consider your life over. You have already given yourself to the Quinarium. It is but a small step to consider your life forfeit. The dead do not fear death, for they have already embraced it. Count yourself among those no longer living, and you will be free."

Caudro locked eyes with the Paladin. "Are we to separate, then?"

"Yes. This next step in your training means that you and I will no longer spend our days together. As much as I have enjoyed your company, Llendshold has need of Paladins, and I would be there for her. You will train with your peers for some years, and when you are ready to face battle, you will be paired with a senior Paladin other than myself."

Jarain knelt and held Caudro's hands.

"In the coming years, you will hear many things, see many things. Your faith will be tested. Your courage will be tried. Your understanding of life itself will be challenged. Stay true to the Quinate, and only the Quinate. Keep the Five in your heart, and you will find your place in this world."

The memories faded, leaving Caudro's mind floating in an endless sea of darkness. Anger filled his heart. If he had to relive the past, why those moments? Why the fateful days which led to his present situation? Why, he asked himself, did he not see the truth of it all sooner?

Hopelessness overtook Caudro. He finally saw the truth, yet he believed it was now impossible to change his future.

"Caudro."

Caudro's eyelids fluttered. He struggled to keep them open, though a part of him said it was pointless anyhow; no matter where he looked, it would be the same stone walls of his cell. Eyes closed, he dragged himself up. The hard floor pressed against his knees.

"Listen, Caudro."

Shaking his head, Caudro squinted and searched for the source, but he saw nothing.

"Caudro!"

Unsteady, he slipped and fell; his mind drifted from the present.

Pain seared in Caudro's knees. Scanning his surroundings, Caudro recognized the chapel. He knelt at the end of a row of twelve Trainees, all nearly ready to face battle and join the ranks of the Paladins. They had been in the chapel for what felt like hours. The skin on their knees threatened to crack and bleed. Caudro silently prayed that someone would come and order him to the training yard, as he would gladly take the most painful of beatings he had ever received over the aches searing through his legs.

"I hear them!" a Trainee shouted. "I hear the words of the Five!"

A Paladin stepped out from a shadowy recess behind the Trainee. "Rise. Join me, and tell me of what you heard."

The Paladin led the Trainee out from the chapel. Those who remained prayed ever more fervently, their eyes clamped shut, wrinkling like stacks of blankets in an overfull closet.

As minutes passed, Caudro's peers left one by one, called to recite the words of the Five as they heard them. No matter how hard he prayed, no matter the words he recited in his mind, no matter which God of the Quinate he called upon, Caudro heard only silence. As hours passed, his body trembled from the agony in his knees. When he thought he could bear it no longer, a hand closed over his shoulder.

"Rise, Caudro. You have knelt for long enough."

"Jarain? You're here?" Caudro looked back, refusing to stand. Tears streamed down his face. "Why have the Five abandoned me?"

The Paladin smiled. "Though rare, not all hear their words. Seeing as we are alone, I will be honest with you. Most hear only the faintest, most meaningless of murmurs. And fret not, you can still become a Paladin. Come with me, should you still wish to serve the Quinarium."

Frigid water splashed over Caudro, ripping him back to the present. The cell door creaked open. Footsteps followed. Caudro knew the familiar, rhythmic *thud-clink* of a Paladin's boots. He wrenched his eyes open to see the man kick aside an untouched bowl of gruel. The contents splattered across a cell wall and the bowl rattled over the floor.

"We should have known you would end up like this, god-shunned. I will never understand why Jarain advocated so endlessly for you. He arrived in time for the Listening Ceremony, as if he knew you wouldn't hear the words of the Quinate. I wonder what he saw in you? Many would have seen you expelled, but Jarain managed to convince us to keep you in the fold. How ashamed would he be to see you now?"

"You have no right to speak on Jarain's behalf, no right to assume what he would believe," Caudro said, his mouth dry and voice cracking. "You hide your face inside your helmet, yet no matter who you are, I know he was ten times the Paladin you will ever be."

The Paladin scoffed. "Your opinion of Jarain is inflated, though at least he died honorably. Did you even know? Your old savior passed while protecting the innocents of Llendshold, honoring the tenets. Unlike you, who betrayed our order, and in doing so betrayed the Five themselves."

Caudro glared at the Paladin. Seeing the sick joy in the man's eyes, Caudro choked back his revulsion. "Jarain would never have stood by for this. The Paladins have lost their way. Scheming to murder innocent people in Cauldhill to start a holy war on a false premise is evil. The Five would never bless the Paladins as they are today. You are heretics. You are self-serving, abandoners of the Quinate!"

The Paladin raised his fist, ready to strike the defiant Caudro, but he instead slowly lowered his hand.

"Better to forget you entirely than to stain my clothes with the blood of a god-shunned fool," he laughed. "Scireth will be here soon enough for your punishment. Then we will see how mouthy you are."

The iron door rattled as the Paladin swung it shut.

Caudro rolled to his side and shivered in the cold. He gazed out the tiny window at the top of his cell as plush white clouds drifted by.

"Ramaia, Almoya, Seraeus, Kosrya, Ilsios... Quinate... please, hear my plea. Please tell me of what I am to do. I stood... I stand for you in defiance of my masters, and see what I have become for it?"

Fear not, Caudro.

The voice filled his head as if it crawled beneath his skin. It was sweet and kind, yet carried a terrible power that sent shivers through Caudro's body.

The Quinate will not rebuke you for defying an order created by Humans, an order which slanders their memory. You sought to protect the innocent, and in doing so turned your back on the orders of Humans, not the Five.

Caudro scanned his cell in a frenzy. "What is this voice? What delusion do I hear? Am I already dead, or dying?"

You are no god-shunned, Caudro. Nor are the voices touted by the Paladins the words of the Quinate.

"Then what are you? Why did I never hear you before?"

You will learn in time. You did not hear us before because it was not yet time for you to hear our words.

"I hear you now... am I to die? If so, at least I finally thought for myself."

All who are of pure heart and desire to stand beside the Quinate will find such a place waiting for them. You too may one day explore the vastness of the skies beyond this world, embraced by the grandeur of the Five. The only question is when you are to join them? And that is not for us to know.

The voice ceased as the cell door screeched open. Caudro, still lying on the floor, looked up to see none other than Scireth, head of the fortress and the one who took him to be tested in battle in the name of the Quinarium. Her round face and soft features, set about a bright eyes and a kind smile, masked a ruthlessly calculating mind.

A Mage hovered behind Scireth, wearing the customary pale linen tunic cut high at the waist and swooping down to her knees at the sides. The crimson spirals adoring the trim denoted her as a Blood Mage, trained in the ways of Ramaia.

Scireth strode over to Caudro, halting when she stood nearly on top of him.

"I had such high hopes for you, Caudro. Jarain vouched for you incessantly, claiming you were the perfect candidate to become a Paladin. He convinced me that having a god-shunned rise among our ranks would be a powerful sign, a demonstration of the grace of the Quinate. I took you personally under my wing, and you impressed me with your dedication. Yet, here we are. What happened to the one known as Caudro? How did he fall so far?"

Caudro burst into laughter. "I am not god-shunned. It is I who stand tall for refusing to support your genocidal mania. The Quinarium no longer speaks for the Quinate, it speaks only for the ambitions of Humans."

"Mind broken before we even begin," Scireth said with a sigh. "This bodes poorly, yet proceed we must. Caudro, former Paladin, you are a traitor to the Quinarium, a betrayer of the Quinate, a self-declared apostate by your refusal to serve as you pledged. You must be punished accordingly. As an orphan, Jarain saved you from losing a finger. Now, we take your eyes instead."

The Blood Mage took a drink of mana and uttered a spell. Caudro, mad with fury, leapt up with a roar. His desperate act of defiance was too late, as slivers of red flew out from the Mage's hand. A writhing mass of slender tendrils, as sharp as freshly honed sewing needles, pierced Caudro's eyes.

The world went instantly black.

Caudro crashed to the ground. As he tumbled over the stone, unbearable pain filled the voids where his eyes once were. He writhed in agony, grunting like a maimed animal and clawing at his face as blood streamed out from his eye sockets. Scireth watched with glee as minutes passed and Caudro shivered and convulsed and drooled.

Pleased with the display, Scireth leaned close and whispered into his ear. "You, my dear Caudro, will make good on your oath to serve. You attempt to turn your back on your duty, but there is no fleeing. Once you have recovered, you will be repurposed as a laborer. You will spend every waking moment in service of the Quinarium, until we consider you to have atoned for your transgressions, or you have died."

Scireth waited, expecting Caudro to respond; instead, he willed himself to remain silent despite the agonizing pain and the terrifying darkness surrounding him.

"Your impudence is remarkable. May your recovery be swift that we might soon put you to work in the name of the Quinate."

CHAPTER 3

Ami stared at her neatly arranged equipment, which rest upon a small patch of short grass. Bottles of mana sat beside her spiked gourd, with two coils of braided rope, a grappling hook, a hooded cloak, dried provisions, and a few potions. Her bow, arrows, and whistling gourd were noticeably absent.

Gazing out from the overlook, Ami felt a strange longing to be back on the ocean. Its rough waters made for an unpleasant ride, yet she couldn't imagine it being less hospitable than the Paladin fortress. Ami shook her head, casting aside the thought.

"I happen to enjoy the company of Catarin and the crew of the Andaira. Absolutely not possible that I want to be on a boat, and I swear to the Five I'm not scared of sneaking about the fortress. Well, no point in musing about pointless preferences. Sun's about set, there's no point in waiting any longer. Mizaina, guide me, please."

Ami stretched as she readied to gather up her gear.

"Stupid Human tunics!" she fumed, swinging her shoulders in wide circles. "Probably an invention of the Quinarium, designed to make Humans hate themselves. 'The less conspicuous, the better,' they all said. What is the point of wearing Human clothing if I have to stay hidden? If I'm caught, they'll see my face and ears and it won't matter that I'm wearing a tunic. Five above, why did I agree to wear this stupid thing?"

Hastily readying hear gear, Ami was soon ready save one bottle of mana left on the grass. She picked it up and traced the bands of silver wrapped around the vessel.

"Delicate and pretty, yet entirely ridiculous. I can't believe I just called these pretty, good thing Dara and Wynne aren't here or I'd never hear the end of it. Well, that's me packed and prepared. Time to see if I can save you, big man."

Ami took a drink of mana, then secured the bottle to her belt. She gave her gourd a tight squeeze, then readied to cast a spell.

"Mizaina, may your waters rise, and enrobe the fields below."

At the sweep of Ami's arm, a wall of fog billowed inside the forest. She descended, darting between trees as the cloud rolled slowly down the hill. Ami paused on reaching the edge of the woods to observe the Paladins atop the walls. She marked time and positions, counting steps and noting the Paladins' expected views from above.

"It's about twenty yards from here to the ditch. Once I'm inside, there's no way they can see from above unless they look down through the machicolations, but there's no reason for them to look if I make my way across quietly..."

Ami drank more mana and pursed her lips.

"Good thing I have a plentiful supply of mana. Fat lot of good it's going to do me if I get caught, though. Five above here am I talking to myself. I haven't done this since I was a lonely, nervous child."

Steeling herself, Ami cast a spell, concluding with an open palm against her chest. Hidden behind a stout tree, she waved her hand back and forth, grinning as her arm diffused into a murky haze.

Peering out from behind the tree, Ami waited until the Paladins reached the ends of their patrol. She dashed out on all fours, moving only a few paces before collapsing flat against the ground. The Paladins continued marching, unable to see Ami through the darkness, fog, and her spell.

A few feet at a time, Ami made her way across the field until she rolled into the ditch surrounding the fortress. Hearing not a sound, she exhaled in relief as she pulled herself up and leaned against the embankment. Ami dusted herself off, then slinked along in the darkness towards a drainage outlet at the base of the walls.

Pale orange light bled out from the arced drain. It was a few feet wide and rose to knee height. Ami inched up from the ditch and peered through. She was relieved to find no signs of the drain being an outflow for latrines or kitchens, with the nearest buildings a few paces away. She watched as Paladins strode across the compound in the distance, but none walked between the walls and the backs of the buildings.

Ami crept into the arced drain. She pressed her shoulders into the largest gap in the criss-crossed iron bars. Ami praised herself for being precisely the right size to fit through the grate as she wiggled and kicked her way through.

Her heart racing, Ami scurried to the nearest building. Pressed flat in its shadow, she looked up to the wall; the angle was severe, and she was certain the Paladins at the top could not see her. Still, voices carried from the heart of the courtyard. Ami's ears prickled and hairs raised on her neck as she listened for footsteps. Holding her breath, she dove to the next building. Ami inched along until she reached the end, when the keep came into view.

The imposing main building of the fortress was three stories tall and constructed of the same enormous blocks of stone as the outer walls. Four Paladins stood guard outside the entrance, with more patrolling ramparts at the top of the keep, while squads of three and four marched across the courtyard.

"May Kahon curse these Paladins with a hundred stubbed toes and a thousand splinters in their asses," Ami murmured. "Third floor, Imreia said. Can't they be normal and put prisons on the ground level? Why at the top?"

Ami struggled to imagine a way in through the front. There were too many Paladins to sneak past, too great a distance through the open courtyard to reach the gate, and the sudden appearance of fog inside a keep would certainly send the entire fortress on alert if she attempted to use a spell to shroud her approach. She thought of using a rope to reach the roof where there were fewer Paladins, yet the sound of a grappling hook striking stone would be sure to draw attention.

Then, Ami noticed narrow windows on the upper levels of the keep. Based on how light scattered over their surface, she knew the walls of the keep were coarse, unlike the smooth stone of the outer walls.

"Climbing it is," she mumbled.

Retreating into the shadow, Ami took a drink of mana. She stretched her hand, but swore under her breath instead of casting a spell. Dirt from the ditch packed her palm, preventing mana from flowing. Ami winced as she splashed water from a flask into her palm, then scrubbed grit away. She reluctantly squeezed her spiked gourd until warm blood wet her skin.

Ami whispered, then tapped the side of the building. She smiled when her fingers clinked as if they were made of metal.

Her preparations complete, Ami patiently observed the patrols for breaks in timing and gaps in their watch. When Paladins reached the end of their walks atop the walls and ramparts, she raced out.

Diving beneath a cart, Ami scanned the courtyard, relieved to see no Paladins moving from their posts. Unable to see the walls, she counted time, then sped forth. Ami rolled to a stop amid a cluster of stacked boxes and barrels. Peering from behind a stout barrel of pungent oil, she waited until she saw only turned backs, then ran to the walls.

Hidden in a recess beside a tower of the keep, Ami took a moment to catch her breath. She stifled a groan after glancing up and faced the task ahead.

Big man, you had better be worth all this effort.

Facing the wall, Ami reached high and wedged her fingers into the gap between two stones. Kicking up with her feet, she jammed the fingers of her other hand into another crevice. Bit by bit, she scrambled up the walls until she reached a window on the top floor of the keep.

Ami peeked over the ledge, relieved to see an unoccupied storeroom. She crawled inside, massaging her softening fingers as her eyes adjusted to the darkness. Sidling past poorly stacked crates, cinched bags, and piles of books, Ami came to a stop by the door. Squatting, she unfurled the diagram of the fortress in the blush of light peeking through the bottom of the door.

Ami twisted and turned the paper to orient herself, staining it with mud and blood as she traced a finger over the diagram. Finding the room she believed herself to be in, she noted the path she needed to take to the prisons, along with potential windows and rooms to flee in should she stumble upon any Paladins in the halls.

Ami rolled up the parchment and prayed to the Five as she pressed her ear against the door and listened intently. Convinced the halls were unoccupied, she eased the door open. The passage, dimly lit by torches spaced far apart, was wide enough for three people to walk shoulder to shoulder. Ami smiled at the quiet emptiness as she scurried out from the storage room.

Tip-toeing down the hallway, Ami counted doors until she reached the prisons. Or at least, where the prisons should have been; instead, she faced a blank wall.

"Well, shit."

Ami unfurled the diagram. She was poring over the paper when footsteps echoed from around a nearby corner. Ami fled back the way she came from, until the stomping of boots and clattering of armor reached her ears from ahead. Bereft of choice, she ran through a nearby open, two-story-tall chamber which was lined on either side by columns and pews, and pushed open a door at the rear.

Back against the door and arms outstretched, Ami held her breath as boots pounded on stone from both directions. The *thump, thump, thump* rose ever louder in concert with her rising heartbeat.

"As They speak!" called a Paladin.

"So we listen," replied two others.

The Paladins continued marching, their boots beating like drums as they passed by.

Ami was ready to duck back into the hall when she paused to inspect the room. Though it was dim, with only scant moonlight flowing in through a few windows at the back, she made out the features of a grand study. Shelves lined the walls, packed with books, scrolls, ceremonial weapons, and wood sculptures engraved with shining bands of metal. Thick rugs covered the floor. Dominating the space was a sprawling ten-foot-wide desk with a single chair.

Ami walked to the desk. Papers and books covered its surface, but a single propped-up painting conspicuously faced the seat. Squinting in the moonlight, Ami recognized the Human it portrayed.

Scireth? The vain bitch! A painting of herself on her own desk? I need to find Caudro, but I wonder if there's anything else of interest in here...

Ami paced back and forth. She desperately fought against the urge to demolish the room; she gleefully pretended to shred the rugs with a dagger, knock over candelabras and sculptures, and swipe shelves clear of their contents. With a sigh, she turned back to the desk and inspected the papers atop it.

The sight of a map of Cauldhill and the edge of the Nomridian Forest—home of the Fae—sent chills through Ami. Notes detailed how Paladins were to sneak into the woods, where they would find caches of supplies to emulate the Fae, and areas of the walls that the village guards would abandon to ensure the attack would be successful. Worse still, Scireth—likely with the support of Cauldhill's own Confessor, Uldrik—had noted which parts of the village were acceptable to destroy, and people particularly worth killing to generate sympathy.

"How can you plot murder and claim it to be in the name of the Five?" Ami seethed.

Grabbing a blank piece of paper from the table and a quill from a pot of ink, Ami scribbled furiously.

The moon had risen well into the sky by the time she finished copying every detail. Tucking the paper inside her satchel, Ami made for the door. As she grabbed the handle, voices echoed down the hall.

Patiently waiting, Ami's eyes bulged when two patrolling Paladins came to a stop outside of Scireth's office. Ami pressed her ear to the door.

"I still don't understand," came a youthful voice.

"Don't understand what?" followed the second Paladin.

"Why are we guarding Scireth's office through the night? It's not like anyone could get past the walls or those posted outside the keep. And besides, we're in the heart of Llendshold. Who would possibly want to break into a Paladin fortress?"

"It doesn't much matter what we think," the second said gruffly. "We're here for the night."

"Want to take shifts? At least we'll get a bit of sleep that way."

"And what if Scireth herself comes by?"

"Oh fine, you're right. Gods, this is boring," droned the first Paladin.

"I spend my night watches reciting prayers. I suggest you do the same."

Ami rolled her eyes. With the door no longer an option, she hurried over to the windows.

Glass panes filled the black iron frames. Ami stifled a scoff at the opulence of a Paladin, a supposed servant to the Five, having windows sealed with glass. Ami pushed the window open and looked out into the night.

Further along the wall, she spied a window filled with an iron grate, which she believed led to the prison. Ami once again cast a spell to harden her fingers and climbed out into the night.

High on the walls and close to the Paladins on the ramparts, Ami timed her movements to match their footsteps. She painstakingly inched along the stone walls in the darkness. Finally reaching the prison window as her arms shook with fatigue, Ami grabbed hold of the iron bars.

Expecting the metal grate to hold her weight, the poorly secured bars instead broke free. Ami scrambled to grab hold of the ledge. The grate tumbled down, clanging against the wall on the way before it landed with a thud.

"What was that!?" a Paladin roared from above.

Though she was unsure if more Paladins were inside, Ami scrambled through the window as fast as she was able. She sat with her back against the wall beneath the open window as Paladins converged on the ramparts above.

"I can't see anything."

"You heard it though, right? It sounded like a sword striking stone, then a thud."

"Could it have been an animal? Maybe an owl flew over the walls and hit the side of the keep?"

"I don't know. I could have sworn it was metal."

"Well, I can't see anything. You go check if you're so worried. Last time Scireth caught someone on night watch not at their post, she put them on latrine duty for a month."

Ami gasped in relief as the footsteps faded. She turned her attention to the prison. Two small torches provided meager light. A row of eight barred doors covered one wall; the opposite had a few tables, chests, and chairs with restraints. Ami crept over to the cells.

The first was empty, but she gasped on looking into the second. A young boy wearing a crude tunic lay on a pile of tattered blankets and whimpered in his sleep. Lesions and bruises covered his arms and legs. Shuddering, and filled with regret she couldn't help him, Ami hurried to the next cell.

She passed more thankfully empty cells until she spied one with a man lying on the ground. Ami leaned against the door and peered in. Though the room was dim, she was certain she had found Caudro.

Ami drank a sip of mana, then took a stout twig from her satchel. She pushed the end into the lock on the door and whispered.

The twig sprouted out, filling the lock while a paddle formed at the opposite end. Ami gave it a twist and the lock cracked open.

"Who... who's there?" Caudro stammered.

"It's me," Ami said, hurrying to Caudro's side.

"Ami?" Countless questions flooded Caudro's mind, but her voice calmed him like a cup of hot tea on a chilly day. "How? How is this possible? You shouldn't have come."

"Sh! Keep it quiet. You don't want the guards coming. And of course I came. I can always find plenty of good use for you, big man."

Caudro sat up to face Ami; she recoiled on seeing the bloodstains around his tightly shut eyelids.

"They took my eyes. I will never see again... I'm useless, Ami," Caudro said with trembling lips.

The defeat in his voice stunned Ami. She grabbed Caudro's hands and squeezed them tight.

"If you were as useless as you seem to think you are, then no one would have been in favor of this rescue. Eyes are but one small part of you."

Caudro shook his head. "A Fae, whose grandfather was murdered by Paladins, has come to rescue an expelled Paladin. Ami, you have gone through all this only to find me broken. You should flee, alone. I can at least be a distraction that you might escape."

Ami patted Caudro's cheek. "You really have a thing for being dramatic, don't you? It would be a terrible waste to go through all this only to leave you behind. And besides, the Paladins have wronged you and me both. It's fitting, not ironic. Now, if you're done being poetic and talking shit about yourself, we have a fortress to flee."

"If you are to take me, can you help me find my armor?"

Ami pulled at her hair. "Five above, you are a right idiot! You tell me to leave you behind, then when you agree to come with me, you ask for your armor? Do you even know where it is?"

"I saw it before they took my eyes. They keep each prisoner's belongings in the chest opposite their cell."

"Fine then. Follow me, keep your hand on my shoulder. And don't you let those fingers go a roaming; hands on my shoulder only!"

Ami grabbed Caudro by the elbow and helped him to his feet, then guided his hand to her shoulder. Caudro froze. After days of feeling only fists and stone, Ami's shoulder, even through her tunic, was incomprehensibly soft.

Ami stepped forward and slipped from Caudro's grasp.

"Psst, hey you!" she whispered through grit teeth. "You have to hold on. I promise I'm not made of daggers!"

Ami returned Caudro's hand to her shoulder. He gripped tightly. A warmth that felt entirely impossible after days spent surrounded by cold stone walls overcame him; it was as if a summer breeze embraced his soul. Caudro had hardly a moment to process the sensation as Ami briskly pulled away. This time Caudro was ready, and he stumbled after.

Ami knelt by the chest, which she unlocked with another twig.

"I hope this Quinarium armor is worth it," she said.

"Even if it comes from the Quinarium, it is mine. It represents who I am... or was," Caudro said.

"No need to disparage yourself, we've already got the armor. They wrapped it all up nicely. You want to bring it along, you need to carry it. Here, I'll get you situated."

Ami pulled the sack of armor across Caudro's shoulders when a feeble voice called out.

"Hello? Who are you?"

Ami spied the boy she had seen earlier. His arms dangled out the cell door.

"No one to you, that's who," she said, tying the sack.

"Are you breaking out?" the boy asked.

"I'm sorry, truly," Ami said. "I would bring you with us, if I could."

"Bring me with you?" the boy spat. "Why would I leave my home? Wait, that's the god-shunned! I heard Scireth talking to him!"

Ami's brow furrowed. "God-shunned? Whatever you want to call him, let's keep this between us, shall we?"

The boy inhaled deeply.

"Sound the alarm! The god-shunned is fleeing!"

"I take it he would rather stay then," Ami said as the boy in the cell continued his shrieking. "So much for my sympathy and kindness!"

Shouts and stomping feet echoed down the hall outside the prison.

"A moment, Caudro. Stay there, and ignore the boy if you can."

Caudro brought his suddenly empty hand to his stomach. He spun in place, uncertain of where he stood, of what surrounded him. The echoing from the halls reverberated between the stone walls, and he could no longer orient himself by sound. A sharp scraping overtook the shouts of the boy and approaching footsteps. It was as if an invisible cage closed around Caudro, pressing ever tighter. His breaths shortened. His heart raced. In that moment, he wished he was an insignificant speck of dirt beneath the notice of all.

Ami's hands closed around Caudro's, and his breathing eased.

"I blocked the doors, but it won't hold them for long; we'll have to climb down. Let's hope there's a way out from the courtyard!"

Thwam!

Paladins rammed into the door, sliding the pile of tables and chests back an inch.

"Time to go!" Ami said, pulling Caudro to the open window.

"Stop! You can't escape!" the boy yelled from his cell.

"Ami," Caudro whispered, "how are we to escape? I don't know if-"

"Shut it, big man. Escaping is my job. You just keep close and don't worry your pretty face," Ami said. She took hold of a rope when her face flushed as the boy continued hollering from his cell. "Oh, come off it, you petulant shit! Enjoy sleeping on stone floors! Enjoy your beatings! Enjoy your meatless meals!"

"I don't think he'll mind the meatless meals," Caudro said, gripping the Fae's shoulder tightly.

"Right, well... it's a bit more of a metaphor than a tease," Ami said as she tied a rope to the door of a vacant cell, then threw the coil out the window she had arrived through. "Anyway, we don't have time to chat. I trust you can still climb down a rope? You aren't looking your best, if I'm honest."

"If you can lead me to the rope, then yes."

The banging of the Paladins grew ever faster. Ami shoved the rope into Caudro's hands and pushed him through the window. The door behind them creaked and groaned, threatening to break as the Paladins battered their way in.

Caudro descended, hand over hand at a measured pace, when Ami blitzed down the rope and crashed into him. They tumbled the last story, clambering for the rope as they landed in a heap on the ground.

"Did you have to move like a worm crawling in the dirt?" Ami scolded as she gathered herself up.

"I... I'm sorry, without my eyes..."

"It's fine... we're fine," Ami said. "No time to worry for the moment. We need to get outside the walls."

"Over them would be quickest. There's no way we can make it to the gate before it's shut and barred, not to mention the Paladins on guard," Caudro said.

A *thunk* came from a few feet away.

"What was that!?" Caudro said.

"A bolt! Back, against the wall!" Ami said, looking up to the ramparts and spying a Paladin reloading his crossbow.

"Which way?" Caudro asked, with arms outstretched.

Ami pushed Caudro into the wall. She pressed against him as she took a drink of mana, musing that she had always thought he would be the one to save her, not the other way around. Ami squeezed her spiked gourd. She summoned a fresh cloud of fog, then sent the haze floating in both directions around the keep.

Caudro flinched when a bolt struck the ground, followed closely by another.

In a flurry, Ami pulled off her cloak and cast a spell into the fabric. Wind billowed inside the cloak as she threw it. The garment flowed through the fog as if Ami ran inside. The Paladins above roared and an alarm bell rang. Crossbow bolts sank into the dirt as Paladins chased after the cloak.

Ami and Caudro clambered up a ladder to the abandoned walls, where Ami prepared a rope.

"Maybe you should go first this time," Caudro offered.

"Fine, but don't make me climb back up to help you."

"I made it down the last rope without issue."

Without comment, Ami guided Caudro to the rope; she then leapt over the edge.

Caudro landed moments later, but when he reached out, his hands found nothing more than air.

"Ami," he whispered.

His head pounded as seconds passed, and he heard no reply.

"Ami?"

Despair struck Caudro's heart as he crouched low with arms extended. He gasped with relief as Ami's fingers wrapped around his wrist. She positioned his hand back on her shoulder.

"Sorry about that," she whispered. "I may have forgotten you need a touch of guidance."

A few minutes later, they reached the forest.

"Well, always a fun time with you around," Ami said, patting Caudro on the shoulder.

"The forest isn't safe."

"Oh come now, can't we celebrate that we've made it out of the fortress? Fine! I know we aren't safe here. We need to make for the docks. Catarin has the Andaira anchored off the coast near Mordinlet."

"Catarin brought you on the Andaira? How can we possibly reach them before the Paladins find us? Scireth won't rest until they have turned every inch of these woods upside down. And while she might not be a Mage, Scireth has been hoarding Mage-enchanted equipment these past months. I can't fight, either."

"Of course we aren't fighting, you silly man!" Ami said jovially. "All we need are a couple of horses, and the Paladins have plenty of them."

Refusing to speak any further, Ami led through the woods until the entrance to the fortress came into view. Scireth marched before an orderly formation of dozens of Paladins as she barked orders. Ami led in the shadow of the trees until they reached the Paladins' stable, a mere stone's throw away from Scireth.

Sneaking inside, they found rows of stalls home to stout horses, still wearing their armor.

"Why keep them armored?" Ami muttered. "Does the cruelty of the Quinarium know no bounds? Poor things should have a moment of respite. Well, at least we can help a couple of them out. Give me a moment, big man."

Ami left Caudro by a stall while she readied two horses. He listened as Ami muttered to herself and bits of metal thudded to the ground. Before Caudro could ask where Ami was or what was happening, she pushed him forward until he bumped into the side of a warhorse.

"Well climb, then, big man! I trust you've done this before?" Ami urged with a whisper.

Caudro stood awkwardly, with one leg raised. Ami sighed, guiding his foot into the stirrup. He took hold of the saddle and heaved up onto the horse. Over-eager, Caudro nearly fell off the other side when Ami grabbed hold around his waist and situated him back into the saddle.

"I'm sorry," Caudro muttered.

"We're all settled now. Think nothing of it," Ami said, mounting her horse. "Ready yourself; we're going at a gallop."

Ami kicked her heels and yanked Caudro's horse's reins.

They burst out of the stables, nearly barreling through a Paladin standing guard. Scireth roared, and the platoon of Paladins sprinted to the stables.

When they were halfway to Mordinlet, Ami yelled out to Caudro.

"They're far behind us, and the distance is growing! Good luck they keep those poor beasts burdened by armor."

Caudro clung tightly to the neck of his horse. "It doesn't much matter how far they are now if we're stuck on the docks!"

"Will you stop your worrying, big man? I've gotten us this far already!"

Alarm bells rang as they flew past Mordinlet. Ami rode hard, straight onto the docks. Hooves thundered over wood planks until Ami brought the horses to a screeching halt, nearly unseating Caudro.

"Success, I see!"

"Catarin?" Caudro called out.

"The very same. I've had quite a fine evening, as it were! Though it seems you've had less than your finest."

"I wouldn't call this success yet," Ami said as she dismounted. "We have some *friends* on the way."

Catarin helped Caudro down from his horse. "Right then, less gawking and talking, more getting onto the boat!"

The three had barely set foot on the rowboat when two of Catarin's crew began rowing in earnest. They were soon gliding over the ocean, laughing as desperate Paladins fired crossbows from the docks. Their bolts crashed into the sea, far behind the rowboat.

"Are you sure the Andaira is fast enough to outrun the ships docked at Mordinlet?" Caudro asked.

"Worry yourself not," Catarin said with a chuckle. "I bought an extra round—or three, in some cases—for every captain and sailor I could find. Those Paladins are going to have a right time trying to find a crew sober enough to make it to the docks, let alone sail."

"Wise as always, dearest captain," Ami said.

"Keep up the compliments and I'll have to make you a part of my crew," Catarin said as her crew members laughed.

Caudro sat hunched on a bench, head drooped. "All this, for me?"

"Yes, yes, you can make it up to me later, big man," Ami replied. "No matter whether you believe me or not, it was Dara and Wynne who insisted that we find you. And I, in my infinite stupidity, volunteered to free you. If you feel in debt, worry not. There will be plenty of days on the ocean for you to make it up to me. You can massage my sore fingers, if you wish. They are in quite a state from climbing the walls of the keep. What would my grandfather say if he saw me so?"

"Dara and Wynne!" Caudro exclaimed, sitting taller. "You said many days. Where are we going?"

Catarin patted Caudro on the back. "Draethhold."

Caudro sat pensively for a moment.

"Any place other than Mordinlet is a welcome place indeed... I can hardly believe I'm eager to make for the southern lands."

"It's alright, big man, you can say it," Ami drolled. "You're happy to be heading there because you're with me."

Chapter 4

Warm morning sun flowed in through a square window. Ami basked in the light. She held the wooden owl charm between her thumb and forefinger and gently traced its smooth surface. She was entirely lost in the charm's faded markings when a cough drew her attention.

Caudro sat at attention in a nearby chair. A white cloth band was wrapped around his head, covering his eyes. Ami inspected his face properly for the first time since they had fled to Draethhold. Despite the cloth, he was still the same Caudro to Ami: gaunt cheeks below high cheekbones, a bold jaw framing full lips, and short, wavy hair the Paladins had thankfully not shaven. Her brow furrowed; his shoulders and chest were leaner than she had remembered.

"You've been quiet," he said, his voice barely more than a whisper. "Can you... can you tell me what you see?"

Ami surveyed their surroundings.

"We're in a study. From what little I've seen of the inside of Human buildings, I would call it simple, but well adorned. There are bookshelves and paintings, all the expected furnishings, but it's rather dull. There's a beautiful forest in the distance—with living trees, as you would prefer to the dead ones of the Nomridian Forest—but it is far away. This Stronghold is cold; it's all stone walls from bottom to top. I don't want to touch anything. I've always felt wrong in Human buildings, but right now... it's like my heart can't understand that I'll be back among the trees soon enough."

Caudro remained rigid, as if he were a statue. "I understand your meaning, despite having grown up in places like this. I'm not sure I belong here, either."

"Well, that's a lovely, uplifting sentiment! And you're one to say I've been quiet. You've been sitting in silence most every moment since we arrived, always with that forlorn expression painted on your face. Why don't you answer a question for me? What are you thinking? Or feeling?"

"Nothing."

Ami readied to break into a lecture when the door to the study opened.

"Dara! Wynne!"

Caudro jumped to his feet, but froze where he stood. He listened to the sounds of rustling fabric, of pats on the back, of wordless expressions shared between friends who regretted the passing of time since they had last seen each other. Then, soft fingers wrapped around his hands and squeezed.

"Wynne, hello."

"It's good to see you, Caudro." Wynne said, her voice deep and calming. "I'm sorry we weren't able to meet you when you arrived. How are you faring?"

"No need to apologize!" Ami cut in. "Besides, we've only been here a couple of days, most of which has been spent cleaning up, eating, and sleeping. I'm doing well enough, but big man, here-"

"I'm alive."

A firm hand grabbed hold of Caudro's shoulder, followed by a bright and airy voice.

"And in living, you have given us and so many others hope and joy immeasurable."

"Hello, Dara," Caudro said.

Ami looked back and forth between the two Mages. Dara cut her formerly long hair short, which only complemented her strong jaw and high cheeks. Wynne, meanwhile, was as Ami remembered her, with wavy hair framing soft features and kind eyes.

"And what of you two? How have you fared these past days? I hoped to see you before I left for Mordinlet, but Imreia said you were occupied by 'matters of import that I need not worry myself over.'"

"She has a great deal more to learn about you," replied Wynne. "Otherwise she would know you let very little worry you. Anyway, we spent some time recovering after we fought the Moderator. Then we followed Imreia for weeks, learning more about the truth of the Quinarium, meeting her contacts in Draethhold, and helping to plan what is to come next."

"And training," followed Dara, "as we're able."

Ami snorted. "I can hardly imagine you two need much training, given what I've seen for myself. I told Caudro all about what happened in Yuvsgrend. Dara flying out of the water to slay the creature, Wynne summoning walls of fire consuming entire tunnels... you two are quite the pair. Only training I imagine you two really need involves quiet nights and a comfortable bed."

"Ami!" Wynne shouted, her cheeks blushing while Dara stifled a snicker.

"You aim to stand against the Quinarium," Caudro said solemnly. "It is wise to train every moment you can."

"You say that as if you don't include yourself among those fighting the Quinarium," Dara said.

"I don't."

Ami sighed. "He'll come around. The big man can't help but be a bit down on himself at the moment, what with his eyes. I don't think he's quite used to it yet."

"Down on myself?" Caudro said, his chin shaking in anger. "There is no being down on myself. There is simply an understanding of reality. I had enough time in that cell to assess my abilities, and have made an appropriate assessment. I have never been much more than two hands molded to fight, and without my eyes, I am of no use."

"You are too harsh on yourself," Wynne said. "You are hasty to discount the contents of your mind. Even in moments when we disagreed, your perspective was always invaluable. And Paladins are the core of the Quinarium's forces. Few know the depths of the order as you do."

Ami playfully punched Caudro's shoulder. "Don't worry about him! I know a useful big man when I see one, and this one here has plenty of use, even outside of his armor."

Dara nodded. "I agree. Please don't forget, Caudro, there's also a powerful symbol in you. A Paladin, one of the most dedicated and zealous servants of the Quinarium, turning away from their lunacy... your defiance means more than you realize."

"Besides, no one needs eyes in the meeting we are about to attend. What do you all make of it?" Wynne asked.

"Imreia, Hawel of the Fae—because of course, that self-important toad would petition to be here—Vinzen of the Dwarves, the Draethhold Lords... it's quite the list of attendees," Ami said.

"I still find it odd that Imreia invited us," Dara said. "We're all young. We aren't Elders or leaders of note."

"Imreia asked for us because of what we know of the Quinarium's plan for the Fae," Wynne said.

"We could have written everything down for her," Ami retorted. "I don't like it. It seems like-"

The door swung open.

"Who is it?" Caudro asked.

Dara's shoulders tensed as she cleared her throat. "Okter."

"And a girl with him," Ami whispered.

"Good to see you too, Dara."

Okter's voice was deep yet crisp. His slicked-back hair framed a dark-complexioned face with a sharp brow and wide jaw. He strode across the room, then came to a stop close by the four, grinning as if he were their old friend.

"Everyone, this is Okter, my former mentor from the Academy of Ramaia. Okter, I assume you already know who everyone is?"

"Of course I do. It is a pleasure to meet you all."

"I heard you were in Draethhold, but didn't expect you to be here," Dara said. "I suppose I should have known you would have made such a meeting your business."

Okter raised an arm missing its hand. He whispered and a misty, wavering skeleton appeared, shrouded in a haze of lilac.

"As with you all, I have quite the history with the Quinarium. In fact, I would wager I understand the institution's immorality better than any, except for Imreia. I would see their many injustices righted. Oh! My manners, caught up in another tirade. Dara is unfortunately familiar with my tendency to ramble. Allow me to introduce Rhoslin, daughter of Lord Kalomar. In Dara's absence, she has become my newest protégé. A touch younger than you four, but capable and eager."

Wynne hooked her arm through her partner's in a reassuring embrace. "A pleasure to meet you both. I've heard much about you, Okter. And I'm sure I will come to know you in time, Rhoslin."

Rhoslin bowed deeply with one hand across her chest and the other stretched wide, palm open.

Wynne grinned and bowed in kind. "I see you've taught Rhoslin our customs, Okter. Thank you, Rhoslin."

Okter chuckled. "Wynne, your mother is one of the few among the Earls and Lords of Llendshold I would still happily bow before. Imreia has told me much of you and Dara as well. That makes you Ami and-"

"That'll be Aminantskeilara for you."

"Ah, yes, my apologies," Okter said, making no effort to mask his smirk. "I am well aware of your people's regrettable naming customs and thought you might prefer the shorter version. Enforcement of Hierarchy is all but the same among Humans, an age-old institutional tool of the Quinarium, and one I will gladly see eradicated. Finally, we have Master Caudro, the former Paladin."

Caudro bowed his head.

"Ami made a thorough report. When I heard of your eyes it pained me deeply, my dear friend," Okter said. "I wish I had the power to help, but I know of no spell capable of healing such a wound. I spoke with Imreia on your behalf, and it is unfortunately beyond her skill as well. My encounter with the Adjudicator's Enforcer was but a modest setback, as I have learned to replicate a hand. But the eyes? A hand is a trifle compared to the eyes, and as I understand it, they shattered yours completely with Blood Magic."

Dara crossed her arms. "Okter, I've been meaning to ask you. Why were we not taught healing spells at the Academy of Ramaia? I've since learned healing spells which call upon Ramaia."

Okter grinned. "The Quinarium is the answer to your question. They dictated exactly what we were to teach. They wanted the Academies to see each other as competitors, not collaborators. As such, I was forced to instruct at their whims. A narrow-minded effort to exert control, especially given the Moderators, Enforcers, and Adjudicators all study the spells of more than one of the Five. I would gladly tutor you again, Dara, should the opportunity arise. You as well, Wynne, and you, Aminantskeilara. Though, from what I hear, you all may have surpassed my ability."

Ami readied to deride the performative compliment when a bell chimed.

"It's time," Wynne said.

Caudro shrank at the sound of departing footsteps, uncertain which way to go, until Ami grabbed his hand and slapped it onto her shoulder. She gave a reassuring pat, then led down long halls, up winding stairs, and through narrow passages.

They finally reached their destination: an expansive room with a sprawling, knee-height square table at the center. Instead of chairs, plush cushions wrapped in a myriad of colorful fabrics surrounded the perimeter. Dozens of round oil lamps dangled from the ceiling, filling the windowless room with a pleasant glow, as if it were sunset on a veranda.

To the right sat the three Lords of Draethhold. They wore simple linen gowns with open-front robes over top which extended to their ankles. The robes were dyed in a rich plum color and covered in geometric patterns made with fine gold thread. Jewelry made of precious metals weighed their fingers, wrists, necks, and ears, though gems were absent; instead, each piece demonstrated an artful mastery of metalworking.

Ami thought the three Lords could easily have been distant cousins, owing to their similar shade of tanned skin, flowing hair pulled back in the same style, and sharp brows framing intense eyes. Behind them stood three guards, dressed the same as their lords, though their clothing lacked gold stitching. The guards carried slender swords, mana bottles, and wore Mage gauntlets.

At the far end of the room sat none other than Hawel, Fae Elder of the village of Keldarna. Ami's face scrunched on seeing him, assuming he used Keldarna's proximity to Cauldhill as justification for being the Fae emissary. She resented breathing the same air as the Fae who was always angling for a higher position among Fae leadership; he must have hopes that attending this meeting would further his status, Ami thought. Hawel twirled his long, silvery hair around a finger as his eyes darted from face to face.

Ami's sour expression faded on noticing her good friend Vinzen the Dwarf, who sat beside Hawel. A thin band of metal, a Dwarf Priest Crown, sat atop his hairless head while the gold talisman Ami had found in Yuvsgrend dangled from his necklace. He winked and grinned for a second, before allowing his face to relax to a neutral expression.

Imreia knelt to the left, her hair pulled back tight as always. Hovering over her shoulder was an unknown, brawny young woman wearing a simple tunic. Though her jaw was rounder and her lips fuller, the woman's face bore an uncanny resemblance to Imreia, with the same high cheeks and teal eyes.

"Welcome! Welcome, all of you," Imreia said with a bow. "Okter and Rhoslin, come sit by me. The rest of you, sit as you wish on the unoccupied side. Allow me to introduce you to Gwelyn, Barden, and Kalomar, the three Lords of Draethhold."

The Lords turned their heads sideways and nodded in greeting.

Once all had taken their places, with Ami helping Caudro onto a cushion, servants arrived and placed a gold cup of water before each attendee. Gwelyn took a deep drink, then set his cup down so gently that it made not a sound.

"As we are all here, you may begin, Imreia."

"Thank you, Gwelyn. Although I recognize the auspiciousness of the present company, I will not mince words. We are all here because we face a dire threat. The Regency of Llendshold and the Quinarium have become so intertwined that they now function as one. As you know, and thanks to the efforts of these four to my right, we are certain beyond any doubt that the Quinarium intends to blame an attack on Cauldhill on the Fae. In doing so, they will instigate a holy war, and will do all they can to commit genocide again."

Imreia looked to Vinzen as she closed; she held her mouth slightly open as if to gasp in silent horror at the genocide of the Dwarves. After allowing the quiet to linger, Imreia readied to speak again when Barden cleared his throat.

"Yes, we have all read your reports, Imreia. And heard your words. Again, and again, and again."

Imreia sat still, unaffected by the Lord's dismissive tone. "We all know that once the Quinarium has completed its *cleansing* of the Nomridian Forest—destroying the Fae as we know them, and completing its genocide of the Dwarves—they will turn their eyes south to Draethhold. We must act before they combine their forces. We must act before they have galvanized the entire nation and filled heads with notions of holy war. We must act before it is too late."

"What you mean," said Kalomar, "is that you believe we should wage a preemptive war against Llendshold."

"How do you believe such a war would go?" Gwelyn challenged with a finger pressed onto the table. "Though our nation is not dissimilar in size to Llendshold considering land, our people are lesser in number. We have precious few Mages, numbering in the dozens. Your Fae allies will bring what, a few dozen more? The Quinarium fields an army backed by hundreds of Mages."

"I would wager a barrel of ossians that the Mages of Draethhold and our Fae Mages are more than twice the warriors of those trained by the Quinarium, but we cannot forget the necessity of mana," said Hawel. "Animal sacrifices provide as we need in times of peace, but war will tax our already strained supply."

Kalomar grimaced. "Where the Fae have their sacrifices, we rely on smuggling mana from Llendshold. War will make this more difficult than ever before. We simply do not have enough mana stockpiled to support a conflict in which Mages will be of critical importance."

A quiet pause settled over the room. Ami looked at Imreia, but the woman's face was blank. Dara, meanwhile, clenched her fists around the edge of her tunic. Wynne sat with perfect posture at Dara's side, though she blinked rapidly.

Vinzen leaned forward. "We would gladly offer our Priest crowns to ward against the Mind Mages, though we have few and crafting more has turned out to be a slow and laborious process. We hope to hasten our speed, but we have only just begun to understand the magic."

"While we appreciate your offer, Dwarf, this talk of mana and Mages highlights another issue," said Barden. "Our economy pales compared to that of Llendshold. They have endless, fertile fields, sprawling farms, deep mines rich in ore, and forests ready for harvest. Meanwhile, much of Draethhold is arid and unsuitable for farming. Our reliance on foraging in the mountains and fishing the seas means our food supply is sensitive. An army will not march on empty stomachs."

"And speaking of a marching army, how will we motivate our people?" Kalomar said, both hands open as he gestured to all the attendees. "You note the Quinarium's plan to incite a genocide by falsifying an attack on Cauldhill, with Humans posing as Fae. You may convince us three of the need to rein in the Quinarium, but will a commoner care of matters so far from their homes? A tenuous peace with Llendshold has lasted for near a generation, with trade even taking place along our border."

Hawel grumbled with his arms crossed. "Even if the armies of Draethhold can be spurred to motion, how are we to face the might of Llendshold? Even if we are to muster all who are able, we are likely to match the forces of only the city of Stellburg, but one of the five cities of Llendshold. Further, our forces are ill-trained to fight in the open fields, which the Llendshold armies are certain to prefer."

Imreia took a drink of water, then set the cup down with a clink. She slowly pushed it further onto the table, then turned it back and forth by the stem until its placement pleased her.

"Lords, Elder, I hear your concerns. Know that I agree with them. I also know that you, Lords of Draethhold, have met before today. You know that war is unavoidable. I believe you also know it is better to start this conflict on your own terms, rather than wait for Llendshold to bring down its unified might upon you. As such, I ask that you state your demands clearly, that we might work together with honesty and earnestness."

The three Lords eyed each other, shuffling on their cushions and adjusting their robes. They shared a silent conversation of twisted and strained expressions before all three finally nodded in agreement.

Kalomar leaned over the table. "We appreciate your candor, Imreia. And as you spoke, I too shall speak plainly. We share a concern. Are you and your allies capable of contributing meaningfully to war, or will Draethhold be left on its own to falter against the might of Llendshold?"

"Yes, we must see your capability," Gwelyn said.

"Prove to us there are cracks in the foundations of the Quinarium, of Llendshold. Prove to us that you and your allies can find their vulnerabilities and capitalize on them," Barden said.

Imreia continued to play with her glass.

"I presume you have specific demands?"

Kalomar's eyes dwelled on his daughter Rhoslin. "There are three demands. First, you must perform a show of supply. As discussed, Mages will be essential in this conflict. While Okter is developing his own institution in Draethhold, and will further gather the support of our scattered Mages, we must be confident that we have all the mana they need."

Gwelyn blinked slowly. "Second is a show of strength. We understand the ways of the Llendshold armies, but the Agents of the Quinarium give pause. Prove to us that we need not be concerned, that you can strike either the Mages or the Paladins with meaningful force. As a show of good faith, we will provide a company of twenty of our finest warriors to fight alongside you. Use them however you will, but you must satisfy our desire to see the Quinarium brought to its knees."

"Finally, we demand a show of honor," Barden said, stroking his chin. "Great power lies in symbols, and we need great symbols to motivate our people. Vinzen wears an ancient talisman of his people. Caudro turned his back on the heretical order of Paladins. In the same way, we would see a symbol returned to us. In ages past, the Quinarium stole a gilded tome from Draethhold. It contains the original recordings which establish Draethhold as a sovereign nation, and documents a dispute to the Quinarium's claims of being the sole and rightful conduit to engage with the Quinate. Perhaps most difficult of our demands, we are certain the tome is held in the Ziggurat of the Fallen, near Evenswall, where the Paladins guard it."

Quiet filled the room until Ami cleared her throat.

"If I may-"

"You should remain silent, Aminantskeilara. Know your place," Hawel spewed.

Kalomar raised one eyebrow and tilted his head. "I am uncertain of all the Fae customs, Elder Hawel, but might I remind you, it was we Lords who invited Ami? She has the same right to speak as we all do. You were saying, Ami?"

Ami gulped, stunned by the sudden voice of support. "Right! I understand your requests, erm, Lords, but I can't help but wonder about the priority. The Paladins are, at this moment, preparing to attack Cauldhill. The seeds are already planted for a rapid mobilization after the attack. We must address this issue with urgency."

"The order matters little," Gwelyn replied. "The Llendshold Regency and the Quinarium alike see every single person at this table, and all of our people, as an enemy they intend to one day eradicate. The only question is the order in which they seek to destroy us."

"Please, pay her no mind," Hawel said, glaring at Ami. "She is naïve at her wisest, childish at her most mature, and does not speak on behalf of the Fae."

"I find it curious our people don't crawl like slugs and snails, if the best representative we can muster is so spineless as you, Hawel," Ami retorted. "You are more concerned with preserving bloodlines and chasing titles than you are about preserving the existence of our people."

"I agree with Ami," Vinzen said in support of his friend. "We Dwarves number in the hundreds, our warriors in the tens, but the Fae have a sizeable force, near equal to one of you three Lords. If we don't stop the Quinarium attack on Cauldhill, if the Humans march on the Nomridian Forest, then this potential alliance may be doomed before it begins."

Barden shifted on his cushion. "If Llendshold sets its eyes north, the early stages of our campaign in the south will be considerably easier," Barden said. "Eyinhill might fall in a day, and Monningburg shortly thereafter."

"Right," Gwelyn said with a nod. "It would take an army a month or more to march from Stellburg to Monningburg. If the Llendshold armies focus on the Nomridian Forest, it would free our armies to strike decisively."

Ami's eyes bulged. "What is the point of capturing a single city if the Fae are overrun? Our entire people might be lost!"

Kalomar clasped his hands together. "I understand our words seem callous, Ami. Yet wars are won by taking the slightest of advantages. Although the Fae might take the brunt of the initial attack, if Keldarna were to fall, it would pale compared to the enormous shift in power that would be the capturing of Monningburg and Eyinhill. And our taking of them would bring reprieve to the north."

Ami's face reddened. "But-"

"Perhaps, Ami, we can consider a Paladin target as one of our options for this show of strength," Okter counseled. "A shame the ziggurat is too small and remote to be appropriate for such a demonstration, but the Paladins have a fair number of fortresses throughout Llendshold, which they consider impervious. Destroying one would rattle the faith of many."

"Rushlet would also make for an excellent target," Imreia countered. "The Quinarium keeps most of its ships near the village, and we could cripple their navy. Though regardless of where we make this show of strength and how we devise a meaningful supply of mana, we don't know when this attack on Cauldhill is to take place. It may well be that supplying mana in the near term will empower our forces, allowing us to better protect the Fae."

"But what if a strike on a coastal village causes the Quinarium to bolster their forces at ports? It may make securing mana all the harder," Ami said.

When Imreia, Okter, Hawel, and Ami began speaking over each other, Kalomar rose from his seat, followed by his peers.

"We have made our demands clear, Imreia. It is up to you and your allies to satisfy them."

"May the Five watch over you all," Gwelyn said.

"Be well," Barden said. "We will begin our own preparations in anticipation of your success."

The three Lords shuffled out with their guards close behind, not sparing a look back as they left. When the door swung shut, Imreia sauntered over to the side of the table where the Lords had sat, and eased into the center seat. Though the others were all on edge, Okter slouched and smiled. Imreia grinned in return, then addressed the others.

"Nothing unexpected, I must say. I anticipated entirely unreasonable demands requiring hours of negotiation, but these three requests? All are within the realm of achievable."

Vinzen methodically rubbed his forehead. "These are not paltry tasks, Imreia. Blood will be spilled."

"I did not say they were insignificant, only that the tasks are feasible."

"I do not know how much we can provide," Hawel interjected. "We Fae must begin our own preparations for the inevitable, in partnership with the Dwarves."

Imreia nodded. "Understood. I ask only one thing before you depart: please release Ami into my service."

Hawel snorted. "I am amenable to such an arrangement."

"Am I not sitting in this room!?" Ami exclaimed, throwing her hands into the air.

"I was about to ask you, Ami, if you are willing to join me, now that we have Hawel's approval."

"Well, seeing as how you all have finally asked for my opinion, I'm all for it. But there are two conditions: first, whatever I am tasked with doing, Caudro joins me; and second, we do whatever we can to stop the Paladins from attacking Cauldhill. Five above, I'm trying harder to protect Humans than most Humans are."

"I'm useless," Caudro blurted out. "Why insist on having me join you?"

Ami sighed. "Because I occasionally need a big, dumb, hunk of a man. That, and without your eyes you need a reliable guide. I assure you there is no one more reliable than me. Shut it, Vinzen, I see that look on your face!"

"Always conditions with you all," Imreia said with a chuckle. "First Dara and Wynne, and now you, Ami. Well, the first request is fair enough and I see no issue with it. As for the second, it is something we must discuss further. We have three intertwined tasks, and I believe we can fulfill your conditions as we devise how we are to satisfy the Draethhold Lords' demands."

"We should leave the show of strength for last," Wynne said.

"I agree," Dara said, placing her hand on Wynne's back.

"Well, of course you would, Dara. Always a yes to every one of Wynne's asks," Ami said with a snicker.

"I mean it in earnest," Dara said, frowning at Ami. "The show of strength will cause all the Quinarium forces to be on edge. It will be easier to find new avenues for smuggling mana and to break into the ziggurat when Mages and Paladins aren't in a state of agitation."

"There is already word of *agitation,* as you put it, since the death of the Moderator," Okter said. "Destroying a fortress would intensify this agitation. I agree the show of strength should come last."

Wynne brushed creases out of her tunic as she sat tall. "We should investigate the cities closest to Draethhold to find our mana supply. Monningburg and Brewardsburg are the obvious choices. Stellburg and Hantsburg are too far, and it would be foolish to approach the capital of Llendswarne."

"I am of the opinion that there is only one choice to source mana: Imreia's old home of Brewardsburg, and the coastal villages of Bramswall and Wilkslet. The mana stores in Monningburg are minimal, owing to the city's proximity to Draethhold," Okter said.

The young woman who resembled Imreia stepped out from the shadows and approached the table. "Imreia, I would join those going to Brewardsburg. Please. I know the city, and-"

"You were a child when we fled, Nireia. Those streets are foreign to you now. I need you here, serving as my liaison and supporting Okter in whatever manner he needs. It is essential that we unify the scattered Mages of Draethhold. Though you are unattuned to mana, your presence alone will be a powerful sign of my commitment and will convince many a Mage. I will lead the efforts to secure mana from Brewardsburg."

Nireia glared at Imreia, then stormed out of the room.

"I'll speak with my dear sister later. I apologize on her behalf."

Okter held his ethereal hand up, as if to examine his nonexistent fingernails.

"Perhaps Nireia would contribute best here, courting the Lords. She may dislike it, but they have quite taken to her. Though, when it comes time for the show of strength I would join you."

"Your presence will be welcome."

Wynne politely cleared her throat. "Dara and I should join you in Brewardsburg. We know the Quinarium as well as any, and can help secure a substantial shipment."

"Don't push too far in the moment," Okter counseled. "We need a spark to start a fire. If you overstep, it may jeopardize our ability to smuggle in the future when mana is needed most."

"That leaves Caudro and I going to Evenswall for the stolen tome, unless you had someone else in mind," Ami said. "It makes sense anyhow. Caudro is the closest we have to an expert on the Paladins, and it's a Paladin stronghold we'll be infiltrating. Getting inside Paladin compounds is turning into a specialty of mine."

"Unsurprising," Hawel drolled. "You've always been a thief, Ami."

Ami threw her hands over her chest in mock surprise. "Hawel!? You're still here? Oh, my apologies, I simply forgot, as you were entirely silent when we spoke of protecting our people. Some emissary you are. But go ahead, brand me a thief once again. At least I raised my voice in support of the Fae while you moaned in the corner."

Vinzen sighed. "Ami..."

Imreia locked eyes with Hawel before he could raise his voice. Like a child faltering under the gaze of a parent after breaking a rule, he retreated into his seat.

"Right then, unless anyone protests, then Caudro and I are off to the ziggurat."

"I protest," Caudro said. "I will only inconvenience you. It was a waste for me to be here at all."

"Of course you aren't a waste," Wynne said.

Okter rolled his eyes. "You are only a waste if you allow yourself to be one. I agree with Ami. Her ability to infiltrate the Paladin Fortress at Mordinlet, and Caudro's knowledge of the Paladins, makes them perfectly suited for such a task."

"And how am I to assist with an infiltration?" Caudro challenged. "I have no eyes. I will be nothing more than a compromising distraction."

"I wonder..." Okter's voice trailed off as he inspected his summoned hand again.

"Well, tell us what's on your mind," Ami said.

Okter tapped his skeletal fingers on the table; with each touch, a small plume of purple haze rose around his hand.

"The method I employ to summon this hand involves a mixture of Blood and Mind magic. The eyes are rather more complex, and seeing as Caudro now lacks them entirely, I wonder if I am thinking about a solution entirely wrong. You should meet with my contact at the Academy of Almoya. It's near Bavenhill. A worthwhile delay, if they can assist Caudro."

"Mind magic to heal a wound of the body?" Dara mused.

"I thought you said you can't help," Ami said. "What makes you think these Mages can do what you cannot?"

"What are eyes, if not a tool to convey the world around us to our minds?" Okter said. "I said I cannot help as I do not know magic to heal such a wound, but I believe there may be other ways to assist Caudro. You must speak with Mages at the Academy of Almoya though, as their ways are beyond my understanding. The Academy is on the brink of revolt, for a plethora of reasons I am sure they will share with you. Many will be eager to assist you."

Imreia stood and clasped her hands. "Then we are decided. The Fae and the Dwarves are to prepare as best they are able. Okter, with Nireia and Rhoslin, will gather favor among Draethhold's Mages. I will join Dara and Wynne in search of a mana supply. Ami and Caudro are to make for the Academy of Almoya on their way to the ziggurat. Once successful, we shall meet in Hantsburg and decide where to make our show of strength."

"Hantsburg?" Wynne chimed.

"Yes, dear Wynne. I have many a friend in the city, and your mother has been reluctant to waste time rooting out allies of mine, no matter how the Quinarium pressures her. I hope you will enjoy your visit home."

Ami bustled about before a row of packs. She inspected, folded, and stuffed spare clothing, bedrolls, pieces of flint, candles, and a wide range of supplies inside. When she reached for a bottle of mana, her tunic pulled tight against her shoulder.

"I cannot get over how horrible this Human clothing is! The design of tunics is positively ridiculous. Every day, it's like I'm putting on a personal prison. At least the Draethhold Lords are supplying us well, though I wish I could try on their clothing."

"I'm sorry."

Ami looked at Caudro. He sat tall, his posture rivaling that of Wynne, though he pulled his limbs in close, like a scared child in a classroom waiting for a strict teacher's rebuke.

"What for?" Ami said. "You didn't design this clothing, nor did you choose where they built the ziggurat."

"I'm sorry that I will be your burden," he murmured.

Ami made a show of exhaling slowly and loudly, half-grumbling all the while. "Big man, if I thought you would be a burden, I wouldn't have asked for you to join me."

"Do you intend to use the gilded tome as leverage when the time comes to decide where we are to make the show of strength?"

Ami set down a tightly bound bedroll and stood before Caudro.

"Yes. Mordinlet makes perfect sense as a target. It's a significant fortress. It's where they held you prisoner, adding to the whole 'symbol' bit, and Scireth calls it home. I will make the others see, no matter what it takes. Even if it means using the tome to encourage them to see the truth of it."

"We have to consider the entirety of the conflict. What if Mordinlet isn't the best strategic target? The forces there might be too strong, or it might not be the most meaningful show of strength to satisfy the Draethhold Lords. What then, if they remain unconvinced, and don't join Imreia as a result?"

Ami scoffed. "Well, you're suddenly chatty. And in case you were wondering, saving my people is the entirety of the conflict to me."

Ami tucked in the remaining supplies until only Caudro's armor remained.

"The Draethhold blacksmith did a fine job repairing your armor. Here, take a look... erm, have a feel."

Caudro recoiled when the breastplate landed in his lap. He felt around the edges to orient himself, then ran his hands across the surface.

"It's as if it were never broken," Caudro said with admiration. "I take it the blacksmith removed the symbol of the Quinarium?"

"Yes. Not a speck of paint left."

"Strange... I still find comfort in holding it. This armor was the heart of my existence as a Paladin."

"Best to make use of everything we can. It doesn't much matter who made what, as long as the pointy end is pointed at the Quinarium. Speaking of pointy end, I don't care for the Draethhold swords and daggers, but these spears seem well made."

"I'm not sure why you're bringing any. You don't fight with spears, and I can't make use of them."

"Better to have them and not need them than the other way around."

The next morning, Ami and Caudro stood outside the stronghold walls with three horses at the ready. Ami was ready to help Caudro onto his horse when a voice called out.

"Don't think you can escape without saying goodbye!"

"Dara! Wynne!"

Ami warmly embraced the Mages. Caudro stood limp, barely responding to pats on his back.

"Have you all decided where you'll start?" Ami asked.

"We'll head east, then take fishing ships to the Llendshold coast," Wynne said. "From there, it'll be a frantic search for people willing to break from the Quinarium's hold and help us."

Ami stood back and smiled. "You two make quite the pair. You're lucky I was there to nudge things forward; otherwise, you might still be staring at each other from a distance instead of turning into a tangle of arms and legs every night!"

Wynne blushed. "You interrupted us as much as you encouraged us!"

"We brought you some things," Dara said, grinning as she handed over a satchel. "It's a shame our time together has been so short."

"Well, all we need to do is tear down the most powerful religious institution in the land, while avoiding death in a war, and then we'll have plenty of time to relax together." Ami peered inside the satchel. "The arrows I expected—and appreciate—but potions? I thought you didn't like these, Wynne."

"These past weeks changed my perspective. I'd rather be there to heal you myself, but unfortunately, it won't be so. It's been good seeing you again, Ami. And you too, Caudro."

Dara wrapped an arm around Wynne as they readied to head back into the stronghold. "Caudro, take care of Ami. She needs someone to keep her in line."

"It's more likely to be the other way around, but I swear to do all that I can."

CHAPTER 5

The setting sun flushed the oblong leaves of towering trees in deep orange. The understory of scattered, squat shrubs and sparse ferns grew out from a floor of decaying leaves. Birds chirped happily, their bellies full of worms and berries.

Three horses, with their leads tied off to a fallen tree and their packs and saddles on the ground, grazed on tall bunches of grass. Ami was busily digging a fire pit with a short-handled shovel when she paused to scan the surrounding woods.

"These forests are strange. I wish there were more plants."

"Do you mean it's strange because the trees are living?" Caudro asked.

"Just because the Nomridian Forest is filled with dead trees instead of living ones doesn't mean it's any less of a forest," Ami snapped.

"I... I'm sorry. I meant nothing by it."

"No, no, it's me who should be apologizing. I've been tense lately."

"Perhaps because you travel with a Paladin again. A blind one at that, who you have to watch over as if he were an infant."

Ami whistled. "Here I was, angry about Hawel of all Fae being selected as our emissary, disparaging me in front of that audience, then happily throwing me at Imreia instead of considering me a benefit to my people. Instead of being mad about that, I could have been funneling my rage at you!"

Caudro sat rigidly. "They are unwise to think so little of you."

Ami smirked. "You don't have to be so subtle with your compliments, big man. Say them openly any time you'd like."

Caudro's stoic expression broke as the corners of his mouth curled up. As if his own reaction caught him unawares, he turned his head down.

"Do you really think we should stop in Almeyhill?" he asked.

"It's on the way to Bavenhill."

"We should avoid the detour and go straight to Bavenhill, to the Academy of Almoya."

Ami set the shovel aside, content with the size of the fire pit.

"We need supplies. It'll be four days to Almeyhill, then another three to Bavenhill. We might save a day if we skip past Almeyhill, but we still we need more food. We'll be stretched as it is, even with me hunting and foraging."

"I'm sorry for being such a burden."

"Gah!" Ami shouted. "Stop with the self-loathing! I brought you for a reason!"

"And what reason is there to bring a fighter who is useless in a fight?"

Ami jumped to her feet.

"Apparently, it is so you can frustrate me to no end so I will feel like I'm back home with my people!" Ami breathed deeply in and out, in and out, then rose to her feet. "We need more firewood, I'll be back-"

A hissing, guttural screech ripped through the forest.

"What was that?"

Caudro turned his head every which way, desperately searching for the source. Ami shoved the shaft of a spear to his chest, then took hold of her bow.

"I'm not sure, but ready yourself."

Caudro clutched the spear with trembling hands.

"Ami?"

"I don't see anything yet. We should keep quiet."

Caudro listened intently. The birds had gone silent. A nearby stream trickled gently, the waters gurgling as they rolled over rocks, when a breeze rustled leaves above. Were it not for the horrifying cry that silenced the animals, the serenity of the forest could have lulled the fussiest of babies to sleep.

Then, a splash came from the stream. A thud was followed by the rattling of tree branches. Caudro spun to face the sound with his spear lowered, but he tripped over a root and stumbled to the ground.

The Fae's bow twanged as she loosed an arrow.

"Ami!"

"I'm a bit busy, big man!"

Ami let a second arrow fly. It soared between trunks, piercing the hide of the source of the screech.

The giant toad, rising to Ami's shoulder in height and with a mouth as wide as it was tall, bounded through the forest on six legs, unbothered by the arrow sticking out of its side. Hardened patches of leathery skin covered its body. It opened its giant maw and croaked, revealing rows of tiny but razor-sharp teeth and a gigantic, barb-covered tongue. The horses reared and kicked, drawing the toad's attention.

Ami unleashed a flurry of arrows as she ran out of the camp. Enraged by the assault, the toad turned and bounded after her. Ami ducked behind a slender tree when the enormous tongue whipped around the trunk, flopping and flailing as it reached for her. Ami dove away as the tongue tightened around the tree, then ripped it from the ground. She reached for her mana gourd, but her hand closed on thin air.

"Teaches me to get comfortable at camp. I guess I'll have to do this without magic!"

Ami dove away from a lash of the tongue. She nocked an arrow as the toad reared back and readied to shoot its tongue out again. When the mouth opened, Ami let the missile fly.

The arrow sailed true, plunging deep into the toad's tongue. Flailing and croaking, the beast slammed its head about as its tongue flopped wildly. The toad finally calmed and flipped its tongue under its belly, clawing until it tore the arrow free.

Slurping its bloody tongue back into its maw, the toad stared at Ami. She stood with an arrow at the ready, glaring. The toad leaned forward and Ami swiftly drew, her thumb coming to a stop by the corner of her lip. With a guttural croak, the toad shuddered, then hopped off into the forest. Ami relaxed her shoulders until the tension was relieved in her bow. She returned the arrow to her quiver, then skipped back to camp.

The sight of Caudro stunned Ami; he crawled on his hands and knees, frenetically searching the leafy ground.

"What are you doing?"

Caudro turned at the sound of her voice. "Ami, you're back! I dropped the spear... I couldn't fight, I didn't know... I was... I was trying to help. You already dug the firepit, I thought I could start a fire, maybe scare away whatever it was, but I dropped the flint, then I... I..."

Ami's joy at the victory over the giant toad was crushed on seeing Caudro's dirt-smudged, panicked, fear-stricken face. She strode over and helped him to his feet, then dusted off his clothes and repositioned a band of cloth around his eyes.

"It was a giant toad. It's run off and I don't think it'll be coming back. Don't be so hard on yourself, at least not until we've met with these Mind Mages. Caudro... I'm sorry for earlier."

"You, of all people, shouldn't be apologizing. You had to face that creature, while all I did was fall over and-"

"Come. Sit by the fire and keep me company," Ami said, taking Caudro's hand and leading him back to the camp. "It's all I need from you right now."

Caudro sat and listened as Ami readied their camp to a chorus of chirping birds, who sang happily now that the toad was gone. Snaps and cracks punctuated the song as Ami broke apart dry wood for the fire. The broken logs clinked and clunked as she stacked them neatly, followed by sharp strikes of metal on flint. Caudro heard Ami blowing to encourage the tinder to ignite. He wistfully imagined the subtle glow of sparks lighting her face.

As the fire crackled, birds quieted and crickets and frogs of a normal size sang into the night. Water sloshed and the flames hissed when Ami snugged a pot against hot coals. For a while, crude chopping and the splashing of vegetables as they slipped into simmering water filled Caudro's ears. When Ami had finished, he heard a pouch being cautiously pried open. The smell of dried meat reached Caudro's nose. He grinned as Ami chewed slowly to mask the sounds, like a child sneaking a bite of sweets. The world seemed simpler in that moment, with the stew bubbling away amidst the song of the forest.

"It's strange I never asked you this, but... How did you come to be a Paladin?" Ami asked.

"Like many in the order, they took me in because I was an orphan."

"Preying on parentless children to fill their ranks; how entirely expected of the Quinarium."

Caudro shook his head. "Most all of us were desperate, whether orphans or poor. There's the saying, 'the Quinarium provides,' but it's false. I had to steal food and still went hungry. When I joined the Paladins, the food was crude, but I never felt hunger again. The indoctrination began with so simple a thing as a bowl of porridge. They took us in at an age where we knew what it meant to lack what we needed in life and fulfilled our needs. Though the Paladin who found me, Jarain, differed from the rest. I wonder if he would have stood against Scireth."

"You said he found you?"

"Yes. I was stealing a loaf of bread when the shopkeeper caught me. Jarain happened by, and I was given a choice: lose a finger, or join him and train to become a Paladin."

"Call me Ami the Nine Fingered, were I in your shoes," Ami said with a giggle.

"A part of me wishes I had made that choice. Once I walked among Paladins, my devotion was total. As children, we all feared losing what we had gained. A bed every night, meals aplenty... the order was strict, but they provided as we had never been provided for. I don't know exactly when it happened, but at some point over the years that fear of loss turned into fanatical devotion."

"The more I hear about these Quinarium sorts, the less they seem *good,*" Ami said, sprinkling a palmful of foraged herbs into the pot. "Maybe I'm a bit sensitive, but they sound a touch restrictive and controlling, not to mention the whole manipulating of orphans, extracting of mana from living sacrifices, and I haven't even started on the whole matter of genocide. Or should I say, *genocides*, if they are to have their way."

Caudro exhaled slowly. "The Quinarium was supposed to be our spiritual guides: the ears to listen to the Quinate, and the mouth to speak their truths to us all."

"If the Quinate are so essential to the lives of all, why is the Quinarium necessary? Demanding that praise to the Quinate be directed through them is quite at odds with what they preach."

"A fair question for which I have no answer," Caudro said softly. "Well, enough talk of my sad childhood and terror that is the Quinarium. What about your childhood? You speak often of your grandfather, but what of your parents?"

Caudro grew uneasy at the sudden change in Ami's breathing as she shifted on her bedroll.

"Do you remember when I said I hated the smell of the ocean?"

"Yes. You said it reminded you of your grandfather, because he loved the coast."

Ami sighed. "I lied. My grandfather was happy as a lark no matter where he was. I hate the ocean because my parents abandoned me when I was a young child. They left me with my grandfather and made for Zanrena, a village as far away as they could get in the Fae lands. I never heard a word from my parents, nor did my grandfather. Any time I smell the ocean air, I'm reminded of them."

"Did you ever look for them?"

"Why would I?"

"I'm sorry, I shouldn't have asked."

"Relax, big man, I'm long past it," Ami said. "Stew seems about ready. Let me get you a bowl, then I'll be off for a quick scout about. I hope the taste is to your liking. I don't often cook for Humans or without meat."

Caudro pondered for a moment if he should accept Ami's deflection or press further, though he instead sat and ate while Ami strode away from the camp.

The remaining days passed without event. Ami and Caudro spoke little as they pressed hard through Llendshold, hugging a forest running along the foothills of an ice-capped mountain range. Though they avoided Human settlements, Ami nevertheless kept her hood low over her face while Caudro wrapped a strip of cloth around the Paladin brand on his wrist, lest they stumble upon anyone unawares.

Ami pulled the horses to a halt as the village of Almeyhill came into view between tall and slender trees topped with rotund clumps of leaves. Wispy clouds drifted across the sun.

"Have you been here before?" she asked.

"No."

"Well then, would you like me to describe it for you?"

Caudro hesitated for a moment with his mouth ajar.

"Yes, please."

"I'm not quite the poet you've proven yourself to be, but I'll describe it as I see it. The village is not terribly different from Cauldhill in size, though the walls are only a few feet taller than the Humans walking about. There is a ditch at the base of the walls, though. Most all the buildings are made of stone instead of wood. It makes the Sanctuary look less out of place, despite towering over the village. All the roofs are painted in a dull orange. Curious, I don't see many guards. There are a couple at each of the gates and a handful walking along the walls."

"Thank you."

"Any time, big man," Ami said. "Now, let's stock up."

"Are you sure it's a good idea to go into a Human village? Maybe we should have stopped at a hamlet instead, somewhere smaller, quieter."

"I've told you my thoughts on this. We need food. There's little more than a day's worth remaining in our packs and better a village than a hamlet. If your hamlets are anything like our Fae settlements, then the smaller the community, the nosier, the more observant, the more questions we would hear."

"You're right, but I can't help worrying what with my brand and your..."

"My absolutely delightful face? Or were you going to comment on my long and delicate ears?" Ami snickered. "Trust me. I've had plenty of time to think about this, so don't you worry your big, handsome head."

Ami continued describing the landscape as they rode to the village. Sprawling fields of waist-high grasses topped with pink and orange flowers gave way to neatly plowed fields home to rows of lovingly tended vegetables. The sounds of the village grew ever-louder, dominated by masons cracking stone and potters stacking shingles and other earthen wares. They stabled their horses outside of Almeyhill, then shouldered their packs and made for the gates.

Caudro's heart pounded as they approached. He desperately wanted to ask Ami what she saw. Step after step, the village grew ever louder with voices carrying out from a market. The packed dirt road was smooth beneath Caudro's feet. He held onto Ami's shoulder, caught between a desire to hold tight and a reluctance to show his fear.

Minutes passed. Caudro kept close; Ami looked over her shoulder to see his eyebrows furrowed and sweat glistening on his face. She smiled and patted Caudro's hand.

"I told you we'd be fine! The guards were all but sleeping at their post. Didn't pay us one bit of mind."

"I'll feel relief when we've left."

Ami followed villagers funneling down the main avenue, assuming they would lead to a market. Although she was not generally keen on crowded cities and villages, whether Fae or Human, the vibrant streets lined with shops lifted her spirits. Ami halted when they reached an expansive plaza.

The Sanctuary stood at one end; its three-story stone walls cast a shadow over half the market. Shops lined the perimeter, home to blacksmiths and carpenters and healers. As they had no need for such services, Ami turned her attention to the stalls filling the heart of the plaza. Colorful canopies with stripes and dots and more intricate patterns danced in the afternoon breeze. Ami spied a cluster of tables covered in fruits and vegetables, with a kindly-looking shopkeeper standing behind.

"Good morning!" Ami called out, approaching the stand. "How are the Five blessing you on this fine day?"

The woman brushed a curl of dusty auburn hair from her face and smiled broadly. "Never a poor day under the watch of the Quinate! And it's about to turn into a finer day for you two. Finest produce in all of Llendshold, right here! Take a gander and grab your fill. Prices are as fair as any you'll find in Almeyhill."

"Thank you!"

Ami happily perused, filling a pack with a bounty of food. The shopkeeper squinted at Caudro as he followed Ami, his hand pinned to her shoulder.

"If you don't mind me asking," the shopkeeper said, leaning close to Ami, "what's with the fellow following you around? He's a bit of an odd sight, what with the wrapping around his eyes and holding on to you like a babe to its mother."

Ami chuckled. "Oh, don't worry, my friend. This hunk is Croda, my twice-removed cousin's half-brother. I'm not sure what makes him twice-removed, I'm terrible with family trees. Anyway, he used to be a right drunkard. Never saw the light of the Five. He started a fight in an inn one day, and a well-placed blow to the head dimmed both his eyes and his mind."

"Oh, dear me."

"Awful as it sounds, I thank the Five for it. Since that day, his eyes may have gone dark, but he's seen the light of the Quinate through the Quinarium. He attends Sanctuary every chance, as pious as a Confessor."

The shopkeeper offered a strained smile. "I'm sorry for being terribly nosy, but why are you with him, then? You seem young to be caring for a blind, distant relative on your own."

"I don't have a sterling past myself, I'm sad to say," Ami said, lowering her head dramatically. "I'm older than I look. I was born early to a mother who failed to pray to the Five and drank herself to a stupor from dawn to dusk. I took after her in my younger years. A quarrel of mine left my ears disfigured. It's why I wear this hood. Though I assure you, I'm a changed woman!

I'm taking Croda to family in Bramswall as a bit of voluntary penance, if you will."

"Oh, Five bless you," the shopkeeper said with a nervous chuckle. "Sometimes it's tragedy that leads us to a happier place."

Ami slid a small stack of guilders across the table.

"Truer words have never been said. As They speak!"

The shopkeeper grinned as she counted the coins.

"So we listen, my dear. So we listen."

Ami slung the loaded pack over Caudro's shoulder, then bowed to the shopkeeper. She led into the market, taking in the excited scene.

"You crafted quite the story. Did you have to say we are related?" Caudro said with a groan.

Caudro felt Ami's fingers weave between his own, deftly sliding across his skin.

"Would you rather I said we are lovers?"

Caudro blushed and coughed to clear his throat.

"At least we can leave the village now. This pack feels like it has enough food for a month."

"It's late afternoon. If we leave now, we won't get far before having to make camp, and a camp strangely close to a village is sure to draw attention. We need a full day to cross the plain between Almeyhill and the mountains to the north. I'll look for an inn."

"Are you sure we should stay?" Caudro said.

"It has been four days since either of us had a proper bath. We smell of smoke and dirt and rotting leaves. I have no intention of riding into the night when I could instead have a warm bath, a hot meal, and sleep in a cozy, dry room."

"You're right, of course," Caudro said. "How long did you practice that routine you put on for the shopkeeper?"

"Let me think... four days traveling from dawn to dusk beside a quiet, brooding man. Plenty of time to conjure up and refine such a story."

Ami hastened through the streets. She passed a few inns that didn't satisfy her discerning eye. Finally, she saw a sign for an inn. Caudro struggled to understand why Ami had selected what must have been the loudest, most boisterous place in all of Almeyhill, but she happily pushed open the door.

Though Ami was ready to launch into a finely crafted story, the innkeeper barely raised his head at the new arrivals.

"What can I do for you?" the surly man grumbled.

"A room with two beds and a bath, and two portions of whatever you're serving brought to our room... please."

"It's four guilders for the room, two for each meal, plus one for the trouble of delivery."

Ami set nine guilders on the bar beside the innkeeper, then winked as she slid an additional tenth over. The man lurched forward and snapped up a coin. He twisted it between two fingers and held it close to the light of a candle.

"Mighty shiny, these guilders."

"My mother always said to keep our mouths clean and our guilders cleaner," Ami said with a smile.

"Right," the innkeeper said, carefully stacking the guilders before sweeping them into his pocket. "Room's this way."

Caudro sat on a chair inside the quarters, listening to Ami bustling about. More than once he heard her pause and inhale, ready to speak, only to resume opening and shutting packs and rearranging items within.

A knock came from the door, which opened before they could respond.

"Here."

The innkeeper set two bowls of stew and a plate with a torn loaf of bread onto a table, then slammed the door shut.

Ami closed the latch behind the innkeeper. Turning to the food, she lifted a spoon then tilted the utensil; the contents fell back into the bowl with a *schlop.*

"Well, the stew's hot, at least."

After eating in silence, Ami gathered up the dishes.

"There's a shallow bath. Not much more than a couple feet deep, but there's a barrel with plenty of water. I'm going to warm some up, if you don't mind me washing up first?"

"Mm," Caudro replied.

Ami stared at Caudro while the water warmed over hot coals. He sat as stiff as if they were in a room filled with Lords. She wondered what occupied his mind for so many hours, sitting without so much as a word. Her thoughts drifted, and she imagined she had been the one to lose her eyes. How would Caudro care for her? Would he guide her with a gentler touch? Would her demeanor be so strained? As she looked back at Caudro, a desire to speak filled Ami, though she was unsure what to say.

When Caudro heard water splashing in the bath, he instinctively faced away.

"Why look away?" Ami said with a laugh, tossing aside her clothes.

"A matter of dignity. If I can't be away from you while you bathe, I can at least offer some semblance of privacy."

Ami exhaled in delight as she slipped into the warm water, then began diligently scrubbing her arms.

"It's only a bath, no need for the formality. Besides, I'm not ashamed of my body. Why are you so sensitive about this? Was everything private with the Paladins?"

"The opposite. I value privacy because privacy is a rarity among Paladins." Caudro chuckled feebly. "I don't even know if I should feel ashamed to be around an unclothed Fae."

"And what precisely do you mean by that?"

"It's a matter of immodesty, is it not? The Quinarium always impressed that matters of... procreation... were private between partners. Not to be shared. Hardly a concern, though, if Humans and Fae aren't able to... pair."

Ami grinned at the sight of Caudro's flushed cheeks.

"How preposterous. My grandfather said that there was once harmony between Humans and Fae. Some went so far as to become lovers, no matter what the Quinarium told you."

Caudro sat with a furrowed brow until Ami finished washing.

"I'm done," Ami said as she stepped out of the bath. "Water's still plenty warm. Let me help you out of your clothes."

Caudro abruptly raised a hand.

"I have little left in the way of dignity. Please, let me do this for myself."

"You need to stop being a right idiot," Ami scoffed. "Let me help you. When you finally let me help you without grumbling, I promise you'll feel less shit. Now come along then."

"Promise you won't look," Caudro said, lowering his hand.

"Childish... child of a man! Fine. I swear to you on the memory of my grandfather, I won't look."

Caudro recoiled when Ami's hand grabbed his and pulled forcefully. Though her thumb was calloused from her bowstring, and her movements were brusque and determined, Caudro all but melted from the softness of her skin. Ami gave him no time to dwell as she lugged him over to the bath. When she withdrew her hand, he felt oddly naked and alone.

Ami plopping into a chair with a grunt prompted Caudro to undress. He reached out for the tub, nearly overstepping and tipping it over, but managed to lower himself in. A nagging tickle ran up his spine as he washed, questioning whether or not Ami would hold true to her promise.

"Oh, you missed a spot on your back," she said with a giggle.

"You gave me your word!"

"Calm yourself, big man, I'm only teasing. Though I must say, I am quite tempted to watch."

"Confounded woman," Caudro muttered.

"Confounded implies unclear and confusing. We both know that I am entirely forward and clear in all I do and say."

Caudro sighed and resumed his scrubbing.

The next morning, Ami and Caudro rose early. The stench of warm ale and cold stew assaulted Caudro's nose as they hurried through the dead-quiet inn. He gasped in relief when they finally exited and a cool morning breeze greeted them. Ami hurried through the streets to the stables.

Ami led Caudro and their horses back through the sleepy village, believing it quicker than riding around. When she came to an abrupt stop, Caudro tilted his head, listening for anything of note.

"What is it?" he whispered.

"There are three people standing in the street ahead, two men and a woman. It's too early in the morning for idle loitering. I don't like the look of them; I'll find a way around."

Ami cut back and forth through a dizzying maze of back streets until Caudro was entirely uncertain which direction they headed. When Ami skid to a stop, Caudro stepped forward until they were side-by-side.

"They found us," she said.

"What do they look like?" Caudro said, clenching his jaw.

"They're not from the Quinarium, if that's what you're thinking. They look like common vagabonds. Short, tattered tunics. I don't see much in the way of weapons, at least."

Caudro stood as tall as he was able, defying the urge to shrink in place.

"Oh, it seems I was wrong about the weapons," Ami said. "They're carrying wooden clubs with a metal spike on the end of each, and they're walking towards us."

"Easy targets today. Nothing more than a little girl and a blind boy," called the man at the lead.

"They might be a sad pair, but the old innkeeper said they carried unusually shiny guilders," said the woman as the three marched ever closer. "I wonder how many more they have?"

"I'd say they stole them, if you were to ask me," said the second man.

The first man chuckled as the three neared to twenty paces away. "I'd say you're right. How wonderful of us three to apprehend these criminals. The Five will look favorably on us for our service. We'll be sure to turn them in to the guards after giving them a proper roughing up."

"Terrible shame they hid all the guilders and refused to say where they were," the woman cackled.

Sweat beaded on Ami's brow. The aggressors outnumbered them, and magic was not an option, not with the attention it would be sure to draw. Worse still, her bow was unstrung and tucked into a horse's bags. She looked to her side at Caudro.

"Stay close to me," he whispered, his fists clenched tightly.

"I would think it's the other way around, big man. You should be the one staying close to me."

"You have something to say to us?" the first man shouted from a mere ten paces away.

The woman cackled and hurried ahead of the men. "Oh, go on, resist, make it fun! Or you can sit and take your beatings. That'll be fine too!"

Ami yanked the bridle of her horse, turning its rear towards the charging woman. She slapped the horse's haunches and it kicked, striking the woman squarely in her chest.

Thrown like a toy doll, the woman smacked into a nearby wall, then fell face-first onto the street.

"Get them!" shouted the first man.

Ami ducked beneath her horse to evade the attackers. She climbed up the nearest stone wall, then leapt over the horse. Flying knees first, she crashed into the first man's chest, slamming him to the ground. He gasped as the air was knocked from his lungs. The man attempted to grapple with Ami when she slapped his ears simultaneously. The man's feet kicked into the air, then collapsed.

Ami hopped off the stunned man and readied to help Caudro, only to see him standing over the third attacker. Caudro wrenched the club from the man's hand and threw it aside. The man punched Caudro's thigh. In retaliation, Caudro roared and twisted the man's arm, dislocating it at the shoulder with a sickening pop.

"Let's go!" Ami said, pulling Caudro off the screaming man.

He reached out for guidance when his hands closed around what was certainly not Ami's shoulder. She responded with a swift smack and returned his hand to her shoulder.

"I'm sorry!" Caudro stammered.

"I appreciate the enthusiasm, but now is the entirely wrong time!"

The two climbed onto their horses and galloped through the town, never looking back until they were near half a day's ride away. Caudro questioned the reason for slowing down when Ami broke into laughter.

"What do you find so humorous?" he asked. "I told you we shouldn't stay in the village!"

"I think you might be dirtier now than you were before you bathed."

"I might look worse, but I at least am feeling a touch better. Nothing like a tumble to get the blood flowing."

"I prefer a different kind of tumble for that effect," Ami muttered.

She smirked when Caudro turned his head in an attempt to hide his flushed cheeks while he pretended not to hear her words.

"We made it away safely, but I still feel useless. Those common brigands saw me as beneath their concern."

"What do you mean? Blind and taken off-guard, without a weapon, you bested that man. Five above, you nearly ripped his arm from his body. Quite the showing, and you looked dashing all the while."

The corners of Caudro's lips turned slightly upward as he sat tall on his horse.

"Thank you."

CHAPTER 6

"It may be the darkening clouds shifting my perspective, but this is one sad-looking village," Ami said, rubbing her horse's neck. "And I mean that considering the other Human villages, which I thought were terribly sad. This is entirely worse."

Caudro shivered as a cool, early evening wind blew down from the mountains.

"What makes it so poor in your eyes? Other than the smell, that is. They must be burning something other than wood. It reeks."

"I don't know what the cause of the smell is—whether it's coming from the village or the soggy ground—but soot covers the whole of Bavenhill and the forest surrounding it. The buildings are made of stone, but half of them are in disrepair. It's larger than Cauldhill, but the streets are nearly empty. There isn't a proper wall, either; a rickety wooden palisade is it. I don't see a single guard."

"Perhaps the guards are all posted at the watchtowers you saw on the way here."

"Possible, though the watchtowers are near half a day's walk from the village. A bit far if their purpose is protecting the residents."

"I hope Okter's information is correct and his contact is ready to meet us," Caudro said. "We are investing a substantial amount of time for this."

"You know, you're quite the skeptic," Ami said, urging the horses to resume their walk with a shake of the reins.

"I'm this way because I trusted the Quinarium blindly. Before, I questioned anything that challenged the Quinarium. Now, with what I thought was my foundation ripped away, I can't help but question nearly everything else."

"Any examples you'd like to share?"

"Well, I don't have a specific event or cause I can attribute this to, but I can't help feeling *something* about Okter and Imreia... it's like they're not always speaking the truth, but neither are they lying. Like the truth is a tool for them both."

"Perceptive. And here I was thinking you're just a looker. You see more since you lost your eyes."

Caudro's brow furrowed. "Do you feel the same about them?"

"Yes. I can't help but admit they are doing more for my people than the likes of Hawel, but I don't exactly love being near them. Though Dara and Wynne seem enraptured by Imreia."

"Who knows, perhaps Okter and Imreia mean well? I'm sure Dara and Wynne will find the truth out about those two before it's a concern. They're each on their own wiser than the two of us together."

Ami chuckled. "I am positively glowing at your assessment of our wits and wisdom! Let's leave the bigger troubles to Dara and Wynne and see what we can find here."

They rode for a few minutes until Ami eased the horses to a stop. Caudro jumped when she scoffed loudly.

"What is it?"

"We have arrived at the *The Squawking Chicken,* as Okter advised. But nearly half the building has collapsed. There's nothing more than a post for us to tie the horses off to, and not a person is in sight."

"Coming to Bavenhill seems to be a rare occasion where being blind has some benefit."

Ami gasped dramatically. "Caudro! Was that a joke?"

"Possibly."

"Caudro has made a joke, and not the worst one I've ever heard. Big man, you should have left the Paladins a long time ago."

"I agree, and for many reasons. Let's hope this Anghara person is here like Okter assured us she would be."

Ami pushed open the creaky door to the inn. The dim interior had no source of light, save slivers of pale gray flowing in through a few small windows and a low fire in a hearth. The innkeeper—a tall, pudgy man with a thick beard and kind eyes—jumped up and smiled wide at their arrival.

"Welcome, welcome!" the innkeeper said, his voice light and airy. "Welcome to *The Squawking Chicken!* I'm Tomas, and I have the wonderful duty of managing this modest little place, the only one of its kind in Bavenhill. Our quiet village, tucked into the forest, high in the foothills of the mountains..."

"Right," Ami said. "We're actually here looking for someone, her-"

"Of course you are! Why else would you come to Bavenhill?" Tomas's eyes drifted to an open window. "We keep to ourselves here. Not much in the way of farming with the marshy ground. Most all the villagers spend their days out foraging. Not much in the way of trade, we keep ourselves going fine as it is. Not much in the way of visitors, what with Llendswarne near enough. Who would stop here instead? One might call me a fool for running an inn in such a place, though I thought it a great opportunity when I was young, and I was too bullheaded to listen to the advice of my mother, who-"

"Excuse me, sir," Caudro interrupted calmly. "Do you happen to know someone named Anghara? We were to meet her here."

"Anghara, you say?"

"That'd be the name," Ami replied.

Tomas took a chunk of black, sticky peat and threw it into the fire. The block sputtered and groaned, but burned brightly.

"Can't say I'm familiar with the name. I keep to myself and most keep to themselves away from the inn. The most common travelers we see are Quinarium folks, but they stay in the Sanctuary instead of here. A village this size with one inn, quite the oddity wouldn't you say? Anyway, seeing as I don't know this Anghara, let me at least get you a meal."

Before Ami or Caudro could protest, the innkeeper scurried away through an open door. Without a better plan at the front of their minds, Ami helped Caudro to a chair at a rickety table.

"Maybe we-"

"Sh!" Ami leaned over the table. "Later. Not until we know what is going on."

Tomas returned after a few minutes and slid loaded plates before Ami and Caudro, along with mugs of fermented berry wine.

"This looks wonderful!" Ami exclaimed.

"Really?" Tomas blurted. "Most who aren't from Bavenhill don't care for our food. They call our diet of foraged greens, mushrooms, nuts, and roots an oddity. We oil and char the ingredients over coals to bring out the flavors, but to most it is an acquired taste."

Ami withdrew, realizing her excitement was because the food resembled that of the Fae. She was suddenly aware of her hastening pulse as homesickness pulled at her heart.

"Oh, well, my family has always said I have eyes—and a belly—for new experiences!" she said.

The innkeeper grinned. "You two enjoy your meal, then. If it turns out you need a place to stay, you're welcome to stay here. I have *plenty* of rooms. Now, if you don't mind, I'll be out for a walk. If I'm not back and you decide to stay, you're welcome to take whichever room you fancy; they're through that door there."

Tomas tapped the table by Ami's plate, then sauntered out of the inn.

"Something's wrong," Caudro said as the door rattled in its frame. "Nosy bloke, bored halfway to madness in an empty inn, and he asked not a question about us; not about me being blind or you keeping your hood low."

"I have to admit I'm a bit sad he didn't question us at all. I had an excellent story about how an abusive uncle smashed the sides of my face when I was a child, so I keep my hood low... it was a real dagger in the heart sort of tale. Wait! Maybe things are not so wrong."

"What is it?"

"He tapped the table for a reason; there's a note under my plate."

"Well, what does it say?"

Ami unfolded the thin, ash-smudged piece of paper.

"It says to go through the north gate, walk ninety paces along the road, then turn left and walk one hundred fifty paces up the hill to the meeting place."

"We have clear instructions. We should get to it," Caudro said, pushing away his plate.

Ami tossed the note into the hearth as they left the inn.

Caudro held tight as Ami pulled him with determination through Bavenhill. The rough cut pavers of the streets were difficult to tread, worsened when a light drizzle coated the stones in a slick paste of ash and rain. Caudro struggled to keep his footing, and his calves ached by the time they reached the gates.

"I'm guessing they meant Human paces, so start your counting," Ami whispered. "There aren't any guards, so it doesn't much matter if you prefer counting in your head or aloud. Ninety before we turn, if you recall."

Caudro had barely made it to fifty when a woman's voice called out.

"Come here."

"Who's there? Can you see them?" Caudro whispered.

"I can't see anyone, but I think the voice came from inside an overgrown, decrepit building. It's covered in dirt and leaves and plants are growing out from all over."

"Stop idling about. You'll be seen!" the voice called. "Come inside!"

"We should go in," Caudro said.

"Are you sure?" Ami shuffled her weight from foot to foot. "I'm starting to have doubts. This doesn't exactly align with the note, which didn't align with Okter."

"At worst, this is a distraction and we can begin again at the gate."

"A Fae and a former Paladin would do well to listen to the summons of the one trying to help them!" hissed the voice.

"We had better go in before she reveals our identities to all of Bavenhill. Either it's someone who can help us, or I'll properly shut her up," Ami said.

Caudro listened intently as Ami crept to the building, but he heard only the pattering of light rain and the breeze whispering through the forest.

"Ugh!" Ami groaned as they stepped through the open doorway. "This place is a mess! The ceiling is almost entirely caved in, the few bits of remaining furniture are broken beyond recognition, and it is positively covered in ash."

"Through here," said the voice.

"Where?" Caudro asked.

Ami gave his hand a pat. "I see the door. Keep close."

"Not that I have much choice, but gladly."

Ami slipped a bottle of mana and her spiked gourd out from beneath the hem of her tunic. She uncorked the bottle and closed her hand around the gourd. Breathing in deeply, she pushed the door open with her foot and boldly stepped through the entryway.

"Who are you?" Ami blurted out.

A tall, slender woman stood at the center of the surprisingly well-furnished room. Lit candles were placed throughout, and chairs were tucked into a table, all showing signs of recent use. The woman wore a Mage's tunic trimmed in light purple, with a hem high at the waist which swept down to her knees at the sides. Her Mage's gauntlet and a mana bottle dangled from her belt. Ami admired the woman's round and warm face, which was attractive despite her gaunt cheeks, bags under her eyes, wrinkles on her forehead, and parched, cracked lips.

"I am Anghara," the Mage said, her voice strained. "I received word of your coming, from Okter."

"How can we be sure you are who you say you are?" Ami said. Her knuckles were white from tightly gripping the mana bottle and gourd.

"If I wished ill of you, then I would be foolish indeed to let you come so close. It would have been easy enough to manipulate your minds from a distance, had I wished. Here, a show of good faith."

Anghara set her gauntlet and mana bottle on the table.

"You'll have to forgive our caution," Ami said, corking her own mana bottle.

"Why did you not meet us at the inn?" Caudro asked.

"Okter designated that meeting location, not me." Anghara wrung her hands methodically. "It is entirely unreasonable for me to stray so far from the Academy."

Ami's head tilted. "The inn is a few minutes away, across the village. I thought you are an Instructor?"

"I am. But you must understand, the Academy of Almoya is not like the others." Anghara took a step closer to Ami and lowered her head like a vulture leaning over dry carrion. "Our existence is torture. We live as slaves."

"Is that why you're so fidgety?" Ami asked, folding her arms.

"Fidgety?" Caudro questioned.

"She's rubbing her hands together to calm their shaking, but she can't control the twitching in her eye."

"These are the symptoms of my withdrawal," Anghara whimpered.

"Withdrawal from what?"

"As I said, all Mind Mages are made to be slaves... to mana."

"Five above... Caudro, we will not trust a mana addict with a twitching eye to cure your eyesight."

"We should listen before we pass judgement," Caudro said. "Anghara, what do you mean by that? Calling yourself a slave to mana?"

"The Quinarium forces new Initiates at the Academy of Almoya to gorge themselves on mana. They drink so heavily in the first months that it forms a terrible addiction, one which scars their very souls. Then, the Agents of the Quinarium—Paladins, mostly—restrict the supply of mana."

Anghara's eyes glazed over as she continued.

"The Initiates are left desperate, only receiving mana if they comply with every command, every demand, every whim of the Quinarium. They also pit the Initiates against each other, providing substantial reward in the form of mana for any who speak up about scheming peers who might consider resisting. All this to ensure the Mind Mages, who are essential for many Quinarium rituals, are ever compliant."

"The addiction... it's like with Failure," Caudro muttered.

"Failure?"

"A long story, for another time," Ami replied. "As for your story, I'm guessing you wouldn't have shared it if you didn't intend to ask something of us."

"Yes. The Academy is on the brink of rebellion. Yet, as weak as we are due to our addiction and lacking access to mana, rebellion is certain to lead to the collapse of the Academy. I cannot imagine any outcome other than the death of all Initiates and Instructors, save a few who remain loyal to the Quinarium. It may be no less than we deserve... many of us have performed horrific acts. None of us are truly innocent. But please, I beg of you, help us.

"I know from Okter's message that *something* is coming. Don't allow us to be used as tools of the Quinarium in the coming conflict. Please, pledge to free us. I know it cannot happen today, but give us hope that we might one day escape this living nightmare."

Ami faltered at the gravity of the request.

"But... I'm a Fae. I hardly know Okter. My people are on the brink of a war with Llendshold, our resources limited. I don't know-"

"I pledge to you, on whatever worth is in my life, that you will be freed," Caudro said, bowing with an arm across his chest

"Caudro! How can you make such a pledge?"

The former Paladin gave Ami's shoulder a gentle squeeze.

"How can I not? They are now as I once was: bound and controlled. Only they are aware of their slavery. I can't leave them in such a state, Ami. Further, imagine if the Quinarium brings dozens of Mind Mages to the battlefield. They would be a terrible force. We must save them, both to end the horrors of the Quinarium and to strengthen our allies."

"Well, I guess there is a big heart somewhere inside that chest of yours," Ami said with a sigh.

"Anghara," Caudro said, "I will be far more capable of honoring my pledge if I can see."

"I can hardly express what I am feeling; it has been so long since I felt anything akin to hope. Know that many of us will gladly serve alongside Okter and those fighting against the Quinarium. As for your eyes, I will take you to the Academy."

"What?" Ami said, her hands on her hips. "I thought you were going to heal Caudro, not take him to this school of mana addicts?"

"Caudro no longer has eyes. We cannot heal that which no longer exists. Yet, it might still be possible for him to restore his sight."

"So you can't heal him, but you can?" Ami grumbled through grit teeth.

"I will take you to a secret chamber beneath the Academy. In ages past, a mana source flowed inside. The echoes of its presence still resonate within the walls, inside a circle of mirrors. When you enter, you will begin a ritual; of what, we cannot say, but all who succeed receive a gift, and that gift may be your eyesight."

"Do all Mind Mages go through this ritual?" Ami asked.

"I hear your doubt through your question. Powerful though the ritual may be, the Quinarium prohibits Mages from undergoing the ritual and have barred access. They do not, however, know of all the entrances. Further, one must drink mana to undergo the ritual, and their control is strict; I see you have brought mana of your own."

"What about the mana you carry?" Ami challenged.

"It takes all my strength not to drink it this very moment. What prevents me from consuming it is the knowledge that my bottle will be weighed on a scale every night, and every morning, and should a drop be missing, I will be punished."

Ami's head hung low at the response.

"What if we fail?" Caudro asked.

"Then you will remain as you are."

"Sounds like you have little to lose, then," Ami said.

Anghara nodded. "Yes, so long as we are not found by the Paladins patrolling the halls of the Academy."

Caudro breathed out slowly through pursed lips, then held his head high.

"I will complete this ritual."

"Come then. Though Paladins and other Agents of the Quinarium are ever-present, I have friends at the ready. We will create enough diversion to ensure you reach the chamber of mirrors and can undergo the ritual."

The heavy, iron-bound doors closed behind Ami and Caudro without a sound.

"I don't see the mirrors that Anghara spoke of," Ami said, the hair on her arms rising.

"What do you see?" Caudro asked, still holding on to Ami.

"Another treeless, stone-bound room. She was right, though. There's no need for a lantern. There's an opening in the ceiling, at the center, and a bit of moonlight is coming in. The ceiling is higher than I thought it would be; it didn't feel like we took that many stairs on our way down."

Ami shivered and drew her arms close.

"Are you alright?" Caudro asked, rubbing Ami's shoulder with his thumb.

"I will be once we're out of this place."

"Thank you."

"For what?"

Caudro withdrew his hand and bowed his head.

"For bringing me here. For giving me hope that I might be useful again."

"Eyes or not, you've been plenty useful," Ami said as she pat Caudro's cheek. "And hold your thanks until you've finished the ritual. Are you ready for your first taste of mana?"

"Strangely, the idea of drinking mana is more intimidating than any challenge I faced as a Paladin. To taste the gift of the Five..."

"I assure you, it is quite safe!"

Ami waited patiently while Caudro stood motionless, his brow furrowed and jaw clenched.

"I'm ready."

Ami pried the stopper out of a mana bottle then placed it in Caudro's hands. He inhaled deeply, then took a sip.

An incredible warmth wrapped around Caudro, like the loving embrace of a parent he had always craved yet never felt. The fire grew until it raged in his belly, spreading through his body, igniting hope and filling him with an urge to roar.

Ami took the bottle from Caudro, grinning at the look of wonderment plastered on his face.

"You alright there, big man?" she asked, licking a drop of mana that had fallen on her finger as she pressed the stopper back into the bottle.

"Yes. Please, lead on."

Caudro nearly jumped when Ami wrapped her hand around his and squeezed instead of placing his hand on her shoulder. The smallness of her hands within his amazed him, and though he knew her as resolute and brazen, she felt delicate. *There was once harmony between Humans and Fae. Some went so far as to become lovers.* Ami's words rattled in Caudro's head as she led him to the center of the room.

With each step, Ami wondered more why she had grabbed his hand. And yet, she was comforted by his touch. Despite the scars across his skin, despite the strength she knew was inside Caudro, he held her with a tenderness that made her wish he would lift her into her arms and hold her close. Ami's face scrunched as a tinge of sadness crept across her skin. If Caudro were to recover his sight, she would miss his touch.

When they stepped into the moonlight at the heart of the room, a monotone chime rang. It grew louder with every second until Ami felt as though her head was going to burst.

"Do you hear that?" she groaned.

"How could I not!?" Caudro yelled. "Can you see where the noise is coming from?"

"No... All around it's the same. Plain walls, and... wait! I see the mirrors now, all around us!"

The room shook as if a tremendous earthquake rattled the ground beneath them. Ami and Caudro stumbled apart.

"Ami?"

The tone faded to a gentle hum as Caudro crawled about on hands and knees, desperately searching for Ami.

"Where are you? Ami? Ami!"

Chapter 7

"Caudro? Caudro, are you there?"

Ami squinted as she rose to her feet, reaching out into the total darkness surrounding her.

"I wonder if I'm to undergo the ritual as well?" Ami said as she ceased her search for Caudro. "Humans have the strangest of rituals. And here I was thinking I would have a boring wait. Then again, perhaps I'm to wait like this; I didn't drink any mana, which Anghara said was necessary for the trial."

"Mana courses through your blood."

The voice came from every direction all at once; it contained a power that made Ami feel as if she should kneel, yet there was a comforting calm that reminded her of her grandfather.

"All I did was lick a drop from my finger," Ami replied. "And I'm not Human."

"Mana courses through your blood. What does it matter that you are a Fae, and not a Human?"

"Am I not in Llendshold?" Ami scoured the darkness, yet she saw nothing.

"A demarcation not born of the Quinate."

"Who are you?"

A shimmer of floating motes appeared before Ami, like bits of dust caught in a ray of morning sun. The particles swirled, billowed, and grew in intensity, forming an orb. Ami blinked and the glowing motes formed the shape of a Fae, with a Dwarf and a Human on either side; it was unclear if they were male or female.

"We are an echo of the Quinate, a whisper of what they once were," they said, their faces unmoved as they spoke. "We are an embodiment of their grandeur, taking on a form that you can comprehend."

Unsure if she should kneel or bow, Ami awkwardly shrugged. "And what would you have me do? I didn't intend to undergo this ritual. I'm simply here for Caudro."

"Mana courses through your blood. Speak honestly, and we shall listen."

"Speak honestly? A trifle."

"For many a trifle, but for you, a terror."

Ami's cheeks burned and her mouth went dry.

"What do you mean by that?"

"Do not pose questions to which you already know the answer, Aminantskeilara. You must face the truth of what is in your heart."

"Fine then!" Ami shouted. "I have nothing to hide."

The three towering figures stepped closer until they were a few paces away.

"Tell me of your deepest regret," said the Fae specter. Though its mouth finally moved and it spoke of itself as an individual, the voice was unchanged from before.

"I try to live life without regrets," Ami said with a smirk. "I am far too busy with my terribly eventful life to dwell on that which has already happened."

"We know your mind."

A dull thumping rattled inside Ami's head. Was she truly speaking to an echo of the Quinate, she wondered? What would happen if she were to defy their demands?

Ami stood defiantly. Slowly, the noise in her head grew until she felt as if a symphony of drums pounded inside. She shook her head and rubbed her temples, hoping to ease the discomfort, but it only ever grew stronger.

Finally relenting, Ami gasped, then spewed her reply.

"Fine! I regret... More than anything, I regret not going with my grandfather to Cauldhill, the day he died. He frequently went to visit Humans, taking arrows to trade. I don't think he even cared about what he received in return. He was so filled with dreams. He thought that maybe people like him, like us, of long names and low birth, could be the catalyst for change. As if somehow our petty trades with Humans might restore the relations between our people.

"I didn't feel like walking so far that day. I wasn't there for him. Maybe if I was, I would have seen the Paladins. I could have told him to stay away, I could have prevented him from dying, I-"

Ami choked back a sob and angrily cleared her throat.

"Tell me of your greatest fear," said the Dwarf, giving her not a moment of pause.

"Well, that's simple," Ami said, wiping away tears. "I'm afraid that the Quinarium will eradicate my people. I'm afraid that I won't be able to do enough, that Imreia and her allies won't be able to do enough. It's like I'm watching the arrival of the end, and I'm scared that the end has already been determined."

"That is what you most wish not to happen," said the Dwarf. "Tell me of your greatest fear."

Ami sighed and closed her eyes. Embarrassment clawed beneath her skin and every inch of her body begged to be scratched, that she might free herself of its presence.

"That I'll be alone," she whispered. "Even though most all of my people detest me, I want to be around them. Even though I can hardly call the Nomridian Forest home, and half of me hates the place, I don't know where I'd go without it. I... I'm more scared of being alone than I am of my people dying."

"Tell me of what you covet most," said the Human.

"Covet? Oh, I'm not much of one for sentimentality. There's my bow, maybe, but now I'm imagining losing it, I don't think I'd be that bothered. Wait! Before you scold me again, there's this." Ami dug the wooden owl charm from a pocket, then held it between two fingers. "My grandfather gave it to me. It's the last-"

"We know your mind."

"Alright, alright! Don't do... *that* to my mind again." Ami took a deep breath. "I think Caudro."

"We know your mind."

"Fine then, I *covet* him!" Ami recoiled from her own scream. She crossed her arms and looked to the ground, whispering as she continued. "But how can I feel this way? He was a Paladin, he walked with those who murdered my grandfather. He left, but does that mean he's redeemed? When I see him, when I touch him, when he touches me, my heart, I... how can I care for the one who, until these last few months, was a zealot against my kind?"

"We are not here to tell you what is right or wrong in the matters of the heart. We are here to assess the content of your mind."

"Then what is your assessment, now you've made me say all the things I wish I never said?"

The Human and Dwarf faded, leaving only the Fae. It shrank as it held out a hand until it was nearly Ami's height. A cup appeared in its palm; the scent of mana drifted out, the sweetness more strong and enticing than Ami had ever smelled before.

"Drink."

Ami was unsure if it was the command of the voice or the soreness she felt from having her heart so exposed, but she complied without comment. When Ami drank the mana, relief washed over her as if soothing ointment were applied to a tender wound.

"What you feel is the power of the Quinate. It is no gift. It is their mark, intended to shape and mold the entirety of this world in their image. Their touch should live in the water as it flows."

The Fae spread its arms and golden mist flowed in an undulating stream around the room. In a flash, the motes evaporated, reforming as a cloud. Droplets fell, coalescing as a misty stream once again.

"Their touch should live in the earth, as creatures live and die."

The stream disappeared, replaced by a thousand saplings. They grew into a forest, only to shed their leaves, go bare, wither, and fall, before new trees rose again. The stream reappeared, flowing through the golden woods.

"So too, should mana rise and fall."

Mages of every race appeared, standing in a ring between Ami and the forest. In unison, they drank mana, silently cast spells, withered and died, then decomposed into the soil. A pile of rocks emerged beside the Fae, with mana bubbling over the top. A new group of Mages materialized by the mana source.

The Fae refilled the cup and presented it to Ami.

"Drink, and be one with mana."

Ami took the cup. She raised it to her lips, but withdrew the moment the mana reached her tongue. There was an overwhelmingly pungent taste, as if an entire bottle of mana were condensed into a spoonful. Ami spat the mana back into the cup.

"It tastes different. Are you sure-"

"Be one with the mana."

Grumbling, Ami closed her eyes and downed a mouthful. She nearly coughed the mana back up when cold filled her belly instead of the expected warmth. Then, a tingling sensation struck. It was as if millions of ants suddenly crawled through her veins and beneath her skin. Ami sensed the mana melding and harmonizing with not only her body, but her very thoughts. Though it was entirely less pleasant than the usual embrace of mana, the connection was undoubtedly something *more,* and the power inside her begged to be used.

"This is incredible, it's-"

Thief.

Ami's eyes wrenched open. Total darkness surrounded her. She spun about, desperately searching for the golden remnants of the Quinate, for the forest and stream, for the Mages by the mana source. Instead, a cascade of voices assaulted her ears in an endless barrage.

Pathetic. Inelegant.

Ami squatted down, pressing her hands tightly against her ears.

"Please stop."

Desecrator.

"Please, stop!"

Despite Ami's pleas, the voices thundered ever louder.

You will never deserve this.

"Please!" Ami cried out as her balled fists trembled. "Please, leave me be. Five above, I thought I was past all of this! Please, leave me alone."

"You never made peace with your past, with the condemnation of your people. All your life, you have attempted to suppress your emotions, but with your mind exposed, your efforts are as useless as a village wall at stopping a hawk from flying through the sky. You may have failed to control your past, and yet, Aminantskeilara, within you is the power necessary to ward off intrusions of the mind in the future."

"How?"

"It is within you already."

The Fae, Dwarf, and Human reappeared. They each raised a hand, and a haze flowed from them into Ami's head. The voices rose, battering Ami anew.

Repent for your foul acts.

"Tell me what to do!"

Unworthy.

We must all live with the consequences of our actions.

"Stop this, please," Ami pleaded.

If you wish this to stop, then make us.

"Please, stop."

Make us.

"Stop!" Ami yelled, clawing at her scalp.

MAKE. US.

"GET OUT OF MY HEAD!"

Ami screamed until her throat burned, until the last of the air was expelled from her lungs and her heart threatened to beat through her chest. As she screamed, Ami felt the mana come alive inside her. It flowed, rising to her head where it pooled within her temples. Then, a shockwave burst free, obliterating the visages of the Fae, the Dwarf, and the Human.

Doubled over, Ami gasped and heaved as the stream, the trees, the mana source, and the Mages reappeared. The Fae, Dwarf, and Human arrived in a swirl of shimmering motes.

"Remember, Aminantskeilara, you alone are the master of your mind. You will never be immune from your emotions. Your memories will always be a part of you. Do not hide from them. However, none may take control of your mind without your approval. We offer you one last gift. Drink of this mana, and take up this bow."

The Dwarf held out a cup filled with mana, and the Human a long and slender bow. Despite her hesitance after the assault, curiosity tugged at Ami's heart. She drank the mana, then took hold of the bow. Her hand felt as if it fused with the weapon, and the mana she drank flowed between the object and herself. Inspecting the shimmering weapon, Ami wondered if it was real or if the trial, bow included, were constructs of her mind.

"Draw."

"There's no arrow," she replied.

"Draw."

"What am I to aim at?"

"Draw."

Ami sighed. "Right. Never can be clear or simple."

Raising the bow, Ami hooked her thumb around the string and drew. An arrow appeared, nocked above her thumb. A tiny barb in the fletching pierced her thumb, and a droplet of blood stained the feather.

"Ow!" Ami said, relaxing her arm to inspect the cut.

"Feel the mana flowing from your body into your arrow. Channel your thoughts as you release. Allow the arrow to be a vessel of your fury, and your spell will manifest as it flies."

"What spell am I to use?" Ami said as she hooked her thumb around the bowstring.

"You are a Mage."

Ami drew the string back to her cheek and readied to release when she saw a disturbance in the trees. A hulking, amorphous blob emerged. The ground rattled as it morphed into a creature Ami remembered all too well: six eyes sat atop an armored head, with a maw large enough to swallow her in a bite; more than thirty feet long, dozens of legs propelled the creature. It was none other than the monster of Yuvsgrend, slain by Dara months ago.

Ami released the arrow, only for it to sail into the darkness. The creature screeched and bounded forth. Ami's second arrow struck its armored shell, ricocheting as the creature grew ever close.

The creature was on top of Ami before she nocked another arrow. Diving away from outstretched claws, Ami rolled over the stone floor. She surged to her feet as the creature readied to charge anew.

Ami thought back to when she battled alongside Dara and Wynne in Yuvsgrend. Back then, she had broken a stone free from the ceiling, which fell and crushed the shell of the creature.

"Mizaina, let this arrow be as your stone!"

As the arrow flew, the end stretched into an orb of rock. It slammed into the creature and cratered a section of its shell. The creature recoiled, hissing as it readied to charge.

Ami's next arrow burst mid-flight. The wood shaft disintegrated while the arrowhead split into a shower of metal slivers which pierced the creatures' eyes. Ami set a final arrow free. It flattened into a thin blade and slipped between the creature's armor by its neck, sending yellow blood spurting out.

The creature gave one final groan with its maw open wide, then fell to the ground.

The Fae, the Dwarf, and the Human bowed.

"Stand tall, Aminantskeilara, Blessed of Mizaina."

"Ami!"

Caudro reached out into the silence.

"Ami, where are you?"

He turned back and forth, taking hesitant steps with arms outstretched, but the only response was the sound of his boots striking the stone floor.

"Ami?" Caudro whimpered, choking back a cry.

"What are you looking for?"

Caudro's head jerked at the familiar voice.

"I recognize that voice. You are the one who spoke to me in Mordinlet!"

"Why do you reach into the darkness?"

"I need Ami to find my way. I don't know where she has gone. Everything is dark."

"Darkness is a limitation of the body."

Caudro shook his head. "All I have is my body. What am I without my eyes? I am no more than a spear without its head, a tool with no use."

"The words of a Paladin, not a free man. If you choose to be no more than your body, then you will be forever blind."

"I am forever blind without my eyes, am I not?"

The voice did not respond.

"Who are you?" Caudro asked.

"I am an Avatar of Almoya. A remnant, an echo, formed of her power, left behind when the Quinate ascended into the sky."

"A voice of the Five," Caudro stammered.

"You speak with fear."

Caudro dropped to a knee and bowed his head.

"I am in awe. I... I never imagined being in the presence of a God's creation!"

"All of this world is a creation of the Quinate. You stand among the Quinate's creations every day. You should fear my presence no more than you fear standing in the shade of a tree."

"Of all the things I fear, death is not one of them," Caudro said, rising to his feet. "But more than anything, I fear being useless. How can I stand against the Quinarium if I cannot see? How can I be a warrior with no eyes?"

"Trust in the Five. Let go of your attachment to the strength of your arm. Become more than a man who finds purpose only in battle."

"How?"

"Give yourself over to the Quinate, as you pledged so many years ago. This time, however, the Quinarium will not stand between you and the Five. The demands of the Paladins will not lord over your servitude. You will serve the Quinate, as you are."

"Then I'm to leave here, as I am?" Caudro said with a furrowed brow.

"You are to trust in the grace of the Quinate."

Tears rolled down Caudro's cheeks. In the days since he heard the voice in his prison cell, he endlessly questioned whether it was real or a hallucination. It was harder to believe now that he was worthy to hear the words of an Avatar of Almoya. This grace, this attention, was more than he had ever hoped for, and surpassed all he had ever desired from being a Paladin. And yet, fear swelled in Caudro at the prospect of living without ever seeing again.

Then Jarain's words crept into Caudro's mind.

Stay true to the Quinate, and only the Quinate. Keep the Five in your heart, and you will find your place in this world.

"As you speak, so I listen," Caudro said, falling to his hands and knees. "I offer myself to the Quinate. I will face the future as They see fit."

"And so rises Caudro, Faithful of the Quinate. You are now prepared to undergo this ritual."

"Was this not the test of my faith?"

"This was a verification of your commitment. Now you are to be tested."

Still kneeling, Caudro grit his teeth and balled his fists, ready to face whatever the challenge might be. A gentle breeze swirled around him. The air grew warm. As his eyelids tingled, a voice called out.

"Rise!"

Caudro knew the word came from a Paladin. His heart raced and his muscles ached and burned, desperate to comply.

Kneel.

The second voice was faint, gentle, pleading.

"I said rise!"

Caudro stood and opened his eyes to see a Paladin, his face hidden by his helm. The world around was a haze, as if a cup of water were spilled on a still-wet painting.

"I can see..." Caudro whispered.

His hands trembled. His cheeks panged from an irresistible smile. Torn between laughter and tears, he wiggled his fingers before his eyes.

"Sit and eat. Today, we train," ordered the voice.

Walk away.

Caudro flinched, his heart torn. And yet, when his vision began to fade, he sat quickly. He landed on a bench, and a bowl of porridge and beans appeared on a table before him. Although the hushed voice nagged at the back of his brain, Caudro complied and cleared the bowl.

"Stand," ordered the Paladin.

Please walk away.

Caudro stood up from the table. The furnishing melted into a haze, reforming as a shield and spear hanging from a weapon rack.

"Take up your shield. Take up your spear."

Set down your arms.

Caudro retrieved the equipment from the rack. He admired the sight of his hand closing around the shaft of the spear, its tip glimmering.

"Thrust!"

The second voice did not protest. Caudro readied his spear and thrust with all his might.

The world went instantly black and Caudro's hands were empty again. Falling to his knees, Caudro's sobs echoed in the cold stone room.

"Rise!" demanded the Paladin.

Do not listen to him, the voice called with rising determination.

Caudro eagerly jumped to his feet. He hesitantly opened his eyes. A smile spread across Caudro's face. He blinked rapidly and the vision cleared, crisper than ever.

"Sit and eat. Today, we fight."

Walk away.

Ignoring the second voice, Caudro sat and eagerly consumed the food.

"Stand."

Leave this place.

Caudro stood at attention, his hands behind his back and head held high.

"Take up your shield. Take up your spear."

Leave this place behind, find peace.

Caudro raised the shield and spear.

"Thrust!"

Do not be their weapon. Do not give in. Let go!

A roar came from behind. Caudro turned and readied to face the attacker. A warrior with a low helm charged, sword raised high. Caudro thrust the spear, striking the warrior in the chest.

Darkness shrouded Caudro's vision.

"Wait! Please!" he cried out.

Caudro stumbled about, clawing at his eyelids, desperate for his vision to return.

"Please, what torture is this? Let me see again. Let me find my way."

"You offered yourself to Almoya, as you are, and yet you cling to sight," said the voice of the Avatar. "Your eyes deceive you. You must see through your mind."

An unseen force pushed Caudro to his knees.

"Rise!" shouted the Paladin.

Ignore him! Forge your own path!

Caudro shuddered as his vision returned. The Paladin stood closer this time. The pocks and dings on his armor were crisp and clear. Flecks of dried blood on the Paladin's helmet should have alarmed Caudro, but his legs stirred and he pulled himself to his feet.

"Sit and eat. Today, we kill."

Don't give in!

Caudro shivered. He attempted to turn, to flee, but his body dropped to a bench. Looking down, he watched as beans swirled inside the bowl, surrounded by half-congealed blood. Moved by an unseen force, his hand reached for the spoon. His muscles ached as he resisted, but he no longer controlled his own body. Shivers ran up Caudro's spine as his fingers closed around the utensil. His stomach churned as the contents flooded his mouth. Up and down his teeth closed on the gelatinous, metallic blood, punctuated with the bursting of mealy, half-cooked beans. He silently screamed, wishing he could gag, when the Paladin called out.

"Stand!"

Flee!

Caudro heeded the Paladin's command as the weapon rack appeared.

"Take up your shield. Take up your spear."

Your hands are your own! Do not comply!

Shutting his eyes, Caudro balled his hands into fists. He clenched so tightly that his arms quaked, but despite his efforts, his fingers wrenched open and the spear and shield filled his hands.

"Thrust!" bellowed the Paladin.

Fight him, Caudro!

Caudro's eyes ripped open to see a young child standing beside the Paladin.

"Kill him!"

Squinting, Caudro gasped as he recognized the boy.

"This is your enemy! Do as I command and kill him!"

A tear rolled down Caudro's cheek as he looked into the face of himself, as a child. He raised the spear high. The point aimed at the boy, Caudro roared. He thrust the spear with all his might.

As the blade brushed against the child's hair, Caudro ripped the weapon aside, impaling the Paladin in the neck. The man twisted and convulsed as dozens of black tendrils crawled out from the wound, wrapping around the spear. Caudro attempted to drop the weapon, but the haft was fused to his hand. The cold and damp tendrils crawled up his arm, grabbing tight like the tentacles of an octopus. They rolled over each other, holding tight until they reached Caudro's eyes.

The world went dark, and the spear faded to nothingness. Caudro hunched over, sobbing, alone.

"And so rises Caudro, a Herald of Almoya."

"Avatar? How is this possible?" Caudro said. "Why name me a Herald of Almoya? I haven't-"

"Done anything of note? Caudro, you have offered yourself completely to the Five, you have turned your back on the misguidance of the Quinarium, and in doing so, have proven yourself worthy of this mantle. As a Herald of Almoya, you must walk this world as Her instrument: protect those unable to protect themselves and free the minds of those whose thoughts are clouded. And as bearer of this title, you are to receive a blessing."

"I deserve nothing."

"That is the Paladins speaking, not you. It is not a matter of deserving. It is a matter of service, and you must move beyond your past if you are to serve in Almoya's name."

Caudro bowed.

"What am I to do?"

"Drink."

A bottle appeared in Caudro's hand. Warmth seeped through the smooth glass surface. Caudro removed the stopper, and the sweet scent of mana filled his nose. Without hesitation, he took a drink.

Bliss filled Caudro's mind, stronger than the day he first stood beside Jarain, when he hoped for a future of purpose and meaning.

"As you have opened your mind to Almoya, open your eyes."

Caudro froze, wondering if it was yet another test.

"But I don't have-"

"Open your eyes."

Caudro inhaled, then exhaled slowly. His heart pounded with anticipation. Despite his doubts, he told himself to trust the Avatar and complied.

Although Caudro's eyelids did not move, a rush of light filled his mind. The brightness eased and he saw the stone walls of the room as if they were a painting made with too-thin watercolors. The blurry and indistinct view hardly bothered Caudro, for he could *see*.

"You have been blessed by Almoya with her sight. It is not the same as what you once perceived with your eyes, but drink mana and you will see as She does. The more you see, the faster your vision will fade, and the more mana you will require. In time, you will adapt and learn to use this gift. Perhaps a demonstration, that you might understand."

In the distance, Caudro spied movement. It began as a simple disruption, like ink dropped on a canvas without purpose. Then, plants grew from the splotch, or at least he thought they were plants; soft, amorphous outlines in various shades of muted greens stretched and climbed with oblong leaves, though no matter how hard he focused, details evaded his gaze.

A glimmer of crimson drew Caudro's attention. It suddenly flew out from the trees, then sprouted wings, flitting through the sky. Wondering how similar this mana-empowered vision was to regular sight, Caudro tried blinking; to his surprise, he was able to 'close' his eyes to the sight at will.

Caudro burst into tears. The weeks of despair, of self-loathing, of fear had faded as he accepted Almoya's embrace.

"Blessed be Almoya," he stammered, his tears falling to the stone floor like rain on shingled rooftops. "What would She have me do?"

"You already know. While a Paladin, you believed yourself to be acting as She would expect. Stand for those who cannot stand themselves. Aid those who are unable to aid themselves. Do all you can to end the deceit of the Quinarium. In doing so, you will bring honor to Almoya's name."

Caudro sniffed back tears and exhaled slowly to gather himself.

"I pledge myself to Almoya. I will not squander this gift, I swear on my life."

"As is your duty. Go forth, Caudro, Herald of Almoya, and serve all in her name."

The plants blurred as a white light overtook the entire room. The brightness intensified until it became painful. Caudro fought to continue looking, as if cutting off the vision would cause him to lose it forever, until the light became unbearable.

In darkness again, a tone sounded. The rumbling tone grew, filling his ears and rattling his head until it abruptly ceased.

Caudro opened his mind to sight, and found himself in the chamber. Looking around, he spied a red form a few paces away.

"Ami!" Caudro shouted.

"Gah!" she replied, grabbing her chest and sighing with relief upon seeing Caudro. "You big oaf, why did you yell so loudly? Caudro, your eyes... well, it's not your eyes, but there's a purple glow over your eyelids. How did you know I was here?"

"I can scarcely believe it, Ami."

Caudro walked up to Ami, then took her hands in his. "You can see? How?"

"There was this voice... after the ritual, it named me a Herald of Almoya. Through her blessing, I can see, in a way. I have to drink mana for this sight, and it is not as it was before, though I can tell well enough where I am and what's around me."

Ami's hands lingered inside Caudro's; she gently traced a crease in his palm with a finger. His hands were comforting, making her worries fade like snow melting on a sunny spring day.

"It seems we both had an eventful time."

"You went through the ritual, too?"

"You're speaking to the Blessed of Mizaina. I wonder if everyone going through this ritual ends up with a fussy title?" Ami said with a snort. "We have some catching up to do, big man. Or perhaps I need to retire that nickname? 'Herald' might have been bestowed by a God, but it doesn't quite have the same ring to it."

"You may call me whatever you wish," Caudro said with a smile.

The door to the chamber swung open and Ami pulled away. A fleeting moment of sadness overtook Caudro. Though he did not expect to use his gift constantly, he realized that with this gift of sight, he wouldn't depend on Ami the same way as before, that he would not feel her touch the same way again.

"Hurry!" Anghara said, peering through the door. "We are to be inspected!"

"Inspected?" Ami said with a squint.

"The Moderator of Llendswarne is coming. This time he comes with a retinue of over twenty, and they have already reached Almeyhill. They will search every inch of this Academy. You must go!"

Anghara hastened down quiet halls. She paused not once to question the haze before Caudro's eyelids, though Caudro's sight had faded by the time they reached the exit of the Academy.

Anghara panted; fear was painted on her face.

"Please, don't forget your promise. I beg you."

"I will do everything in my power to help," Caudro said, closing his eyes. "I swore to you on my life, and if I were to die and rise again, I would swear it all again."

Ami rolled her eyes. "Alright, you poet, enough with the drama. Anghara has places to be, and we have a place we shouldn't be, and that is right where we are standing. We need to go!"

"Thank you. Both of you. Hope is more than we have had in many years. Few are more motivated than we Mind Mages to enact our revenge on the Quinarium. Uphold your vow to free us, and you will have yourselves a powerful ally."

Anghara waved as the two fled into the night.

INTERLUDE

Sweat dripped from Neia's brow. Her arms glistened and muscles rippled as she gripped her halberd tight. She glared at the enemies before her: an array of logs, with branches for arms, sticks for weapons, and sacks filled with sand for heads filled an outdoor arena at the edge of a forest.

Neia burst forward. Though her figure was hulking, she was deft on her feet and made not a sound.

She swung her halberd at the first target, cleaving the head in two. While sand still flew, she impaled a second target with the spike at the end of her weapon. A mighty kick sent the log rolling away.

Neia feinted left, then right, then engaged the third target. A downward slash severed one arm. She effortlessly flicked her halberd up, splitting the other arm in half. Raising her halberd high into the air, Neia brought the weapon down with all her strength. Two halves of the log tumbled away as the halberd's blade sunk into the ground.

With a heave, Neia pulled her halberd free. She threw it at another target; the weapon flew as if it were a light javelin. The point disappeared into the log, which tipped over from the force.

Drawing her sword, Neia leapt at the nearest target. She slit its throat, then sped away. Neia jumped and rolled over a target, slicing bark away with a flurry of blows. Turning to the last standing target, Neia threw her sword. The log wobbled, then fell.

"Well done. Though I wish you invested yourself in matters more important than cutting bits of dead wood, Nireia. And that sleeveless tunic looks ridiculous."

Neia glared, red faced, as Imreia entered the clearing.

"The tunic's comfortable. And this is what I know."

"What you know?" Imreia scoffed. "I taught you *everything* other than whatever this is. You know far, far more, Nireia."

"I wish you would call me Neia. You know I prefer it."

"Don't be ridiculous."

Neia crossed her arms. "Whose choice was it that I learned all those things? Formalities and customs, rules and etiquette, your time would have been better spent teaching anyone other than me."

"There was no choice."

"There is always a choice."

"A childish fallacy," Imreia said coldly. "You speak as one with far less tutelage, less training, less *everything* than you have been afforded."

"And you speak as if you were always here with me," Neia said, striking her chest with a fist. "I see you a few days at a time, sporadically, at your leisure, with little more than scant words scribbled in cryptic letters between. Who are you to lecture me as if you've been a doting mother? As if you were my mother?"

"Don't insult the memory of our parents."

"It is YOU who insults them by treating me this way! Parading me around, sending me as a showpiece to make Lords and other leaders of Draethhold feel like YOU are committed. I am capable of more!"

Imreia paced back and forth, glaring at Neia's fists.

"You mean you wish to fight?"

"Yes!"

"Fighting is for the boors," Imreia said, waving her hand dismissively. "You are destined for more."

"I DON'T WANT MORE!"

Neia's chest heaved as she grabbed her halberd. She cleaved a log in half, then swung again when Imreia leapt out and parried with her sword.

"You are such a selfish bitch!" Neia screamed. "Why don't you leave me be? Being alone would be preferable to whatever it is you're doing now. You go on about how fighting is for the boors, but look at you! Better trained than me, always diving into battle. You're such a hypocrite!"

"Hypocrite? I do what is necessary," Imreia said, sheathing her sword. "Unlike you, I will gladly hang up my sword when this is all over."

"When exactly will this all be over? When you sit on the throne of Brewardsburg? Or Llendshold? Do you even see me in this future?"

"If you would stop being a petulant idiot and acted as I've taught you, then I would see you by my side."

"You mean in your shadow," Neia seethed.

"Cry all you want. Keep making yourself out to be a victim, but my words are genuine."

"You're genuine with no one, Imi."

"Don't call me that."

"Why not, Imi?"

Imreia glared, her eyes burning like a blacksmith's forge. "You know."

"But you always tell me to move past Mother and Father's passing, Imi."

"Silence!"

Neia eyed Imreia as she pried her halberd out of a log. "There's the Imreia I know."

Imreia breathed deeply and brushed a wrinkle out of her tunic. "This is about more than what happened in Brewardsburg, Nireia. No matter what you think of me, I wish to free the people of Llendshold."

"Why should I care?" Neia spat. "You don't let me step away from this forsaken place, to be a part of anything. I haven't stepped foot in Llendshold a single time since we fled."

"I need you here. This is the best way for you to be a part of what is to come. I know you are a capable warrior, but every battle carries the risk of death. I will only employ you when I absolutely must."

"How many times do I have to tell you to stop speaking falsely to me!? It isn't my fault that I'm not attuned to mana, but not being able to cast a spell doesn't mean I'm incapable of fighting!"

"That is not my belief. That is your own insecurity," Imreia said.

"Fine then. Say what you will, believe what you want, but until you're willing to let me stand by your side, leave me in peace. I can do all you've asked without you lording over me," Nireia said, throwing her halberd aside.

Imreia smiled as she watched her sister storm away.

Chapter 8

Oars lapped rhythmically against the surface of a placid lake in the late afternoon. The calm of the waters contrasted starkly with the ominous clouds which billowed in the sky above. The warm, humid air promised rain would soon fall.

"I hope we can make it to the island before it starts pouring," Ami said. "Don't want our provisions to get soaked."

"Is that your polite way of saying that I'm rowing too slowly?" Caudro asked with a smirk.

Ami surveyed their surroundings from her perch at the aft of the boat. They had been in the rowboat for a few hours, and the shore of the lake was far in the distance; trees looked like tufts of moss. The island ahead had seemed like a logical stopping point, but Ami questioned their choice of destination with every passing moment as the sky darkened.

"Of course not. I am propelled by a Herald of Almoya, a hero among common folk! I trust you to make yourself useful. Though blessed as we both may be, it might be a good thing you can't see how dark these clouds are getting. It's a bit of a shame that Almoya didn't see fit to let you see all the time."

"I will see when there is need," Caudro said. "I hardly need vision to row. It's a strange feeling; the last time I held an oar was when we were with Dara and Wynne, on our way to that forsaken island in search of the mana source... while we still served the Quinarium."

"And now?"

"I have purpose. It feels strange to call myself Herald, especially since I'm not entirely sure how I'm supposed to fulfill my oath. It's not as though I am to go around announcing myself in such a way. As a Paladin, I was recognizable on sight with all the armor and symbols of the Quinarium, but what will people think of me as I am today?"

Ami gazed at Caudro. With his eyes closed and headband removed, he looked almost peaceful, at rest, despite the effort of rowing. Her eyes drifted to his hands, which gripped the oars tightly, and his forearms, which tensed and relaxed in a calming rhythm. The urge to reach out and trace her hands along his skin filled her heart, with the hopes he would wrap his arms around her and hold her close in return. Looking back at his face, she was struck with a tinge of sadness that he was so uncertain of himself, despite all she saw in him.

"In your entire life, have so few people liked you?"

"Paladins aren't known for their affection," Caudro said with a chuckle.

Ami grinned. "I'm not sure I'll ever get used to hearing you laugh."

"Should I restrain myself?"

"No. It's pleasant."

Caudro smiled broadly as he rowed.

"Your gifts seem quite useful."

"It's more a matter of putting them to use than receiving them," Ami said. "I can't help but think the talk in there was more important than the blessing I received. I will say that cutting my thumb to empower arrows is far from pleasant. It is such a sensitive place compared to the palm. I would rather it worked as with you, simply drink mana and be done. Though,

I'm grateful you don't have to cut your eyelids or something awful to release mana and see."

Thunder rumbled.

"Perhaps we should have kept the horses and ridden south, instead of going across the lake," Caudro said as he hastened his rowing.

"The innkeeper assured us this is the most expedient way to Evenswall. I still don't understand why he felt the theatrics were necessary with Anghara, but he otherwise seemed genuine. Bah, this storm is making me question our decision as well. At least we've nearly reached the island. It looks like there's some sort of building there, with a pier."

"Does it look inhabited?"

Ami leaned forward, resting her hands on Caudro's shoulder. He suppressed the urge to lean into her touch. Ami's scent—of a forest on a cool spring morning—intoxicated Caudro. He swallowed when she sat back at the aft, leaving his shoulder bare.

"It looks abandoned. The walls are a cream color, though they might be brighter in the sunlight, and ivy is growing over the whole thing. There are two stories, with a three-story tower of sorts on one side. The red clay shingles are a nice touch, but quite a few are missing. It might have been charming when it was maintained, but it has fallen into decay. I expect we will be alone."

The gentle patter of a drizzle urged Caudro along. He rowed with purpose as the rain progressed from a delicate shower to a torrential downpour. Ami scurried about, protecting the food as best she was able with oiled cloths and spare clothing. Caudro smiled at her profuse cursing, thinking the discomfort was well worth hearing the fury that grew in Ami. Her mutterings grew louder as a wind blew in and lightning flashed, chased by thunder.

"Ease up, we're almost there!"

Caudro raised the oars as Ami stepped past. He listened as ropes creaked and groaned from Ami cinching them tight, and the rowboat gently bumped against the pier. She helped Caudro out from the boat and loaded him with packs before pulling him by the hand into the building.

Winds howled behind them like a pack of wolves, though the pelting rain sounded comforting from inside the shelter. Ami lifted the bags from Caudro's shoulders; he listened as buckles clicked and clattered against the tiled floor.

"Let me help you," Caudro said. "It'll take but a sip of mana and then you won't have to do everything on your own."

"I won't complain," Ami replied. "It looks like we'll be here for the night anyhow."

Caudro reached for his hip. His knuckles brushed against the glass bottle; he was still unused to the warmth emanating from the walls of the vessel. Taking hold, he took a hesitant sip.

In a blink, light filled Caudro's mind. He inspected the surrounding room: they stood near an open kitchen, with a hulking brick-lined hearth; a bar jutted out into the room, separating the kitchen from a tangled mess of half-decomposed chairs and tables. A stairway to one side led up to the second floor, while a spiraling staircase on the opposite wall led up the tower. His gaze landed on Ami; staring at her hazy figure, he wished he could see her clearly.

"There's something different about this place."

"Different in what way?" Ami asked.

"The walls of the Academy of Almoya, both inside and out, were a deep shade of grey. It's far brighter here, despite the storm."

"Maybe that's normal?" Ami said, her voice wavering. "Perhaps things will look different depending on where you are."

"I suppose I will learn in time. Do you see anything of note?"

"Ah, well, it's all rather boring," Ami said, her nonchalance returned. "Some sort of clay lines the walls. It's worn down and chipped here and there, but it's holding together well enough. I don't see any signs of anything living here, or having been here recently. The oddest thing is that it's not terribly dirty. No mountains of leaves or dirt piling in the corners. Aside from that, nothing you would miss, I think."

"We should look around to be sure it's safe."

"So says the hero, so must we do!" Ami said with a sweeping bow. "Right then, let's get to it. Why don't you take a look in the tower? I'll see what's to be seen upstairs."

Though the building was large for an inn, there was little of note, and the two explored its entirety in a matter of minutes. Ami found lodging rooms with leaky ceilings, rotting beds, and vines growing through holes in the walls; Caudro, meanwhile, determined the tower to be a simple attraction for guests, with a commanding view of the lake but no other obvious purpose.

Back in the main room of the inn, Ami prepared a stew, then set about attaching metal barbs to a handful of her arrows. She regretted the idea of cutting her thumb with the arrows, but the colorful thread she used to bind the barbs tempered her distaste.

She pulled a knot tight, then set aside the arrow. Taking a peek into the pot, she looked over at Caudro. He neatly spread the two bedrolls with more care than a Lord's servant. An impish grin spread across Ami's face.

"Are you ready to try some fish?"

Caudro sighed deeply. "I can hardly believe you've convinced me to eat... flesh."

"Come now! You have entered a new phase of your life. The Paladins are in the past and you're a Herald of Almoya now. You don't have to heed the demands of the Quinarium, and it was only them saying not to eat meat. You saw the people of Draethhold happily eating fish."

"I did not *see* them, as such," Caudro said with a smirk.

"Right," Ami said, dragging the word. "You were there when the people—*Humans*—of Draethhold ate fish. You even confided that it smelled delicious before you knew it was meat."

"I will do this, but only because you have asked me so many times that I am desperate to finally live for a day free from you asking me."

"I will do this," Ami said mockingly. "Come now. I tried your stupid beans. I tried that horrendous Paladin bread that damn near broke my teeth."

Caudro grimaced as a wooden spoon scraped the pot.

"I pray the Five won't think worse of me for what I am about to do."

"We have been through this! It is not the Five saying to not eat meat, otherwise all the peoples outside of Llendshold wouldn't be eating it."

Ami thrust the bowl into Caudro's lap. He raised the dish and inhaled. His stomach grumbled; an aroma of herbs and onions danced around the sweet brightness of the fish.

"Fine. I will eat this, but if I am suddenly struck down by the flames of Ilsios, barreling down from the sky through the storm, then know it was your doing!"

Ami stared expectantly. Caudro first took a drink of broth, thickened with ground potatoes. Smacking his lips, he raised his spoon, then plunged it into the bowl. As Caudro raised the utensil, Ami reached out and slid a hunk of fish on top. He took the whole bite, his head tilting as he chewed.

"Well, then?" Ami asked, watching expectantly as Caudro licked a drop of broth from his lip.

"The taste is strange, and the texture stranger still. I can't say that I like it, but it isn't entirely unpleasant."

"A rousing success, then!" Ami said, raising her own bowl. "Seeing as how a divine fire hasn't consumed you, I think we can agree that you will be fine, you overgrown baby of a hero."

"Perhaps divine fire has not consumed me because the Five are too repulsed by our actions to watch."

Ami and Caudro burst into laughter, but their humor was short-lived when a crash came from above.

"Did part of the roof cave in?" Ami said, setting down her bowl.

"It didn't sound that large. Maybe the wind blew something over," Caudro said.

"Or maybe there is something living here, and we missed it. Perhaps it's an ancient denizen, a cursed guest. Stuck on the island, a malevolent inclination overtook them and they murdered everyone else in the inn and performed a powerful spell, extending their life by draining vitality from the dead!"

"I would have seen if there was something living in the tower," Caudro said, ignoring Ami's outlandish tale.

"You didn't check upstairs."

"We should look then. An extra sip of mana will be well worth the comfort of knowing we're alone when it comes time to sleep. I think we should stay together this time."

"No complaints from me," Ami said. "How about you go first?"

Caudro took the lead with a spear at the ready. He scoured every inch of the stairs for a red glow among the pale grey walls and the occasional intrusion of green vines. Ami kept close behind with a mana bottle and her spiked gourd in hand.

Gale winds rattled the building as they reached the upper floor. Caudro inched forward and peered into rooms for signs of life. A wailing screech came from within, as if a soul were screaming out in pain, then suddenly ceased. The door to the room swung open; Ami drank a mouthful of mana and squeezed her gourd, while Caudro charged into the room with a roar.

Ami entered to find Caudro standing at the center, his shoulders relaxed. He raised his spear, pointing to a hole in the wall. A gust of wind rose, and howling echoed through the opening. Ami sighed in relief.

"It was as you said. Just the wind."

Bang!

They both jumped and turned to find the door to the room had blown off of its hinge.

"Blustery night, sleep is going to be diffi... hey, what's going on?"

Ami ran after Caudro, who was already halfway down the hall.

"It wasn't the wind!" he called back. "I saw something! It was a strange hue of purple, and its footsteps leave a glowing trail. This way!"

Caudro followed the footprints down the stairs to the main room of the inn.

"Did you see anything purple during the ritual?" Ami called after.

"No, only grey and green and red."

A crash greeted them as they reached the main room of the inn.

"The footsteps lead to the tower," Caudro said, resuming his sprint.

"The cretin knocked over the pot! I worked hard on that stew!" Ami yelled. "Five as my witness, I will end whatever thing did this!"

"Whatever it is, I don't think it's large," Caudro said as they jogged across the inn. He paused by the stairs to the tower. "I saw no signs of it when we arrived, and you didn't see anything concerning. Is it possible, whatever this thing is, that it's not a foe?"

"It's an enemy to me. It wasted the stew I made for you... us," Ami growled.

They scurried up the stairs by twos and threes until they reached the top. Harsh winds blew the rain nearly sideways, soaking their tunics.

"Not a trace," Ami said, scanning their surroundings. She looked up to the roof, which swayed in the wind, threatening to blow free.

"There!" Caudro shouted, pointing over Ami's shoulder.

She spun about to see a blur of a shadow leaping off the tower. They hurried to the edge; Ami saw nothing in the darkness.

"It disappeared. Not much chance of sleeping, knowing some creature is on the prowl."

"There are footsteps leading to a cellar, tucked against the side of the building. The creature ran from us. Perhaps it is afraid."

"It had better be afraid!" Ami shouted into the storm.

Caudro turned to Ami with a wry smile. "If I knew how you felt about the food you cooked, I would have spoken of the fish with more enthusiasm."

A few minutes later, they stood in the driving rain before the cellar. A rusted lock secured the rickety doors. Caudro strode forward and kicked, sending fragments of half-rotted wood tumbling down the stairs. He confidently marched into the chill of the pitch-black cellar with Ami close behind.

The darkness engulfed Caudro. A flash of lightning revealed a cobweb-covered oil lantern; Ami ignited the wick with a bit of flint, then examined the cellar. Caudro stood ahead of her between rows of shelves stuffed with broken crates and cracked vases, which ran the length of the room.

"It's cold, and there's only one way out. What creature would seek solace in here?" Ami said.

"It's an odd thing, whatever it is."

A vase crashed the floor. A hiss echoed through the cellar as Caudro readied his spear.

"Face us, beast of the night!"

"Wait!" Ami yelled, grabbing Caudro's arm.

She took a bit of dried meat from a pouch, then set the lantern down. Crouching low, she cooed as she inched forward with the meat held at arm's length. Nails skittered over the floor.

"It's alright, little friend," Ami said, sitting and placing the meat on the ground.

Out from the darkness hopped the creature. It sniffed the morsel, then chirped before gnawing on its end.

"What is it?" Caudro ventured.

"A strange creature indeed," Ami said. "It can't possibly weigh more than a few pounds. It has the head of a weasel, the wings of a bat, the tail of a squirrel, and the hind legs of a rabbit. Though I say it bears resemblance to those animals, the relation is entirely wrong when you look at it as a whole."

"I have never heard of such a creature. Glowing purple... Should you use a spell to control it?"

"Control it?" Ami scoffed. "A creature this cute and so easily plied by a bit of meat? I think not, my hero. Besides, purple is the color of Kardef, or Almoya as you Humans call her. Given we came from the Academy in her name, the color must be a good sign. A little creature like this needs food and love, not to be controlled. Isn't that right, my friend?"

The creature snapped up the morsel of dried meat then scurried up Ami's arm, coming to a rest on her shoulder.

"Oh, its fur is so soft! What a delightful little friend. I think I will call you Plug."

"Plug? Like a stopper to a bottle?"

"You say that as if it isn't a perfect name." Ami stood and gently pet the creature's head. "I can already tell that it has plugged a hole in my heart—a desperate need for tender companionship—that I was previously unaware of."

Caudro sheathed his sword and exhaled slowly to calm his heart. "Hardly the worst imaginable outcome. Though, I regret drinking mana only for us to find a harmless little pet."

Back in the inn, wearing dry clothes and huddled by the fire, Plug enamored Ami. The creature, having eaten its fill of their second batch of stew, hopped in and out of her lap, playfully begging for belly rubs and head scratches. Ami looked at Caudro; the purple haze had faded from outside his eyes. She stared at the lines where his eyelids met, wishing she could lock eyes with him again, that Caudro might see the look on her face when she gazed at him in quiet moments.

"How curious Plug is," Caudro said, pulling Ami from her stupor.

"Curiously wonderful! I wonder why Plug appeared such a strange color in your vision?"

"Perhaps it was exposed to mana?" Caudro mused.

"Possibly, but whatever the cause, I am infatuated. Who knew that in an abandoned inn, caught in a storm, we would find a mighty ally?"

Plug hopped onto Ami's knee, let out a furious, tiny roar. It leapt, then glided around the inn, kicking off tables and walls as it flew about.

"Energetic thing," Caudro said as he lay on his bedroll.

"Why shouldn't he be? He's happy!"

"He?"

Ami crawled closer to Caudro, then leaned close to his ear as she whispered. "There are certain... indicators of gender. Let me know should you ever need instruction; I'm an excellent teacher when it comes to matters of procreation."

Caudro's face burned hotter than the fire crackling in the hearth as Ami leapt away with a giggle. She hummed and sang a wordless song until Plug slowed his frenzy. He landed on her shoulder and cuddled against Ami's neck.

"You sing and whistle often," Caudro said. Regret struck him as Ami ended her song to reply.

"Is it a problem for you?"

"The opposite. It lifts my spirits. But if you don't mind me asking, why do you sing?"

"Are all the Humans of Llendshold so boring? So reluctant to find joy in life? Why not sing if I fancy it? Songs are simply a way of letting things out when it's too much to keep everything inside."

"The songs you sing, they are of your own creation?"

"Of course."

Caudro smiled as he leaned up, propping his head on his hand. "I should call you my joyful minstrel."

Ami breathed deeply as she stared out an open window. The storm had eased, and the glow of the moon broke through the clouds, casting the lake in a delicate silver light.

"I sing happy songs because they're all my grandfather would sing."

Quiet filled the air. Plug's cooing melded with a gentle breeze rustling leaves outside. Ami hummed softly, joining in the song of the tranquil night.

"It is my life's greatest regret," Caudro said, his voice cracking.

"What is?"

"Being a Paladin." Caudro sat quietly for a moment with his head turned down. "I served—with my hands, my heart, and my very soul—an order that committed atrocities in the name of the Quinate. Atrocities like murdering your grandfather."

Ami inspected Caudro's face, hoping to see an expression that matched his words, but he remained stoic.

"Ah, so you admit the truth now."

"I was scared before, and in denial. I was wrong to doubt you. While I can't undo the wrongs of my past, I will dedicate myself to stopping the order I once served."

"Do you mean by ensuring that Mordinlet is the target for the show of strength, and that we stop your old master Scireth?"

"Oh, well, I-"

"I wonder how Vinzen and the Dwarves are doing?" Ami shifted the conversation cheerfully. "It seems a challenging task to craft new crowns."

"He sounded hopeful. Excited, even."

"If only they had enough crowns for every Human of Llendshold, it would make our work heaps easier."

"I wonder if it is possible to fold mana into armor and weapons?" Caudro said. "As powerful as the crowns seem to be, such equipment would be an incredible advantage in war."

Ami stretched on her bedroll; Plug burrowed deep inside.

"I'm sure it's possible, given Mages can enchant objects well enough, when the purpose warrants the mana. I imagine the weaving of mana into things would be a fascinating study, once the war is over."

"A time without war..." Caudro's voice faded.

"What? Am I not allowed to dream?"

"I wish I better knew how to dream. I grew up training, told my only purpose was in my ability to fight until I die, if need be. Everything I did was in support of that purpose. I struggle to imagine all the possibilities that exist outside of battle."

"Well, start trying. I don't intend to do... *this* forever."

"Thank you."

Ami chuckled. "For what? Demanding you start dreaming?"

Caudro exhaled slowly through his mouth, then brought his lips together as he inhaled through his nose.

"Whenever I'm with you, things seem to go better for me."

Ami opened and closed her mouth over and over, mulling over how to reply.

"That's not what you said when I captured you, Dara, and Wynne in your little boat on your way into the Nomridian Forest."

Caudro chuckled. "I hear your meaning, though you know what I say is true. From the Jackal den to sailing into the Zanerian Archipelago with Dara and Wynne, to you saving me in Mordinlet, to hauling me across Llendshold, you have been instrumental in me being where I am today. I would be lost, likely still serving as a Paladin, were it not for you."

Ami lay back, tracing the wooden beams of the ceiling with her eyes, content at his reply.

"Well, I must say I am quite touched. Unfortunately for you, however, you must now fight for my affections, as I am preoccupied with the disastrously sweet creature known as Plug. I think I'll make him a special pouch for my belt, so he can always be as close as he deserves. Goodnight!"

Caudro lay awake for a while, listening as Ami's breaths slowed. The occasional breeze whistled sweetly through the inn, joining the sizzle of the fire. Caudro imagined turning his head to see Ami, to gaze at her in a peaceful rest. Though he lamented that even with mana he would never see Ami again as he did before, Caudro smiled, glad for the time he had at her side. With a sigh, he attempted to clear his thoughts and drift to sleep.

CHAPTER 9

The following day, Ami and Caudro rowed across the lake beneath tranquil skies. It took them three more days to follow a narrow pass down from the mountains, cross a wide plain, and press through a dense forest until they reached a rocky overlook above Evenswall. The village shone beneath the mid-afternoon sun. Constructed almost entirely of sandy stone, it was nestled into gently sloping mountains which stretched to the coast. Dozens of piers jutted out over the ocean near the village walls.

The Ziggurat of the Fallen stood between the overlook and the shore. Towering stone blocks devoid of decoration formed a stepped pyramid at the heart of a field. It was a profoundly strange structure, unlike any other in all of Llendshold. Imposing walls wrapped around the field; a compound of a few buildings stood outside the lone gate.

Caudro raised a few mana bottles, then looked out from their vantage point.

"Maybe we should have gone slower. Drinking mana was a luxury when we crossed the fields; we might have saved a bottle or two."

Ami punched Caudro's shoulder playfully. "Better to make good time and make sure we weren't caught. Anyhow, I still have a few untouched bottles. I'm more worried about how we're supposed to get inside this place. A hoard of stolen treasures...

I wonder if we'll find antiques from the Fae and Dwarves alongside those from Draethhold?"

"The Draethhold Lords were quite certain their gilded tome is inside. As for breaking in... Paladins are taught that appearance is second only to the strength in their hands. My understanding is they built the ziggurat to look impressive, but the number of Paladins guarding it is quite modest. It's the inside I'm worried about."

"That many guards?"

"I doubt we will find a single person inside."

"Oh come now, you can't say that and not explain!"

"The ziggurat serves as a crypt, a final resting place for Paladins who die honorably in combat. A procession arrives for burials, but the crypt is otherwise empty, so that Paladins might rest in peace. But tombs are in the upper levels. Supposedly the lower levels took more than a century to build."

"Excuse the interruption, but what qualifies as an honorable death?"

"Dying in battle, in the name of the Quinarium," Caudro said grimly. "Dying while acting in service of the Quinarium qualifies, too, so as to not exclude those who die of old age but remain dedicated to the end."

Ami snorted. "Interesting you say Quinarium, and not Quinate, or the Five."

"I say that because they are the words of the Paladins. We always focused on the Quinarium, as they claimed that the Quinarium alone speaks on behalf of the Quinate. I was too stupid to realize the deceit."

Ami chewed at her lip. "So... you were saying about the lower levels?"

"Exactly what lies below is a secret, but I do know there are many layers of security. To reach the lowest levels, you must either have a key, carried only by designated Keepers, or pass the tests."

"And these tests might be…?"

"I don't know." Caudro turned to Ami. "All we were told is that anyone unfamiliar with the Paladin code would fail."

"Lovely you bring that up now!" Ami said. "You seemed entirely disinterested in coming at all when I said you should accompany me to the ziggurat, all for me to find out that I would have failed without you! Five above, what a hero."

"If I didn't join you, then I would have shared everything I know before you left!"

"Right, so I could die alone, with a small understanding of why I died."

Plug popped up from a pouch on Ami's belt. He scurried up her chest and lounged atop her shoulder.

"Maybe Plug will be of some use inside?" Caudro said.

As if to reply, Plug yawned, then closed his eyes and fell asleep.

"I somehow think that to be unlikely," Ami replied. "Wonderful little companion he may be, but I wouldn't expect such a sweet creature to face a trial. You are right about the guard, at least. The patrols cover long paths, and there are periods when not a single Paladin stands by the gate. Rather shoddy, if you ask me."

"It should be easy enough to enter under the cover of nightfall," Caudro said.

The two spent the ensuing hours readying themselves. Though dwindling supplies were a worry during their travels, the ability to stuff their provisions and equipment into two packs was a boon as they prepared to infiltrate the ziggurat.

The last sliver of the sun slipped below the horizon while Ami and Caudro hid behind trees near the edge of the compound. A bell chimed, and the Paladins patrolling by the gate marched into a building, leaving the open entrance unattended.

Caudro darted out from behind the tree and sprinted to the gate as fast as he was able. He grabbed onto the giant door to slow himself, motioning for Ami to hurry through. They scurried away from the gate and through the empty courtyard until they stood before the imposing Ziggurat of the Fallen. The stepped walls tapered into the night sky, as if the building were a pathway to the stars above.

Doors creaking open and shut as guards changed shift pulled Ami and Caudro from their stupor. The two ducked inside, shutting the doors after.

"Well, this is sad," Ami said, inspecting their surroundings.

"Even with my sight as it is, I agree."

Thin rays of moonlight flowed in from square windows set high around the foyer, but not a single adornment of any kind graced the walls. There was one pair of doors on each side of the room, with no sign of what lay beyond.

"Stairs down should be through the door ahead. I'll lead," Caudro said.

"No complaints from me."

Caudro opened the doors, revealing a small room before a stairway leading straight down. Strange bronze lanterns sat in a row on a table; they were round and full of oil, with a wick at the center and three chains leading to a metal ring for a handle. Ami lit one and raised it, pleased with the light.

They descended for more than two stories' worth of stairs until they reached a landing. Another long stretch of stairs stretched to the right. With a shrug, they began their descent.

For more than an hour, they trudged down flight after flight. Their legs ached and burned when the stairway finally ended at a narrow doorway.

"I am not going to enjoy going back up," Ami panted.

"Don't worry," Caudro said between strained breaths. "You have a big man to carry you if your legs get tired."

"Not sure that name quite fits you anymore. You've moved on; no longer a Paladin, Herald of Almoya, and all that."

After massaging their aching legs to restore the feeling in their feet, they pushed open the doors, revealing a passage no more than ten feet wide and twenty feet long. Scenes were carved into three sections on the walls, mirrored on either side.

"Can you see well enough to tell what these carvings depict?" Ami asked, running her hands over one of the motifs.

"No. Can you describe them for me?"

Ami sidled down the hall, stopping at the center of the first section.

"I see a person standing before rows of kneeling people, holding up a scroll. Nothing odd about the person reading, but the scroll is enormous. It says-"

"Abandon your past, serve in the present, forgo the future."

"I take it this has some special meaning?"

Caudro nodded. "It's the Paladin's oath. I suspect this means each of these carvings relates to a test we must pass, based on the Paladins' tenets. The first test must pertain to the oath."

Ami eased over to the second section.

"This one shows people placing offerings before effigies of the Five. There are all sorts of things: guilders, animals, food, armor..."

"Fealty to the Five, the second of the tenets. That means the last section depicts Paladins in battle."

"Yes. Paladins fighting a variety of creatures and people, with five pairs of eyes watching over them."

"Strength eternal." Caudro paced back and forth before the door at the end of the passage with his hands on his hips. "The three guiding tenets of the Paladins: remain true to your oath, be always obedient to the Five, and stand with strength eternal. Three tests for the three tenets."

Ami grabbed Caudro's hand; he halted and turned to face her. The softness of her hands eased the fear which gripped his heart.

"I trust you, Caudro."

A smile spread across his face. "Then we have but one thing to do."

"It sounds more like three, based on what you were saying. But yes, let's get to it!"

Ami pulled away and pushed the door open.

They entered a wide chamber, where three simple stone altars stood in a row some ten feet apart, dividing the room in half. Miniature braziers at the corners of each altar billowed with flame. When Ami and Caudro took a few steps forward, the door slammed shut behind them.

"Good thing I trust you," Ami said, glancing over her shoulder as Plug nuzzled against her cheek and yawned. "There's no backing out now."

"Right. Three altars. Each one must relate to a part of the Paladin's oath. We should see if there are any inscriptions describing which one is which, and what is expected of us."

Caudro led them to the first of the altars. The top surface was inset a few inches, with only a small bronze placard on the raised edge.

"Do we really have to go through this?" Ami said with a yawn. "There's plenty of space between the altars and the door is right there. We should see if there's another way to open it."

Caudro threw his arm out as Ami walked towards the gap. "Watch."

Caudro took a piece of bread from his pack, then tossed it between the altars. A grid of spears thrust down from the ceiling, striking the floor. The spears slowly rose, leaving crumbs scattered across the floor.

"I can't imagine the Quinarium would allow us to simply walk past the tests," Caudro said. "Mages and craftspeople toiled for years to construct them. Supposedly a great deal of mana was expended, though we never learned of the spells they used. What we did learn was that testing the Quinarium's bounds was never a good idea."

"Fair enough," Ami stammered, staring at a chunk of bread.

"Is there any writing?" Caudro asked as he walked back to the first altar.

"Ah, sorry. I forget your vision has its limits."

Caudro chuckled. "I was half-illiterate before anyhow, and what little I read clearly did nothing to improve my intellect."

"Let's hope, then, that you can make some sense of this," Ami said, wishing she had a better reply. "It says *abandon the past: give that which means most to you.*"

Caudro stared into the distance, or at least Ami thought he was staring into the distance. She realized it was entirely impossible to judge where he was looking, and for a moment imagined all the mischief she could cause if she had such an ability.

"So... we are thinking..."

"The altar is a vessel. It must be awaiting an offering. We must each give something that best represents our past. If we offer the right objects, then we will fulfill this facet of the oath."

"Abandon the past... give that which means most to you..." Ami's voice faded to barely more than a whisper as she stared at her feet.

"Are you alright?"

"What are you thinking of offering?" she said, ignoring his question.

"Please don't laugh."

"You already know I'm going to; it's in my nature. Besides, your feeble request makes not laughing all the harder."

Caudro fished inside a pouch and retrieved a short length of tattered rope.

"I've kept this scrap of rope from my childhood. I had seen delvers and other travelers with ropes on their packs, and when I found this piece, I thought it might be important one day, when I was living a life of adventure. I abandoned those thoughts when I joined the Paladins, but for some reason I kept the rope."

"Well, now I can't laugh," Ami said in mock frustration. "It wasn't entirely wrong for you to hold on to it, though; you've ended up with me, and time with me is always an adventure. Oh, and don't think I've forgotten about you saying that you aren't sentimental. I was most certainly right when I called you sentimental after you held on to a Jackal's tooth. Anyway, might as well toss it in."

Caudro tossed the rope onto the altar when an unseen bell chimed.

"Run!"

"What?"

Caudro grabbed Ami by the waist and tackled her, spinning as he fell so he would be the one to strike the ground.

"Five above, what was that for!?" Ami yelled, lying atop Caudro. She playfully slapped his hand, though in truth she quite enjoyed being wrapped up in his arms. "If you wanted to lie with me, there are a few conversations we need to have first!"

"This is not a time for joking! That was the sound of failure," Caudro said. He wheezed, his face stricken with fear, as he held Ami close. "That bell always rang when we were to be punished. My offering was wrong."

"Punishment? I fail to see what punishment has been dealt, other than you bearing my weight. Besides, being close to me is very much a reward for anyone with reasonable sensibilities."

Ami slipped free, then sat up. Caudro reached after her when a twang came from the far end of the room. Out from the darkness flew a volley of arrows, passing inches above Ami's head. She watched as the projectiles shattered against the wall behind them.

"Good thing I'm precisely the right height," Ami said, her eyes open wide. "Were I a taller woman, then you might have to finish this alone."

"How can you be cavalier?" Caudro asked as he sat up beside Ami. "You were almost impaled by a dozen arrows."

"Well, I wasn't, was I? Hardly my first scrape with death," Ami said boldly, though her heart raced. "Pick something better this time, my dear protector."

"Maybe you should try offering something?"

"I already know what I have to place on the altar." Ami's voice faded as her hand settled over a pouch on her belt. She looked up with a grin. "Besides, I'm Fae. We should make sure this works with a Human before I place something inside. If the wonderful Uldrik, Confessor of Cauldhill, was any indication, those who made this place would not likely look kindly upon Dwarves or Fae taking part in their sacred tests."

Caudro rose to his feet. His mind raced as he pondered what to offer. Back and forth, he paced before the altar as minutes burned by. Ami hummed patiently, playing with Plug, until Caudro abruptly threw off his pack and undid his belt.

"Excuse me," she called out, "If I may, I think this is not quite the appropriate time to be so forward as to disrobe. I understand that carnal thoughts may rise to the top of mind when facing death, but let's plan on making it out of here, shall we?"

"My armor."

"What of it?"

"Can you think of anything that more represents who I was, of what meant the most to me? I must forgo my past, and my past was that of a Paladin. I am now a Herald of Almoya; it is time for me to let go."

Caudro stacked his greaves and gauntlets onto his breast-plate and marched up to the altar. As he set it inside, a soft light filled the inset area and a bell chimed, this time sweet and light.

Caudro sighed in relief as he backed away and stared at his armor.

"How do you feel?" Ami asked.

"Naked."

"Are you making a proclamation, a proposition, or a request?"

"How can you speak in such a way when we are in this place?" Caudro asked, shaking his head.

"Maybe I'm a touch desperate for attention," Ami said in a breathy voice.

"Makes two of us," Caudro muttered.

"What?"

"Your turn to place something inside."

Ami took a step, then faltered. "Do you think the altar might be satisfied with one offering?"

"No. There are two of us here, and if we both are to proceed, I believe it will require an offering from each of us. Paladins demanded individuals each make a sacrifice, and through the sum of the sacrifices, the whole became stronger... or so they said. Are you worried you don't have something appropriate to represent your past?"

"It's more that I have something too appropriate," Ami said coolly. "I don't want to part with it."

Ami trudged to the altar with her grandfather's owl carving in hand. Tears fell from her eyes as she rubbed its surface between her fingers. She knew her grandfather would encourage her to toss the owl in, that it was nothing more than a little trinket, and that he would be proud of her for giving up the charm for their people. And yet, she felt as if she would lose a piece of her soul by letting go of the owl. She trembled, silently crying as she faced the cold stone altar.

Caudro's hand appeared, warm and comforting on Ami's shoulder.

"Oh, I'll be fine," Ami said, wiping away tears. "Everyone needs a good cry once in a while."

"I've never seen you like this," Caudro whispered.

"There's a lot of me you haven't seen," Ami said, smiling despite the tears in her eyes.

She gently placed the owl on the altar. The bell chimed again, and the light grew stronger.

"All this for people who don't even like me."

"Are you alright?" Caudro asked as Ami turned, his hand falling away from her shoulder.

"Well, I donated my last, most important remembrance of my grandfather to the Quinarium. An institution seeking to kill my people. Other than that little insult, I'm doing splendidly."

"Ami, I-"

"Next altar, then?"

As they approached the second altar, a life-sized statue of a Paladin made of stone and clad in real armor rose from behind it. A bowl rested inside its hands. Dozens of fist-sized bronze sculptures were strewn across the altar; Ami noted a spear, a shield, a miniature Sanctuary, and a wheel, before losing interest in the array.

"It appears we don't have to give something up this time, the altar is filled with miniature sculptures."

"Does the inscription give any indication of what we are to do?"

"Let's see... it reads as follows: *service to the Five, service to the Paladins, service to the people, all are one.*"

"I believe we are to choose a sculpture which exemplifies a Paladin's service—representing the Five, the Paladins, and the people—and place it in the bowl."

"There must be thirty sculptures here. I can't see some of these having any bearing on your service," Ami said, holding a bronze casting of a bundle of wheat.

"A Paladin's service... we rarely spoke of effigies or representations outside of the Five."

"Why don't I tell you everything that's here, and you tell me if I should set it aside as a possibility?"

Ami spent the following minutes sorting the bronze sculptures and describing them to Caudro. She placed the last one, the head of a bull, back among the rejects.

"You've selected a human heart, the symbol of the Quinarium, and a shield. Why these three?"

"The human heart might represent a Paladin giving over their life in service to the Five. The symbol of the Quinarium is because the leaders of the Quinarium consider themselves to be the only true connection to the Five, though that doesn't really represent service. The shield represents how Paladins claim to serve: protecting others."

"And which of the three?"

"Service to the Five... service to the Paladins... service to the people... the heart is more a matter of giving oneself over, but is that not what service is? The symbol, more the institution... hm..."

Ami bit off a piece of apple and fed it to Plug while Caudro leaned against the altar, mulling over the options.

"The shield," he said.

"You sound certain," Ami said encouragingly.

"A Paladin's shield is the heart of their service. It is central to the way they fight and is their favored symbol. The leaders always spoke of how a shield was the most essential item a Paladin carries, whether addressing wild beasts attacking a hamlet or facing serious threats like the Dwarves or the Fae, false though those might have been."

"Alright then!"

Ami tossed the shield into the statue's stone bowl. Before it came to a rest, the warning bell chimed.

"Five above!" Caudro yelled.

Ami needed no instruction this time. They dove back together onto the hard floor as an array of arrows flew past. Plug hopped onto Ami's face and licked her cheek before crawling into the top of her pack.

"I'm sorry. I thought... I-"

"Caudro, stop apologizing. You aren't a Paladin anymore. Clearly, all the people involved in creating this place were fanatical monsters. Not that lying beside you is the worst of things to happen to me."

"That's it!" Caudro exclaimed, jumping to his feet.

"What? Are you saying that you enjoy lying beside me?"

"The designers, creators, whoever they were, must have been absolute fanatics. To them, there would be no higher service than to the Quinarium. It has to be the symbol!"

Ami returned to the altar and cautiously picked up the symbol of the Quinarium then tossed it into the bowl.

A bright ring echoed through the room as a muted light filled the basin.

Ami pulled Caudro in by the collar and planted a kiss on his cheek, then pushed him away. Caudro's face flushed bright red and his head pounded. His skin tingled as the softness of her lips overwhelmed his mind and filled his heart with delight.

"I..."

"Come on then! Still one more to go."

Ami scurried away to the final altar, which matched the first with an inset basin. She watched Caudro half-walk, half-skip his way over, with a dumb look of joy smeared across his face.

"The inscription here says: *forgo your future, abandon all except for your duty,*" Ami said as Caudro came to a stop beside her. "Sounds a bit dumb to me. The future is the only thing that keeps me from dwelling on the past."

"A Paladin is also supposed to forget their past. Giving up one's future, when the past has been forgotten, means Paladin can dedicate themselves totally to the Quinarium," Caudro said as he rummaged through a pouch.

"You're certain this time? Not like the rope, is it? Maybe you should slow down, be really sure."

"I am certain."

Caudro revealed a Jackal fang which he promptly set it on the altar. The bell chimed sweetly and a light glow filled the basin.

"A Jackal fang?" Ami questioned with arms crossed. "You kept more than one. Care to explain?"

"No."

"Oh, come now! Why not?"

"I don't want to."

"If you tell me, it will make it far easier for me to select the right thing. Or would you rather we go diving away from arrows again?"

"Fine," Caudro said, shaking his head. "The Jackal fang represents many things. I took it from the Denmother's lair after facing combat honorably, which was important to me then. It was also when I stood strongest beside Dara and Wynne, and they give me the most hope that Llendshold might have a good future. It was also the first time I stood beside you in such a way."

"Standing close beside me... Was that a pressing thought for you then, or one that has only emerged in recent days?"

"This isn't an inquisition!" Caudro said, his voice shrill. "Your turn!"

Ami chuckled as she thrust a hand inside her tunic. She yanked her fist out, then opened it over the altar. Caudro was unsure what Ami had placed, but the bell told him it was an appropriate offering.

"What was that?" he asked.

"Trickery of the Fae," Ami said with a snort.

"That is hardly fair! I told you exactly what I placed on the altar!"

Ami laughed boisterously as she threw a potato between the altars. It rolled across the floor without a sign of spears falling from the ceiling.

"Two trials left, my protector. Come along then!" Ami called as she strolled to the exit.

Chapter 10

Bang!

Ami and Caudro flinched.

"Why must all the doors slam shut?" Ami fumed. "Whoever designed this place went through the trouble of making doors that can close on their own. Why didn't they design them to swing smoothly?"

"I have no doubt the doors slamming is intentional."

"And what do you make of the appearance of *this?*" Ami said as she set down her lantern.

Caudro took a drink of mana and scanned the room as the purple glow before his eyes strengthened. Torches billowed into flame around the perimeter of the square room, which was some fifty feet across. Five statues representing the Quinate dominated the space, spread in a wide arc. Mats lay on the ground before the statues, while vaulted ceilings rose high above. Statues aside, there was not a single decoration in the room. A door waited at the center of the far wall.

"Fealty to the Five. The arrangement, the mats for prayer… it reminds me of our lessons about dedication to the Quinate. They were particularly harsh and reinforced with physical punishments, even when we were guilty of no transgressions. The leaders droned for hours on end about deceit and truth, and how the only way to navigate past the falsehoods of mortals and find absolute truth was through an unwavering adherence to the Five."

"As told by the Quinarium," Ami followed.

"Only ever through their interpretation."

"What do you think will be expected of us here?"

Caudro stood tall. "I assume something to do with the statues."

"You... you're joking again! I don't know if I'll ever get used to you joking, but I have to admit, I quite like it."

Caudro headed for the nearest statue with a pep in his step.

"Can you describe it for me?"

"It's rather... dull? I think it's made of metal, but the surface is blackened. The face is masculine. Wisps radiate out from his head, ending in slender blue crystals. If this is meant to be Panvano—Seraeus, for you—I wonder why there is no mask over the lower part of his face. What do you imagine we are to do before the God of Air?"

"Seraeus... the God I have the least familiarity with," Caudro said.

"Well, there is the mat. Are we supposed to kneel?"

"It couldn't hurt."

"Excuse me, but I will have to stop calling you my dear protector if you fail to remember recent events like spears falling from the ceiling and walls spitting arrows at us," Ami said. "I am quite certain there are plenty of ways in which this trial might hurt us!"

"Should we remain standing, then?"

"No, I think we should kneel."

As soon as they knelt before the statue, a whistle tickled their ears and a gentle breeze sent loose hairs flying. Ami peered at Caudro out of the corner of his eye. She was admiring the lines of his jaw when a voice boomed.

"You do well to kneel."

They looked up at the statue.

"Give praise to the air which surrounds you, for without air, no living creature could breathe."

"Five above," Ami whispered. "The mouth moves... it looks like flesh. Positively unsettling."

Caudro bowed with his hands in his lap until his forehead nearly touched the ground.

"Blessed Seraeus, God of that which we breathe, we thank you for your gift. May we forever remember you, in our days working hard when your grace fills our lungs, and at night when we dream in your embrace."

"Go, and breathe well."

Ami glanced back over her shoulder as they walked to the next statue. "That felt deceptively simple, did it not?"

"I agree, but what else are we to do? Unless you have another idea?"

"Nothing at the moment. Right then, who's next?"

They went from statue to statue, offering praise for blood to Ramaia, for earth to Kosrya, and for fire to Ilsios, before concluding with thanks for consciousness and the mind to Almoya. With all five prayers complete, Ami and Caudro stood, waiting, by the exit door.

"So..."

Ami's voice trailed off as Plug's head popped up out of her pack. The creature inspected the room, then dove right back in, resuming its slumber.

"You were right," Caudro said. "Praying before statues was far too simple."

"I wasn't asking you to say that. Nice that you did, though. I'm more curious about what we're to do now."

"Maybe we should look at the statues more closely."

"Sure. Staring at statues is one of my *favorite* pastimes." Ami said mockingly.

Caudro's eyebrows rose as he looked at Ami. "I didn't take you for a lover of art. Not that I expect I will be, with my eyes as they are."

"My favored ways of passing time might surprise you. Though what I find most entertaining is rather more active... engaging... physical... than staring at Quinarium sculptures."

"Ahem!" Caudro's loud cough echoed.

"Such as archery," Ami said.

"Well, let us pass some time inspecting the statues."

Back at the statue of Seraeus, Ami pored over its surface. She huffed as she leaned away.

"I see positively nothing remarkable. What about you and your sight?"

"Mundane as a rock."

"Wait one moment. When we first arrived, you mentioned truth and deceit as a part of your lessons of fealty. The statue demanded we pray, yet nothing has come from prayer. Do you think it will respond if we ask it questions?"

Caudro immediately knelt before the statue.

"You do well to kneel. Give praise-"

"What must we do?" Caudro asked.

"A question with many answers."

"What are you?"

"I am an effigy of Seraeus, that which you breathe, the embodiment of air, God of the Quinate."

"And what would you ask of us?"

"I ask no questions."

Ami knelt beside Caudro.

"What is your purpose?" she asked.

"I am an effigy of Seraeus, that which you breathe, the embodiment of air, God of the Quinate."

Ami grumbled at the repetition. "What must we do to pass this trial?"

"A question which you must answer."

Caudro leaned over to Ami. "Frustrating thing. I wonder if it's possible that the magic used to create this has faded, or perhaps even failed, with the passage of time?"

Ami held a finger over her mouth as she pondered what to ask the statue.

"I think you're lying," she said sweetly.

"A representation of a God does not lie."

"But what if that is lie? Liars claim to speak no falsehoods. As sure as the Five graced this world with mana, I know you lie. Tell us the truth. What must be done?"

The lips of the statue pursed tightly together.

Caudro leapt to his feet. "I will not kneel before an effigy of a God which speaks as if it contains the power, the righteousness, the holiness of the God herself! Tell us, pretender, what must be done?"

The statue smiled, revealing pearly white teeth. "Each of us has a task for you. Ask for your task, discern which of the five is telling the truth, and then complete the task."

"What would you have us do?" Ami asked, rising beside Caudro.

"One must strangle the other."

"Excuse me?" she blurted out.

"Only one may leave," the statue hissed like winds passing through a narrow passage. "One must strangle the other."

"Right, let's hear what the next statue has to say," Ami said with a shiver.

They were halfway across the room when Ami stalled.

"Is it not strange that the statue listened to a Fae?"

"I doubt any in the Quinarium would imagine that a Fae would ever enter the ziggurat. I'm sure they considered the effort of enchanting these trials to discern between Humans and others to be unnecessary."

"Fair enough. I can't say I would have ever expected a Fae to come into such a place, let alone the Fae being me."

Caudro slowed as they reached the statue of Ramaia. A low hum emanated from the statue's parted lips.

"It would have been nice if Dara were here," he said. "This one makes me particularly uncomfortable."

"Then let us to be done quickly," Ami said, approaching the statue. "Effigy of Ramaia, what would you have us do?"

The statue groaned, as if an impossible-to-reach itch were finally scratched. "One must shed the other's blood."

Ami sighed. "And let me guess, only one may leave?"

"Only one may leave."

Ami marched to the statue of Kosrya with Caudro hurrying after.

On arriving, she eyed the statue's gown. Delicate carvings of plants climbed up to the neck, where vines formed a collar.

"What is your task?" she demanded.

The statue chuckled, its voice booming like boulders tumbling down a mountainside. "One must bludgeon the other."

"Right. And only one may leave?"

"Only one may leave."

Although the Quinarium constructed the statues and the moving mouths were unsettling, the beauty of the statue of Ilsios enthralled Ami. She wished Caudro could see the vibrant streaks of red and orange tracing up the sleek statue, though she wondered why it appeared more like a fire than the sun.

"The task?" Caudro asked.

"One must immolate the other," the statue cried out, its voice roaring like a blacksmith's furnace.

"Another liar," Caudro said with a shiver. "The last one must be the truth-teller."

"Only one may leave," the statue whispered as they strode away.

Ami rubbed the back of her head furiously as they stood before the statue of Almoya. Unlike the others, it bore no decorations of any kind.

"Something is off," she said.

"You mean with four statues telling us to kill each other?" Caudro said with a laugh. "You heard the statue of Seraeus. Four of these statues are liars, and the last four statues have said the same thing. That leaves one telling the truth: this final one."

"Let's hear it then."

"What is your task?" Caudro asked of the statue.

"Choose a game and play the game; the loser must take their own life," the statue said with a snicker. "Only one may leave."

Sweat beaded on Caudro's brow. His head pounded as he stepped away.

"Well, that is without question the most unpleasant thing I've heard today, and I just listened to four statues tell me to kill you," Ami said. "Maybe we should rest a moment and see if we've missed anything."

Ami took a few steps away, then plopped down onto the stone floor. Plug ran up and down her arms and darted around her legs, chirping all the while. Caudro joined Ami; he chewed on dried berries as he rested his chin on his fist.

"You have any ideas for us, Plug?" he asked.

The creature dove beneath Ami's knee; seconds later, snores came as a reply.

"It wouldn't be a test if it was easy," Ami said.

"I can't imagine killing each other is the truth of it. It goes against everything the Paladins taught... not the killing part, Paladins happily kill. But to kill an agent of the Quinarium would be unconscionable to a Paladin. All five statues said that one is telling the truth..."

"You said it's poor form for Paladins to kill Quinarium folks, but I'm no Paladin. Come to think of it, you aren't a Paladin anymore either," Ami snickered. "Don't look so serious, my protector! I promise I won't kill you. At least not unless we are *absolutely* certain it's the only way forward."

"Charming and reassuring as always, Ami."

"Wait!" she shouted. "It said to find the one telling the truth. We didn't ask them what must be done, only what task they would have us do. We assumed the statue of Seraeus was honest when it said we needed to find the true task, but what if it was lying? Whoever created this trial may have designed all five to tell the same lie when asked about a task. We didn't ask the other four about how to pass the trial."

"My head is spinning," Caudro groaned. "I suppose we should speak with the other four then."

"Shall we start with Ramaia?"

Caudro marched over to the statue, then kicked away the prayer mat.

"What must we do?" he demanded.

"One must shed the other's blood."

The statue licked its teeth, staining their white surface in a sheen of red.

"That is the task you stated before, but I ask of you, what must we do to pass the trial?"

"Each of us has a task for you. Ask for your task, discern which of the five is telling the truth, and then complete the task."

"Who are you to have the authority, the right to order people to commit murder?" Caudro roared.

"There is no murder, only a proving of fealty."

"It's a damn circle," Ami said. "Is there something I missed earlier when I inspected them?"

Ami walked to the back of the statue. She leaned her forearm against its side as she pored over its surface, when she gasped and stumbled back.

"Are you alright?" Caudro asked, rushing to her side.

"It... it feels like skin. It's warm, too. Go on, touch it!"

Caudro hesitated until Ami gave him a gentle push. He slid an open palm against the surface, then immediately retracted his hand as if he had touched a scalding pot.

"What is this madness?"

"You said the lessons of fealty involved deceit and truth. Is it possible that *all* the statues are lying?"

"Ami... I think you're right."

"Of course I am," Ami said, beaming. "If I am right, though, what are we supposed to do with them? What does the Quinarium consider an appropriate punishment for those not part of their order who claim to speak for the Gods?"

"To imitate the Five is an affront of the highest degree," Caudro said softly. "They view it as worse than murder. The punishment for claiming to represent the Quinate... is death."

Ami and Caudro looked at the statue.

"Would you like to do the honors?" Ami asked. "You are the former Paladin, after all. It seems fitting for you to be the one to cut it down."

Caudro drew his sword. The flickering light of a nearby torch reflected off the honed edge, casting wavering ribbons of white across the statue. Caudro pressed the blade against its throat. The false effigy of Ramaia gasped and held its breath. Caudro pulled the sword with all his strength, slicing into the statue. The statue wheezed as blood spurt forth and splattered across the floor. The mouth opened wide in a silent scream as blood dripped out. Its head slowly drooped, then hung still.

Ami scampered away. "I start my days thinking of the many things—both good and bad—that might happen between dawn and dusk. Never, ever have I once considered that I might watch a statue be cut open and bleed."

Caudro wiped his sword clean with a rag. "It seems we have a few more to take care of."

The unpleasantness of what ensued haunted Ami and Caudro for many days after.

They found the statue of Seraeus solid, impervious to cuts and strikes, and too heavy to push or move. As they stared at the statue, a delicate, light whisper crept into their ears. They followed the sound to its source: the statue's mouth. Unable to pry it open, they wrapped a spare bowstring around the effigy's neck; as Caudro and Ami pulled tight, it wheezed and groaned until the whisper finally ceased.

A previously unnoticed scent of oil greeted them at the statue of Ilsios. They ran their hands over its surface, finding it had the texture of painted wood. Ami struck a flint at its base and fire enrobed the effigy. It screamed and hissed like the burning of wet logs until the flames charred the entire statue.

The statue of Kosrya was, by all measures, a normal statue. The two pondered how to destroy it, when Caudro leaned against the statue and it wobbled at his touch. With a push, the statue fell and shattered into thousands of pieces, revealing the center to be hollow.

Ami and Caudro stood before the final statue, the pretender of Almoya.

The statue's mouth quivered. "What is to become of me?"

"You statues are depictions of what the Quinarium considers pretenders, those speaking for the Quinate with no authority to do so," Caudro said. "And yet, the Quinarium itself falsely claims ownership of the words and messages of the Quinate."

"How apt that we—a former Paladin and a Fae—are the ones to dismantle false idols representing the Quinarium's false interpretation of the Five. They made these statues act as pretenders, when they are pretenders as well."

"What is to become of me?"

"It speaks as if it were alive. As if it has a soul," Ami said.

"What is to become of me?"

"Perhaps it is right for you to be left here," Caudro said, his arms crossed. "A reminder that all living creatures are fallible. We are all prone to falling under the sway of liars, the Quinarium being no exception. A false idol of Almoya... may you wallow in your isolation and descend into madness, forever lost and alone."

The statue's lips parted, revealing its teeth in a half-smile, half-grimace; the expression sent shivers down Ami's spine. She looked across the room to see the door at the back of the room had opened.

"You keep finding opportunities to speak like a poet," Ami said as they made for the exit.

"I seem to only find my voice when I'm with you. It's a shame there is no one else to hear, save you and a demented statue."

Ami glanced back over her shoulder. "I wonder if the statues were made in the same fashion as the crowns of the Dwarf Priests?"

"A likely theory."

"It is strange, though. Did Humans and Fae never learn the craft? Was it protected by the Dwarves? Or was it lost, forgotten to time?"

"All questions that I would one day love to hear answered. For now, though, only one trial remains."

"I can't imagine it will be more unpleasant than this one."

CHAPTER 11

"More stairs. Lovely." Ami glared at the stairway waiting through the doorway. "These ones are spiraling, though. Quite different from before."

Caudro's head tilted. "The change gives me pause as well, though we have little choice but to take them. The door behind us didn't open."

They descended for a thankfully short few minutes before they reached a broad, open chamber. Caudro took a drink of mana as his sight began to fade, while Ami raised her lantern high.

"Are these living chambers?" Caudro asked.

"Beds, a kitchen, common areas. What else could it be?" Ami circled the room, lighting ancient coals which filled braziers, sconces, and lanterns. "There must be twenty beds. Five above, why would there be living quarters this far into the ziggurat? Who would live down here? It was an utter slog going down all those stairs. Can you imagine carrying food and water all the way?"

"I imagine there is another way down. A lift, perhaps, that the Keepers would have access to, hidden in the walls somewhere."

"You know, it would have been nice if you climbed a bit higher among the Paladins before your unceremonious exit. If you were a Keeper, this all would have been a touch easier."

"I agree," Caudro said, stepping to the center of the room. "It would have taken only thirty or forty years for me to ascend to such a role if I managed to keep in the good graces of the leaders, and didn't die fighting some horrible beasts. Then, with me as Keeper, entering the ziggurat would have been a trifle."

Ami peered over at Caudro. The corners of his eyes creased despite his attempts to hide a grin. "Humor is a good look on you."

"I..."

"Let's look around, see what we can find." Ami yanked open a chest at the foot of a nearby bed. "I'm not sure if you noticed, but there's a rather large set of doors at the back. I'm guessing the last test waits through them. Maybe someone wrote something down that will give us an idea of what to expect."

"I, unfortunately, must follow your lead in this," Caudro said. "I can't see much in the way of details, especially not when reading is involved."

"Unfortunately? You haven't seemed to have any issues putting your hands on me when you aren't empowered with sight from drinking mana. Should we consider you blessed or cursed by Almoya, I wonder, now that you can roam on your own from time to time?"

Caudro blushed. "Always a blessing to be in the presence of a trickster of a Fae."

Ami snickered as she took off her pack then tore through the room; she opened chests, rifled between blankets and stacks of clothing, pulled covers off beds, and flipped through books. Caudro, unable to assist, sat on a bed beside Plug.

A few minutes later, Ami marched over to find the two taking turns munching on bread topped with a piece of dried, salted cheese. Caudro would take a bite, then hold out the snack for Plug to nibble.

"Glad to see you two are hard at work," Ami said, snatching up her own portion of bread and cheese. "While you two layabouts stuffed your faces, I found a journal in good enough condition to read."

Caudro coughed and grumbled, breaking his bread in two and tossing the smaller piece to Plug.

"Anything of interest in it?"

"I'm not sure yet," Ami said between mouthfuls. "I figured I would read it with you."

"Why wait?"

"Oh, I don't know... perhaps so that you would feel included. Perhaps in case I missed anything while reading. Perhaps because you're the former Paladin, and would notice if anything were amiss in the writings?"

"Ah. Thank you. I promise to be your most dedicated, fastidious listener."

"Barring interruption from the audience, I'll paraphrase as best I can. The writings are from a Trainee. The opening page says she had been here for a few *weeks* when she decided to start writing. Here's a bit saying she thought it was an honor at first, but now feels very much stuck... blast it, Wynne made it look easy but reading and condensing at once is quite challenging. She goes on to list off the names of... fifteen Paladins. There's a note beside a few of them, marking them as fellow Trainees."

"Strange," Caudro said, rubbing his chin.

"How so?"

"Trainees—once they have left the confines of the fortress where they began their training—are kept separate until they become full Paladins. Even if we were to face battle with other Paladins, we would camp separately. Close quarters like this were unheard of, unless perhaps traditions were different in the past."

"No matter the case, they were nice and snug down here. Moving along... the Trainee wrote very little, but here she says there's a rumor that there will eventually be no Paladins underground—seems like the rumor turned true, given its present state—but more curious, she says Mages were working on *something*. They weren't told exactly what, and none dared to ask, but then she goes on to call the first two trials a supposed 'trifle' compared to what was being done by the Mages."

"A trifle?"

"Her word, not mine. Anyway, there's a lot in here about being bored. Then the last entry says that the next morning they were to report to the chamber, and she hopes it'll be their last day. That's it."

"Something is wrong," Caudro said.

"Right. That is about the greatest, most ridiculous understatement you could possibly make at this moment. We had to give up cherished belongings, only to dispatch four statues through bleeding, garroting, immolation, and shattering. And now, we sit in a perfectly preserved room that might as well be a tomb, ready to head into a chamber where Mages toiled for days on *something*. How this could be anything but *wrong*, I do not know!"

"Did you find anything else?"

"Aside from plates set out like mealtime was coming, cards dealt for a game, and packs ready to go? Not a thing."

"Then I suppose there is but one thing for us to do."

Plug hopped, then glided to Ami's shoulder.

"Are you going to help us this time, my dear little friend?" Ami asked.

The creature dove into Caudro's pack as he slung it over his shoulders. They then marched to the doors, side by side.

"How are you feeling without your armor?"

Caudro's brow furrowed. "Both liberated... and naked. I feel uncomfortably exposed, marching towards the unknown without my usual protection."

"Hm," Ami murmured, glancing at a bed as they walked by.

"What do you mean by that?"

"As far as I can see, you're definitely not naked right now."

"You say that as if I should be."

"Only if you wish."

"But... why would you say that?" Caudro stalled while Ami scurried ahead. "This is a preposterous time to joke in such a way!"

Ami struggled with a metal ring on the door by the time Caudro caught up to her. Shaking his head, he grabbed the ring and heaved open the foot-thick, iron-bound wood door. A short passage greeted them, with a bright light emanating from the room ahead.

Caudro led the way, clasping his spear tightly as he crept through the passage like a cat through an alley. His shoulders slacked as he exited.

Ami stepped around Caudro and gasped. The lantern dropped from her hand. It was as if she were transported back to Yuvsgrend, but in miniature. The path led to an oval-shaped platform at the heart of the cavern, with a great void beyond. A stair led down either side of the platform. The ceiling towered above, with a white crystal at its apex, casting down streams of white light. As with the sunken Dwarf city, the air was dank and musty.

Glancing back over her shoulder, Ami gulped.

"Caudro, the doors shut by themselves. Gods, why did it have to be quiet this time? I complained about the other door slamming, but shutting quietly is somehow much worse. And there are marks all around the doors. Can you see them?"

"Yes... it's as if people tried to pry them open. There are grooves running from the walls into the doors. It seems they tried to make their way out using the leftover materials scattered on either side of the passage. Is that a placard on the doors?"

"One says *STRENGTH*, and the other *ETERNAL*. Caudro, why would they put such a message on this side?"

"That phrase was an ever-present reminder," Caudro said, his hands tightening around his spear, "of Paladins' total commitment to the Quinarium. Paladins are trained to yell 'strength eternal' in battle, when they believe they are about to take their last breath."

"That is not reassuring at all, given it looks like someone, or many someones, tried to flee this chamber." Ami squinted and looked at Caudro. "You didn't yell the phrase when we faced the Jackals."

"I foolishly did not believe I would die. Not with Dara and Wynne there anyhow."

"What about me... why you..."

Caudro marched onto the oval platform.

"Are you sure it's a good idea to go out so far? You remember me telling you of the creature in Yuvsgrend?"

"We aren't in the Dwarf city. Besides, we should see what lies below."

"How far is below, I wonder," Ami said.

Ami hurried to join Caudro. She eyed the messy heaps of construction materials left behind on either side of the passage: hefty beams, thick iron fittings, bolts, and more.

"They didn't take the time to tidy after themselves, it seems. I tell you, this is uncannily like Yuvsgrend, from the platform to the stairs to the light shining from above."

"Maybe Dwarves helped build this place, back in a time when relations with Dwarves were still friendly," Caudro said.

"Or this was already built, and the Quinarium stole it. Or they forced the Dwarves to work as slaves. Based on the journal, this place was constructed not long after the flooding of Yuvsgrend. The Quinarium might have taken some Dwarves with them from the city. Well, seeing as this platform is vacant, let's take the stairs down and see what we can find."

"But what of the third trial?"

"What of it? I see not a thing," Ami said, waving at the empty cavern.

"I can't imagine-"

A booming rumble shook the walls of the cavern. Plug darted out from Caudro's pack, soaring back into the depths of the passage.

"Caudro, please tell me there was a particular meaning to that sound."

Caudro slung off his pack and raised his spear. "You know how you were asking about how I felt without my armor? The answer now is that I wish I had it. I have never heard such a sound before."

The thunderous echoes faded. As white columns of light lazed about the cavern, Ami and Caudro heard only their own breaths.

Ami shuffled, her eyes darting back and forth, searching for any sign of movement.

"Maybe if we hurry, we-"

The rumbling reverberated through the cavern again. A crunching, grinding cacophony followed, as though a smithy were uprooted and dragged over cobbled streets. Ami and Caudro flinched when a shrill wail struck their ears.

An enormous skeletal hand, nearly as large as Caudro himself, grabbed onto the edge of the platform. Metal chains took the place of ligaments. An ethereal, crimson-purple glow clung to the bones. A second hand pounded onto the platform, sending Caudro stumbling back, while Ami slipped away and nocked an arrow.

The amalgamation of bone and metal pulled itself into view. A strange mix of pieces of Paladin armor and coffin lids formed armor around a skeletal torso, composed of thousands of bones lashed together. Skulls encased in molten iron formed its head, surrounded by a skin of shoulder blades. White flames burned in place of eyes. The amalgamation raised a tremendous mace with a coffin-lid head and a handle that was as stout a ship's mast. Nearly fifteen feet from its waist to the top of its head, it hovered over the void.

"I really, really wish I had my armor!" Caudro shouted, bracing himself.

"I believe in you," Ami said, nocking an arrow. "Though do try to avoid being hit."

"Intruders are not tolerated in these sacred halls!" bellowed the amalgamation. "This sanctuary houses treasures meant for none other than Paladins, and I see no Paladin before me! I am the Keeper of all Keepers. I will not abide by this incursion!"

Ami and Caudro dove away as the Keeper slammed its mace onto the platform, sending cracks radiating out through the stone. Ami loosed an arrow; it ripped through the Keeper's eye. The flames dulled for a moment, then reconstituted as if nothing had happened.

Caudro roared as he leapt forward, driving his spear into the Keeper's hand. He wrenched the shaft to the side, sending bones scattering over the platform before he withdrew and readied to strike again. Meanwhile, Ami sent arrow after arrow into the Keeper; the missiles rattled against bones and metal braces as they tumbled through its body.

When the Keeper clenched its fist, the scattered bones glowed in a red haze, then flew back to their places. Caudro stood defiantly as the Keeper raised the mace with a restored hand.

The Keeper swung the butt of its mace at Caudro. When he stepped aside, it abruptly changed course, sweeping the head of its mace across the platform. Caudro jumped but was struck in the leg, sending him spinning and tumbling to the ground.

Ami couldn't spare a second to worry as the Keeper raised its mace high. She grabbed a barbed arrow, then released as she murmured a prayer to Mizaina. The head of the arrow hardened into a steel orb as it flew. Bones shattered as the arrow struck the Keeper's shoulder.

Though the blow was mighty, the Keeper brought its mace crashing down. Caudro narrowly evaded the strike as Ami sent a second metal arrow blasting through the cheek of the monstrous amalgamation.

"Ami, I'll distract it. Go for the stairs!"

"Cau... Five above, you heroic idiot!" she yelled as Caudro dashed away.

Taking hold of a huge wooden beam, Caudro charged. He shoved the beam into the Keeper's open hand, knocking its mace away and scattering bones as it pierced all the way to the amalgamation's elbow. Caudro desperately held tight as the Keeper swung its arm from side to side, dragging him across the platform.

Ami dashed for the stairs. She was mere feet away when a skeletal hand crashed down and blocked her way. The Keeper shook Caudro free then pulled the beam from its arm. It threw the timber at Ami; she slid over the platform as the beam passed overhead, shattering when it struck the cavern wall.

Caudro took up a shield from the wreckage and sprinted at the Keeper. Sliding between its outstretched arms, he hurled his spear with all his might.

Ami watched as the spear pierced the Keeper's chest, then burst through its back and struck a metal ring anchored to the cavern wall. A thick metal chain ran from the ring to the Keeper's back; Ami spied four of the chains before its outstretched hand forced her to run.

While Caudro battled the Keeper, Ami nocked an arrow. She winced as she drew; the side of her thumb was a tattered mess from the barbs. Ami called on Mizaina as she let the arrow fly. The point twisted and stretched as the arrow flew, forming a wide blade. It struck the chain, shattering a link.

Rearing its head back, the Keeper wailed. Ami sent a second and third arrow flying. Her arms burned with fatigue while blood dripped from her hand, staining her cheek, shoulder, and arm. Ami readied a fourth and final arrow when a skeletal hand reached for her.

The Keeper ignored Caudro as he hacked wildly at its chest with his sword. Forced to retreat, Ami dove into the passage. Her bow slipped from her hand as she scrambled away on her hands and feet. Back against the doors, Ami recoiled as the Keeper reached after her, when Caudro's roar carried down the passage.

He leapt through the air, clutching a giant beam. Caudro heaved the timber to the ground, cleaving through the Keeper's arm. Ami dashed past the twitching severed limb and picked up her bow.

She emerged from the passage to see Caudro raise his shield as the Keeper's fist struck. He went flying back, landing in a pile of rubble beside Ami.

Hands trembling, Ami nocked an arrow; the barb cut nearly to her bone as she let it fly. The arrow passed between the Keeper's outstretched fingers, shattering the last of the chains.

The amalgamation of bone and metal desperately scrambled to hold on to the platform. It wailed as its eyes flared, then faded. The hollow eye sockets stared at Ami as the Keeper slid off the platform, falling into the depths of the cavern; a faint crash followed shortly after.

Plug hopped onto Ami's shoulder, bringing her to her senses. She rushed to Caudro and found him sitting in a daze.

"Are you alright?" Ami asked, running her hands over his arms and shoulders, as though her touch would heal his wounds.

"I've had better days, but I'll survive," Caudro said. "Is the Keeper truly gone?"

Ami sat beside Caudro. "Seeing as it hasn't come back from its tumble, I think so."

"Five above, who created that thing? How did they create it?"

"If I had to wager a guess, I'd say perhaps it was Mages and Paladins? Who knows the how, though? Some awful magic must have been involved."

Caudro shook his head. "I have never heard of nor seen its like."

"I imagine it was one of a kind. It explains the lack of guards inside, given *that* was waiting to face intruders."

Plug jumped from Ami's shoulder into Caudro's lap, where the creature nuzzled into his hand.

"Useless beast. At least you made it through unscathed. Caudro was near flattened and I all but cut off my thumb. Did you enjoy your nap in the dark of the passage, hm?"

Caudro chuckled as he uncorked a potion. "I'll have to thank Wynne again for preparing these. I was hoping we wouldn't need them. You should take a sip too, Ami, if your thumb is as poorly as you say."

Ami and Caudro sat content for a few minutes as the potion eased their pain. Ami was mindfully wrapping a bandage around her thumb when a small wooden object on the platform caught her attention. She walked over to retrieve it before sitting beside Caudro again.

"What did you find?" he asked, the glow nearly faded from his eyes.

"A necklace. It must have fallen from the Keeper."

"Can you describe it for me?"

"It's made of wood, in the shape of an animal. Maybe a fox, or a dog? I thought you were the only sentimental Paladin," Ami said.

"Jarain," Caudro whispered.

"Who?"

"My mentor, the one who brought me to the Paladins... Jarain... that is his necklace."

Ami's shoulders drooped as she placed the trinket into Caudro's hands. "Do you mean to say-"

"I think there is only one possibility," Caudro said, closing his fist around the necklace. "They must be taking the bones of Paladins and adding them to the Keeper. You saw, hundreds of skulls formed its head. Who knows what horrible magic they used to create such a monster, to sustain it for so many years?"

"But why? Why use Paladins, instead of, I don't know, anyone else?"

Caudro took a deep, slow breath. "Remember what you said about fanaticism? I'm sure that is a part. Perhaps they consider it a form of final service. Perhaps they made it with the bodies of dissenters as a form of punishment. I've been wrong about the Quinarium at most every turn, and I have been overly hopeful that there might be glimmers of good within. Yet I believe, without any question, that Jarain would never have gone along with any of the injustices we've seen or heard of. I had made peace with his death many years ago, but this... to find his necklace here, it's like an old wound has been reopened."

"Maybe he can finally rest now," Ami said. "Maybe all those caught in that horrible thing can rest."

"I am glad it was my... our hands that freed him from such shackles."

"Sit still." Ami took Jarain's necklace and secured it around Caudro's neck. "I think he'd want you to have it."

"Thank you."

Ami ruffled Caudro's hair. "Here's to hoping we're done with strange monsters! At least of the non-Human kind, we still have a few choice Humans to deal with. Should we see what lies at the bottom of the stairs?"

"Five above, it had better be the Paladins' hoard."

"Let's get to it, then. Come here, you adorable oaf, and lean on me. Come on then! Don't be scared, I'm stronger than you think I am."

Caudro chuckled in resignation and set Plug atop his pack. They hobbled across the platform and down the arcing stairway, with Caudro doing his best to carry his own weight, while Ami wrapped her arm around his waist.

At the bottom of the stairway, Ami took a peek over the edge of a low railing. Her stomach dropped at the endless dark. She turned away to face the simple door which led beneath the platform. It slid open with a gentle push.

Ami's mouth fell open.

"Caudro... I wish you could see this place. I'm now entirely convinced that Dwarves were involved. It is remarkably similar to the Dwarf Priests' storage in Yuvsgrend. There is a hall, maybe fifty feet long, with two shelves on either side. I can't begin to describe all the treasures."

"I've never been one to care for treasures. There are other things I would rather see..."

Caudro's voice trailed off as he was suddenly aware of the warmth of Ami's hand on his waist, with no armor in the way. In that moment, he would have gladly given a hand to see Ami, to know she was alright after their battle with the Keeper.

"I wonder if they stole designs or forced Dwarves to work here," Caudro said. "And why copy Dwarf designs at all, I wonder?"

"From what I've seen of Quinarium buildings, they are in dire need of more inspired architects. According to Dara, Dwarves are far better workers of stone than Humans. Anyway, why don't you rest yourself and not worry about 'wasting mana,' as you say? I'll see about finding that tome."

Ami helped Caudro down, then patted his cheek before stepping away.

Caudro felt as though he were in a dream as he contentedly listened while Ami roamed the hall. He heard the mischief in her hands as she picked up and set objects down, stifled laughter, and muttered to herself.

A cold metal object abruptly dropped into Caudro's lap.

"Hey there. Did you fall asleep? The audacity to sleep while I'm here toiling away, rifling through countless, immeasurably valuable treasures."

"What is this?" Caudro asked.

"New armor for you. Don't worry, it's not the gilded sort. I'm actually quite unsure why it's here. The armor is rather mundane in appearance. There are no markings, but it's well made. The chest is in three articulated pieces instead of one, and there's chain mail to cover the arms and legs instead of scales. The whole thing is light and flexible. I bet you could dance like a troubadour with this on. There are also gauntlets and greaves to match. Oh, and weapons too, in good condition. I stocked up on arrows and nabbed a spear for you."

"Are you sure we should take from this place?"

"Five above, what is it with you and Wynne!?" Ami spewed in mock frustration. "Let me tell you precisely what I told her. Whoever it belonged to before won't have any use for it now. We might as well find a good use for things the Quinarium stole. I forgot to mention, there's a helm too. A rather simple one, but it'll keep your pretty face looking pretty."

Caudro grinned. "Did you find anything for yourself?"

"Of course I did. There are heaps of things stolen from the Fae down here. I found an armguard; it runs from wrist to shoulder with thin layers of plate. Nice and light, yet flexible. It'll offer some protection while not impeding my ability to use my bow."

"It would have been nice to see you wearing it."

Ami smirked. "Sometimes sight is overrated. And why worry about seeing me when you still have your hands?"

"What?" Caudro blurted.

"What?"

"I asked you 'what' first. You can't ask me that back without answering first!"

"Never you mind," Ami said. "Since you didn't ask, allow me to inform you: I found the gilded tome as well. It's a fair bit smaller than I expected, but it's hard to miss a book covered in gold."

"Did you look inside?"

"It's me. What do you think?"

Caudro grinned. "Did you find the contents intriguing?"

"It's filled with an ancient script of some sort. I can't read a word."

"You're sure it's the right book?"

Ami scoffed. "My dearest protector, I appreciate your concern, but I assure you this hall of treasures is not lined with gilded books. This was the only one of its kind."

Ami took the armor from Caudro and stuffed it into a spare pack, then helped him to his feet. He spread his arms to steady himself, grinning as Ami slipped her shoulder beneath his outstretched hand.

"What is your intent with the book?" Caudro asked.

Ami halted and spoke words devoid of emotion. "I will do what I must to aid my people."

"I know you, Ami. Unless I am greatly mistaken, you will use the book to bargain, refusing to turn it over to Imreia unless she agrees to target the Paladin Fortress at Mordinlet."

"Yes. Does that make you think differently of me?"

Caudro listened as Ami's breath shifted, hastened, and grew thin.

"I can judge no one for doing what they believe to be right. Besides, Mordinlet is as good a target as any. Striking there should sufficiently satisfy the Lords of Draethhold while affording the Fae time to prepare."

Ami's breathing eased. "Well... that's a bit softer of an agreement than I'd hoped for, but at least you're coming around."

"If you're done with your looting, then perhaps we should see if there is a way out?"

"Looting!?" Ami shrieked. "And there you go, saying *we* should see about a way out. Unless I'm greatly mistaken, you're the one hanging on to my shoulder, following me like a sick lamb after a shepherd! Come along then, I see the way."

Caudro grinned at the joyful rise and fall in Ami's steps as she led to the exit.

A cool, fresh breeze rushed into the passage as Ami pushed the doors open. They drank in the air, relieved to finally be clear of the stagnant ziggurat.

"What a sweet scent!" Ami exclaimed, stretching as she passed the threshold. "Good fortune for us, I can't see a single sign of Humans anywhere. There's a small grassy clearing inside a tall forest. It looks like we've come out on the east side of the mountain, opposite the ziggurat."

The door behind them ground shut of its own accord.

"Good riddance to that place," Caudro said. "Odd that the Quinarium would keep such treasures so close to the surface without a guard of some sort."

"There's no handle on this side," Ami said. "And it bears the symbol of the Quinarium. I wager any commoners who stumbled on this place would flee without a speck of thought towards finding a way in."

"Personally, I have no desire to go back."

"That makes two of us," Ami said, striding into the woods. "I'll find us a place to camp for the night. I've had enough of this day."

CHAPTER 12

"Five above, my feet are aching," Ami groaned. "At least the lands are pretty."

"What makes the view attractive?"

"Do you get tired, holding on to my shoulder?" Ami asked, evading Caudro's question.

"One of the favored ways of punishing Paladin Trainees is to make them hold their arms out, with a stick balanced on the backs of their hands. If the stick falls, the instructor beats the Trainee with it."

"What a strange way of saying you like having your hands on me," Ami said. She slowed to inspect their surroundings. "The fields to our right are lush and green. Short grass spreads over rolling hills, with these bulbous tufts that wobble with the breeze. To the left, the forest is filled with trees bearing nettles instead of leaves. Their pointed tips seem to scratch the sky. And ahead, our path stretches on, and on, and on to the horizon. A part of me agrees with you, that we should have taken horses from Bavenhill instead of the boat."

"I'm not always wrong, you know."

"Oh, I know. Though I assure you, it is a very small part of me wishing we had skipped the lake." Ami chuckled and reached into a loose cloth pouch hanging from her belt. "Because if we hadn't taken the boat and stopped at that island, we never would have found Plug, the most essential of our allies."

"Yes, the lovely creature which so helped us in the ziggurat," Caudro snorted. "Plug is also quite skilled at eating food. He consumes a substantial amount for so small a creature."

"Don't think I haven't noticed you sneaking him bits of whatever you're eating at every turn," Ami chided, resuming their march. "Though, our food supply is dwindling. We'll have to stop by Dorslet before continuing on to Hantsburg. At least we have a bit of mana left, thanks to your stinginess."

"Mindfulness."

"Whateverness! Enough chatter. The sun is low in the sky. This is as good a spot for a camp as any. Why don't you take a sip of the mindfully preserved mana and get camp started while I hunt us a rabbit or something for dinner?"

Caudro sighed as his hand dropped away from Ami.

"I swear on my grandfather's memory, the Five will not smite you for eating meat! You've had bits and bites the last three days and you're still breathing. If they were to unleash their wrath upon you, they would have done so long ago." Ami set her pack down and punched Caudro's shoulder. "Go on then! I expect a tidy camp by the time I get back."

The last rays of sun illuminated the canopy as if a tapestry of gold were laid atop the trees when Ami returned with a rabbit in hand. She grinned at the sight of bedrolls laid out on either side of a neat fire, with a bubbling pot of water tucked against the coals. Ami swiftly cleaned the rabbit and tossed it into the pot, along with a mix of roots and greens she had foraged.

She stared at Caudro as the purple haze before his eyes faded. He sat tall, as if to greet the coming darkness.

"I thought staying in Draethhold for a few days would change you a bit more," Ami said, lounging on her bedroll. "They eat fish at most every meal, and dried varieties as a snack between."

"I promise you, I will eat the rabbit and not throw it aside."

"I didn't mean it as a condemnation, more of an observation. It's curious to me how different the people of Llendshold and Draethhold are, despite all being Humans."

"Mm," Caudro grunted in agreement. "The separation is likely in part due to the Quinarium, though I suppose the Regency bears equal blame."

"You speak as if they're different. Imreia speaks of them as one thing."

"She may be right to speak of them as such," Caudro said. "They always talk about being separate entities which work in harmony to better life for the people of Llendshold; one governing the people, the other shepherding praise to the Quinate. Perhaps their being intertwined is what has led the leaders of the Quinarium to be so arrogant, to believe they are beyond reproach."

"Dara and Wynne certainly taught the Moderator of Stellburg that he was within reach of a thorough rebuke," Ami said.

"I thought they said it was Imreia who killed him?"

"Psh, I'm sure his death was only possible because Imreia had Dara and Wynne protecting her," Ami said as she tossed a bundle of herbs into the pot. "I wonder how much coercion, blackmail, that sort of thing goes on in the Quinarium?"

"What do you mean?"

"I had the fortune—or perhaps it was misfortune—of talking to some of Imreia's friends," Ami said as she lazily stirred the stew. "They told me that the Quinarium would do awful things, even going so far as to kill the children of Lords and Earls who did so little as show signs of dissent. They spoke of less extreme cases too, where Earls would quietly have misfortunes befall their businesses; animals falling ill, caravans getting lost, farms burning, never enough to accuse the Quinarium, but Imreia's friends believe the Quinarium was the cause."

Caudro's shoulders slumped. "Much the way I suspect Jarain's death was intentional. At least we now stand against the Quinarium and can prevent more atrocities."

"I don't understand why Humans don't let people worship the Five in their own ways." Ami scooted close to the fire, resting her chin on her knees. "Even in Draethhold, they had their own customs about the Five and were reluctant to hear of other ceremonies or preferences."

"I can neither explain nor justify it, but for the Quinarium, it seems to be entirely about control and power, and not praising the Five."

"How perverse."

"Indeed."

As a cold evening breeze rolled down from the mountain, Ami ladled out the stew. The two enjoyed their hot meal by the warmth of the fire before crawling into their bedrolls and drifting to sleep beneath the moonlit sky.

A twig snapped beneath Caudro's foot. The echo carried through the tranquil forest, momentarily interrupting the joyful afternoon birdsong. Though a cool fog hung low through the morning, the sun had long ago burned away the low-hanging mist.

"I still wonder if it was right for me to drink mana," Caudro said.

"I told you I heard riders last night," Ami said over her shoulder. "We're fortunate they didn't see our fire, or if they did, that they didn't stop to investigate. You only need to drink until we reach the plains, then it will be much easier to guide you. We can buy horses in Dorslet, and it will be easier still."

"I don't see how it will take any less than five days to reach Dorslet. Hardly an easy trek."

"It'll be fewer days with you walking on your own. And stop worrying, you've been plenty mindful with the mana. We still have a few bottles, and you aren't consuming a whole bottle each day. The others should have plenty more once we reach Hantsburg."

"I wonder how Dara and Wynne are faring," Caudro said, hastening his steps until he was beside Ami.

"Are you worried about them?" Ami said, smiling at Caudro's appearance by her side. "Dara and Wynne are each on their own more capable than you and I combined. Not to mention they travel with Imreia. If you had seen her fight, you would be less concerned."

"Fairly said. In some ways, their task sounds easier than ours, yet in others it seems far worse."

"Worse!?" Ami hissed. "Did you forget the monstrous bone-thing that was the Keeper? We just re-killed your dead mentor, along with countless other Paladins! Not to mention the other trials! Worse, he says. They went to pretty villages to talk to people."

"We simply had to acquire a single object. They must establish a supply line, one which will sustain through war, and it depends on stealing from the Quinarium. And they have to do so quickly."

"Well, I still think you're an idiot for thinking that nudging some people into a little light theft is somehow worse than what we've gone through."

"I also said that in some ways, their task seemed easier."

Ami groaned as she looked up at the leaves above. "What is the 'some' of it? I swear to the Five, you can be such a thick-"

Caudro threw out his arm. Caught up in their conversation, they had not realized they drifted into a clearing and were a mere twenty yards from a confrontation.

A grizzled old farmer stood outside a small wooden house on a low hill; a quaint field with tidy rows of crops stretched behind him. The man's thick, greying beard matched his wiry and windswept hair. He wore a simple, short tunic; its edges were tattered and worn. His tremendous arms rippled with muscle as he leaned on a scythe.

Ami stared at the tool as she had never seen its like. The scythe was taller than the man, with a three-foot-long blade. A ray of sun pierced the canopy, and the honed edge glimmered. The handle was covered in brackets and braces and bindings from years of repair.

A squad of guards stood in an arc before the man with their swords drawn. Their horses lazed about at the edge of the woods.

"Stop denying it," seethed the captain of the guards.

The old man stared back, his face calm and voice bold. "Deny what?"

"We are here on the authority of the Elder of Evenswall, and speak with the blessing of the Confessor! You owe your tax, you owe your tithe, and you have paid neither, Maric."

"How many of you guards are there? Eight, is it?" the old man said, gazing over the aggressors. "You rode how many days to my little farm, all to harass me for a pittance of guilders?"

"If it is a pittance, then pay."

"And what should happen if I don't?" Maric said, crossing his arms with the handle of his scythe tucked inside his elbow.

"You will be branded a heretic for turning your back on the Quinarium, and you will be branded as a tax evader for refusing to pay your due," the captain said. "Then we will collect an equivalent sum of what you owe from your belongings."

"I pray to the Five every morning and every night. I feed myself well enough on my little plot of land. I need nothing from the Quinarium, and they have done nothing for me. Same for the Elders, Earls, Lords, and the Regents themselves of Llendshold. If you care to assess my piety, come inside. I'll cook a meal for you, and you can see my shrine to the Quinate."

"We are here to collect your tax and your tithe!"

"And I already said..."

Maric quieted as a guard turned away.

"You there!" the guard shouted, pointing at Ami and Caudro.

"Shit," Ami muttered.

"You two, don't move! Who are you? Friends of Maric?"

"Keep your hood low," Caudro whispered, facing the ground to hide his eyes.

"Worry about yourself. You're the one with glowing eyes and a Paladin's brand on your wrist," Ami replied, tucking the edges of her hood close to her cheeks.

Three guards broke away from their compatriots and marched towards Ami and Caudro.

"I do not know them," Maric said. "They have no quarrel with you. Let them pass."

"You are not in a place to order us around, and I do not trust your word," the captain said, pointing his sword at the farmer. "The man carries a spear and the woman a bow, and they have an unsavory look about them. We will determine whether they are a trouble that needs seeing to."

The approaching guards suddenly froze.

"The man. His eyes! They're glowing!" shouted the nearest guard.

"I don't see how that's business of yours or mine," Maric droned. "You came here for my taxes. Why don't we all calm ourselves? You've had a long ride. I'll get a stew going and there's plenty of bread already baked. Let us share a meal, then we can continue our discussion in a civilized manner."

"Quiet!" shouted the captain, his helmet wobbling as his head darted back and forth between Maric and the new arrivals. "I speak with the authority of the Quinarium and Regency, through the Confessor and Elder of Evenswall! You will speak only when I say you may speak! Find out who those two are!"

"You, girl, show us your face," ordered the nearest guard.

"Not much point in hiding now," Ami muttered as she threw off her hood.

The guards immediately raised their shields and swords.

"It's a Fae!" shouted the nearby guard. "What is a Fae doing here!?"

Maric chuckled. "What matter is it to you? There is no law that forbids Fae from traveling in Llendshold."

The captain marched towards Maric with his sword still raised. "You were told not to speak unless I told you to. Shut your mouth or we'll take your tongue as a part of your tax."

"Please, let us pass," Caudro called out. "We were simply-"

"Yes, tell us where you were off to, man of the glowing eyes, accompanying a Fae!" shouted the captain.

"We... We..."

"Oh great thinking, really deft with your words today," Ami said to Caudro under her breath. She puffed up her chest and hollered to the guards. "Kind of you to invite us into this little chat you all are having, but I assure you, we are quite busy. Please, let us hurry on by and you'll never hear a word of us again!"

The three guards nearest Ami and Caudro laughed and resumed their march.

"I think we'll have some fun with you two," said one. "Maybe take you back to Evenswall as a prize for the Elder? A Fae and a man with glowing eyes. I'm sure he'll find you interesting."

"Stand down!"

Caudro's voice boomed through the forest, spoken as if he were a Paladin rebuking mischievous Trainees.

"Who are you to order us around?" the guard demanded, despite the trembling of his hands and the quivering of his voice.

Caudro threw off his pack and gripped his spear with both hands.

"I am Caudro, once a Paladin, now a Herald of Almoya! I will not be harassed by petty guards who threaten an innocent man, who clumsily wield false authority, who slander the name of the Quinate under the guise of representing the Quinarium!"

The forest went quiet as the guards looked amongst themselves; a grin stretched across Maric's face.

"Well, now you've done it!" Ami seethed.

As the soldiers broke into a charge, she threw off her cloak and took hold of her bow. Ami and Caudro braced for a fight when Maric raised his scythe. As the captain moved to strike, the farmer beheaded him with a single swing. The captain's head slipped free from its helmet and rolled down the hill; his body slumped to the ground and Maric walked slowly by.

Three of the remaining guards froze in place, but one charged to avenge his captain. Maric sliced through the guard's leg. As he attempted to crawl away, the tip of the scythe plunged through his back, impaling him to the ground.

Ami and Caudro had hardly a moment to process the sight as guards closed the distance with weapons drawn. The first ran too fast, unsteady, as he sprinted over the forest floor. Caudro timed his strike, evading the outstretched sword as he thrust his spear. The point shattered the guard's armor and pierced his heart.

An arrow flew over Caudro's shoulder. It came to a stop in a guard's neck, sending him tumbling.

Caudro backed away and stood close to protect Ami, but the remaining guards fled for their horses. Before they reached their mounts, Maric was upon them. He dispatched the guards with precision, slicing with his scythe calmly, as if he were pruning unruly shrubs.

Ami and Caudro hardly knew how to act when Maric walked over. Blood dropped from the tip of his scythe, staining the forest floor. He came to a stop close enough to speak comfortably, but left ample space so as not to seem threatening.

"I am sorry, my friends, truly sorry," he said, wiping a blood splatter from his cheek with a rag. Piercing azure eyes were set above his full beard. "You came seeking no quarrel and stumbled upon my troubles. Allow me to make amends. Nightfall is nearly upon us, and from the look of you, your travels have been far from pleasant. Spend the night in my cabin. You can eat hot food, bathe, and sleep in a clean bed. Five as my witness, I assure you I mean you no harm."

"I... we..." Caudro stammered. "I'm not sure if-"

"Thank you!" Ami chimed. "It would be terribly rude of us to turn down your offer. We've had quite the travels, as you say."

Maric nodded happily, leaning against his scythe. "The guards introduced me well enough to you. Whom do I have the pleasure of speaking with?"

"I'm Ami, and this is Caudro."

"Do you think it wise to use our real names?" Caudro muttered.

"He cut down six guards with absolute ease, like a cook chopping onions," Ami whispered back. "If he were a threat, we would have been in the thick of it already. Besides, he tried to get the guards to let us go. Hardly the way to act if he meant us ill."

"Why don't you head inside and I'll take care of all this," Maric said, looking over his shoulder. "It seems your days have been longer than mine."

Ami and Caudro sat on the opposite sides of a square table inside the well-crafted cabin. Though the single room was designed for one person, a bunk bed was tucked against a wall opposite a broad bed with a thick green blanket on top. Little carved wooden figures lined shelves placed sporadically throughout the cabin. A fire sang in the hearth as it burned through sap-filled logs.

"Are you alright?" Caudro asked.

Ami's chest rose and fall as she breathed deeply. "I'll be fine. What about you?"

"It was my first time," Caudro said, hunched over in his chair.

"First time doing what?"

"Killing a Human."

Ami blinked rapidly. She leaned over to inspect Caudro's face. The glow was gone from his eyes and though he slouched, his face was emotionless.

"I thought that, you being a Paladin, you might have killed a Human before. Don't Paladins protect hamlets from bandits and whatnot?"

"They do," Caudro said, his jaw tense. "Though I hadn't had the opportunity yet. The Jackals were my first time in a proper fight. Even then, those were mindless beasts."

"I'm not sure these guards were much more than the Jackals. They completely refused to listen to reason."

Caudro faced Ami. "Have you killed a Human or Fae before?"

"No."

The softness of Ami's voice faded into the crackling of the fire as they both sat listening.

"It weighs heavily on me, too," Ami said. "No matter what I say, it feels awful. It doesn't matter that they tried to kill us. I wish it didn't happen."

"As you said, we had no choice."

Ami sighed. "We always knew this was coming. If not now, then soon enough we would have faced Agents of the Quinarium on the battlefield. Maybe it will get easier."

"I don't want it to get easier," Caudro said as he rubbed the back of his neck. "The finality of taking a life is something I should have to live with forever."

Ami looked at Caudro with a wistful smile. Her eyes settled on Caudro's hands. She wished in that moment he would reach out and hold her, reassure that all would be alright; that somehow through his touch, the sickening emptiness filling her stomach might fade away.

"Although I hate it, you're right," she said. "This feeling is a terrible reminder to avoid killing whenever we can."

"Do you hate that I'm right, or do you hate the feeling?"

They laughed half-heartedly until the door creaked open.

"Don't mind me," Maric said, shuffling in without a hint as to the grisly task he had completed. "You two are sitting as stiff as if you were attending service in a Sanctuary. Please, make yourselves comfortable. There's water and mead in those jugs—I ferment the mead myself—and bread in that basket there. Help yourselves while I get the stew going."

Ami eyed Maric's bloodstained tunic as he bustled around the hearth.

"Are you certain you don't need help outside?" she asked.

"Not at all." Maric spoke under his breath, pausing for a moment and staring into the fire. "They're tucked away well enough. There are plenty of creatures in the woods that will take care of what remains."

The farmer set a few logs in the fire while he hummed a joyful tune.

"How did you come to live out here?" Ami asked.

"A simple question with a complicated meaning, which I believe you intended when you asked it," Maric replied. "Please, rest your worries. I know there are few reasons for a Fae and a former Paladin to travel together. I can only assume your experiences have led you to believe all Humans in Llendshold are under the sway of the Quinarium, all-reaching as they seem to be. Yet there are many dissenters, such as myself. You see me as I am, because this is fate for those who are open in their defiance."

"This is not by choice, then?" Caudro asked.

"It is entirely by choice, but it is the Quinarium that made this choice."

"Will you share your story with us, that we might feel at ease when telling you ours?"

Maric chuckled. "It has been years since I have heard such a creative framing of words. Yes, young one, I am happy to do so."

A wooden cutting board scraped against the table as Maric slid it into a position of his liking. Gourds and squash and a wide range of vegetables clunked atop the board, followed by the clink of a broad cleaver.

"Apologies, my dear Fae; I have no meat, but I do have eggs. Master Caudro, do you object if I add a few to our stew?"

"Ami has... influenced my dining preferences," Caudro replied.

"You've set him a certain way," Maric said with a chuckle. He took up his cleaver; the blade glided through vegetables in an unwavering cadence. "As for my story... I was once a quiet farmer, as I am now. Long ago I lived with my sister and her husband, their three little children—Alsy, Toma, Hedda, sweetest little creatures, true blessings of the Five—and my husband. We lived happily for many years. Our farm was near Monningburg, and we traded with hamlets of Llendshold and Draethhold alike."

Maric took the cutting board to a pot by the fire and slid the vegetables inside. He poured in a few drops of oil, then stirred as the vegetables sizzled.

"That all changed when a spat broke out between the Lord of Monningburg and the Lord of the neighboring Draethhold city. They never even told us his name. All I know is that one day, guards arrived from Monningburg to conscript me."

He poured water over the browned vegetables, then retrieved glass jars of dried spices and herbs from a tidy shelf. Back at the table, Maric chopped the seasonings into a fine powder.

"We trained for a few weeks, then the Moderator from Monningburg arrived. She blessed us, then it was off to battle. The next day, and for many days after, I fought as I was commanded. I fought in the name of our Lord's greed, even as I received word that my sister and her family, and my husband, were forced to move. The Quinarium deemed our lands necessary for the 'holy war' that the Lord had undertaken. They were told the Quinarium would provide equivalent lands further north."

The back of the cleaver groaned and stuttered against the cutting board as Maric slid the herbs into the pot. An enticing aroma filled the cabin as he stirred.

"A Quinarium messenger handed me a letter one day. I unfolded the paper to read a cursed message. My husband. My sister. Her husband. Alsy, Toma, Hedda, the three most precious blessings in my life. All of them, dead. Some malady on the road. The letter went on to say their deaths were no doubt a condemnation from the Five. That the Quinate did not save them because our piety was unsatisfactory. That my service to the Lord would be sufficient atonement, as decreed by the Quinarium. I deserted that night, and have lived on my own ever since."

Maric tapped eggs against the edge of the pot, then dumped their golden yolks into the simmering stew one-by-one. He stirred aimlessly; the handle of the spoon ground against the rim of the pot in a hypnotizing rhythm.

"I see the surprise on your face, young man," he said to Caudro. "The Quinarium would have everyone—young Paladins, young Mages, the people of villages and cities—believe their hold is total and unwavering. Yet I am hardly unique, and there are many with stories like mine."

"Your past is a travesty," Ami said, her voice barely above a whisper. "Though we are fortunate to be in your company now."

Caudro cleared his throat and sat tall. "We are here in support of Imreia. We aim to do no less than tear the Quinarium apart, destroying all that the institution has become, and reform praise of the Quinate in Llendshold."

Maric shifted in his seat. "Imreia? So it is true that she lives? I thought the Quinarium used her name in rumors to instill fear, to keep the masses compliant; that perhaps they merely resurrected the idea of Imreia, and that she had, in truth, died long ago."

"I would have thought the same, had I not met her myself," Caudro said.

Maric looked up to the ceiling of the cabin. "I think we can consider ourselves in the company of friends. As a friend, would you satisfy my curiosity: what motivates a Fae to fight the Quinarium?"

Ami cast her gaze aside. "The Quinarium intends to attack Cauldhill while placing blame on the Fae. They believe such an act will unite Llendshold in a holy war to destroy my people."

"I am sorry," Maric said, stroking his beard. "I am certain my lack of reaction is a disappointment, and yet it does not surprise me that the Quinarium would conspire to commit such an act."

"You are a capable fighter. You should join our cause," Caudro said.

"I am an old man. A shell of what I once was."

"A shell?" Ami blurted out. "If we saw a shell fight today, then what fury did you wield on the battlefield in your prime?"

Caudro leaned onto the table. "We cannot allow the Quinarium to continue on this disastrous path. There may have once been good in the Quinarium, but there is none left. As deep as the roots of evil run, so too has the strength of their arm grown. We need all the support we can gather."

"I don't disagree, but I am a tired old man," Maric said, huddling over the stew.

"Ami is right," Caudro pressed. "You may feel a tired old man, that you are no longer a warrior, but we saw you today. There is nothing tired or old about you. You lost everything, and we can never bring your loved ones back, but we offer a chance for you to exact your revenge on the institution responsible."

"If I ever was to stand against the Quinarium, it would not be for revenge," Maric said. "I buried my thoughts of revenge in decades past."

"That may be, and we are glad to hear you have found peace, but we hope to prevent others from facing the fate that you have," Ami said. "The same fate that might befall my people."

Maric set two bowls onto the table and filled them with generous portions of stew.

"You two eat up," he said. "I have a few things to take care of outside. I'll eat later."

Realizing the hunger which had grown in their bellies, Ami and Caudro ate in silence until their spoons scraped the bottoms of their empty bowls.

"He's quite the cook," Ami said, chewing on a crust of bread.

"A good cook, and a better warrior."

"Hm..." Ami's eyes roamed the cottage, from pots hanging in a tidy row to neatly folded blankets, from a clean butter churn to the little glass vials filled with foraged herbs. "I think he'd rather be a cook than a warrior."

"Ami... I..."

"Yes?"

"I'm sorry."

"Oh? For which transgression?" Ami said, twirling a curl of her hair.

"The most severe of them all. I am sorry for not supporting you in protecting your people. I should have lent you my voice back when we were in Draethhold. I should have pressed for Mordinlet to be the focus of the show of strength. I..." Caudro grinding his fists into his thighs. "It is time for me to stop following blindly. I have lived in fear of what it will take to atone for all my years serving as a Paladin, all the while not seeing that all I must do is before me, now, with you. The Paladin Fortress at Mordinlet is the only place for the show of strength. I will do all I can to ensure we march on it."

Ami leaned across the table until Caudro felt the warmth of her breath on his ear.

"I could just kiss you right now," she whispered.

"And will you?"

"Nope!" she said with a giggle, rising from the table. "Maric mentioned cleaning up, and I am desperate for a wash. I'm off to find him and see what sort of bath he might have. Enjoy the rest of your supper!"

INTERLUDE

Imreia looked out from a balcony at the ocean. Cresting waves glowed beneath the moon. A pleasant breeze sent her light robe billowing.

"Wine?" a deep voice called.

"Please," Imreia replied.

Okter, wearing a similar robe, sauntered over with two glasses in hand.

"Hantsburg," he said, standing beside Imreia. "I doubted I would ever return. Though it is not my home, of all the cities in Llendshold, it is the one I most wished to see again."

"The great Mage Okter, taker of what he wishes, thought a desire of his might go unfulfilled?" Imreia said with a chuckle.

"Yes."

Okter leaned on the railing and looked to the streets below. Wood-soled shoes clomped on the cobbled streets as residents passed by; the faces of even the most busy and determined workers bore expressions of joy at the pleasant evening. Okter raised his ethereal hand and surveyed the ocean through its lavender haze.

"I must admit, losing my hand to the Adjudicator's Enforcer lessened my confidence. For a while, at least."

Imreia leaned in. Okter greeted her with a kiss; their lips lingered until Imreia pulled away.

"I, for one, am glad to see your confidence returned. And that we have returned to Hantsburg."

Okter took a sip of wine. "This is only possible thanks to you and your network of allies. While I expected Lord Pharadrax to decline the Quinarium request to root out any potential allies of your family, your reach here is still far greater than I anticipated."

"I have not sat idly by all these years. The Quinarium—from Confessors to Moderators, Adjudicators to the Voice himself—have inflated confidence that they hold sway over all the people of Llendshold."

"Your survival is an excellent example of their arrogance. The hubris to use rumors of you, to boast of your power, to fuel fear in an effort to strengthen control... in truth, I thought those rumors to be inflated until I met you. I have found them to be pleasantly true, in many regards."

Imreia watched as a singular ship sailed away into the night.

"You and I have only ever talked about our dealings with the Quinarium. Tell me, what would you do if we did not have to worry about the troubles of today? What would you do with all the freedom, resources, and time you desire?"

"My position at the Academy of Ramaia was in equal parts a palace and a prison. I only ever wanted to learn more, to do more, with magic. All the tools I needed at my fingertips, yet I was never allowed to press against the walls placed around me. The Quinarium was ever watchful, ever controlling... it was both tantalizing and maddening."

"What if those walls did not exist?"

Okter smiled like a child told to run free in a toy shop. "Time."

"What of time?"

"Through Blood magic, we can augment speed. Mind magic can change the perception of time. And yet, those both focus on the person. So far, none can control time. I would be the one to unlock its secrets."

"A lofty aim," Imreia said.

"One I believe possible. Since I've been allowed to teach in my way, I see magic as never before."

"I take it Lord Kalomar's daughter is a capable student?"

"My expectations were nonexistent at first," Okter said, smirking. "I thought I need merely placate the Lord to fund the school. It turns out his progeny is truly gifted. Though I wish Rhoslin would show more interest in Blood and Mind spells, I can't help but encourage, and be encouraged by, her affinity for Seraeus and control of the Air."

"I wish you had brought her along. I would have liked to see her tested."

"As would I, though she has a gentle spirit. She is holding back, despite my pressure. I don't think it's the right time to unleash her, capable though she may be. Not to mention her father, being Lord Kalomar. I don't think he would look favorably upon us taking her from Draethhold so soon. Speaking of proteges, what of your sister, Nireia? Why not have her accompany us?"

Imreia sighed and set down her glass. She leaned with her back against the rail and looked up to the night sky.

"Neia is a liability. I love her, and I know I can't keep her locked away forever, but she is entirely too headstrong, too hotheaded, too filled with a desire for revenge. If I let her loose in battle now, it would destroy any chance of her learning to control herself."

Okter eyed Imreia hungrily; the thin robe outlined her powerful yet lithe and elegant figure.

"Quite the opposite of what is needed in a time of war."

"Yes. Interesting that we both find it necessary to hold back Neia and Rhoslin, though for quite different reasons."

"Would you perhaps consider us hypocrites for happily employing other young and capable fighters?"

Imreia squinted at Okter, meeting his attentive gaze. "You mean Dara, Wynne, Ami, and Caudro?"

"Precisely."

"They are the future. You make it sound as though we are taking advantage of their zeal, their yearning for justice. I would call it irresponsible to not have them involved in our efforts. I need more people I can trust than you and Neia in the coming age."

Okter sidled closer as he leaned against the rail until his arm brushed against Imreia's.

"The handling of Mages is one of the few aspects of the Quinarium I quite agree with. Bringing in Initiates at the cusp of adulthood, allowing them to have a sense of self and identity, then leading them to the conclusion you desire, creates far more powerful adherents than the ridiculousness of Paladins. Indoctrinating children results in little more than mindless insects, incapable of independent thought."

"Especially powerful are followers who think their every act is of their own volition. As for the Paladins, I consider Caudro a rare exception. He acts as if he is simple, but I have heard enough to believe he is capable of more. I assume you agree, given you sent him to the Academy of Almoya."

Okter chuckled. "A rare exception indeed. I wonder if it was his time with Dara and Wynne that opened his eyes. Lacking their influence, he might have been as brainless as the rest of the Paladins."

"Yes. Dara and Wynne have proven themselves quite capable."

"I see your pride in Dara and Wynne. Do you think it wise to deceive them? Wynne takes after her mother, Lord Pharadrax, in many ways. She notices more than she speaks."

Imreia laughed. "There is no deceit. Further, Dara and Wynne both stated their demands, and I happily agreed to them."

"I must say, recent experience tells me you are not one to care for demands placed upon you."

Imreia ran a finger along Okter's jaw. "It was all quite sweet. They demanded that we assist the Fae by disrupting the attack on Cauldhill; that we free Caudro, which thankfully Ami took care of almost entirely on her own; that their involvement be limited to the dismantling of the Quinarium; and finally, that they stay together through this all."

"No mention of you retaking your position as Lord of Brewardsburg?"

"I explicitly told them they would need not take a single step on my behalf."

Okter tilted his head. "I take it then that your parents' title is not what you seek. What then, do you believe is the end for the mighty Imreia, rightful Lord of Brewardsburg?"

Imreia drank the last of her wine, then turned to face the city. A breeze flowed through the streets of Hantsburg, rustling her hair.

"I will not push Dara or Wynne to assist in my ambitions; nor Ami or Caudro, nor anyone else. And yet, in striving to dismantle the Quinarium, they will all battle the Regency of Llendshold. Not unlike my parents, who stood against the Quinarium. Unfortunately, their ambition for the title of Regent was their undoing."

"You share their ambition."

"I am owed what the Quinarium stole."

Okter rested his hand on Imreia's back. "You have amassed an impressive array of allies these past years. It seems you are finally ready to take that which is rightfully yours."

"If I am to rule, I will need a powerful partner to stand beside me," Imreia said. "To aid me in leading with authority, yet with a gentle touch. And I will need someone to create a new order of Mages, loyal to me."

"And do you have someone in mind?" Okter said as he pulled Imreia into his arms.

CHAPTER 13

"Do you think Maric will join Imreia?"

Ami looked back to the cabin. Maric was busy in the nearby field, whistling as he tended to his crops. Any passerby would be none the wiser that the day before he had effortlessly hewn down a host of guards.

"I'm not sure," she replied. "No matter his decision, I am encouraged that the Quinarium's control is not so complete as they portray it to be."

Caudro held onto the saddle of his horse, listening as Ami readied their supplies. "He seemed happy enough to aid us; we're taking nearly everything the guards had. I worry that a larger contingent of guards will come once they realize the first group won't be returning."

Ami heaved a pack filled with food onto the back of a horse. "It would take quite the number to give Maric issue. I'd love to see him duel Imreia. He moved so quickly, so effortlessly, all without the power of mana."

"He is precisely the kind of ally we need when facing the Quinarium."

Plug slipped out of Ami's tunic and hopped to her horse's saddle. He lazed across the seat, stretching and purring.

"As if Imreia didn't already have all the army she needs with the mighty Plug!" Ami said, rubbing the creature's chin.

"Need I remind you of his propensity for disappearing at the first sign of danger? Did he even once come out of your tunic since we fought the guards yesterday, until now?"

"He knew we would be fine! I'm sure dear Plug is holding back his immense power, waiting for the right time to unleash his might."

Ami and Caudro laughed as they rode away to Maric's fading song.

The horses stomped through a shallow stream a few days later as the village of Dorslet came into view. Ami would have described the village as boring and plain—with its stone walls surrounding buildings nestled against the foothills of a towering, sparsely wooded mountain—were it not for the odd sight in the nearby fields.

"Caudro, there is something going on outside the village. There are tens of carriages parked in a circle, with colorful flags all around. I think it's a carnival!"

"How awful."

Ami's mouth fell open. "Excuse me? What do you mean by that?"

"I mean there will be a large crowd," Caudro said, his shoulders slouched. "We need to stay hidden."

"My dearest protector, if anything, a large crowd means it will be easier to avoid notice. I'd wager that everyone will be so consumed by the carnival we can pass freely wherever we wish." Ami inhaled sharply. "In fact, we should go to the carnival! We deserve a bit of fun after all we've been through."

"I disagree."

"Why? It's only midday. There's more than enough time to stock up on supplies and rest after we enjoy the carnival."

"What about avoiding attention?"

Ami squinted at Caudro's clenched jaw. "You aren't worried about unwanted attention. There's something else. Tell the truth, you deceptive weasel!"

"Fine," Caudro said. "I was an orphan, then I joined the Paladins. I never really had time for fun."

"Are you scared?"

"Not the word I would use," Caudro said, raising his chin and facing away from Ami. "A bit more uncomfortable, I'd say."

"Well, it's time for you to be uncomfortable. I've never been to a Human carnival, and I want to see one. I'll find us an inn first, if any have a vacant room left, then we are going to the carnival."

Ami urged the horses into a canter, refusing to listen to Caudro's protests. On the way, she spied visitors flowing to the carnival from a sprawling encampment of tents and lean-tos at the foot of the mountains, about a half mile away. Impromptu stalls and stands dotted the path as opportunistic merchants attempted to profit from the attraction.

After stabling their horses, Ami pressed through the crowded streets of Dorslet. The village was abuzz as residents hurried about, filled with an urgent desire to see the carnival. Frustrated with the rowdy throng, Ami made for the first inn she spotted.

The doors to *The Laughing Badger* swung open. She expected to find a boisterous crowd, yet the inside was as quiet as a morgue. The innkeeper was draped over a table like a cast aside coat as he languished over a mug of ale.

"Here for a meal?" the innkeeper said, leaping from his seat.

"And a room, if you have one," Ami said. "The streets are chaos. Please tell me you have at least one bed not yet claimed?"

"If only my inn were as crowded as the carnival. You'll be happy to hear that near every room is presently unoccupied, as precious few want to stay within the walls," the innkeeper lamented. "The spectacle will be a boon for us all, or so the Elder said, happily collecting guilders from all us merchants to entice the carnival. Despite his assurances, the cretins, the layabouts, the hooligans from the surrounding hamlets camp outside our walls. Dastardly cheap bastards, all of them, refusing to pay for proper lodging."

"Well, we need just the one room, but we are happy to pay," Ami said.

"Perhaps a meal for you two as well?"

"This evening, please," Ami replied. She set a few guilders on the bar; the innkeeper took his portion, then slid one shiny coin back.

"Right then, enjoy the carnival," he said, slouching into a chair. "Don't eat too much of their slop and I'll make you something proper. Nothing else for me to do, as it were."

Minutes later, Ami dragged Caudro out through the gates of Dorslet. They walked on an impromptu road of packed dirt, made by the excited feet of villagers on their way to the carnival.

"You're being stingy," Ami chided. "Take a drink of mana and enjoy yourself."

"I am not being stingy. Mana is a precious resource. There is nothing wrong with being mindful of its use, especially when we know how the Quinarium extracts mana from innocent people," Caudro retorted. "Besides, I think a man walking around with glowing eyes would undoubtedly attract attention."

Ami patted Caudro's hand, pressing it into her shoulder. "Come now, you can say it if you want to touch me."

"That's... that's not it. I'm not trying to touch you!" Caudro stammered. "Wait, I mean, it's not that I don't like touching you. Wait! That came out wrong... it's just that..."

Ami giggled as she skipped along with Caudro in tow.

The sounds of the carnival grew ever louder as they neared. Performers hollered and hooted and roared, while attendees laughed and cheered in response. Strange smells filled Ami's and Caudro's noses, cutting through the stench of a dense crowd on a warm day; unfamiliar herbs, spices, and flowers shifted with the breeze, the exact aroma never quite discernable.

"Welcome, good madam, welcome good sir!" shouted a greeter. He wore a strange gown of interwoven cloth ribbons in bright greens and blues. "Please step through, step in, step among the sort you will only ever see in the Menagerie of Delight! You are most fortunate to have arrived today, for today is the last day we will be in Dorslet. Enjoy yourselves!"

"Thank you!" Ami said, bowing as they passed by.

Though Caudro heard the joy and levity in Ami's breath and felt it in the way she bounced with each step, his trepidation grew. Shoulders bumped against him. A hand pushed against his back. A foul-smelling man grumbled inches from his ear. Back and forth, Ami wove through the crowd, while Caudro clung as the crowd pressed ever-closer.

They passed vendors shouting about the rarity of their wares, which they were willing to part with for a pittance, performers telling stories of heroic adventures, musicians playing strange instruments Caudro had never heard before, and games where contestants cheered with joy and cried out in sadness in equal numbers.

Ami finally came to a stop. Guilders clinked, then Ami thanked a woman who grunted back.

"What-"

"Ah ah!" Ami said, pressing a finger against Caudro's lips. A shiver ran through his body at her sudden touch, and the cacophony assaulting his ears dulled. He felt a sudden urge to pull her close, to be closer.

"Eat up. Then we can talk."

Caudro resigned himself to Ami's command as she led him to a table. He felt his way around a broad bowl and found a spoon with a strangely curved handle. When he lifted the spoon to his mouth, he found a smooth dumpling, coated in a vibrant and herbaceous broth. Caudro took a hesitant bite; a myriad of vegetables poured out. He joyfully dived in for more until he scraped his bowl clean.

As soon as Caudro set down his spoon, Ami grabbed his hand and yanked him from his seat.

"What is it? What's the rush?"

"I'll tell you in a moment!"

Caudro stumbled after Ami until she came to an abrupt stop. She aggressively haggled with a vendor; their words were entirely unintelligible to Caudro, yet from the tone it was apparent both enjoyed the exchange. Then, a thin band of cloth wrapped around Caudro's head and soft padding pressed against the outline of his face. Ami chuckled as Caudro ran his hands over the object.

"You can take a sip now."

"What have you done to me?" he pleaded.

"You sound like I've thrust a dagger into your belly!" Ami said, poking him in the gut. "It's a mask. I'm wearing one too. It's a shame you can't see yourself. The vendor was right, a fish was the perfect choice for you. It has a great big open mouth and tiny eyes!"

"A fish? And what precisely did you pick for yourself?"

"A chipmunk. Wonderful little creatures."

"Mischievous. How fitting," Caudro said. "No matter about the masks, I can't bring a bottle of you know what out in a crowd."

"Oh you handsome, tiring, boring Ogre of a man!"

A bottle pressed against Caudro's lips. Not wishing to spill the precious mana inside, he opened his mouth and the sweet liquid poured in. The carnival appeared around him.

"Are you sure this is safe?" he muttered, casting his gaze to the ground.

"Caudro, think about who we are. Think about where we are. We might as well have a bit of fun. We can't always be worried if the next moment will be our last. Besides, the mask covers up your eyes completely and plenty of people are wearing them. I can't see the slightest hint of glow."

"I still think-"

"Oh, stop trying to think! Let me have this day, Caudro. I need this."

Caudro breathed in deeply. "What would you like to do?"

Ami grabbed Caudro's hand, sliding her fingers between his. She leaned her head on his shoulder as they strolled through the crowd.

They came to a stop by a small stage where a short-statured Human posing as a Dwarf and a real Fae performed before a tightly packed audience. The Human had shaved his head—eyebrows included—and wore a bulky tunic over loose pants. Darkened cylinders of glass, held together by thin metal bands, covered his eyes. The Fae, meanwhile, wore a caricature of Fae clothing. Her oversized poncho extended nearly to the ground, and gourds dangled from straps all across her body, clinking against each other with every move.

The Fae bared her teeth, revealing fake fangs. "Children, gather close! Come to the front, yes, up here. Listen to your parents, listen well, lest I catch wind of your misbehaviors. Defy your parents, and I will creep into your rooms in the dark of night and eat your noses!"

Children squealed and covered their faces while the rest of the crowd chuckled.

The 'Dwarf' cupped his hands around his face. "Eat their noses? Five above, I'm from underground, I can hardly see knees from a nose! This sun! This sun! Dwarves are not meant to burn in its glare!"

When the Fae smacked the 'Dwarf' on the top of his bare head, the crowd burst into laughter.

"Petulant fool of a Dwarf," she sneered. "If you can't see a nose, then I'll eat your ears!"

The 'Dwarf' clasped his hands and tilted his head, spoke with feigned adoration. "Oh my dearest, were you to eat my ears, then how would I hear the sweetness of your voice?"

Ami pulled at Caudro. "Let's go. This is a gross spectacle, making fun of Fae and Dwarves like this."

They turned to leave when a hulking man stepped in their way.

"What's it to you, little girl, where we get our laughs from?"

Ami glared at the man's wart-ridden nose. "Sorry, it just happens that I'm a person with morals, class, and taste."

"What's that supposed to mean?" he growled.

"It means you're too daft to discern the difference between humor and horror," Ami spat.

"If you have something to say, say it simply or I'll show you what I'm thinking with my hands!"

Caudro grabbed Ami's shoulder and pulled her away. "Think nothing of it, sir. My apologies. We had too many rounds at the inn before coming to the carnival. No trouble meant."

"Get your woman in line, boy, or else someone will do it for you!" the man yelled after.

When they were comfortably far from the belligerent man, Ami yanked her shoulder from Caudro's grip and crossed her arms.

"How could you let him say that?" she spewed.

"Ami, I assure you I would have loved to plant his face in the mud. But you cannot correct ignorance in a moment, and that man was not willing to be corrected by the likes of us. He was wrong. The show is awful, and I'm sorry, but now is not the time to attract attention with a brawl."

"Fine. You're right."

"I'm sorry. It's not my place to explain away your feelings, which are justified."

"It's alright, I promise," Ami said softly.

"I don't mean to..."

Caudro lost his thought on noticing a group of children happily chewing on circles of crisp, sugary dough as they joyfully bounded through the crowd.

"Are you alright?" Ami asked.

"Yes... it's just that I didn't expect to see children."

"Caudro, we saw children at the show. And we're at a carnival. Why would you expect there to be no children?"

"We were never allowed to play," he said, barely above a whisper.

"Excuse me? Did I hear you say you were never allowed to play?"

"Not as Paladins."

"Five above, no wonder you are so childish!" Ami said.

"What?"

"Today you get to be a child. Come, pick a game, and play!"

"I don't know what to do."

"Whatever you feel," Ami said, playfully shoving Caudro towards a row of stalls with games.

Caudro meandered back and forth until he made his choice. Chest puffed up as if he were ready for battle, he stepped over to a narrow table covered in rope rings. An array of wooden posts protruded from the ground beyond the table.

"Come closer, my good man!" cheered the game's officiant. The woman's cheeks were rosy and her smile was as inviting as a beloved grandmother's. "Fancy a try at the rings?"

"Yes. Please," Caudro said, still rigid as a hewn log.

"The game is as simple as can be. A guilder gets you five rings, and each ring on a post gets you a chit. Collect five chits and win a prize!"

Ami stood on tip-toes, leaning close to Caudro's ear. "Are you sure a game where crisp sight is an advantage is the right one for you?"

"I have chosen," Caudro whispered back. He placed a guilder on the table. "I'll try once."

"Right you are!" the officiant cheered. "Take your five rings, good sir, and may the Five guide your hand!"

Caudro ran his fingers along the woven rope. He squeezed and flexed a ring, bounced it in his hands to test the heft and estimate its flight. He finally raised the ring, balancing it delicately between his fingers, then sent it flying.

Ami snickered when the ring sailed past the posts. "A little eager, aren't we?"

"A test! A trial! Practice for the next," Caudro said.

The officiant patted his shoulder. "Four to go, plenty of tries! Five chits to earn your prize!"

Caudro exhaled slowly through pursed lips. The second ring bounced off the post. The third sailed true, spinning about the top of a post where it came to a stop.

"It's hanging from the post!" Caudro shouted, pointing with a shaking hand. "It counts, right!?"

"Toss one more!" said the officiant. "If the ring falls on, it will count!"

Caudro hastily threw his fourth ring, which sent the dangling rope tumbling away from the post.

"Five above!" he shouted.

Ami hooted. "One ring left, and it takes five chits for a prize. No pressure on this one."

His face flushed, Caudro flippantly chucked the last ring, then turned to leave when the officiant's cries brought him back. At the base of a post rested the fifth and final ring.

Caudro jumped, nearly sending his mask tumbling from his face, while Ami and the officiant clapped. He looked to Ami, then back to the game. Marching to his place at the line, Caudro slammed a guilder down.

A short while later, the officiant happily counted a stack of guilders. Ami sat atop the table while Caudro threw yet another ring. He squealed with delight when it wrapped around a post, joining four others already at the base.

"Five rings, five chits, one prize it is!" declared the officiant.

Ami grinned. "My *friend,* you paid nearly as much for this game as we did for our inn."

"We might as well have a bit of fun," Caudro said, mimicking Ami.

"You dare turn my words against me! Dastardly man. Fine then, pick your prize and let's carry on."

The officiant opened a small chest of trinkets. Caudro positioned himself between Ami and the baubles, feeling his way through until he found an item to his satisfaction. They bowed to the officiant and eased into the crowd.

"What did you choose?"

"A trifle."

Ami snorted. "I'd wager that trifle will stay in one of your pockets or pouches for the next decade or more, you sentimental buffoon."

Caudro walked along with a dumb smile pasted on his face and his fist clenched tight around his trinket. They roamed for a while until a voice carried over the carnival.

"Come one, come all, show us your prowess with a bow! The penultimate event, with the finest prizes in all the Menagerie!"

The arbiter of the competition waved at passersby. His tan hair was curled into a slicked wave. A wide mustache, waxed into pointed ends, framed his broad smile.

"Ami, you have to compete!" Caudro said, prodding with his elbow.

"Who says I have to?"

"I do."

Ami's cheeks flushed at the command. She was glad for the moment that Caudro couldn't see the sudden change in her skin. "Well then, getting your woman in line now, like the man said?"

Caudro choked and gasped for air.

"Relax," Ami said. "I'm merely joking. Alright then, let's see how I measure against the finest of Dorslet."

Ami took position at the end of the line. The round white targets painted with blue rings waited thirty yards away. Back and forth the arbiter marched, until all the archers stood at the ready with a bow in hand and three arrows in a quiver before them.

"The rules are simple," said the arbiter, his voice booming. "Three arrows each. The archer with most arrows in the center ring—of their assigned target—wins. If we have more than one archer with the same number of arrows in the center, then we'll measure the shortest distance from the center. Pace yourselves as you wish, loose when you are ready!"

One young man instantly nocked an arrow and drew. He released, only for the arrow to sink into the ground a few feet away. While his face burned at the jeers of the crowd, the other archers released their arrows. The arbiter cheered and jeered and riled up the cloud as missiles flew; some true, some horribly astray.

Ami raised her bow calmly. She drew and released fluidly. Her arrow landed squarely in the heart of the target. A smile crept across her face when her second arrow struck a hair's breadth from the first.

"Miss, if you don't mind me saying," whispered the arbiter, leaning close, "I find your grip fascinating, drawing with your thumb instead of your fingers."

Ami's eyes grew. She peered down the line to see that every Human pulled their bowstring with three fingers, while she followed the traditions of the Fae and hooked the string with her thumb.

"My family always was of the strangest sort."

The arbiter smiled. "Never a worry, my dear. If I may share a secret—one I think you might want to know—the victor is to dine with the Elder and Confessor this evening."

"Thank you, friend," Ami said.

"I'm friend with plenty of folk from the forest—I'm sure you've seen more than one in our carnival—and I don't want to see you in an unpleasant situation. If you strike, say, the third ring, you should come in second," he said with a wink.

The arbiter addressed the crowd anew as Ami raised her bow. She sighed, adjusting her aim and sending the last arrow into the designated ring.

Once all the archers had exhausted their arrows, the arbiter hurried to the targets. He leapt atop and knocked over and danced around those with poor scores until he reached a target with three arrows in the center and declared the winner.

A losing contestant screamed and snapped his bow in half over his knee. In the blink of an eye, two carnival guards appeared, wearing shiny steel armor and wielding maces with oblong heads. Fear overtook anger and the contestant shakily counted out guilders to pay for the broken bow.

"What happened with your third arrow?" Caudro asked Ami.

"It would seem you were right, that we might be noticed. The master of the competition kindly informed me that the prize for winning is dinner with the Confessor and the Elder."

"I would say you placed your third arrow perfectly."

Ami selected her prize in the same fashion as Caudro—hiding her selection—though she felt a touch disappointed when he didn't ask what she chose.

They happily strolled through the carnival, taking in sights and sounds as the sun descended on the horizon. Ami contemplated taking hold of Caudro's hand again when a woman abruptly stepped between them, hooking her arms into theirs.

"Dear friend, would you be willing to part with the little pet in your pouch?" she asked, half-singing in a willowy, light voice.

"And who might you be?" Ami said, glaring at the woman.

The intruder had a lithe build, with flowing hair styled into a tall plume. Mischief glistened in her green eyes. She wore a colorful tunic; the lower half was a tangle of bright ribbons, some of which were no more than an inch long, while others nearly dragged on the ground.

"Oh, dear me! My manners. I would apologize for my lack of them, but I somehow lost my sensibilities some years ago and never managed to collect them again. As for who I am, I am Erswein, ringmaster of the fine carnival you are presently attending. And about the pet?"

Plug's head appeared from a pouch on Ami's belt. The creature hissed, then ducked back inside.

"There is your answer," Ami said.

"How did you know he was there at all?" Caudro asked. "He hasn't stirred all day."

Erswein gave Caudro's arm a friendly shake. "My good man, as leader of the carnival, I must have an especially discerning eye for that which might be called special. It would be poor form if I wasn't aware of such a thing. The same way it would be poor form were I not to take note of a Paladin and a Fae attending my carnival in disguise."

Ami and Caudro froze in place, their arms stiff inside the carnival leader's embrace.

"Never you mind. Your secret is safe with me, I assure you. You have not a thing to worry about. I merely found your presence curious, and being a purveyor of the curious, I had to say hello. If I might pry a touch, as I always do, would you be so kind as to share where you are headed? Oh, but please don't tell me all of the why. I like to know what I can but also know what I shouldn't. I am quite certain your motivations are most certainly a matter that I should not know about."

"West," Caudro said.

"Excellent! West... if it is Hantsburg you seek, then I will arrange a boat for you. Traveling by river will save you some days." Erswein's eyes darted back and forth between Ami and Caudro. "I sense you don't trust my offer. Head west in the morning. When you reach the river, you'll see a small craft waiting for you, with a yellow flag flying from the bow. Take it if you please, leave it if you don't. With that, I have other matters I must attend to. Farewell!"

Erswein bowed with a flourish and disappeared into the crowd.

"Should we-"

"What of-"

Caudro shook his head as they both laughed. "Perhaps we've been here long enough. My vision is beginning to fade."

"I agree. We are both long overdue for a proper bath and a comfortable bed."

"I don't understand why you insisted on putting a curtain around the bath," Ami said, reclining in the tub of warm water. She scrubbed her arms, awaiting Caudro's response. When he did not reply, she called out anew. "What's on your mind?"

"I..." Caudro breathed slowly. "I'm finding it hard to know what I'm feeling at this moment."

"You tend to hide your feelings away. It's good for you to let them out once in a while."

"While true, I don't think this is even about hiding. I've simply never experienced this before. My childhood passed with hardly a day of fun. Until today, I never truly realized what I missed, what I dedicated myself to, and what the Quinarium demanded in return."

"If I knew a game of rope toss would bring this out of you, I would have made the game for you myself," Ami chuckled. "Caudro... I say this with all seriousness: I understand your meaning. You don't have to hold things in all the time. You can be open with me. The Five know we've been through too much together for you to worry about my judgement."

"I don't know if I will ever be as happy as I have been today," Caudro said as a tear rolled down his cheek.

"And why is that?" Ami asked, leaning her head back until the water covered her scalp.

"Despite all the uncertainty about what the future might hold, today... having been through so much with you, today has meant more than I ever imagined... it's... Five above, I don't even know what I'm trying to say."

"Are you trying to say that you have feelings for me? And I don't mean the contempt you had when we first met."

Caudro's head drooped as he contemplated Ami's allegation. She spoke as if in jest, yet his heart pounded. He could hardly deny his fondness for Ami grew ever since they met in the Nomridian Forest. Were it not for the lingering claws of the Quinarium holding him back, he might have sooner realized, sooner spoke of his feelings.

"Is it possible for a Human and a Fae to feel what I think I feel?" Caudro said. "I question if I feel this way only because I have lived a life so starved of affection, but something burns in my heart, deep inside, and it grows stronger every moment I am with you. Have I misunderstood your words? Have I misread your touch? Please, tell me if I have, and I will never speak of such things again."

"You are a stone-headed oaf of a man," Ami said. "I assure you, Humans and Fae are more than able to bond. At least if you trust the words of my grandfather, which I do."

"What will your people think?"

"I don't care."

"Is it so simple for you?" Caudro asked.

"Should it not be? I've spent my entire life treated as something less because of my birth, because of something I can't control. I'll happily make my choice and live with it."

"Would you have rather you were born with a short name?"

"No. If I were born among them, my life would have been far too simple, too dull to become such a delight," Ami said. "And what of you? Would you rather you weren't born an orphan?"

Caudro stood at the sound of water sloshing, followed by wet footsteps approaching. "Ami, I…"

"Yes?"

"I wouldn't change a thing about my past, if changing it would mean not meeting you." Caudro raised his hand, reaching out for Ami, then recoiled. "Not seeing you is a nightmare. I'm afraid that I might one day forget your face."

Ami took Caudro's hands and placed them on her cheeks. "I'm here. There's nothing to forget when I'm in your hands."

"Ami, I have never felt for another the way I feel for you. When I was locked away by the Paladins, my only light in that world of nightmares was the dream that I might see you again. The Five have blessed me more than any in all of Llendshold, that I have been able to spend these past days with you."

Ami gently touched Caudro's eyebrows. Her fingers lingered, tracing the outlines of his cheeks and down to his jaw.

"Caudro, you don't need eyes; you already see me."

Wrapping her hands around his neck, Ami pulled Caudro in. He moved slowly, uncertain in the dark; Ami guided him until he felt her breath against his skin. Held close, he gave himself over to her embrace. Ami lunged forward, pulling Caudro into a kiss.

They had hardly a moment to enjoy the embrace when bells rang through the village. Ami threw open a window to hear screams in the distance.

Screams and cries echoed into the night as Ami and Caudro ran through the streets with hoods pulled low over their faces. They reached the gates to find them shut; guards loitered about nearby.

"What's going on?" Ami spouted. "Why were the alarm bells rung? Why are you all standing idly?"

"Look at these two," sneered a guard. "Hoods low and carrying weapons like they're about to do something. Get back to your inn, or the alley, or wherever you planned to sleep. We locked the gates because the troubles are outside."

"Troubles?" Caudro said. "If there are troubles, why are you not riding out to provide aid? There are hundreds of people from the nearby hamlets camping out there!"

The guard and his compatriots laughed.

"If those people wanted our protection, they should have paid for lodging inside the walls," said the guard. "Protecting Dorslet is our job, not riding to fight whatever it is out there."

Caudro pushed the guard aside and strode up the stairs to the walls with Ami close behind.

"Hey! You aren't supposed to be up there," the guard said, stomping up the steps.

Though Ami saw little in the darkness, Caudro spied dozens of creatures swarming the encampment. A few harassed the carnival, though the carnival guards kept them at bay.

"Wyverns," Caudro said. "We have to help!"

"Wyverns?"

"Overgrown lizards. They're twenty feet long with scale-covered bodies, long tails, broad wings and no arms. Their legs are stout, with sharp claws, and their mouths are like that of an enormous bear. They don't fly well, but can jump to glide and are quite agile on their feet. They live in the mountains, usually hiding from capable foes, as a single Wyvern is not terribly difficult to fight. But they are clever hunters, and-"

"Right, enough lessons," Ami said. She glared at the guard marching up the stairs. "It's not our fight, but we can't leave the people to those monsters."

Caudro faced the approaching guard. "Will you not protect your fellow Humans of Llendshold?"

The guard laughed. "I already told you. They're outside the walls, and as such, are not our problem. They made their choice."

"Your Confessor will condemn this!" Caudro roared.

"Who do you think you are? The Voice of the Five?"

"Fine then. If you won't fight for them, I will. Open the gates!" Caudro demanded.

"First, he thinks he's the Voice, now he's trying to order us around like he's a Paladin," the guard said with a sneer. "Get off my wall."

"This way!" Ami called. "We'll get off your wall, you useless sack of pig shit!"

Ami tied the end of a rope to the ramparts, then threw the rest outside the village walls. She helped Caudro over, expecting the guard to complain, but he simply chuckled as they rappelled down.

Caudro broke into a run as soon as his feet touched the ground.

"Maybe we should have gotten the horses?" Ami yelled between heavy breaths.

"It would have taken longer to run back across the town. Besides, horses are scared of Wyverns."

Ami took a drink of mana as they ran and situated the arrows in her quiver. As they neared, the screeching of Wyverns sent shivers through their bones; no better were the cries of people fleeing from the beasts. The red-scaled Wyverns appeared in flashes, leaping into the light of torches around the encampment, only to disappear as quickly as they arrived.

"I can hardly see them," Ami panted as they paused between the carnival and the encampment.

"I see them all," Caudro said. "There are some thirty of them. It's a small group by the carnival. The cagey beasts are cycling in and out, making it seem like there are more of them than there really are."

"We could use those guards at the encampment."

"You're right. With every strike, the Wyverns are pressing in closer, and I don't see anyone armed or able to fight them. I'll rally the carnival guards. Do what you can to protect the others, but stay safe until I can join you!"

Ami grabbed Caudro's armor at the neck and pulled him close. She gave him a peck on the cheek, then sprinted for the tent city.

Caudro silently prayed to the Five that Ami would be safe as he ran to the carnival.

The guards brandished their clubs at first, uncertain of who approached in the night. Caudro sped past without a word. He leapt off a crate and landed on the back of a gliding Wyvern as it came into the light. He thrust his spear clean through the back of its head until the point burst through its mouth, spraying the field with black blood. The Wyvern's tail flailed one last time, then the beast fell limp.

Another Wyvern screeched as it charged over the ground, its wings outstretched. Caudro recognized the tactic: the creature attempted to look huge by holding its wings high, yet it left the Wyvern vulnerable and unsteady.

He grabbed his spear by the butt then swung, tearing through the Wyvern's wing. As it recoiled, he plunged his spear into its chest. Through the darkness, he spied a third, hunched low. When it charged, Caudro threw his spear. The blade sank deep into the Wyvern's side. It stumbled for a few steps before collapsing.

Caudro retrieved his spear then jogged back to the guards, who clumped together with elbows tucked close by their sides, their hands barely holding fast to their weapons.

"You all protected your people bravely, but please, join me!" Caudro said, banging his bloodstained spear against his chest. "We must protect the innocent people in the encampment!"

"Our job is to protect the carnival," stammered a guard.

"He's right. We're more practiced at throwing out drunks than we are using our weapons."

"How many of them are there?" pleaded a third. "There are only eight of us. What can so few do against so many?"

A scream pierced the night. Caudro watched as a Wyvern pounced on a man in the encampment. It reared its head, ready to strike, when Ami slipped out from behind a tent. She unleashed a hail of arrows, sending the beast flapping in retreat.

"Have heart!" Caudro said. "These Wyverns fly in from cover of darkness, attacking only where they believe none can fight back. Show these mindless beasts the strength in your arm, show these mindless beasts the valor in your hearts, and we will be victorious! Those willing, fight with me! Fight, and become the saviors you are destined to be!"

Ami stalked between tents, keeping low to avoid the attention of the Wyverns. A glimmer of light in the darkness caught her eye.

"Caudro?"

A Wyvern glided in with its wings stretched wide. Ami sent a barbed arrow flying. The Wyvern rolled to the side to evade the approaching missile, but the arrow arced tightly, striking it clean through the heart. Ami smiled as it crashed to the ground, when a gust of air rustled her hair.

She dove forward as jaws snapped shut inches from her neck. Ami looked back to see her bow on the ground between her and the crimson-scaled Wyvern. She hastily called on Mizaina and swept her hand. The Wyvern squawked and flapped its wings, backing away from the fog which rose from the ground.

Ami snatched up her bow as a Wyvern soared by. She nocked an arrow and sent it into the back of the passing Wyvern. Ami ignored its screeches of pain, turning her attention to a Wyvern which prowled through the encampment. It grabbed the crudely placed poles of a tent and ripped them away, revealing a little girl clutching her knees to her chest, sobbing and quivering.

Ami unleashed arrow after arrow as she marched towards the Wyvern. The beast crumpled in place; its tongue rolled out of its fanged mouth beside the child's feet.

Rushing to the stunned girl's side, Ami took the child's hands in hers.

"You'll be alright," Ami whispered. "Go there, under that cart. Hide until you're sure these monsters are gone."

When she was certain the girl was safe, Ami rose with an arrow nocked. Launching magic-empowered arrows until her thumb trembled and blood trailed down her hand, she grew furious as the attacks seemed never to cease. The Wyverns pressed in from all sides, ever more frequently.

A crash sounded as a Wyvern smashed through a row of tents. Thin fabric blew over torches, bursting into flame and shrouding the moon with smoke. Forced from their hiding places, people scattered throughout the encampment as the flock of Wyverns descended in unison. Despite unleashing arrows until her quiver was nearly empty, Ami's efforts did little to stem the tide.

To the right, three Wyverns surrounded a man. Ami winced as the beasts dove in, cutting the man's cries short. Across the encampment, a Wyvern glided in from the darkness and knocked over a fleeing group with its wings.

"Caudro, where are you!?"

Refusing to give in to desperation, Ami raised her bow when an enormous Wyvern landed mere feet away. She stumbled away from its snapping jaw, falling over a tent and losing her bow in the tangle of cloth and rope. Clambering up with her dagger drawn, Ami faced the Wyvern.

Its ridged, leathery skin shone brightly in the light of the torches. Rows of hand-length fangs dripped with saliva. The Wyvern's black, forked tongue flicked in and out of its snapping mouth. Wide eyes framed by tall brows glared at Ami. Black smoke billowed behind the Wyvern as it spread its wings and raised its head, poised to strike.

Ami ducked, but before it could lunge a spear pierced its wing and sank into its side. Caudro leapt in with a roar, rolling over the Wyvern's back with his sword drawn. He howled with fury, stabbing and hacking until he nearly decapitated the Wyvern. Its legs twitched even as the rest of its body lay still.

Standing over the beast, Caudro looked to Ami. "Are you alright?"

"I had things under control," Ami said, her voice shrill as she stared with wide eyes. "There are still so many though, I'm not sure if you and I-"

"For Erswein! For the Menagerie!"

The shouts of the carnival guards carried over the pandemonium which consumed the encampment.

"We are not alone," Caudro said with a grin, turning to the guards. "By the will of the Five, slay them all!"

Though the guards were far from battle-hardened, they proved capable fighters when following Caudro's orders. In a matter of minutes, they overwhelmed the Wyverns, killing more than half of the beasts before the survivors fled into the darkness.

Caudro and Ami stood at the edge of the encampment together while the guards jumped and cheered their victory.

"How are you?" Caudro asked, gently touching Ami's back.

"I have to say, my heart is racing a bit differently than I expected it to tonight."

Caudro beamed. "Regrettable though the interruption may have been, I long ago learned that days and nights with you rarely go as expected."

"Well, now that we've taken care of the Wyverns, I suppose it's time to head back to the inn. It's a shame we didn't ride the horses, I don't fancy a walk. Come to think of it, I don't think you've ever *seen* me ride." Ami stood on her toes and grabbed Caudro's arm tight as she whispered into his ear. "Maybe I can show you how I ride when we've returned to our room."

"Oh!" Caudro blurted out before wheezing consumed him. His face burned nearly as hot as the torches scattered throughout the encampment. "Well, I... I... ahem..."

Ami relinquished her grip when Plug's head hopped out of his pouch.

"Oh, my precious little friend, are you well?" she said.

Plug chirped as Ami pet him.

"I see how your pet, in all his heroism, aided you at every turn. How well he earned his praise," Caudro droned.

"Plug did precisely what I needed him to do: his mere presence gave me all the confidence I needed."

"I should have known it was you two," called a familiar voice. "Who else would leave the safety of the village walls and make themselves known in such a way?"

Ami and Caudro pulled their hoods back over their heads as they turned to greet Erswein.

"I apologize for commandeering your guards," Caudro said.

"Oh, no need for an apology! They are undoubtedly more capable fighters after this experience. And more than the brawn, but the brain! How confident they must feel having driven off the Wyverns. And more than your unnecessary apology, I owe you my thanks. In fighting the Wyverns here, you kept the fight far away from my lovely carnival. I am in your debt."

"You offered us a boat freely," Ami said. "Consider this our payment."

"The boat is to be a gift, and it would not be a gift if I accepted payment for it." Erswein looked around as villagers emerged from tents to survey the burnt wreckage and corpses littering the encampment. "Come, let us chat as we walk. The air around the carnival is more... not nosy."

Erswein snagged a lantern as they passed through the encampment. She waved as they exited and the guards stalled, leaving ample space for her to speak privately with Ami and Caudro.

"I think we are far enough from prying ears to speak openly," said the ringmaster, walking between the two. "Earlier today, I said that your purpose is something I shouldn't know. Having seen you fight, I find myself thinking quite the opposite. If you are willing, might you share your reason for sneaking across Llendshold?"

Ami glanced at Caudro and to see his brow furrowed. She caught herself wondering if his tendency to scrunch his eyebrows would fade now he could no longer see.

"We mean to tear apart the Quinarium before they can commit genocide against my people," Ami said. "We do this in support of Imreia."

Erswein went quiet for a moment, nodding her head like a chicken pecking at scattered seed.

"A name rarely spoken, and one only spoken in choice conversations. Quite the accusation you level against the institution which calls itself the conduit of the gods."

"It is not an accusation, it is a truth, heard by Ami and myself, among others. What is your opinion of Imreia?" Caudro asked.

"The idea of her intrigues me. Seeing as I have never met her myself, I cannot properly form an opinion. Though if you two are the likes of her supporters, then perhaps the Quinarium speaks ill of a person who does not deserve to be spoken ill of."

Ami grabbed Erswein's wrist. "You have Fae in your employ, and-"

"Achoo," Erswein said.

"I mean to say-"

"Achoo!" Erswein exclaimed, staring directly into Ami's eyes. "My sincere apologies. I'm allergic to details of matters which I have no business knowing the details of. You were saying, about the Quinarium?"

Ami took a deep breath to calm her anger. "You see, and hear, so much. You must know more than most any other person in Llendshold of the madness which embroils the Quinarium."

"The rot runs deep," Caudro followed. "Look at the refusal of village guards to protect their own people. Neither the Elder nor the Confessor ordered them to protect the innocent."

Erswein smiled wistfully. "You speak the truth."

"What then will you do?" Ami asked.

"My first and foremost and most forefront responsibility is to the Menagerie. These people trust me with their lives, and their trust would be poorly placed were I to speak openly against the Quinarium. And yet..." Erswein grinned impishly. "I might know a certain someone, who knows a certain someone, who knows some things about something to do with defying those who wish not to be defied. If I mention that a particular former Lord of Brewardsburg is involved, there are a fair few even among the carnival who will be excited to lend their *expertise.*"

"Your aid would be most appreciated," Caudro said.

"Please, temper your hopes. More than you two are in need of me."

Carnival workers crowded in the spaces between carts and stands, watching as the three approached with the guards in tow. Erswein smiled, then ran ahead. She climbed atop a carriage and addressed the onlookers.

"My wonderful people, this night we were saved from those contemptible, craven beasts by none other than these two fine travelers and our lovely guards. Let us shower them with their most deserved praise!"

Ami and Caudro shrank under the thunderous clapping and cheers, though the guards happily joined their compatriots to receive embraces of thanks. Erswein winked at the two, then raised her hands to calm the crowd.

"My dear friends. Let us celebrate. The Menagerie of Delight has concluded in Dorslet, we have survived the night with two new friends to join us..."

Erswein's voice trailed off as she looked to the village.

"My new friends, our dear saviors, I fear you must make yourselves scarce and miss our celebration. Your victory has attracted the attention of the Elder and Confessor of Dorslet, who are marching this way with a contingent of their entirely worthless guards.

"My friends, at times I have asked for your most essential discretion," Erswein said, addressing the carnival workers. "This is, in its entirety, one of those times. Gullico! Take our new friends to your carriage and hide them inside. Jerith, Aeron, when the village is properly slumbering, slip into *The Laughing Badger* and retrieve their belongings. The rest of you, let us make a show of celebrating our most wondrous guards, who drove away these beasts tonight, without the aid of any others. Everyone know your part? No questions? Then it is time to put on a show. Crack open the barrels, bring out the food, and make merry!"

The carnival workers flew into a frenzy. Tables appeared from nowhere, followed by food and drink of all kinds. Musicians played, acrobats somersaulted through the air, and dancers tapped across tables. Ami and Caudro had hardly a moment to gawk as a stout man pulled them across the carnival grounds.

Upon reaching the appointed carriage—an enormous construct near the size of a small home—Gullico unlocked the door and held it open for Ami and Caudro. He peeked inside after they entered, chuckling impishly as he swung the door shut. The carriage was unexpectedly well insulated, dulling the sounds of a wild party which filled the night outside.

Ami blinked until her eyes adjusted to the dark carriage, which was lit by moonlight creeping in through two small windows in the roof. A bunk bed was at one end; at the other, a small table and seating. Chests, racks, and hooks packed with bags crowded the space.

"I suppose we shouldn't light any candles," Ami said.

"Pointless for me anyhow. My vision has all but faded."

Ami unstrung her bow and stowed it in a corner with Caudro's spear before helping him out of his armor. When she unbuckled her belt, Plug leapt from his pouch to a high shelf and purred. Ami rifled through the carriage until she found a bladder of water and bits of cloth; sitting at the table, the two quietly cleaned themselves as best they were able.

"It seems that combat causes your vision to wane quickly," Ami said, scrubbing her neck.

"Yes. A mouthful lasts nearly a half-day when walking in the forest, but fades in mere minutes when fighting." Caudro traced the edges of the damp cloth, then mindfully folded it. "How do you think Erswein knew we had left our belongings at *The Laughing Badger?*"

"She is well connected, and seems reluctant to reveal any of her secrets. Something tells me she will be a powerful ally for Imreia, if not in ways that are outwardly visible. That feast out there rivals the finest of harvest celebrations in Keldarna. I don't believe for a second that it's only Erswein with secrets. The whole carnival is an oddity."

Caudro nodded. "Odd though they may be, Imreia needs all the support she can get. The Lords of Draethhold had such severe demands. Hopefully tearing down the Quinarium will lead to a lasting peace between both nations."

"It's more than the Quinarium," Ami said. "From everything I've heard, the Llendshold Regency is all but one with the Quinarium."

"A fair point. At times I could hardly tell where a Confessor's responsibility ended and an Elder's began," Caudro said. "It was much the case with Uldrik and Maren in Cauldhill."

"Maybe because it's more about power than responsibility. The Quinarium lusts for the fealty of all Humans."

"A problem for another day. I'm exhausted."

"You certainly exerted yourself tonight," Ami said, eyeing Caudro in the moonlight. "I didn't take you for such a leader. The guards followed your every command as if you were their captain of many years."

"A lifetime spent listening to Paladins barking orders. I might be daft, but I remember some of their ways; enough to emulate, at least. It was nothing more than modest encouragement to help them find their resolve."

Ami rose from her seat and sauntered over to Caudro. "As I recall, you were in the process of finding your resolve before we were so rudely interrupted by the Wyverns. Perhaps we should pick up where we left off?"

"Perhaps..."

Caudro wrapped his arms around Ami as she slid into his lap. She moaned softly as he pulled her close, hungering for her touch. Ami teased Caudro ruthlessly; again and again she brought her mouth a hair's breadth from his, only to suddenly pull away, until his neck craned and his hands clawed at her back.

Finally relenting, Ami locked lips with Caudro. Her every worry faded, as if being in his embrace shielded her from all the horrors of the world.

Ami leapt up as the door abruptly swung open and the sounds of the party flooded the carriage.

"Are you two alright?" a carnival worker asked.

"Yes!" Caudro squeaked, wiping his glistening lips. "Ahem! Yes, thank you."

A second worker peeked over the first's shoulder.

"The self-important idiots from Dorslet are making their way back to the village. Erswein is winding everything down. No point in wasting all the good food and wine when we'll be on the road in the morning."

The first of the two workers stepped inside and lit a candle. She grinned as Ami and Caudro looked away with flushed cheeks.

"Oh ho, sorry for the disruption! How was your time in the quiet dark of the carriage?"

"Move on in then!" called a third worker. "Oh, we'll be snug in here tonight! I don't mind the floor, just roll out a blanket; our guests can share a bed, we're short on them. That leaves one bed for you two; Jerith prefers sleeping on top of the carriage anyhow. I'll leave a blanket up there for him. My sincere apologies, our dear saviors. There's not much privacy to be had in a carriage!"

Chapter 15

A gentle rap on the door woke Ami. She grumbled and peeled open her eyes. The inside of the carriage glowed with a touch of orange. The air was stuffy. Looking down, Ami realized why she was uncomfortably hot: she lay atop Caudro, who slumbered peacefully. Although it was not quite the night she desired, she smiled at the peaceful calm on his face.

A knock came again.

Ami slipped off of Caudro and went to the door. She opened it a crack to see Erswein smiling.

"I thought you might like to sit beside me once we get these lazy oafs moving?" Erswein looked over Ami's shoulder as Caudro sat up. "You two rested among entertainers. The buffoons will sleep for many hours yet. Come, we have a glorious day ahead!"

Ami and Caudro groggily climbed onto the lead carriage. From the perch, Ami watched in awe, while Caudro listened. Erswein bustled about, barking orders, rousing sleepy workers, and tossing guilders and slices of candied fruits to those who moved with gusto. Tables and stands, banners and flags, fences and gates were folded and packed and loaded onto carts and into carriages. The carnival had seemed as well built as the walls of Dorslet, yet within minutes, beaten grass and a few holes in the ground were the only signs that remained.

Erswein hopped up onto the carriage. She gradually lowered herself between Ami and Caudro, forcing them to slide to opposite sides of the plush bench. Grinning all the while, the ringmaster unwrapped a parcel to reveal three miniature round loaves of bread. Handing one each to Ami and Caudro, Erswein tore hers in half, revealing a filling of roast vegetables and cheese. She took an enormous bite, then took up the reins. Without so much as a wiggle or a command from their master, the team of horses happily began their march, with the rest of the carnival following behind.

"If I might ask," Caudro said between mouthfuls, "how did you come to know so much about... well, everything?"

Erswein chuckled. "Much is a relative term, and everything is an all-encompassing one. Your question is a curiosity of all and some at once. But if you mean how I know so much about you, then it is simply my good fortune that I employ many a uniquely skilled worker, and they are all too happy to satiate my nearly insatiable curiosity.

"If you mean how I know so much about *other* matters—such as those pertaining to a certain former Lord of Brewardsburg—then it is because the plentiful wine and ale which fill joyful days and nights in the carnival have a wondrous way of loosening tight lips."

"You must have an endless supply of information," Ami said.

"That I do! The joy of extracting the unextractable from stalwart keepers of secrets, of turning the prudish pride of those who believe their knowledge to be safe only with themselves into blubbering tell-alls... it rivals my joy of leading this lovely carnival."

"We are most appreciative of your discretion, as well as for gathering our belongings," Caudro said.

"Think nothing of it!" Erswein said. "It's poor business to blab without purpose. Oh, now is as good a time as any to tell you we unfortunately were unable to recover your horses. It would seem the stable hands recognized the brand of the Evenswall guards. We thought it best to leave them behind."

"No matter about the horses," Ami said. "If it's not too uncouth to share, might you tell us your best bit of gossip?"

"Best is an entirely subjective! Hopefully my best satisfies your fancy, as I have heard many a tale over many years from many voices in so many places. I suspect my best will satisfy you, as my favorite rumors and secrets are those told by Agents of the Quinarium."

"Please, do tell!" Ami said.

Caudro sighed.

"Is something the matter?" Erswein asked.

"She is incorrigible."

"He means that I am curious and delightful," Ami retorted. "You were saying, about the Quinarium?"

"Word of the Moderators is unfortunately rare. They stay rather secluded, almost as reclusive as their superiors the Adjudicators. Well, there was the unfortunate end of the Moderator of Stellburg, which I presume you might know something about, though I wish to know no more of that matter than the little I already do. Meanwhile, rumors swirl around Mages and Paladins, so much so that I can hardly lend half a thought to more than half of what is said. The best stories are those about the Confessors."

"What makes those particularly enticing?" Caudro asked.

"Below the Moderators, above Mages and Paladins, as heads of Sanctuaries they have some power and control, yet none of them seem satisfied with their station. Being in the middle of all the things offers a unique perspective, and unique opportunities to match. The Confessors get up to the strangest of activities. Just yesterday I heard of a Confessor traveling all the way to Mordinlet and I cannot possibly fathom why. Quinarium festivities are held in the cities, not villages, and the Confessor of Mordinlet is alive and well. This particular Confessor also has no reputation for trysts in the night or any other acts of extravagance, which makes it all the more unusual."

Ami's eyes grew wide. "Which Confessor?"

"The one from Cauldhill."

Caudro nearly leapt from his seat. "That means-"

"It's Uldrik! Erswein, do you know when he left Cauldhill?"

"If the rumors are to be believed—and I only cite rumors which I believe—then he left three days ago."

"Do you have a map?" Ami asked.

"More than one. Here."

Erswein stuffed the last of her bread into her mouth, then spread a map across her lap.

"If Uldrik left from Cauldhill, he would likely stop in Stellburg," Ami said. "That makes this northern pass his most likely route. He would take the river road. It crosses our path at the confluence of these rivers!"

Erswein set aside the reins and leaned so close to the map her nose nearly touched it.

"If you take the boat I mentioned, then you should reach the crossroads at least a half day or so before Uldrik. I take it the Confessor is a person of interest to you?"

"He is one of the two behind the plot to incite the genocide of my people."

"Achoo," Erswein said slowly. "You'll have to excuse me, not sure what came over me. It's not important I know the little details about your little goings-on with this little Confessor from the little village... oh, which one was it again? As for the matter at hand, would you like for us to drop you off by the boat? It's no trouble, as we are on our way to Rushlet."

"Should we not make haste for Hantsburg, that we not delay what comes next?" Caudro whispered. "Besides, we are only two. What if Uldrik is well guarded? Mages might accompany him."

"Ha!" Erswein slapped her knee, then rolled up the map. "Confessors are far too low to warrant so significant an escort. I would wager no more than one or two guards, and no Mages."

"All the more reason to act now," Ami pressed. "We can stop him now, before he meets with Scireth. We have to do this."

Caudro nodded. "As you say. I'm with you."

"Ooh, my darling Fae, you have worked wonders on this handsome Human." Erswein chuckled. "It would seem we will part ways soon, as the road breaks away from the river. I wish you all the best. And perhaps some people I know might soon speak with some people you know about some things we all know need to be done."

"You have our most heartfelt thanks," Caudro said with a bow.

"I can hardly express how grateful we are," Ami followed.

"You two must stop! I will start to think far too much of myself if you carry on this way. I simply hope there is a day I can take the carnival to the Nomridian Forest without complaint from the Lords and Elders of Llendshold. You can thank me when that day comes!"

The boat, little more than a wide canoe, bobbed along the shallow, placid river. As Erswein had advertised, a quaint yellow flag at the bow flapped lazily in the breeze.

Thoughts of Uldrik had preoccupied Ami since they said farewell to Erswein and the carnival the day before. She hardly noticed the passing of time and spoke with Caudro only when necessary. A bee buzzed uncomfortably close to her ear before zipping away, drawing her attention to the landscape.

Birds flitted over the stubby, blue-gray grasses beneath a sky filled with streaky white clouds. Short coniferous trees with clusters of nettles along their twisted limbs clung to stones which pierced through the earth. A breeze carried a sweet floral scent from patches of bright pink flowers.

"Would you like me to describe our surroundings?" Ami asked.

"I'm alright," Caudro replied, smiling. "As with you, I have plenty on my mind at the moment."

"What did you make of Erswein?"

"I sense she is genuine. But why ask me? You're usually the first to assess others and are often reasonable in your judgement."

"Often reasonable? You mean I make judgements with impeccable correctness. Let me remind you, I thought positively of you while you were still a Paladin," Ami said. "Dastardly man though you may be, I agree with you about Erswein. I wasn't sure at first, seeing the entertainers making a mockery of the Fae, but I can't deny the act drew a large crowd."

"At first I thought the performer was a Human dressed as a Fae."

"I know my people when I see them, and there's no question that Erswein has a few of us in her employ."

Caudro tilted his head back, reminiscing about the day spent roaming the carnival. "I wonder how she managed to collect such interesting individuals? Creating the spectacle that is the Menagerie must have taken an age and a fortune."

"I find it more curious that you never heard of the carnival, which I am sure is famous throughout Llendshold."

"I blame the Quinarium."

"As do I."

Caudro grinned at Ami's frank declaration. "What do you suppose Erswein will do? Do you think she will aid Imreia?"

Ami stared at a passing cloud. "She gave us plenty of food and this boat, not to mention the bottles of mana."

"I wanted so badly to ask how she managed to get her hands on mana."

"You wanted to ask badly? Think of me! I about burst, holding myself back. Though, we were right not to question the gift. Somehow, I think mana is far from the oddest thing she has hidden away."

Ami's gaze fell on her pack. A buckle glimmered in the sun, reminding her of the tome inside. She felt suddenly overwhelmed, as though a veil of darkness wrapped around her mind and pulled tight.

"We found the tome a few days ago, yet it feels like it was a different life entirely," Ami said. "Strange that this journey is nearly at its end. I hope we've done enough to convince the Lords of Draethhold."

"Destroying the Paladin Fortress at Mordinlet will be enough to convince them. We cannot let the Quinarium start a genocide of the Fae."

They floated along until a sprawling inn came into view late in the afternoon. It was wider than three typical inns, with a stable by the crossroads and a dock stretching out over the river. Farms sprawled over the distant hills.

Ami secured the boat, then helped Caudro onto the pier. The crowded stables gave her pause, though she told herself that the stables of an inn at a major crossroads must often be full.

The door to the inn creaked open and Ami stepped inside.

She had never seen an inn so full. Visitors crowded around twenty tables, piling over each other on squat chairs and rough benches made of hewn logs. The innkeeper and three assistants ran about, struggling to control the chaos.

Ami waved and shouted repeatedly until the innkeeper finally bustled over. His eyes darted back and forth between Ami, who had her hood pulled low, and Caudro, who wore a band of cloth around his eyes.

"Welcome... All are.. All welcome... Right, welcome," the man stammered, his bushy mustache flopping up and down. He flinched when a dish shattered in the distance.

"Sorry, good sir," Ami said, her words sweet as fresh picked berries. "I unfortunately bear disfigurements which make my figure a disturbing sight. My partner here lost his eyes some years ago. Here we are, at your doorstep, one with working eyes who shouldn't be seen, and one with no eyes who's easy on the eyes."

"What can I do for you?" the innkeeper asked, his attention already drawn to a rowdy group at a small table.

"We need a room, and we docked our boat at your pier. First, though, it's been a long day. Might we have a drink and a meal?" Caudro said.

"Five guilders apiece," said the innkeeper. "Stew's hot. I'll grab you mead, as mead's all we've got. Oh, and only our smaller, second-floor rooms are open. You two will have to make do."

"Any room is splendid after days on the road!" Ami said cheerily.

The innkeeper motioned to a few of the only open chairs in the inn tucked against the bar, then bustled away.

"You spoke like Erswein," Caudro said as Ami helped him into his seat.

"I fancied the way she sounded, thought I'd give it a go," Ami said, her voice nearly lost in the din. "Kind of you to invite us to eat down here. We should have gone straight to the room."

"Rushing away to our room would have been conspicuous. No telling who is in the crowd. Besides, do you hear them? Most every soul in here is drunk halfway to the point of passing out. We'll be fine."

The innkeeper sped by, depositing two bowls of stew and two mugs of mead on his way. Ignoring the food, Caudro leaned close to a neighboring man and woman.

"Good day!" he shouted.

"Hm," the man and woman mumbled in reply.

"The inn is bustling today. What brings you here, fellow travelers?" Caudro asked.

"We're not travelers," said the man.

"Local farmers," clarified the woman.

"All the better then! We," Caudro said, motioning towards Ami, "are so used to seeing other travelers, it's good to meet with local folk. Well, Gurda here sees them, I only hear."

"Right..." the man replied. "Well, if it's the same to you, we'll get back to-"

"What brings you here today? It's not yet evening, and the inn is full of cheer."

"A Confessor is coming!" the woman replied.

"Five above!" Caudro shouted. "Gurda, you hear that? We are indeed blessed to be here! Do you know when the Confessor will arrive?"

"By all accounts, he should be here this evening."

"Gurda, hurry! We need to finish eating and clean up so we don't reek of the road. Wouldn't do to meet a Confessor in this state. Dear friends, thank you. As They speak!"

"So we listen!"

Ami smirked as they finished eating without further disruption, then made for their lodging.

The innkeeper's description proved apt: their room was simple, with two chairs beside a tiny square table, an old chest, and a single bed. Ami said not a word as she guided Caudro to a chair. She heaved the chest in front of the door, then set their packs on top. Plug emerged from his pouch at Ami's waist then dove into the depths of the bags.

"What was that scraping?" Caudro asked.

"Oh, I blocked the door to make sure we aren't interrupted," Ami said. "Quite the show you put on back there."

"I thought it was our best opportunity to find out when Uldrik would pass through. It's fortunate that word travels swiftly in places such as this."

"Did you really have to call me Gurda?"

"It was the first name that came to mind. Besides, an unpleasant name is hardly a slight compared to the stories you've crafted about me," Caudro said with a grin.

"I never took you for a sweet-talker."

"I can speak well enough, when the occasion calls for it."

"Hm," Ami hummed. "Strange how you've never thought to speak in such a way when you're around only me."

Caudro's mouth opened and closed repeatedly as he floundered over how to respond.

Ami giggled. "I'm going to wash up. There's no bath, but there is a bucket of water and cloths. Thankfully, it's a warm enough day. You should clean yourself too."

"We need to plan for Uldrik's arrival," Caudro said.

"There'll be time for that later. It's late enough in the day, and there's no possibility of him making it to another hamlet or inn before nightfall. He'll spend the night here, meaning our best opportunity to confront him will be in the morning, after he leaves. Now, clean up. There's water in the bucket by your feet and a cloth on the table."

Ami stared as Caudro undid the wooden toggles down the front of his tunic. He shuffled in the chair, lifting his tunic up to his waist. He froze, then tilted his head.

"Is there privacy?"

"Plenty."

Caudro lifted his tunic over his head, then folded the garment into a neat square. He set it aside, then dipped the washcloth into the bucket. Ami gazed with longing at Caudro. She had teased him relentlessly for being a big man, though he was, in fact, quite lean. Scars covered his body, permanent reminders of his time as a Paladin.

Ami cleaned herself as she watched Caudro, her chest rising and falling as her breaths deepened. His hands gripped the damp cloth tightly as he traced the outlines of his forearms, slow and methodical. Punctuated by dips into the water, he worked his way up his arm, across his shoulders, dwelling along his collar for a moment before wrapping around his neck and continuing down his other arm. Ami stifled a sign as Caudro scrubbed the smooth skin of his chest before descending to his abdomen.

Satisfied with his upper half, Caudro kicked off his boots. He slipped out of his trousers, folded them, and then placed them on his tunic before sitting again. Ami's eyes traced the tense muscles of Caudro's back as he scrubbed his legs. She washed her skin in rhythm with his motions.

Caudro sat back up, then set his cloth on the table. He reached for his trousers when Ami's hand darted out and closed tight about his wrist.

"Ami?"

"No. It's me, Uldrik. I've come early and decided to say *hello,*" she replied. "Of course it's me, you Ogre. Why call my name as if it were a question?"

"I thought you said there was privacy."

Ami's hand drifted up Caudro's forearm. *"We* are in private."

"What do you mean?" he asked, shivers running up his spine from her delicate touch.

"Sometimes I worry about you," Ami said, resting her hands on Caudro's chest.

"Worry?"

"Yes, worry. That perhaps you've forgotten how to think. It's been two nights since we were so rudely interrupted, but we have this moment now... nothing to interrupt us... and there's only one bed," she whispered.

Caudro groaned from Ami's breath in his ear and at the electrifying touch of her hands on his skin. "I see... I mean, I understand."

Ami kissed his cheek. "It's time for you to take what you've earned."

"I can hardly take what I cannot see, I-"

"Caudro, you have two hands, and you can feel. I am naked."

Ami grabbed Caudro's arms and wrapped them around her waist. Spurred on by her invitation, Caudro stood and leaned over Ami. His fingers pressed into her skin as he leaned in for a kiss when Ami ducked away. She giggled as he craned his neck, lips pursed, desperate to find Ami as she evaded his every move.

Ami slipped from Caudro's grasp, cackling as he reached out after. She grabbed him by the neck and pulled him into a deep kiss. He nearly fell over, his every muscle melting from the warmth of Ami's lips.

Caudro nearly cried out when Ami pulled away, but she gave him not a moment to think as she shoved him in the chest and she kicked his leg out from beneath him. Ami giggled mischievously as she dove after Caudro as he tumbled onto the bed.

"Yes, yes, blessings of the Five upon you all. May you always be in their light. Remember their words, and you will find peace. Be well!"

Uldrik slammed the door to his carriage shut. He exhaled in relief as he leaned back into his seat and brushed wrinkles from his purple stole and black vest. A sideward glance revealed a crowd of onlookers, still gathered outside the inn. Though

Uldrik reveled in the attention from a rapt audience during his sermons, the boors of the inn had tested his patience.

He pursed his lips and smiled thinly, then yanked a curtain over the window.

Minutes passed, and the sound of locals chatting and milling about grew louder. Uldrik slid across the cushioned bench and leaned out the opposite side of the carriage, only to find his driver and guard leaning down from their perch and happily taking gifts of bread and mead and cheese.

"What are you two doing!?" Uldrik hissed. "It is time to leave! We are on a schedule!"

The guard and carriage driver glared at Uldrik as he disappeared back into the carriage. They smiled and offered a final thanks to the kindly locals. With a shake of the reins, they were on their way, rolling down the packed dirt road.

The guard—a portly man whose buckles strained to hold his armor together—grumbled as a fog drifted over the road.

"Cloudy morning, and now this? I can't see shit," he groaned.

The weasel-faced driver snorted as she adjusted her grip on the reins. "At least the Confessor keeps to himself down there. I don't think I can stand much more of his rambling. Of all the people I've ferried around for the Quinarium—and I'm always on time, mind you—they had to stick me with *him.*"

"I was wondering the same. Who did I wrong to be stuck with this oaf? He couldn't even be bothered to properly smile to those locals. All they wanted was to show him some kindness."

"Fortunately, they were so blinded by his presence that I don't think they noticed his sour mood. Anyway, we should reach Mordinlet the day after tomorrow, on schedule. What's next for you?"

"I'm to join a trade caravan on its way back to Cauldhill. And you?"

The carriage driver sighed, leaning back in her seat. "We always receive our instruction when we arrive, never in advance. I'm hoping I'll be ferrying an Initiate to an Academy, and preferably a poor one. The job's always pleasant when you're hauling a wide-eyed newcomer with no notions about their status."

"Same for me, yet I somehow always end up on assignments like this. Makes for-"

A strange whistle sang through the fog.

"What was that?" the guard said, his head whipping back and forth like the arm of a metronome.

"You're the guard, not me!"

The driver pulled the reins, slowing the carriage to a stop. She grabbed a crossbow from beside her seat, then hooked a lever to its string. With a grunt, she drew the string back and locked it to the nut, then set the lever aside.

"Shouldn't we be speeding up?" the guard asked.

"Carriages are too slow to outrun riders on horses, so our best chance is for me to hit whatever's making that sound before it hits us. If I miss, you best be ready!" the driver said as she placed a stout bolt into the crossbow's groove.

The guard drew his sword as the whistle sounded again, this time from the opposite side of the carriage.

"That way!" shouted the guard.

"I know! Do you not see the end of my crossbow pointed properly at where the noise came from!?"

The whistle hummed from behind the carriage.

"There's more than one! Get us moving!"

The driver moved to snatch up the reins when an arrow flew in, pinning the strap to the carriage. The driver and the guard scrambled atop the carriage and stood back to back with their weapons at the ready.

"What in the name of the Quinate is going on out there?" Uldrik shrieked, leaning out of the carriage window.

"We're under attack!"

Uldrik retreated with a squeal as the whistle echoed through the fog. Hooves pounded from the left, then the right, and back and forth. The guard and the driver spun in place, avoiding each other's weapons as they tried to face the unseen foe. When the whistle steadily circled the carriage, the driver raised her crossbow. She squeezed the lever and the bolt flew into the fog.

The whistle abruptly ceased, and the stomping of hooves faded.

"Maybe you..."

"Five above, I think I did it!"

"You did it!" cheered the guard. "You-"

An arrow sailed in through the fog, striking the blade of the guard's sword and knocking it from his hand. The carriage driver's hands trembled as she attempted to hook the crossbow string with the lever when hooves thundered through the fog.

A man, wearing steel armor and with a glowing purple haze before his eyes, leapt onto the carriage from his galloping horse. A swift kick sent the crossbow tumbling to the ground. Before the guard could raise his hands, the man struck him squarely in the nose.

The carriage driver fell to her knees beside the fallen guard. Both raised their hands above their downturned heads as they pleaded and whimpered for mercy. Cackling broke through the fog as a woman rode out of the fog.

A few minutes later, the guard and driver sat wrapped in cord with their backs against a wheel of the carriage.

"I think we should deal with these two first," the woman said from beneath a low hood.

"I agree," the man said, readying his spear. "On your feet!"

The guard looked up; a trail of dried blood ran from his nose to his chin. "Please sir! Don't-"

"I said on your feet!"

The driver and the guard pushed against each other and the carriage, wobbling until they were finally upright.

The woman brought over two horses, then tied the reins to the driver's and the guard's bindings.

"Run back to the inn, and make sure these horses find their owners," the man said.

"Do you mean-"

"What about-"

"Rah!" the woman screamed.

The two wailed as they bolted down the road. The guard stumbled and fell on his face, crying out until the carriage driver returned to help him to his feet. After scrambling and wriggling his way up, the guard wordlessly fled into the fog, with the carriage driver close behind.

"Do you think I hit the guard too hard?" the man asked.

"His nose didn't look broken. He'll be *fine,*" the woman said. "With that taken care of, shall we see how our old friend is faring?"

Uldrik quivered inside the carriage. He sat on the floor, scrunched into a corner, too scared to look out a window, too scared to run. Shadows appeared over the curtains. Uldrik shrieked when the door swung open. The sun peeked from around the cloud in the distance, shrouding the faces of a man and a woman in shadow.

"Please! I am a Confessor!" Uldrik sobbed. "I promise you, the Quinarium will not seek retribution if you allow me to go free. May the light of the Five shine upon you, that you find mercy in your hearts!"

"What is that stench?" asked the man.

"That is the odor of a pathetic man who has pissed himself," the woman said with a groan.

"Lovely. How his tone has changed now he's outside of his precious Sanctuary."

"Your assurances, Confessor, would be more comforting were I not one of the people you aim to eradicate," the woman said as she leaned against the door frame and pulled back her hood.

"A Fae!" Uldrik squeaked.

The man took one step into the carriage and leaned forward until his face became clear. "You, dear Confessor Uldrik, have encountered the two of the worst imaginable people for you in all of Llendshold."

"You... you were Scireth's Trainee!" Uldrik said, pointing with a finger weighed by gold rings. "The dissenter. The abandoner. The one stolen from Mordinlet!"

"Stolen?" Caudro challenged. "You speak as though I were property."

"What is a Paladin if not a tool of the Quinarium? Though you turned out to be a deformed piece of slag," Uldrik said with a dismissive scoff.

"He really is a mouthy one. What to do with him, I wonder?" Ami said.

"We can't deal with him as simply and swiftly as we did his escort."

"Quite right. The Confessor thinks himself special. We should provide a *special* treatment."

"What did you do to the others?" Uldrik stammered. "Please... please don't torture me."

"It's no less than you deserve," Ami spat. "Lucky for you, we aren't a part of the Quinarium, for whom acts such as torture and genocide are commonplace."

"You weaklings!" Uldrik roared. "You are too late! No matter what you do to me, the Fae are finished! Too much is in motion. None can stop the coming of the righteous cleansing!"

"Maybe we should reconsider our stance on torture," Caudro said casually.

Ami nodded. "Come to think of it, we never established an official position. I'm sure Imreia would be fine if kept the torturing to Confessors and the like."

The color drained from Uldrik's face as he pulled his urine-stained legs in tight. "Did... did you say..."

"Imreia? Old friend of ours," Ami said with a wink. "We should get moving. We have a long day ahead if we're to make it to our rendezvous before nightfall."

"Should one of us stay in there with him?"

"I refuse to share a carriage with a piss-soaked pile of filth," Ami said. "Let's bind his hands and mouth. He'll survive the day well enough on his own."

CHAPTER 16

The carriage rolled on through the uneventful day. Despite Ami and Caudro's appearance, not a single traveler stopped to wonder where the duo was taking a Quinarium carriage. The reins sat limp in Ami's hands as the horses happily trotted on the stone-paved road. Ami scooted close to Caudro, then leaned her head on his shoulder.

"Can you tell me what you see?" he asked.

"Your hands," she replied, running the tip of a finger across his skin with the gentlest of touches. "They're conjuring memories of last night..."

Caudro swatted away Ami's hand. "I mean our surroundings!"

"How boring," Ami said with a dramatic sigh. "Well, if you must know, the river beside us is quite beautiful. As I'm sure you can hear, it has grown wide. Its waters run deep and blue. Reeds crowd along the banks. There are little yellow flowers atop the stems, surrounded by butterflies. I'd prefer a forest, but I have to admit the fields are beautiful. The grass is waist high, wavering in the wind."

A tear rolled down Caudro's cheek.

"Are you alright?" Ami asked, squeezing his arm.

"Yes," Caudro said, turning his head as if gazing over the world around them. "The loss of my eyes is painful at times, yet my blindness is a fair penance."

"Penance?"

"Yes, penance. I don't know if I can ever repay the debt I have incurred for serving as a Paladin."

"They took you as a child. It's hardly your fault."

"Fault doesn't change my actions," Caudro said. "I served the Quinarium willingly."

"Ah, I understand now," Ami said. "You're the one I should blame for planning the genocide of the Fae. I wonder what that makes me for bedding you?"

"You would call what happened last night bedding me?"

"You sound as if you think it were the reverse."

Caudro grinned. "I seem to recall some details-"

"If I hadn't approached you wearing nothing at all and told you I was wearing nothing at all and pushed you, quite literally, then you would still be hiding behind a curtain!"

"There's the fire I so adore. Maybe if we conjure the image of a former Paladin and a Fae intertwined, Scireth will simply die?" Caudro said.

"A Fae and a former Paladin together will be sure to shock many," Ami said.

"I wonder what Hawel will think of us?"

"I don't think the old codger could possibly think less of me," Ami said, pulling at a loose thread on her sleeve. "He would probably say it's entirely expected."

"How can Hawel think so poorly of you? He must be blinder than I am."

"It's not only him. Most all of my people think this way of me," Ami whispered. "Maybe one day I break free from the notion that lowborn Fae can't achieve greatness. Maybe they'll finally see me as someone worthy of adoration."

"You are that and more to me."

"Right, and as soon as the Fae care about the words of Humans, it'll be fantastically helpful that you hold me in high regard," Ami said as she jokingly punched Caudro's shoulder.

"I wonder what caused Humans and Fae to grow so distant? Is the Quinarium responsible for such a rift?" Caudro said.

"I don't know if the Quinarium is the sole perpetrator, but I can't imagine it took much to drive our people apart. It's easy to make minor differences seem larger than they are. Since you're asking me, I'd wager the Quinarium was happy to nudge things along. Spreading rumors, pointing fingers, whispering about the evils of the Fae..."

"A shame."

"What's brought this about?" Ami asked, nuzzling into Caudro. "Has a recent experience perhaps made you feel differently about the Fae?"

"It would be a lie to say the experience was anything but life altering."

Ami grinned. "Keep being a good partner and you'll have plenty more life-altering experiences."

Caudro wrapped his arm around Ami. "Are you trying to motivate me? Because if you are, I assure you, the tactic is highly effective."

"I know it's not you who needs convincing," Ami said, poking Caudro in the ribs. "I'm worried about Imreia. Hopefully, she sees things as we do."

"She will."

Hantsburg came into view as they crested a hill in the late afternoon. The unmistakable scent of ocean air greeted them. Farms stretched across the land, nearly to stone walls of the city which dominated a broad plateau by the shore. Ship masts punctuated the horizon, hurrying for the docks as the setting sun cast the tops of waves in gold.

"Strange we'll be walking right under the nose of Wynne's mother," Ami said.

"I've heard a great deal about Lord Pharadrax. She has a reputation for being pragmatic and cunning, yet also the most soft-hearted of the Lords."

"I somehow doubt she'll be soft and merciful, should Imreia be caught."

"There are precious few alive who know what Imreia looks like," Caudro said. "Unless she goes around advertising herself, I'm sure she—and we—will be fine."

"Have you forgotten who we are? I'm a Fae and you still bear the Paladin's brand on your wrist."

"We'll have to trust Imreia's contact. She has Dara and Wynne's trust, and I have to believe we can trust her, too."

Ami inhaled the salty air. "Of all the things, the ocean is making me homesick. It reminds me of Vouliona... I suppose it makes sense. They are the same waters, after all."

"Homesick..."

"What? Because I'm a bit of a pariah, it means that I can't be homesick?"

"Not at all. It's just that I never thought of being homesick before. I'm not sure I even know what it means to be homesick, or even have a home, really. Paladins took me in as a child, and service to them consumed my childhood. They claimed to be giving me purpose, when in fact they stole what it meant to be me."

Ami swung her legs onto Caudro's lap as she snuggled against his chest.

"Maybe I can help you find a place to call home, if the Nomridian Forest is still standing after all this. And assuming we survive. The Fae do love taking in strays, like the Dwarves. Why not add a reformed Paladin to the list?"

"What future are we even heading towards?" Caudro pulled Ami in close. "We are taking the gilded tome to a woman who claims she wants nothing more than to tear down the Quinarium and reclaim her rightful seat as Lord of Brewardsburg, yet all I see in her is a lust for revenge."

"Is the revenge such a problem if it's directed towards the Quinarium?"

"I wonder the same about myself," Caudro said. "Since leaving the Paladins, I have existed to stop the Quinarium. If we are victorious, then what will be left of me?"

"Your future will finally be your own. What to do will be your choice, and yours alone."

"You make it sound simple."

Ami exhaled through her mouth. "I spent many, many hours alone in the forest, to the degree that my people think I'm crazy. Perhaps it's a touch crazy to believe it can be simple for you, but it is what I believe."

"If you are a touch crazy, then perhaps it is time for me to leave my past behind and try being a touch crazy, too."

The carriage eased to a stop outside an inn a half hour's ride from the walls of Hantsburg. A man waved lazily from his perch atop a stack of crates.

"I wasn't expecting a carriage," he said in a thin and raspy voice.

Ami glared at the man. He was middle-aged, with thick eyebrows and a slender jaw. A surly look was pasted on his face.

"Loraen, I take it? We have plenty to tell you."

"Tell me inside."

The man hopped from his perch and waited for Ami and Caudro to descend.

"We need to address the contents of the carriage before we go in," Caudro said.

"And the contents are?"

"Uldrik, the Confessor of Cauldhill and conspirer against the Fae. We intercepted him while he was on his way to Mordinlet," Caudro said.

Loraen wiped his brow on his sleeve. "This was not a part of your task. This is a distraction, a waste of time, and will not be simple to deal with."

Ami stood with her hands on her hips. "Excuse me, but given what we are trying to do, we thought it prudent. If we only perform assigned tasks at the direction of... her... then we are being entirely shortsighted. We had to capture him when the opportunity presented itself, given he is one of the two main conspirators against the Fae."

"It was reckless."

"As is being in Hantsburg. We could have met her out here. I support her only because she is a pathway to protect my people. I will not bow to her as though she is the Regent of Llendshold and I am a peasant Human."

"Can you take care of him?" Caudro asked.

"I'm sure she will have something in mind. I will ensure he is held appropriately in the meantime."

"Right then, inside it is," Ami said.

Loraen led to the cellar of the inn, taking position on the opposite side of a small table.

"You are the last ones," he said. "The rest are already in the city, waiting for you. As they have been, for some days."

"I wager it's been a touch awkward for Wynne," Ami said.

"You needn't worry yourselves about Wynne or the others. Instead, worry about your own tardiness," Loraen chided. He was entirely unbothered as Plug popped up from the pouch at Ami's waist and hissed ferociously.

Caudro leaned forward on hearing Ami inhale sharply. "I assure you we came with all possible expedience. I understand you have papers for us, that we might enter Hantsburg?"

"The contents of the carriage show that you did not come with all possible expedience."

"It was hardly a half day's delay!" Ami spewed. "Now, give us the papers!"

"I was instructed to see the tome first."

"I already sent word that we recovered it," Ami said.

"It is simply confirmation," Loraen said, dragging his words. "No need to be so defensive."

"What if we weren't successful?" Caudro asked.

"Then Imreia would have dispatched others to retrieve the tome, and you would not be entering Hantsburg."

"You mean to hold this over us?" Caudro fumed. "After all we've done for Imreia, she-"

A thud on the table interrupted his rage.

"There."

"Thank you, Ami," Loraen said, running his hands over the gold binding. He cracked open the cover to peek inside, then swiftly closed it again.

"Satisfied?" Caudro asked.

"Yes. Here are your papers," Loraen said, handing over two squares of folded parchment. "Do not let go of them. Lord Pharadrax is more lenient than the other Lords in enforcing this new requirement, yet we cannot expect her leniency to be universal. Agents of the Quinarium linger about, and they hunger for any reason to cause trouble, as if harassing commoners is somehow exacting revenge for the culling of the Moderator of Stellburg. If you lose your papers, you will be assumed to have involvement in his death, and will at best be imprisoned."

"We'll keep them near to our hearts," Ami said.

"Do not treat this matter lightly. It is especially perilous for the two of you. If found without papers, or if your identities are revealed, the result will be cataclysmic. Now, hurry along. Imreia is waiting. You'll find saddled horses outside. If asked, you are delvers in search of a new contract, which should provide sufficient reasoning for your appearance. Caudro can lean on you, Ami, owing to a wound for which you will seek a healer."

Ami pursed her lips. "That's a rather underhanded way of saying we look a mess."

"I could speak plainly if you prefer."

"And here I was, thinking you had a kind face, until you spoke."

Caudro smirked, though Loraen remained unmoved.

"You are to make for the house of Broderick. I've marked it on this map. The distance from the gate is slight. Do not tarry. Do not delay. They are expecting you."

Caudro swayed side to side as his horse ambled along the stone-paved road. The ocean breeze tugged at his tunic. The squawking of gulls and terns intensified as they neared the city. While the sound of waves crashing and rolling onto the beach was comforting, Caudro couldn't shake the growing tension in his neck and shoulders.

"We're nearly there," Ami said.

"You sound unsteady."

"I'm a Fae, riding into a Human city, with the knowledge that some, if not many, of those inside would happily see my people eradicated. Of course I'm unsteady."

"I would like to think the people of Hantsburg differ from those poisoned by the words of Uldrik and Scireth," Caudro said.

"And yet those two were beyond certain that all of Llend-shold would gladly unite to destroy my people."

Caudro's brow furrowed. "From her reputation, I can't imagine Lord Pharadrax would support such a thing."

"Then why would she have Mind Mages posted at the gates?" Ami said, slowing their pace.

"Perhaps it was not her decision. Whatever the case, we have to trust the echoes of Almoya, that our minds are warded from the intrusions of such Mages."

After stabling their horses, they approached the gate. Caudro wrapped his arm around Ami and pretended to lean on her, though she felt not the slightest bit of weight on her shoulders. Before they reached the entryway, a guard strolled out to meet them.

"Let's see your papers," she said, not questioning the hoods covering half their faces.

Ami passed the bits of parchment over.

"Please don't mind the Mages. The Quinarium types can't help but stick their fingers in near everything, but they mean well enough," the guard said as she scanned the papers. "Coming from Evenswall? I hope the journey treated you well, and you find what you need in Hantsburg."

Ami and Caudro offered their thanks, then marched to the gate. The Mind Mages frequently motioned for passersby to stop, though Ami and Caudro walked by without incident.

"I think we made it," Ami whispered, leaning close to Caudro as they pressed through a bustling street. "Strange how the guard spoke of the Mind Mages."

Caudro tilted his head. "It's as though the Quinarium is overstepping. I wonder if what happened in Brewardsburg so long ago kept the other Lords in line and the influence of that event is fading, or if perhaps Hantsburg is unique in its distaste for the Quinarium's reach?"

"If Wynne's mother is the influence which leads the guards to say such things, then she had better be cautious lest she end up like Imreia's parents."

Caudro closed his hand around Ami's shoulder as she pulled ahead. The bumpy cobbled streets felt strange beneath his feet after weeks spent traipsing through forests and across fields. Voices reverberated off stone walls in every direction. Thousands roamed the city, and the crowd seemed to press in from every direction.

Buskers enticed onlookers at every turn. Caudro smiled, imagining the performances which elicited cheers and applause. They passed shops with open windows stuffed with arrangements of fragrant cut flowers, still bearing the scent of freshly disturbed earth. A door opened and the smell of baked bread flooded Caudro's nose; his stomach churned with hunger.

Ami pulled onward, and a few minutes later the bustle of the city eased and they heard the ocean waves again.

"Finally, some plants," Ami said.

"Have we arrived?"

"Yes. The manor is enormous. It's three stories tall, with an iron gate around a courtyard full of short trees and flowers. Not many windows, though. I'm not sure if we're supposed to go in or we should knock. I wish Loraen-"

The door to the manor opened and a young woman wearing a simple cream-colored tunic bustled out. She crossed the garden with her hands clasped over her stomach. Her head was remarkably still, despite her wobbling gait.

"You are expected," the woman said, her voice stern despite her tunic's mid-thigh hem. "Please, follow me. Broderick is waiting, as are the rest."

"Are all of Imreia's friends this brusque?" Ami whispered to Caudro as the woman opened the gate.

"Please do not speak that name until we are inside," the woman said, heading to the manor without a backward glance.

Ami's mouth dropped as she passed the threshold. A cavernous foyer greeted them; the ceiling stretched up the full three stories. A gilded shrine to the Five was tucked between two sweeping staircases covered in ornamental woodwork.

"I will take you to your room first, where you will find food and clean tunics," the woman said. "Please make yourselves presentable. When you are ready, I will take you to the meeting. Might I remind you, your presence is long overdue. Please do not keep the others waiting any longer than is absolutely necessary."

"Well, excuse me..." Ami's voice trailed off as the woman marched up the stairs.

Caudro took a drink of mana upon reaching the room that he might ready himself without burdening Ami. Ignoring the opulence of the space, they wiped away dust and sweat from their faces. Plug, meanwhile, glided around the room before curling into a tight ball on a plush pillow.

Ami stared at the tunic she was to wear. The fabric promised to be soft and light, and bore a delicate black and green trim. She scooped up the garment and yanked it on, fussing over the fit despite the tunic being all but perfectly tailored to her frame.

As ready as she would ever be, Ami retrieved the wrapped tome from her pack. She lay it on a bed and gently unfolded the cloth. Tears threatened to flow from Ami's eyes as she stared at the gilded cover.

Caudro wrapped his arms around Ami and held her tight.

"I'm with you."

Ami and Caudro marched down the halls after the young woman. Thick rugs and hanging tapestries dulled their footsteps. Candles atop silver trays on furnishings and in wall sconces provided a calm, muted light. They passed the occasional servant, but none spoke a word.

Caudro's heart raced. The march reminded him of his time as an orphan, walking the halls of the Sanctuary. The short-tempered Confessor detested the sounds of children, even their breathing. Each infraction would lead to punishments ranging from lectures to the assignment of unpleasant chores, all done in the name of the Quinate.

A bright floral scent reached Caudro's nose. Ami had found a tiny bottle of perfume in their room and giddily applied it to her neck before departing. Though Caudro hardly understood her elation, the refreshing scent comforted him greatly. While the fragrance calmed his nerves, he wished Ami felt at ease; her increasingly erratic and heavy breathing betrayed her mood.

They finally reached a dining hall, dominated by a long, narrow table designed to fit twenty people. The ornate carvings and polished surface of the table were so dazzling that the room itself seemed to be built in honor of the table. Cabinets and shelves surrounded the room, topped with candles, vases, paintings, and other useless yet pretty decorations.

Imreia sat at the left end of the table, with Okter sitting by her side nearest the door, while Dara, Wynne, and a Draethhold Captain, who Ami recognized as Owain, sat on the far side. Broderick, despite being the owner of the manor and their host, sat in an unceremonious position a few seats away from Owain. They all wore ornate clothing similar to Ami and Caudro; while Wynne looked quite at home, Dara sat rigidly with her elbows pinned at her side.

Ami grinned broadly and waved at Dara and Wynne, who shared her joyful expression. Noting the two seats pulled out beside Okter, Aim and Caudro took their places.

Peering inside a trio of glasses, Ami spied wine, water, and ale. She took Caudro's water glass and slid it close to him, then took a sip of wine as Imreia opened the meeting.

"Welcome, Ami and Caudro. I am overjoyed to see you well."

Ami faltered; Imreia was nearly unrecognizable in a formal tunic made of fine cloth with delicate detailing. The brusque, harsh warrior she was accustomed to was now disarmingly gracious and elegant.

"We didn't expect such a welcome," Ami said.

"Are we certain this is a safe place to meet?" Caudro asked.

Broderick stood and bowed low before returning to his seat.

"My manners, goodness, my apologies! I left it for my guest to welcome you. How uncouth. Allow me to introduce myself properly. I am Broderick, a humble Earl of Hantsburg. Welcome to my home. I assure you we are quite safe, or at least as safe as such company can be in Llendshold.

"Regarding my staff, I personally vet every person under my roof and provide for substantially to ensure their loyalty. I designed this manor for privacy and solitude first, and comfort second. In my role as Earl, I spend many hours petitioning for action to be taken to either verify Imreia is dead or to find her and make her so—more of the latter, since the Moderator of Stellburg's passing—to ensure the Quinarium considers me an ally. I am often mocked for my zeal, but it has earned me freedom from scrutiny. And so, please, trust, you are safe in my company. Excuse me, I grow long-winded, when I am here to host and listen, not speak. Imreia?"

"Thank you, Broderick. Caudro, your time with me has been shorter than the rest, but you need only ask Dara, Wynne, and Ami. You can trust me. I only enter dangerous situations when I am certain victory is certain, as is the case today. Wynne, will you please provide a recounting of our efforts?"

"Oh, right!" Though she was used to the performing before high audiences, Wynne was caught quite off guard by the request, given Imreia had been present for their activities. "Imreia, Dara, and I laid the groundwork for a steady and reliable supply of mana. It turns out there are many Mages dissatisfied with restrictions placed upon them by the Quinarium. In meeting with carefully selected contacts—many of whom were found courtesy of Okter and Broderick—we secured agreements to siphon mana from shipments destined for Academies and Sanctuaries, in exchange for ample payment and protections once conflict begins."

Dara took hold of Wynne's hand. "Further, there are a few Quinarium carriage drivers who assured us that the occasional bottle gone missing in transit is hardly of notice. Fishers in Bramswall, who are friendlier with the people of Draethhold than most, gladly accepted a deal to transfer unopened packages to Draethhold ships."

"I have to admit I was worried at first," Okter said, smirking as he gazed at Imreia out of the corner of his eye. "Each of these sources—Academy shipments, Sanctuary stockpiles, shipments on carriages—is miniscule on its own. However, in total they should be sufficient. As for progress in Draethhold, it was similarly sufficient. Rhoslin and I spoke with dozens of Mages, most of whom saw reason. The others will see the truth in time. While the Quinarium maintains a sizeable advantage, our force is substantial and will only grow as the dissenters fall in line."

"Fall in line? You mean by force, or coercion?" Caudro challenged.

"Neither." Okter's voice boomed as he slammed his ethereal hand onto the table. Recovering his calm, he leaned back into his chair. "I am no longer a part of the Quinarium, and as such, I will no longer employ their methods. Seeing Rhoslin's prowess so early in her training is all the convincing the Mages of Draethhold required; they desire the same power, and through me they shall have it."

"So they are mercenaries?" Ami asked.

"Tools, and ones which are necessary for war," Imreia replied. "Mages are in short supply. We require many to fight the Quinarium. I care not how we recruit them as long as they are dependable in a fight."

"A host of Mind Mages is ready to fight for you, but we must liberate Bavenhill first," Caudro said.

Imreia squinted. "Bavenhill? You mean to liberate the entire Academy of Almoya?"

"I see you met with Anghara," Okter said. "I assume it was a fruitful meeting, given the haze before your eyes."

"It was fruitful in many ways. The Mind Mages are all but enslaved by the Quinarium. I swore to free them, and they pledged to support you, Imreia," Caudro said.

"We should speak on this further, though now is perhaps not the right time," Okter said, raising a finger to his lips.

"I swore on my life."

"I would see your pledge honored, but such a task involves many details, details which must wait," Imreia said. "We have more pressing matters to attend to. Ami, Caudro, we await only your report."

Caudro gave Ami's thigh a reassuring squeeze under the table as she inhaled deeply. Sweat beaded on her brow.

"We overcame all the trials in the Ziggurat of the Fallen," she said.

Imreia smiled hungrily. "Yes, and according to your message, you recovered the tome. Shall we see it?"

"I'm surprised the dragonfly made it," Ami said, still holding the tome tight.

"I told you they were reliable," Wynne said with a smirk.

"You'll have to excuse me, but sending a message to a Llendshold city via a Quinarium Mage's methods is still questionable, if you were to ask me, which no one did," Ami said as she slid aside glasses to make room.

"Not as though you could have used whistling gourds to send word," Dara said, suppressing a grin.

"You two are incorrigible!"

Ami set the gilded tome on the table.

"A prized token of Draethhold," Broderick said as he stood and craned his neck for a better view. "This is a powerful bartering tool indeed."

"A gift, as it were," Imreia said. "You two are to be commended for your efforts. I understand it was no simple task to recover. Thank you."

"You speak as if it were yours," Caudro said, his brow furrowed. "We have conditions."

"Oh?" Imreia glanced at Okter, then to Dara and Wynne. A grin broke across her face. "I am becoming quite accustomed to conditions. And what might yours be?"

"The show of strength... it must take place at the Paladin Fortress at Mordinlet," Ami said.

"And on whose authority *must* this happen?" Imreia said, her words as cold as a winter storm.

"The authority of the one holding this tome," Ami said, placing her hand on the gilded cover.

Imreia glared at Ami. "Broderick has been a most gracious host. Let us not make a scene in his home. Need I remind you, we are allies."

Ami jumped up from her seat. "I will not support you if we will not take the course of action which best protects my people!"

"The best, and only, way to protect your people is to cut the head off of the Quinarium. We must do this with unemotional precision," Imreia said, unmoved from her chair. "You speak with an emotional plea. It is one I hear and empathize with, especially as one who lost nearly everything to the Quinarium. However, I cannot let your feelings influence the most strategic course of action. Such is war."

Caudro stood beside Ami. "It is not an emotional plea! This would stall the Quinarium's planned genocide while we gather our forces and make that decisive strike."

"This is, without any question, an emotional plea. Look inside yourself too, Caudro. Are you not influenced by your own desire for revenge?"

"I assure you revenge has nothing to do with it!" Caudro said, his fists tightening. "I am focused on the injustice, the immorality of even considering a different target, which would mean abandoning the Fae!"

Imreia snorted. "Do you mean the Fae, or is there perhaps one Fae in particular you're speaking of?"

"If I may," Okter said as he swirled his glass of wine, "allow me to return us to the task at hand. We have already narrowed the options to two: the Quinarium's naval garrison at Rushlet, and the Paladin Fortress at Mordinlet. Destroying either would be a substantial blow. It is true that the fortress is the better fortified of the two. However, it is also more important to the Quinarium. If we destroy their navy at Rushlet, they will simply buy or borrow what they need from the Regency. Further, killing a high-ranking Paladin such as Scireth would send a profound message to the Quinarium and the Lords of Llendshold and Draethhold alike. I believe we should strike the Paladins."

Okter's proclamation stunned Ami and Caudro.

"I agree," Dara said, locking eyes with Ami and offering a reassuring smile. "Further, we've learned the Quinarium has worked hard to twist the truth of what happened to the Moderator of Stellburg. The events taking place in a Hamlet, with no witnesses, made their task easy. The destruction of a Paladin fortress would be impossible to hide."

"My vote is for Mordinlet, if we are indeed voting," Wynne followed. "If you remember, Imreia, your pledge to Dara and I included doing all we can to avoid harming innocent people.

The Quinarium facilities are interspersed with those of civilians in Rushlet. It would be difficult to avoid harming those who deserve mercy."

Imreia's face remained stoic. She took a long, slow drink of wine.

"Owain," she said, looking to the Draethhold Captain, "you've been quiet this evening. Might I trouble you for your thoughts?"

"Twenty Draethhold warriors wait on the ship, along with a few Fae and Dwarf volunteers. Our force is modest, even with many Mages at our side. I don't trouble myself with thoughts of surviving, but I wonder if we have a force necessary to overtake a stronghold of Paladins. Would the docks not be a more prudent target?"

"We can more than take the fortress," Ami said.

Owain blinked slowly. "Are you so sure?"

"I saw the fortress end to end when I freed Caudro. I am certain such a force is capable of destroying the garrison. We will have to be smart in our approach, but it can be done."

"It seems there is consensus, then. We sail for Mordinlet tomorrow," Imreia said. "I have some further business I would discuss with Owain, Broderick, and Okter. Why don't you old friends share a meal? Catch up, and enjoy each others' company."

CHAPTER 17

Ami stared at the opulent spread of food before her: curls of steam rose from a creamy stew which smelled of exotic herbs, roast vegetables dressed in a bright red oil still sizzled, stacked loaves of bread had a variety of sliced onions pressed into their surface in the shapes of flowers, and many more dishes aside.

"Are we really safe here?"

"We're fine, Ami," Wynne said, ladling soup into bowls. "My mother spoke often of the Earls. She considered Broderick trustworthy, though his apparent obsession with Imreia was an annoyance."

"Perhaps he is too forward with his act," Dara said. "I understand your concern, Ami, though we've been here a few days and Broderick appears to be genuine. I was more worried about you two getting into Hantsburg."

"The guards here are quite different from those elsewhere in Llendshold," Caudro said, chewing on a morsel of bread.

"I was close with a few of the guards, enough so that I had some concern one might recognize me," Wynne said. "My mother made it a point to befriend all those in her employ. She said that by seeing people for who they are, and showing them a bit of yourself in return, you can win lifelong loyalty. And for those who are loyal, it is appropriate to set high standards and offer high rewards."

"Didn't realize we were here for lessons. Speaking of high rewards... Do they extend to Dara? Or perhaps you might call them low rewards, depending on the where and the how of your delivery?" Ami said with a smirk.

"Ami!" Wynne exclaimed, her cheeks flushing bright.

Dara grinned as she speared a chunk of crisp potato.

"I'm sorry for her," Caudro said, shaking his head.

"I can apologize for myself, should I say or do something worth apologizing for," Ami said indignantly.

"It must be strange for you to be here, Wynne," Caudro said.

"Yes... I can't imagine the questions my mother faced after Dara and my departure from the Quinarium. Maybe one day I can walk the streets with her again."

Dara brushed an errant strand of hair from Wynne's face, then gently stroked her cheek.

Ami took a bite from a rolled pastry stuffed with finely chopped vegetables, chewing brusquely as she wished it were a roast sausage instead.

"It's interesting that the guards here seem flippant, almost irreverent, about the Mages," she said.

"It was, and is, an exhausting labor for my mother," Wynne said. "She carefully demonstrates respect for the Quinarium, yet does all she can to keep her distance. I suppose her tendencies have found their way into the guards. She doesn't reserve that approach for the Quinarium, though. She acts sweet and friendly yet is discerning with every person she meets, ever slow to trust, and forgetting nothing."

"Not unlike Imreia," Ami said, hacking apart her pastry with two knives.

"There are similarities, yes."

"For a wary person, Imreia was quick to trust us four," Caudro said.

Quiet overtook the room. Caudro raised his bowl and took a long drink of soup. The moment he set the dish down, Ami punched his shoulder.

"You certainly have a way of killing the mood!"

"Why strike me so?" he said, recoiling in mock fear. "It is an earnest thought, and one I thought safe to share among those I trust most."

"A thought fairly shared," Dara said.

Wynne toyed with her utensils, lining them up with precision, only to muddle them anew.

"Imreia found us at the perfect moment. I'm certain she knew she had a unique opportunity to recruit us for her cause. We already doubted the Quinarium, defied their orders, and seeing Yuvsgrend would change even the most stalwart believer's perspective. Taking us to the extraction did little more than hasten our arrival to an already determined conclusion."

"We trusted her then, and continue to trust her now, because we know she fights against the injustices we saw," Dara said. "We experienced it, too. I don't doubt they planned for us to fail our Rite of the Faithful."

"Well, that plan could not have reversed more spectacularly," Ami said.

"I can relate, given my past as a Paladin," Caudro said softly.

"I suppose we all have motivations against the Quinarium, more so than most. Of all the Fae, my grandfather would probably have loved to see me sitting at a table in Hantsburg dining among Humans. Still, I didn't expect Imreia to be so supportive of my presence, Mage or not."

"The Fae are among her greatest allies, and you are quite skilled. There are many reasons for her to want you here," Wynne said.

Dara cleared her throat loudly. "We also demanded that Caudro be found. Imreia was happy to go along, and she has been quite vocal about Caudro's importance as a symbol. Meanwhile, we were certain you would happily involve yourself in our efforts, Caudro, owing to your attraction to Ami."

Caudro coughed.

"Of course he's attracted to me. I am positively magnetic. Only boors like Hawel don't adore me," Ami said, tossing an olive high into the air and catching it in her mouth.

Plug jumped out of the top of Ami's tunic and landed beside her plate. He happily munched on the remains, chirping with glee.

"Oh, my!" Wynne said, leaning over the table. "What a curious thing."

"Dara, Wynne, meet Plug," Ami said, piling food onto her plate for the creature. "We found him alone on an island after leaving Bavenhill. He has been our steadfast protector ever since."

"Protector?" Caudro scoffed. "Plug has fled at every turn. He ran from us when we first saw him. He slept through the ziggurat, he... ow!"

Laughter filled the room when Plug chomped Caudro's finger, then sped across the table towards Wynne.

"He quite reminds me of Reggie, a ferret and resident troublemaker at the Academy of Ilsios," Wynne said as Plug spun about inside her hands. "What a sweet and tender creature. I've never seen anything quite like him."

"Speaking of sweet and tender creatures," Ami said when Plug ran up Dara's arm and nuzzled against her neck, "how has sharing a bed been for you two?"

Wynne coughed mid-drink, sending water dribbling down her chin. Ami snickered gleefully.

"We are well, thank you," Dara said, suppressing a smile while Wynne dabbed her face with a cloth.

"You're one to point fingers and make insinuations," Wynne said, rolling her eyes. "You two seem rather close."

"It seems that way because it is that way," Ami replied. "You two knew it was only a matter of time before I made him see reason. Unlike you two, though, I'm not ashamed of it."

"Caudro, you've been quiet," Dara said.

"There's not much for me to add when I agree with Ami."

Wynne smirked. "I see. The nature of your relationship is quite clear."

"What?"

"Don't trouble yourself," Ami said, patting Caudro's cheek. "You sit there and keep looking pretty. Save your energy for when we're marching on Mordinlet. Or for bed tonight."

"Ahem!" Caudro spewed. "Dara, Wynne... Have you fully recovered? Are you ready for battle?"

"We're back to ourselves. Ow!" Dara rubbed a red spot on her forearm, the site of a vicious pinch.

"Dara is overconfident about her progress," Wynne said, glowering at her partner. "I'm all but recovered, but her arm-"

"Works. It's a bit stiff, a bit slower than I'd like, but I'm fine. I've switched sword hands and can fight as well as ever. Thank you for asking, Caudro."

"We owe you an overdue thanks as well," Caudro said. "Your potions were essential, Wynne."

"I'm glad," Wynne said. "Dara aside, it seems we're all physically well enough. Hopefully, we can say the same after what comes next."

"Assuming we all walk away alive and well from Mordinlet, what might that be?" Ami mused. "Imreia says her focus is singularly on the Quinarium. But is that all she has her eyes on? She always speaks of the shadowy side of the Quinarium, yet she walks in the shadows herself."

"While Imreia holds back much, and at times seems like she's explaining away questions, she has yet to lead us astray," Wynne said. "Nor can I blame her. Imreia has been a target of the Quinarium for many years. Such attention would make anyone nervous."

"We can at least be confident in our actions against the Quinarium," Dara said.

Ami inched forward to the edge of her seat. "I still have so many questions. What happens once the Quinarium is gone? Who will march with Imreia on Brewardsburg? Will the Regency—if it is left in place after the Quinarium is undone—recognize her as a rightful Lord? And how did Okter become so involved? He speaks as her equal."

"I'm sure Imreia sees Okter as a useful ally," Dara replied. "A harsh, calculating, and exceptionally capable Mage, his skill is second only to Imreia as far as I've seen."

"I don't care about how capable he is. I care about his intentions," Ami said.

Wynne sighed. "I wish it was Sionan with us, instead of Okter. She may not be his equal in combat prowess, but we need calm and collected minds."

"Your old instructor?" Dara pushed away her plate. "I would rather we have both her and Okter, instead of one or the other."

"No matter who is here, no matter what Imreia wants, my aim is to stop the Quinarium, and in doing so, preserve the Fae," Caudro said.

"We are all aligned on that," Wynne said.

"But why does Imreia speak only of the Quinarium?" Ami swirled sweet berry wine inside a delicate glass cup. "The Quinarium and Regency seem inseparable; your mother being the exception, Wynne. Imreia can't simply march into Llendshold, destroy the Sanctuaries, Temples, and the Basilica, then leave. And what will the Draethhold Lords expect after it's all over?"

Dara stared at a flickering candle. "I'm not sure what we can do, other than take things one day at a time. For now, at least."

Ami slid her elbow across the table and rest her head on her hand. "There's the Dara I know and love. Though you're right. Not much else we can do when Imreia's the best way for me to protect my people."

"We'll learn more after we stop Scireth," Wynne said. "Good fortune you two already took care of Uldrik. I wish I was there to see him cowering."

Ami chuckled. "You do not. He pissed himself before we opened the carriage. The stench was abominable."

The four laughed for a moment, filling empty glasses and picking at the remains of their meal.

"Then we all agree on what must come next," Caudro said. "It will be good to fight alongside you once again. We've all grown in the months since we destroyed the Jackals."

Wynne stood with a smile, though she cast her gaze to a dark corner of the room.

"If I may… might I ask that we four pledge to stand together and stay true in our purpose? We must do all we can to stop the Quinarium, whether or not that is with Imreia. Stopping the Quinarium and protecting the Fae, that is what matters."

Ami raised her glass. "I could agree to that."

"You two are the first. Head inside."

"Lovely to see you too, Loraen." Ami bowed deeply, smiling at the man's scowl. "How is our dear friend?"

Loraen pushed off the wall of the inn with his shoulder and took a few steps until he was uncomfortably close to Ami and Caudro.

"You'll be happy to hear that your *dear friend* is healthy, alive, and has been properly handled. There is nothing else for you to know."

"We were the ones to capture him," Caudro said. "I would think we have a right to know the details."

"You placed an inconvenient trouble on my doorstep. Though he may one day be of use, until that day he is a waste of time and resources. You know all you need. Inside."

Recognizing the futility of arguing, Ami and Caudro entered the inn.

The innkeeper—a stodgy woman wearing a filthy apron—slid two plates laden with roast potatoes beside fruit drowned in entirely too much honey and cream onto a narrow table. She bustled away before the two could offer their thanks.

Ami plopped down beside Caudro and pulled her dish over. Sitting with their arms pressed against each other, Ami poked at her meal.

"How are you feeling?"

"A touch crowded, but I'll take this over the tunnels," he replied, recoiling when Ami jabbed his side. "I can't imagine how many years it took Broderick's family to dig those tunnels. The walls felt like solid rock. Shame they are only designed for leaving the city in haste, not entering; it would have made our arrival much easier. I wonder if Lord Pharadrax knows they exist?"

"I wouldn't be surprised if she does, and is waiting to use that information should a need present itself," Ami said. "You must know I wasn't asking about you physically. We'll be in Mordinlet tomorrow... What's on your mind?"

Caudro set his fork down. "I hadn't much thought of it. The fortress is the right place for the show of strength. My past, my emotions, they don't matter. I can face that all after it's done."

"You're treating yourself a bit harshly."

"It's how I was raised."

"We'll have to see about undoing your upbringing once this is all done." Ami said. "You know that if you won't worry about yourself, then I have to. No theatrics, no heroics in the fortress, alright?"

"Being with you, I've learned to thirst for life like never before, but it doesn't change that I will do whatever I can to stop Scireth. I may no longer be a Paladin, but I know my place, Ami. I'm expendable."

Ami felt as though her heart fell into a bottomless well. Walls pressed on her soul from every side as she was forced to consider death as a possibility. Ami looked at Caudro; he sat calm and stoic despite the severity of his words. She wondered if he feared as she did; not so much that she might die, but that Caudro might, and she would be alone once again.

Ami clung to Caudro's arm as tears trickled down her cheeks. "Please, never call yourself expendable. You are anything but that, to me."

A few minutes later, the door to the inn swung open. Ami wiped her face as Imreia strode in, followed by Okter, Dara, Wynne, and finally Loraen.

"Ah, I see we are the late arrivers this time. Broderick's family tunnels are perhaps not the most comfortable, yet sliding out of the city has me feeling like a little girl again." Imreia pulled a broad table next to Ami and Caudro, then sat uncomfortably close to the two. "Owain and his company have already set sail, along with the majority of the supplies, while Loraen has readied our horses. Eat quickly, the road awaits."

Ami stared at her half-eaten plate of potatoes. "And then what?"

"Whatever do you mean? Did you hit your head in the tunnels?" Imreia snickered. "We are to destroy the Paladin garrison."

"And then what?" Ami whispered, still holding to Caudro's arm.

"Ah." Imreia stared into Ami's eyes. "I understand your meaning. The support of Draethhold will enable us to stop the Quinarium, dear Ami, and ensure the safety of your people. I will not take a temporary victory, only to forget our dearest friends. The winds are favorable. Eat up, lest Owain arrive before us."

"Why do we not sail with them?" Dara asked.

"They sail on a cramped fishing ship, its belly half-filled with half-rotting fish to cover the supplies. If you wish to sail with such fine company, you are welcome to gallop to the docks and join them. Horses will be of use in the assault, yet thirty of us can hardly ride to Mordinlet without detection, and I would rather not spend even a minute on such a ship. Any other questions? No? Then fill your bellies."

They followed an ancient, half-decayed coastal road for the next two days. It wove along a mesa above a narrow beach to one side and an open plain on the other. The flat landscape had little in the way of trees, though windswept shrubs with triangular leaves speckled the land. Dense vines covered the rocky face on the ocean side. Whenever a horse strayed near the edge, flocks of tiny white birds emerged, filling the air with song.

Imreia broke into a gallop in the late afternoon of the second day. She cheerily stormed up to the meeting spot atop a squat hill near the shore, where Owain had already prepared a map on a knee-height table. Draethhold soldiers hauled supplies back and forth between the boat and the hill like a colony of ants. Owain waved as the arriving party dismounted and joined him.

"How many do we expect inside?" Owain asked as the group crowded around the low table.

"Paladin fortresses typically house a garrison of one hundred, and occasionally host a Mage or two," Caudro said. "There may be another twenty Trainees, though they are unlikely to fight."

"So many..."

"Are you certain this drawing is accurate?" Loraen asked.

Ami snorted. "These are Imreia's plans, with Caudro and my notes. You're welcome to steal some plans or scout ahead yourself."

"Thank you, Ami and Caudro, for providing this crucial information," Imreia said, raising her voice slightly. "The fortress is well designed."

"Perhaps we should have considered Rushlet," Owain grumbled. "Attackers should have a numerical advantage, and they outnumber us near four to one. We don't have the time or equipment necessary for a siege, nor do I see how we can breach the fortress should our initial attack fail to break the gates."

"We have five Mages. Though Paladins are indeed formidable in combat, we have all the advantage we need."

"Imreia, you know I am with you, and the hour is late, but will five Mages be enough?" Loraen's eyes were fixed on Ami's sketch of the fortress. "We have reports of Paladins increasingly wearing equipment enchanted to ward off spells. Who knows if there are Mages in the fortress as well? Even one will greatly enhance their strength."

Okter leaned over the map. "We are already here. The battle has been chosen. It is now a matter of execution, of details."

Imreia grinned. "Ami, would you please share how you entered before, that we might ease the worries of Owain and Loraen?"

"There's a drainage opening here." Ami pressed her finger against the diagram as the others huddled close. "I squeezed through unnoticed, but we could bend the bars so that others fit."

"It is too slow and vulnerable for us all to enter in such a way," Okter followed. "I will go with Ami and Caudro. Once the three of us are inside, we will ensure the gates remain open, so the rest may enter freely."

Imreia grinned, her eyes set on Okter. "I will lead the main force. We can get close yet remain unnoticed, here in the woods by the stables. Dara and I will ride in first to draw their attention; Owain, gather as many additional horses from the stables as you can and lead the rest, Wynne and Loraen included. The Paladins will struggle with a scattered fight."

"Any orders, other than to kill all we see?" Owain asked.

Wynne's eyes bulged. "We should provide an opportunity for the Paladins to surrender once we gain the upper hand."

"Our objective is to destroy the fortress and kill Scireth," Imreia said, her voice chillingly calm.

Okter raised his ethereal hand and inspected its surface. "And the Enforcer. I have assurances the Adjudicator's lackey is here, no doubt meeting with Scireth regarding their plans to attack Cauldhill. Our meeting is long overdue."

"You chose a late hour to share this information," Dara said.

Loraen furrowed his brow. "An Enforcer? This entirely worsens the already substantial challenge."

Owain nodded. "We should make for Rushlet. As I hear it, an Enforcer is the worst of all Mages. We don't have the force we need to-"

"Please don't trouble yourselves over the Enforcer," Okter said. "He is a matter for me to resolve, and resolve him I will."

Nervous eyes glanced across the table as silence settled in.

Wynne stretched her neck. "We should make every effort to capture Scireth and the Enforcer first. Then perhaps the Paladins will surrender."

Caudro faced the ocean. "Scireth will never surrender. She is a fanatic without rival."

"Nor will an Enforcer," Okter said. "Though I must say, Wynne, your desire to preserve life is appreciated in a moment when the value of life is easily forgotten."

"Although we shall seek their death rather than their surrender, Scireth and the Enforcer are then our priority," Imreia said. "Okter, Ami, Caudro; once you three secure the gates, you will be close to the keep and far from the heart of the melee. Make your way inside with haste and find the leaders while we keep the garrison busy."

Dara rested her hand on Wynne's leg. "If there are still Paladins alive after Scireth and the Enforcer are dealt with, then we should give them the opportunity to surrender. Though we might need a larger ship, depending on their numbers."

"I would as soon leave survivors as take them prisoner, though a larger, faster, cleaner ship would be preferable to this vessel," Imreia said, waving at the fishing ship in the distance. "It reeks from here and we're upwind. Owain, send a few of your company to the docks with the sailors. Have them ready the swiftest ship, and sabotage all the others that they can."

"Are your soldiers ready, Owain?" Okter asked with a sideward glance.

Owain sat tall. "It is my duty to express doubts, but I lead the finest fighters in all of Draethhold. We will fight to the last, and I have the same assurances from the Fae and Dwarves who join us."

Imreia beamed. "Rest as you are able, eat as you wish; the sun will set in a few hours. It begins at nightfall."

CHAPTER 18

Ami cursed under her breath as she slid into the muddy ditch. While the gentle mist provided excellent cover, it turned the ditch outside the walls of the fortress into a slick mess. Caudro and Okter landed moments later, their boots squelching into the mud. Ami crept forward at the lead until they reached the drain. A steady, narrow stream of water trickled out.

Plug popped out of his pouch when Ami came to a stop. The creature examined his surroundings, then fled back inside.

"Will your little pet keep quiet, or will it cause us issue?"

Ami clasped her hands over her chest. "Okter, my good sir, I assure you I keep only the most capable and reliable of allies in my proximity. You should be honored to stand beside the wonder that is Plug."

"Forgive me," Okter said with a chuckle. "I offer my most sincere apologies for questioning its honor."

Caudro stared through the grate; the purple glow of his mana-fueled vision filled his helmet.

"It is strange to stand here, ready to break into the very place you saved me from mere months ago."

"The time has come for your revenge," Okter said. He held out a hand when Ami readied to climb in. "Please, allow me."

Okter leapt into the drain. Sliding up to the grate, he took a drink of mana. He whispered, then placed a finger against a bar. The metal glowed bright red for a moment; Okter moved his hand to reveal a thin gap. He repeated the spell until a section of the gate fell free, creating a wide opening.

"Fair trick," Ami muttered as she followed after.

The three dashed to the back of a nearby building. Okter peered around the edge.

"The distance is too far to worry about spells or arrows," he said, kneeling in the shadows with Ami and Caudro. "You two stay put while I run to the gates. I should be able to catch the Paladins by surprise before they can react, but I'll need your supports once they realize what's happening. I'll block the portcullis winch first, then we can worry about the gate. Are you-"

Okter stared, dumfounded as Ami stepped out from behind the building. Nocking a barbed arrow, she raised her bow and called on Mizaina.

Flecks of blood trailed the arrow as it sailed across the courtyard. Not a single Paladin noticed until the arrowhead, elongated into a metal cylinder, sank into the portcullis winch with a thud.

"Ring the bell!"

Paladins along the walls by the gate hurried over, when an arrow with a wide, sickle-shaped head severed the rope holding up the alarm bell. The giant bronze cone fell to the ground with a dull thud. Paladins hollered into the night, lighting torches and taking up arms.

Blood trailing down her hand, Ami readied a third arrow. Crimson stained her bowstring as she released.

The third arrow wobbled frantically as the head morphed into an orb of steel. It struck the upper hinge of the massive doors. The multiple-layers-thick wood door fell askew; its end plunged into the mud, rendering the barrier immovable.

Although the bell was unusable, Paladins flooded into the courtyard at the calls of their compatriots. A sheen of white danced across their armor, shining in the dark of the misty night.

Okter moved to pull Ami back into the shadows when an orb of white flame exploded over the gate, showering the courtyard with rubble.

Ami silently cheered Wynne's display when Imreia and Dara galloped into the courtyard. They leapt from their horses with swords drawn, cutting down the nearest Paladins before the defenders could raise their shields. As the two Mages carved through the disorganized defenders, Owain and Loraen rode in at the head of their company. Paladins retreated from the courtyard as those on the walls fired crossbow bolts at the attackers.

"Enough watching," Okter said.

The three retraced Ami's steps from months ago, following the darkness between the backs of buildings and the walls. Reaching the end, they rushed towards the keep.

A Paladin caught sight of the three and moved to intercept. Okter dropped to his shins and slid across the mud, evading the Paladin's spear. He stabbed his foe in the back of the leg with his sword and pulled himself up as the Paladin fell to his knees. A flash of light cut through the dark of the night as Okter slit the Paladin's throat.

Ami froze for a moment, aghast at the gleeful look on Okter's face. She broke from her stupor when Caudro shoved her aside and a crossbow bolt sank into the mud inches away. Ami sent an arrow flying. It found its mark, and the Paladin crumpled on the wall.

They entered the keep to find it eerily quiet.

"Shouldn't there be more Paladins inside?" Ami whispered.

"Paladins are of a singular mind. They will rush to the sounds of battle and organize themselves there," Caudro replied.

Okter waved dismissively. "There is an Enforcer in the keep. Scireth is likely unworried, as long as she has such a guardian. Ami, can you take us to her quarters, that we might teach her the error of her ways?"

"I took quite a different path last time, but it's me you're asking; of course I can."

Ami sprinted down the hall when a group of Paladins rounded a corner. Ami nocked an arrow, but the Paladins fled.

"Why?" she wondered as their footsteps faded.

"Because they aren't needed," Okter said, nudging Ami's shoulder. "Keep on. The sooner we take care of Scireth, the sooner we leave this place."

Ami led them up a winding stair, then down a narrow hall until they reached the antechamber outside of Scireth's office. Columns flanked the space, and stone pews were oriented to towards a lectern.

"Scireth's quarters are through the door at the back," Ami said.

As the three made for the door, a man stepped out from behind a column. The simplicity of his clothes alarmed Ami: he wore a plain brown knee-length tunic with a simple white symbol of the Quinarium over his shoulder, cinched beneath a wide belt holding bottles of mana all the way around. A sheathed sword hung at his hip. His face was the picture of dull normality, with not a discerning feature that might cause attention were he seen among Lords or commoners.

Okter pulled Ami back with his ethereal hand; the chill sent goosebumps racing along her arms and up her neck.

"Here without mother dearest, I see," Okter said, strolling into the chamber.

"You were banished," the Enforcer replied.

"I so enjoy your company that I couldn't help but come back."

"You left a bit of yourself behind in Llendshold. A hand, if I recall," the Enforcer said as he inspected his own fingers.

Okter snorted. "I lost little of import in our last encounter. The Adjudicator should have ordered you to take my tongue or my head, not my hand."

"And yet it was important enough a loss for you to return, whimpering."

"Think of this as me simply returning your favor before finding the Adjudicator." Okter advanced until he was a few paces away from the Enforcer. "Last we met, you caught me unawares. Now, we face each other as equals. Are you prepared?"

"We are not equals, Okter. You are little more of a Mage than Initiates beginning their Rite of the Faithful. You will forever be my lesser, in the eyes of the Quinarium, in the eyes of the Quinate, and in the wielding of steel and spell."

Okter's lip curled. "Let us see if your words are true. Ami, Caudro, hurry along. I'm sure Scireth will be overjoyed to see you."

Ami and Caudro bolted away, skirting along the sides of the antechamber. They recoiled when a piercing clang struck their ears.

Okter stood with his back to them, his sword locked with that of the Enforcer.

"What are you waiting for? Hurry along."

The Enforcer bared a mouth full of pearly teeth. "Sending children to their death. How brave of you."

"Unlike you, I have allies I can trust, including these two young ones. Were the Quinarium not to hoard power, you would see how much potential there is in the most unexpected of places."

"Potential?" Enforcer said, pushing off Okter with his sword and returning to the center of the room. "You are one to speak of potential when you yourself are a failure."

Okter flourished his sword as he strode after. "You will find me quite the changed man."

As if a mirror were placed between the two, Okter and the Enforcer each raised a bottle of mana and drained the contents. Swords raised, they tread slowly in a circle opposite each other.

The Enforcer mumbled a spell; Okter hissed, the only intelligible word being *Ramaia,* as he called on the God of Blood. They lunged forth at an impossible speed.

Though Ami and Caudro had reached the door to Scireth's chambers, they watched in awe. Two swords swished and sliced, glimmering like the wings of dragonflies skittering over a moonlit pond. The weapons rarely struck each other as the duelists predicted and evaded the honed edges, slipping away, and then retaliating without pause.

A swing sent Okter reeling backwards. He spun about and flung a spear of flame at his foe. The Enforcer muttered as he dove aside, summoning a tremendous gale to lift and hurl a stone pew at Okter.

The Mage ducked beneath the hurtling bench. It struck a column, sending cracks rippling all the way to the ceiling. The duelists drank more mana then bounded at each other, their swords ringing through the keep.

Footsteps danced over the stone floor. Okter and the Enforcer traded blows until they were beside a column. The Enforcer sprang from the ground and ran up the side of the pillar with Okter in pursuit. On reaching the ceiling, they flew into the air, their swords clashing as they descended.

Okter kicked the Enforcer as they landed, sending his foe tumbling away. He glanced over his shoulder to find Ami and Caudro staring.

"Less gawking, more dealing with Scireth!"

Stirred into motion, Caudro rammed through the door shoulder first. Ami followed close behind, scurrying through the entrance as the door swung shut by its own weight.

Scireth stood by her desk, mindfully tucking papers into a satchel. Though she wore her armor and moved with determination, her expression was calm. Moonbeams flowed in through the tall windows at the back of the room; the peaceful, calming light melded with the glow of a few scattered candles.

"Stop!" Caudro shouted.

Scireth chuckled as she carried on. "Is that young Caudro, ordering me around as if I were a petulant Trainee?"

"Surrender, Scireth," Ami said. "There is no way for you to escape."

"A Fae and a failed Paladin. This is what Imreia sends to face me? This is an insult," Scireth snarled.

Caudro stood tall and readied his spear and shield. "We are plenty enough to stop the likes of you. I have grown, Scireth, beyond the limitations of the Paladins' training. Beneath the Academy in Bavenhill, an Avatar of Almoya declared me one of Her Heralds! I will fulfill my oath to Almoya, my oath to protect those unable to protect themselves, by stopping you. On my life, you will never step foot in the Nomridian Forest!"

"Herald of Almoya?" Scireth secured the buckles to the pack and set it atop her desk. "Claim grandiose titles induced by hallucinations all you wish, but know that you will never become more than what I allow you to become. You were a disgrace before, Caudro, and you are no more than a disgrace as you stand here today. Your very existence is an insult to the beauty, the grace of the Five. Taking you in was an error on the part of Jarain. I failed to correct that error when I took you as my Trainee. It is time I remedy my failure."

"Call off your Paladins!" Ami shouted, her voice strained. "Order them to stand down. Let them live. You can still live."

"Stand down?" Scireth scoffed. "Surrender to Imreia? I am a Paladin! We who stand in the light of the Quinate in this fortress, we are Paladins! We stand as the foundation of the might of the

Quinarium! We are the righteous warriors of the Five! Never will we bow to the likes of *you.*"

"Give up, Scireth," Caudro pleaded. "We already made it past your Enforcer. You have no chance."

Scireth burst into laughter. "Oh, I saw Okter out there. I wager he is well on his way to losing his other hand once the Enforcer is done toying with him. Imreia stands to lose much today. I will enjoy my time with her. Now, enough talking. I thought I was done with you once before, Caudro. Today I will be thoroughly finished."

The feathered plume at the top of Scireth's domed helmet wavered as she pulled it on. She pointed a hulking mace with a spiked head at Caudro.

Ami loosed an arrow, but Scireth raised her shield. The missile protruded from the wood surface, wobbling as Scireth swung to parry Caudro's spear. A second arrow, its point morphed into an orb, struck Scireth's shoulder. The Paladin stumbled back, yet the missile glanced off her armor, clattering to the ground.

Scireth lunged rapidly despite the heft of her armor and her hulking frame. She shouldered Caudro aside, then kicked a candelabra. The iron structure flew across the room, forcing Ami to dive away.

Caudro thrust savagely with his spear, desperate to find an opening in Scireth's defense. Shield against shield, spear against mace, they fought in a furious tangle that prevented Ami from striking.

The Paladin deflected a blow, then pinned Caudro's spear to the floor with her mace. She struck its wooden haft with the edge of her shield, shattering the weapon. Caudro rammed the edge of his shield into Scireth's stomach. She caught herself with a backward step as an arrow bounced off her pauldron, then threw all her might forward, striking Caudro's chest with the butt of her mace. She swiftly followed with a blow to his shoulder.

Scireth stood above her former Trainee and raised her mace high when an arrow struck her wrist. Though protected by her armor, the weapon fell from her hand. Caudro scurried to his feet, drawing his sword and striking before Scireth could recover her mace.

Backed into the corner by the tall windows, Scireth charged. Unbothered when Caudro's sword slit her thigh, the enraged Paladin ran around her desk and gave it a thunderous kick. Wood groaned and splintered from her boot as the desk struck Caudro's leg, knocking him to his knees. As an arrow pierced her shoulder, Scireth struck Caudro in the head with her shield, sending his helmet crashing through the window.

Ami screamed as she released her bowstring, sending a barbed arrow at Scireth. It split into a hundred darts, peppering Scireth's face through her helmet. The Paladin cried out as blood poured from one of her eyes. Ami ducked when Scireth flung her shield, but before the Fae could flee, the Paladin was upon her.

Scireth grabbed Ami's bow and yanked it from her hands. The Paladin smashed the bow against the wall as she advanced, heaving and grunting like a wild boar. Though Ami was deft, Scireth wrapped her arms around the Fae then threw her against the wall. Her head spinning, Ami stumbled to the ground. Scireth dove after, pinning the Fae's arms to the floor with her knees.

"Disgusting beast, not worthy of mana, not worthy of life!" Scireth shouted, frothing at the mouth. "I will cleanse this world of all your kind, with my bare hands if I must!"

Ami watched, helpless no matter how hard she struggled, as the Paladin raised her fist. The steel gauntlet shimmered in the moon's light. Scireth tensed, ready to strike, when Plug crept over her shoulder.

The creature sank his fangs into the Paladin's neck and ripped out a chunk of flesh. Scireth clawed about until she grabbed hold of Plug, then hurled the creature across the room.

"Now where was I?"

Scireth's first blow filled Ami's vision with stars as she nearly blacked out. The side of her face went numb.

Ami's legs kicked involuntarily as Scireth struck again.

"Caudro," she whimpered as the Paladin raised her fist.

Scireth ignored Ami's cries as she pummeled the Fae relentlessly.

Then, a roar of fury and hatred filled the room. Caudro struck Scireth's arm with her mace, cracking bones. She stumbled off of Ami and reached for her shield, when Caudro mashed her hand into the ground. Scireth rolled back, hollering in pain when Caudro swung the mace a final time, cratering the Paladin's helm. Scireth's body fell limp as blood streamed out from her helmet.

Caudro dropped the mace and rushed over to Ami. He lifted her battered face into his lap as Plug crawled over and nuzzled against her neck. Caudro's shoulders trembled as his tears fell to the cold stone floor.

"Why there you are," cracked a feeble voice.

"Ami!"

"Crying my name as if you'd find someone else here," she wheezed. Her hand quivered as she touched the battered and bruised side of her face. "At least you can't properly see. Scireth made a right mess of me... I don't think I'll be able to use this eye again."

"All I care is that you are here, alive, with me."

"I would have liked Scireth to live long enough for me to give her a bit of a beating, though you and Plug seem to have quite taken care of her."

"Here, drink this," Caudro said, uncorking a potion as he eased Ami up.

She leaned against his shoulder, her hands shaking as she tilted back the bottle.

"I don't think this potion will save my eye," Ami said. "Now we have only the one good eye between the two of us. What a pair we make."

"Less than a pair, if we're counting eyes."

Ami chuckled feebly, her breathing easing as the potion took effect.

"Can you walk?" Caudro asked. "Perhaps you can lean on me?"

Ami patted Caudro's cheek. "Unless I'm mistaken—I might be, as my head took quite the beating—she hit only my face, and not my legs. I'm sure I can manage."

"You'll have to forgive me, I took quite a blow to my head as well. Both dumb and blind, quite a pair indeed." Caudro looked over at Scireth's body. In Caudro's vision, the corpse had already faded to grey. "I'll see if I can pry Scireth's helmet off. I hope Okter has dealt with the Enforcer."

Ami and Caudro hobbled out of the office to find Okter and the Enforcer still embroiled in their bitter duel. Empty mana bottles littered the floor. Ami squinted, astonished that there was not a scratch on either one.

Swords sang, clashing as the two sped past each other.

"Wait there, dearies," Okter said, grinning like a child with a bag full of sweets.

"Yes, wait for your turn to die, heretics!" the Enforcer called after.

They raised mana bottles in unison, draining the vessels. Okter raised his sword then bowed, flourishing his weapon. The Enforcer returned the gesture.

Seconds stretched as they stared. Then, like diving falcons, they sped forth. Swords clanged as they blitzed past each other. Okter rushed into a fresh assault when the Enforcer hooked his blade under the hilt of Okter's sword and flung it aside.

The Enforcer laughed, raising his blade casually, ready to deliver a fatal blow.

He flinched upon seeing Okter's ethereal hand meld and sharpen into a blade, but the Enforcer was too slow to stop the sweeping strike. Okter grunted as he stood close to the Enforcer, whose eyes bulged.

At the gentlest of nudges, his head fell from his body and rolled across the floor.

"You took my hand, yet I have taken your head. It is clear who the better of us is on this day," Okter said as his ethereal hand reformed. His gaze drifted over to Ami and Caudro. "Ah, you have Scireth's helm, an excellent token. Let us share this news with our friends and the remaining Paladins."

CHAPTER 19

Okter waltzed through the halls, gleeful despite the sounds of battle raging outside and the bloody head of the Enforcer in his hand. He glanced over his shoulder and sighed, slowing his pace until Ami and Caudro caught up. Okter huffed impatiently the rest of the way out of the keep, though his bright smile returned on reaching the courtyard.

"Ah, the rain has stopped!"

A cascade of fiery spears arced through the night sky. The bolts showered a tightly packed group of Paladins, piercing gaps in their armor. They cried out and dropped their weapons and shields as they clawed at the burning skin trapped beneath steel. Ami traced the streaks back to Wynne, who stood on the wall above the gates amid piles of empty mana bottles.

An unnatural gust of wind surged through the courtyard, knocking over Draethhold soldiers before they struck the charred Paladins. Imreia stormed across the wall. She leapt over a group of Paladins, evading their spears. Shouting a spell as she landed, Imreia pressed her hand against the ramparts. A block of stone broke free, striking the Mage responsible for the gust. She marched forward and dispatched the Mage before returning her attention to the Paladins.

Down in the courtyard, Dara kicked off a building. She soared over a line of shields, landing amidst a group of Paladins wielding crossbows. Grabbing the arm of one, she aimed his crossbow and kneed the trigger. The bolt plunged into the chest of a Paladin. As the others attempted to retaliate, Dara moved like a feather caught in a wind, slipping around spears and swords and evading bolts as she tore through the warriors of the Quinarium.

Though many a dead Paladin littered the fortress, Draethhold soldiers lay among them. Ami spied a fallen Fae. Ringing filled her ears. She closed her eye and clenched her teeth to quell the trembling in her jaw.

Okter took Scireth's helm from Caudro and skipped to the heart of the courtyard. He took a drink of mana, then raised the Enforcer's head and Scireth's helm.

"Paladins!" he bellowed, his voice sending tremors through the walls of the fortress. "Your leaders are dead. You have lost this day. Lay down your arms, and we will treat you with dignity as the Five would demand. Fight on, and we will cut you down like wild dogs!"

A few Paladins hesitantly set down their weapons and raised their hands.

"Traitors!" shouted a Paladin, raising his spear to strike a compatriot who sought to surrender.

A bolt of flame sped through the air, piercing the shouting Paladin's neck. As his body crumpled, those Paladins still bearing arms charged wildly in a final, desperate attack.

"How wasteful," Okter said. "What an entirely unnecessary, tedious affair. Ah, I may as well hasten things along."

While Okter dove into the fray, Caudro held Ami close and half-dragged her across the courtyard. The two stumbled to the ground by the gates.

"I'm sorry, I couldn't protect you," Caudro said. "I failed you."

"Failed?" Ami said, her chest rising and falling slowly with every breath. "I'm still talking to you, aren't I? Don't be so hard on yourself. You squished Scireth's head like an overripe tomato. I would say you did fine."

Caudro fussed over a piece of cloth, attempting to pull it into a bandage.

"Five above!" he seethed through grit teeth, his hands shaking furiously. "I can't even prepare a simple bandage."

"Please, sit with me for a moment," Ami said. "It's all I need, Caudro."

Caudro wrapped his arms around Ami as she leaned against him. Her breathing eased as she squeezed his hand.

Minutes passed, then all went quiet.

"Ami!"

Wynne ran down steps in twos and threes, skidding to a stop beside her friend.

"Ilsios, grant me your healing light," she whispered.

Wynne's hand glowed brightly as she brought it beside Ami's face. Caudro exhaled in relief as Ami's breathing strengthened.

"Her eye," he said as his own vision faded, "I can't see, but is it possible..."

Wynne struggled to form words when Dara came over and embraced her.

"I'm afraid it is as yours," Dara said. "I don't think there's a spell that can heal such a wound."

"Oh, stop worrying," Ami chided. "One eye is plenty. We have only half a mind between the two of us anyhow. One peeper will keep us from being overburdened by seeing too much at once."

Caudro's shoulders shook as he pulled Ami in close, his tears pattering against his armor like a light spring rain falling on clay shingles.

Meanwhile, Imreia laughed and cackled as she paced around the courtyard. Beaming, she ran up the stairs to the walls and stood over the gate.

"Stand tall! Stand proud! Revel in victory!"

The soldiers gathered to listen.

"Tonight the Five have shown who they favor, and on this night it was us, and not the Quinarium! You have proven they are not the only ones upon the whom the Gods will shine their light. We stood together as peoples of all walks. United, we are stronger than when alone.

"Some may say this was but one small victory. To that I say, this one small victory is the snip in the fabric that will spread into an uncontrollable, unstoppable tear as we rip apart the heretical tapestry of lies that is the Quinarium. We are the righteous storm! We are the bringers of light! We are the true Quinate's faithful!"

Applause and cheers filled the courtyard. Dara and Wynne looked on, clapping politely. Imreia glanced out from the ramparts towards the ocean.

"Our time draws short," she said. "Soon the guards of Mordinlet will realize something is amiss. Bring in carriages and carts, whatever you can find. Bind the prisoners, but treat them with dignity, and take everything of value. Make haste!"

Needing no further instruction, the soldiers scattered. A few brought in carts and carriages from the stables, while the rest split between binding the captives and ransacking the fortress.

Soldiers flowed in and out of buildings in the courtyard and the keep, loading the carts with arms, food, gold, and mana. Wynne and Dara, meanwhile, helped Ami and Caudro to a cart and tended the wounded.

The sound of clinking glass drew Imreia's interest. Peering inside a crate, she found it neatly packed with bottles of oil. Strolling through the chaotic flurry of soldiers, Imreia set a few by each building in the courtyard, then set the half-full crate inside the entrance of the keep. When bells rang in the distance, Imreia approached Wynne.

"My dear, I am quite out of mana. Will you please set the bottles of oil aflame?"

Caudro stirred from Ami's side. "What of the dead?"

"What of them?"

"We can't abandon them! There are soldiers of Draethhold, and Fae, among the slain Paladins. They sacrificed their lives to stop the Quinarium. We owe them our respect. We should extend that respect even to our enemies. What does it say of us if we cannot treat the dead with honor?"

Imreia spoke calmly, yet she glared with her hands on her hips. "This is war. All who joined us knew of the risk and volunteered for it."

"And because they knew what fate might await them, we should abandon our duty to treat them with honor?"

"Do you not hear the bells?" Imreia said, her voice rising. "I will not waste time and put the wellbeing of those still living at risk by attending those incapable of thanking us for our efforts. Wynne, if you please, the oil."

Caudro's knuckles went white as he gripped the rails of the cart. "What else will we abandon alongside our morals? How far will we sink in the name of victory before we are wading in the same heap of shit as the Quinarium?"

"I have said all I care to say on this matter. Wynne."

"Imreia, I..."

Dara wrapped her arm around Wynne. "I understand time is precious, but Imreia-"

"Oh, come now!" Okter said, chuckling as he sauntered over with an open bottle of wine in hand. "We are victorious! It is time to celebrate, not argue. We can discuss methods and morals another time. Everyone, make ready to leave!"

Okter held his open hand near his mouth and blew gently. A cloud of fiery wisps flittered into the night sky before settling on the bottles of oil. All at once, the glass vessels burst. Flames lapped at the buildings, and soon their glow filled the fortress.

As the procession of horses, carts, and carriages passed through the gates, bells rang in Mordinlet. Okter kicked his horse into a gallop and broke away. Drinking mana as he approached the village, he brought his horse to a stop before the walls, outside of arrow range. A contingent of guards marched out of the gates.

"The fortress lies in ruin! Lay down your arms!" Okter bellowed. His augmented voice rattled heads inside helmets; the guards faltered. "Cower in the presence of Imreia! Hide within your walls! Flee those who will gladly obliterate you should you take one step further!"

Against the commands of their captain, the guards stumbled over each other and scurried back into the village as the carriages roared past.

Hooves and wheels thundered over the docks. The Draethhold sailors waved from a two-masted caravel. The sails unfurled as a flurry of Humans, Fae, and Dwarves unloaded the carriages and carts.

Though Imreia and Loraen stood watch, expecting guards to charge out from Mordinlet at any moment, not a single person ventured forth. Despite all the fury that had consumed the fortress a short while earlier, they sailed quietly into the night.

Ami leaned against Caudro, grinning in the warmth of the morning sun. They sat on the edge of the ship's deck with their feet dangling over the edge and their arms resting on a low rail.

Ropes groaned as the full sails pulled against the mast. Birds flew over the distant shore, their squawks and caws faint over the ocean. The rhythmic lapping of waves against the hull of the caravel put all at ease, as if every splash were a reminder of the growing distance from Mordinlet.

Plug rolled to his back and stretched his legs in a not-so-subtle request for attention. Ami happily complied, though she never took her eye off the passing coast.

"I should have gone with you," Dara said, sitting next to Ami.

"*We* should have gone with you."

Wynne sat beside Dara and stretched out her hands and feet, relishing the ocean breeze.

"It was my... our fight," Caudro said. "We may not have left unscathed, but we left alive while Scireth is dead."

"And Uldrik is in captivity," followed Ami. "Okter said that with the Enforcer there, at least one Adjudicator is sure to be involved, but the destruction of the fortress will delay them for some months."

Wynne smirked. "You still owe us the entire tale of how you captured Uldrik."

"We have a few days before we're back in Draethhold. Plenty of time to recount everything," Caudro said.

"I do want to hear it all, but you two also need rest."

"My dearest adoptive mother Wynne, I hardly think talking will be such an exertion that it will impede our recovery," Ami said.

"I'm glad we have more time together," Dara followed. "One night was hardly enough."

"A single night is never enough, especially when spent with this one," Ami said, jabbing Caudro's side.

"Ami!"

"What? I say that as an endorsement of your company! Every girl should be so lucky." Ami leaned over the rail and squinted at Dara and Wynne. "And what about you two? How go your evenings? Every night one for the records?"

Wynne looked away before Ami had the pleasure of seeing her cheeks flush.

"I missed your company, Ami."

"Of course you did. I, on the other hand, am surprised you two have lasted this long without me watching over you."

"You are indispensable, of course, though Imreia has done well enough keeping us out of trouble in your stead," Dara replied.

"You believe you are in her debt?" Caudro asked.

"Not as such; it's more that we can credit her for watching over us."

Ami gazed into the ocean. "I'm not sure I trust her or Okter."

"Better than the Quinarium, at least."

"Caudro, that is far from a lofty standard to surpass," Ami said. "What I don't want is to be trading sideways when the Quinarium is gone."

"On that we agree," Dara said.

Caudro breathed in deeply, then exhaled through his mouth. "I'm not sure why, but it irritates me that Okter knew the Enforcer would be there."

"He and Imreia have exceptional networks," Wynne said. "It's how we... they have been successful thus far."

"As long as our purposes are aligned, I'm overjoyed for their successes. But what do they hope for once the Quinarium has been taken care of?" Ami wondered.

The door to the lower deck creaked open and Owain peered out.

"Wynne! Can you help us? Some of the wounded are taking a turn for the worse."

"Of course!" she replied, hurrying to her feet. "We'll have plenty more days to discuss the past and our futures."

"I'd best join Wynne and help as I can," Dara said, slinking away.

"No need to make excuses to excuse yourself from the company of malformed layabouts such as us," Ami said. "Nor do you need to make an excuse to spend more time with your beloved!"

Dara shook her head and chuckled as she disappeared under the deck alongside Wynne.

"It's good to be with Dara and Wynne again," Caudro said, leaning his chest against the rail and letting his arms dangle over the ocean.

"I wouldn't mind spending a night or two with them. They positively glow together."

"Ami! They are a couple!"

"I didn't say I was going to try to separate them!" Ami said, giggling. "Much more a thought of bringing them together, with me happening to be there too. Are you perhaps a touch jealous of my dreaming?"

"That is not what I said at all."

"Oh, you aren't worried about me casting my eyes—well, just the one eye now—on others, and having covetous thoughts?"

"Not in the slightest," Caudro said, casually swinging his feet back and forth. "I know you well enough to know when you're serious. Which is almost never. I also know better than to frustrate myself by trying to restrain you. You're only yourself when you're free to do as you please."

"It's as if you've bared my very soul." Ami rested her head on Caudro's shoulder as he pulled her in close. "For the first time, I'm glad you're blind... at least you can remember my face as it was before Scireth tore it half to pieces. Well, if I'm honest, I should confess that I've enjoyed your touch when I'm guiding you around."

Caudro smiled. "Whether or not I can see, whether your face is broken or whole, nothing can change how beautiful you are."

Ami rested her hand on Caudro's chest. "A half-blind pariah of a Fae and a blind, would-be poet of a former Paladin with no place to call home. We really are quite the pair."

"We have each other. I am here for you, forever and always."

"Even if that means traipsing back through the dark, scary land of dead trees that is the Nomridian Forest? The place you were so fearful of before?"

"Even with mana, I won't see it the same. I like to think that if I had my eyes, I would see the forest differently, as I see you now." Caudro tilted his head back and drank in the salty ocean air. "I wish I could have met your grandfather."

Ami smiled wistfully as she examined a curl of hair which hung over Caudro's ear, wavering in the breeze. "He would have liked you."

"You think so?"

"Caudro, have you been asleep these past months? Wandering in a dream? You partnered with a Fae and fought—continue to fight—to protect us from our greatest threat. You're what my grandfather hoped to one day see: Fae and Humans standing side-by-side. A silly dream, given he was a fletcher, and I was destined to be one until I stole mana."

"Maybe he would have been happy with both of us. You are proof his dream was right, after all."

Ami chuckled. "Maybe."

Ami's head drooped as a sullen quiet settled over the pair.

"I'm sorry, I shouldn't have brought up your grandfather," Caudro said.

"It's not that at all. It's..." Ami chewed at her lip. "Are we doing the right thing, supporting Imreia?"

"We had to work with her to protect your people. Also, I trust Dara and Wynne, and they seem to trust her. Perhaps she will gain our trust in time. For now, we should rejoice that the Quinarium—without its two architects in Uldrik and

Scireth—have been substantially delayed in their effort to incite a genocide. And that Draethhold will stand against them."

"You sound different," Ami said.

"I am finally free. The Quinarium, the Paladins... they no longer own any part of me."

"Well, hold tight, my protector, because you traded them for me."

"Will the Fae accept me as your partner?" Caudro asked.

"I'm already an outcast. A smashed face and a Paladin for a bed mate can't possibly worsen my people's opinion of me. And even if it did... Five above, I'm too tired to care anymore."

"You speak as if your existence is a problem for your people. I assure you, everything you've done, everything you do, everything I've come to know about you, it serves only to further my care for you. The Fae will have to see you differently, as I do."

"Here I was, all these months, languishing, wondering if you would finally wake up."

Caudro cradled Ami's cheek with the gentlest of touches. He leaned forward, hungering for her touch; for a fleeting moment, Ami thought of teasing, of pulling away, when a deep need welled inside her heart. She leaned into his embrace, her lips greeting his.

Their kiss was not one of passion or burning fire, rather it was an embrace of safety, of comfort, of reassurance that one day all would be right, so long as they were together.

Ami clung tightly to Caudro's tunic as they eased apart.

"I promise you, Ami, I am awake, and now I finally see."

About the Author

Brendan Corbett grew up in a military family, always on the move. Books, particularly fantasy, were both stabilizing and the ultimate escape, companions to other worlds that could journey with him even when friends could not. As an adult his career turned away from the arts, though a wide range of experiences have brought him back to his love of writing.

He now resides in Oregon with his wife, son, dog and two cats. While writing consumes much of his time, you might also find him at one of his ever-growing list of hobbies, including cooking, gardening, hiking, gaming, archery, and woodworking.

Keep up to date with Brendan by signing up for his newsletter at his website, authorbrendancorbett.com, or by following him at one of the following:

instagram.com/authorbrendancorbett/

bookbub.com/profile/brendan-corbett

goodreads.com/author/show/6473803.Brendan_Corbett